Kingdom of Ash and Briars

HANNAH WEST

HOLIDAY HOUSE / NEW YORK

For my parents, who always encourage my wishful want-tos,

and for Sarah, who wishes them as hard as I do

Text copyright © 2016 by Hannah West
Map by Jaime Zollars. Copyright © 2016 by Holiday House, Inc.
All Rights Reserved
HOLIDAY HOUSE is registered in the U.S. Patent and Trademark Office.
Printed and bound in June 2016 at Maple Press, York, PA, USA.
www.holidayhouse.com
First Edition
1 3 5 7 9 10 8 6 4 2

Library of Congress Cataloging-in-Publication Data
Names: West, Hannah, 1990– author.
Title: Kingdom of ash and briars / Hannah West.
Description: First edition. | New York : Holiday House, [2016] |
Summary: Sixteen-year-old Bristal discovers she is a shapeshifter, one of three
remaining elicromancers tasked with guarding the realm of Nissera against dark
magic while manipulating three royal families to promote peace.
Identifiers: LCCN 2015048226 | ISBN 9780823436514 (hardcover)
Subjects: | CYAC: Shapeshifting—Fiction. | Duty—Fiction. | Characters in literature—
Fiction. | Identity—Fiction. | Fantasy.
Classification: LCC PZ7.1.W4368 Kin 2016 | DDC [Fic]—dc23 LC
record available at https://lccn.loc.gov/2015048226

KINGDOM:
VOLARRE

FAMILY:
LORENTHI

King Errod······Queen Lucetta ⟨⟨⟨⟨⟨⟨ Duchess Lysandra ······Duke Aidric

Princess Rosamund — — — — — — — — — — Elinor

KINGDOM:
CALGORAN

FAMILY:
ERMETARIUS

King Riskan·······Queen Dara

Orrin - - - Prince Charles ∞∞∞∞∞ Prince Anthony

KINGDOM:
YORTH

FAMILY:
VELOXEN

King Thaddeus·······Queen Estelle

Prince Nicolas

······· *indicates marriage*

| *indicates children*

∞∞∞∞∞ *indicates siblings*

- - - *indicates cousins*

Prologue

History might be whittled down until all that remains are shining fables of fairy magic and curse-defying kisses. War might go unmentioned in the polished children's tales of the two girls with rose petal lips and hair of spun gold, the girls whom I was tasked with making queens.

The coming generations may forget that the price of the peace they will enjoy was paid in blood.

But for the historians, the truth-seekers and the curious: here is the light and the dark of it. Here is my story.

Part One

ONE

*E*ach icy gust bit me to the bone. A daydream of roasting next to a fire in the kitchens while eating fistfuls of hot, flaky bread made the cold feel even harsher, the wind wetter and my stomach all the more empty. But the thought of death made me coldest of all.

I took inventory of my kidnappers' weapons. Two were armed with daggers while the other two carried bows and fully stocked quivers. Maybe they would cut me open like a sack of flour or snap my neck like a fattened, frantic chicken. Maybe they would leave me to freeze to death and I wouldn't be found until spring.

"You'll get no ransom, if that's what you want," I said to Hagan, the redheaded gardener. My arms were wrapped around his freckle-spotted neck, numb from taking the brunt of the snowy gusts. My teeth chattered so often I could barely prize them open to force out the words. "You ought to have kidnapped the lord and lady's daughter. You could have asked a fine price for Hazel."

Hagan snorted with laughter. "Aye, if I managed not to kill her in the meantime. I wouldn't go to that trouble for a thousand aurions."

"But you know Patsy doesn't have the means to purchase my freedom, and the lord and lady aren't going to pay a thousand aurions for me, or even fifty."

Hagan shifted my weight on his back, hooking his arms under my knees. His bow dug into my ribs. I didn't complain for fear that they would force me to walk again on numb feet. "I know better than to demand a price for the cook's help."

Hope left me like a last breath. They didn't want ransom, and I had ruled out the possibility that they planned to use me for pleasure. Plenty of opportunities for that had passed by now. I could only wonder what fate awaited me.

My kidnappers had seemed so sure of themselves when they snatched me from the kitchen cellar of the manor and hauled me alongside the snowy road leading north. But as we stood at the outskirts of the Forest of the West Fringe, I felt a tremor in their resolve.

Once we plunged into the woods, the snowfall grew so dense, we faced the danger of hitting a tree nose-first before we caught a glimpse of it.

Hagan glanced nervously over his shoulder, his breath puffing out like pipe smoke in my face. "Let's rest a bit, eh?" he said to the others, who studied their surroundings before nodding their heads. No one, not even hardened men like these, could feel at ease in the Forest of the West Fringe.

"This spot's as good as any," said the uncomely, squash-faced fellow with gray teeth, pointing at a cluster of evergreens. The men unburdened themselves and gathered beneath low branches that dipped under the weight of the thickening snow.

Hagan relinquished me with a relieved sigh. I lost my footing, but he grabbed me by the arm before I fell. "Don't you go runnin' off now, Bridget," he warned, as if I were an errant child.

"Bristal," I hissed, twisting out of his grip. But I stayed put as he asked. We both knew I wouldn't make it far in these woods, not without a proper cloak and winter boots.

While the four men pulled kindling from their packs and labored over a sputtering flame, I sat with my back against a tree, swallowing hot tears. They ate a meal of pork and bread, casting cagey looks over their shoulders. In the olden days, these woods had been rampant with terrible and beautiful creatures. Some said that if you journeyed deep enough, you could see shadows of things long thought to have fled the realm of Nissera.

"Should we give her something to eat?" the blond man, who I thought was called Elwood, asked the others.

"Why waste it?" asked the ugly fellow with the gray teeth, poking indelicately at the feeble fire. "This lass will be nothing but a drowned corpse in a few hours."

My stomach dropped. Drowning. I tried to slow my breathing, to comfort myself with the thought that it might merely feel like falling asleep. These men could surely think of worse ways to kill me if they wished.

"Why are you doing this?"

No one answered, though Elwood offered me a chunk of bread and meat. I wanted to turn it down, but he unfastened his cloak and swept it over my shoulders. This small act of kindness overthrew my resolve and I accepted the food, thankful that the bitter wind dried my tears before they fell.

"Don't worry," Elwood said. "You may survive."

"Don't make any promises," said the fourth, who had been

silent the entire journey. "Thousands have touched the Water and died. Do you know how many have lived in the last few centuries, girl?"

The fear latching onto my stomach got an even fiercer grip and twisted hard. I had heard stories of the Water, a pool that lay deep in the forest, deadly to most who dared touch it. Amid my shuddering, I barely managed to nod my head. But I knew. Everyone knew about Brack and Tamarice.

"Two," he said, holding fingers up as his cold blue eyes bore into mine from underneath severe black brows. "Of all those people, only two were worthy to receive an elicrin stone. This bloke thinks you may be the third—I think he's a fool."

"I tell you, Trumble, I've seen her do magic!" Hagan said.

"Magic?" I asked in disbelief. "I don't know the first thing about magic. If I did, do you think I would be the cook's help? And wouldn't I have escaped by now?"

"Don't lie, brat," Hagan snarled. He shivered and brought his hood up to cover his bright red hair. "Maybe you can't control it, but I know what I saw."

"Plenty of folks can do small magic, Hagan," said Elwood. "Every proper household in the three kingdoms has a fairy these days, and they're good for nothing but chores and parlor tricks. The cook herself is said to be a witch. I bet every last one of them would turn belly-up in the Water, and this one here doesn't even claim to be their kind."

"Wouldn't that be nice," said Trumble, the cold one with the blue eyes, breaking branches the size of my neck and tossing them onto the fire. "Throw all the witches in with their worthless brews and incantations. If every thesar wasted on that horse dung came to me, I'd be the richest man in Nissera."

Hagan leaned over the flames. "It wasn't small magic. I saw her change into a rabbit. She was in the snow and then pop! I hadn't even blinked. I nearly fell off the ladder whilst I was thatching the roof of the garden shed, didn't I, Gilroy?" He turned to the ugly man, who affirmed his account with a nod. Hagan went on. "That was when I knew she might survive, like one of them elicromancers in the history books."

All four pairs of eyes turned on me.

Turn into a rabbit? Such power was only heard of in stories from the old days, when elicromancers had their own city, culture and language. But only two people had survived the Water to receive an elicrin stone in the last few hundred years. I opened my mouth to argue—to say that I hadn't become a rabbit, that I couldn't have, that I should be elbow-deep in dishwater right now rather than wandering through the forest in my apron—but I choked on my words. Hagan had been violent with me before when I managed to be inconvenient.

"Whether it's true or you were up to your bollocks in ale makes little difference to me," Trumble barked at Hagan. "It will only cost the cook's brat if you're wrong."

"Aye, and maybe a few fingers!" the ugly man named Gilroy said as he rubbed his hands together to keep warm. "But it's better this way, with the snow. They'll think she wandered off and froze to death in the woods. If it doesn't work, none will be the wiser when we're back."

That tale sounded likely enough, as I made a habit of roaming off after finishing my chores to escape the heat and clamor of the kitchen, not to mention the ridicule of the lord and lady's daughter, Hazel. She thrived on watching me finish my chores, only to soil what I'd cleaned or dishevel what I'd straightened.

"Didn't you come from the woods, anyhow?" Gilroy went on. "I've heard the story. You were covered in blood, speaking some nonsense language. All you knew was your name. Everyone but the cook thought you'd been whelped by wild dogs."

"That'll do, Gilroy," said Elwood, voice hard.

I could stomach Gilroy's torment. I had endured Hazel's cruelty for years, and grown smarter for it. A reminder of my past could hardly crush my spirits. It was the truth, after all. Patsy, the cook at a manor house in Popplewell, had taken me in after I was found wandering at the edge of the woods. She brought me from town to town, hoping someone might recognize me and point her to my mother or father. When no one claimed me, she took me in and cared for me. The lord and lady of the manor were kind folk who allowed Patsy eight extra silver aurions a year for my care, as long as she made certain I was useful. They felt obliged; Patsy was so fine a cook that everyone in the nearby border villages suspected her of being a witch. Sometimes I wished she were. Perhaps then she could summon memories of my parents.

Other times, I preferred not knowing how I had turned up roaming the streets like a stray dog.

As I inched closed to my kidnappers' fire to warm my purpling fingers, I thought about how it would take Patsy at least a day to realize I was nowhere to be found. She wouldn't think to go prying for gossip about the manor gardener or three other townsmen who had happened to vanish for a day. It would be too late by then, anyhow.

We started off again, my hands now bound around Trumble's sinewy neck.

The man who had given me the food and cloak leaned close

to me. His pale hair and brows softened the edges of his square jaw and straight nose.

"We may not even find the Water," he said. "The elicromancers put up gates and laid an enchantment upon it. It keeps itself veiled from those it does not welcome, moving throughout the forest and only permitting those who may be worthy." He wore a meager smile, and his colorful, captivated tone reminded me of Patsy's storytelling voice, which I had heard so often as a girl. "I think Hagan's right about you. And if he is right, do you know what will happen should we find the Water?"

I lifted my head, a small hope stirring inside me. But Hagan cut him off before he could say anything more. "That's enough, Elwood," he snarled. "If you tell her any more, things could get dangerous when she comes out of that Water."

"Dangerous?" Elwood repeated as he trudged through the snow beside me. "She's just a kitchen maid, and a slice of a girl."

"Likely to piss herself soon, by the looks of her." Gilroy's laugh reminded me of the raucous little tawny-tits that crowed at dawn. I gritted my teeth and determined that no matter what befell me, I wouldn't piss myself.

"Aye, but look at those eyes," said Hagan. "Sharp and gray as moonlight." He clamped his fingers around my jaw and squeezed. "She's got streaks of magic in her blood. We'll see what that looks like soon enough!"

Gilroy gave another tawny-tit laugh and Elwood fell silent, fixing his gaze on the road ahead. Anger and fear warred in my pulse, but I did nothing, recalling the bruise Hagan's fist had left on my face years ago when I caught him stealing aged sherry from the food cellar. He would no doubt do worse to me now; since I had grown older he'd started calling me "pretty one," and I had felt the urge to squirm under his gaze. I was old enough now to understand what had happened when I was young and saw him coerce one of the maids into the shed, a firm grip on her arm. I would rather jump into the Water than be next.

I tried to recall the legends of the Water, the stories Patsy and the maids had told me. It determined the fate of anyone who dared touch it—like the thousands dead before me. It either bestowed immeasurable power in the form of an elicrin stone or pulled you into its depths and destroyed you. The bodies of those it rejected were never recovered.

In olden days, many people had survived the Water, retrieving a powerful stone from the depths that made them ageless and immortal elicromancers. But a civil war between two factions of elicromancers had wiped most of them out a few centuries ago. After the Elicrin War, magic had greatly weakened in Nissera.

A man named Brack had been the first to survive touching its surface, and after him, a woman, Tamarice. Every soul in the three kingdoms knew those names. Not a soul would know mine.

Little as I wanted to, I clung tightly to Trumble. I feared what lay ahead much more than I feared even him.

"Look at that," Hagan breathed in awe. Streaks of silver flashed in the distance, barely perceptible in the fog. Mist rose from the forest floor and wind whispered through the barren branches.

"Impossible," Elwood muttered breathlessly. "We've already reached the gates."

Trumble handed me off to Gilroy, who smelled like a wet weasel. The men suddenly seemed to have an air of reverence—no, of fear. Their steps slowed and their breaths softened.

We drew cautiously near and saw silver trees glinting in the muted light. The two foremost were woven together to create a set of narrow gates stretching into unknown heights. If the mist hadn't been rippling like ghostly apparitions, the sight would have been more beautiful than fearsome.

Gilroy set me down, but kept a firm grip on my arm. "How are we supposed to get through?" he asked, voice lumbering through the eerie silence.

I looked up at the silver branches looming in the fog. Perhaps we would fail to even reach the sacred pool to begin with.

"Eh! What's this?" Hagan exclaimed.

All eyes followed his pointed finger. Gilroy dragged me forward so that he could get a closer look.

"It's an elicrin stone," Hagan mused.

Where there normally might be a lock, the gates held what looked like a jagged, uncut gem, blue as a sapphire and clenched in ornate silver garniture. Hagan extracted a knife and prepared to pry it off, but the cold man, Trumble, seized his arm.

"A fool you are!" he spat. "This place reeks of old magic. There's power here that would make even an elicromancer tremble, and you come pilfering like it's a jewelry box." He released Hagan's arm. "Let's do what we came here to."

Hagan made as if to argue but instead sighed, disenchanted. Eyes locked on the translucent gem, he slowly sheathed his dagger.

Gilroy seemed to recall the reason we were there and shook me by the shoulders to make sure I hadn't forgotten, either. "Well, go on then, boys!"

Hagan and Trumble pulled with all their strength, but couldn't budge the gate an inch. The elicrin stone flickered even in the absence of sunlight.

"Come off it, Elwood!" Hagan growled. "You going to help?"

We turned to Elwood, who looked pale and uncertain.

"Never mind that," said Gilroy, who held me fast, icy fingers at my nape. "Make her try."

After a hushed moment, they nodded at one another in agreement. Gilroy cut my bonds and the men retreated into the haze. I took a cautious step forward, watching the snowflakes kiss the earth.

"Get to it then!" Hagan prodded.

"What am I supposed to do?" I meant for my voice to sound sharp, as callused and strong as my hardworking hands, but it emerged feeble and thick with fear. I already knew the answer. I looked at the elicrin stone, trying not to notice what lay beyond the gates as my fingertips prickled in anticipation. The light reflecting in the gem seemed to shift and bend, revealing a multitude of rich, rippling hues.

I looked back at my captors, but the flash of a knife in Trumble's hand told me hesitating would only make matters worse. I faced the gates again.

I had worn fairy charms before, even held a stone that a traveling peddler claimed carried traces of deep magic. Those trinkets had produced a sort of chill, a peculiar tingling that traveled across my palm and under my skin, proving its mystical qualities. Closing my eyes, I pressed my fingertips to the stone.

Heat coiled around my veins and burst through them like strands of fire consuming me from inside, only I felt no pain. My blood surged, carrying a shudder of heat to my core. This was no trinket.

The silence grew thick as I drew back and waited. Nothing happened. If it didn't work—if I promised never to tell what they had done—perhaps I would be allowed to return home.

But the uppermost branches began to untangle themselves. The silver slid away, revealing wet brown bark beneath. I gasped as the trees shrank, straightened their branches and grew sparse coronets of withered leaves. Only the tree embedded with the sparkling stone remained unchanged.

Hagan's voice barreled through the dense silence. "Ha! You see that? I'd say I well deserve my three quarters."

"Half," Elwood corrected, voice low. I turned around. He and Trumble hung back, stiff with hesitance.

I dug my heels into the snow as Gilroy dragged me forward, hauling me over the threshold. "You aren't getting scared now, are you, pretty one?" he goaded, making a show of his gray-tinged teeth. "We're nearly to the good part!"

With mounting terror, I watched the fog snake away from the Water. The surface shone silver, but I could see fragments of light breaking up the darkness, rays of color cast in all directions, tricking the eye so that its depth could no more easily be determined than the distance of the stars.

The men formed a half-circle around me. Gilroy shoved me toward the Water's edge.

"Please, I'm not what you think I am." I attempted to break

free from the heavy hands on my shoulders, twisting to face Hagan. "My guardian is a witch," I lied. "The powerful sort. But me, I've never done magic. I don't know how to do any of it, common or not." At least that part was true.

There was a touch of doubt in Hagan's hard eyes. He looked at Trumble. "What if it was the witch? What if she finds out and punishes us?"

Trumble's tone was final. "The girl opened the gates. She's coming out with an elicrin stone or not at all."

I turned to Elwood, my last hope.

"Please," I begged, the word emerging as a hoarse whisper. Elwood bleakly returned my gaze.

Trumble chuckled. "Don't be cross with him for not taking up for you, sweet. He has his reasons. Don't you, Elwood?"

Elwood stared at Trumble. He stiffened his jaw but kept silent.

"That's what I thought," Trumble said. "You can play the hero another day."

I felt a fresh round of fiery tears well up as Trumble tugged off my borrowed cloak and clamped a large hand on my shoulder.

"No!" I shrieked, beating my fists against his solid chest until the word became nothing but a scream. He yanked me close to the shore, dangling me so that my feet still touched the earth but the rest of me was poised over the Water. My warped reflection showed a sopping mess of dark hair, a stained apron and eyes alight with fear.

My left hand nearly touched the surface. I made a defiant fist.

"Shall I drop you in?" Trumble growled into my ear. I

shuddered as the cold caress of a knife trailed along the back of my neck.

"She's scared enough!" Elwood pleaded.

Trumble didn't react. "Let's put it this way: you got a better chance of living by touching that water than by disobeying me."

Biting back a sob, I uncurled my fist. The distance between the Water and my hand was imperceptible.

I shut my eyes and grazed the surface with my fingertips.

A ghostly calm swept over the world. Seconds passed, sinister in their silence, before an invisible force from below clenched my forearm with an icy grip and pulled me into darkness.

As I sank far beneath the surface, I heard a sound like crackling wood and watched in horror as a sheet of ice closed over the Water. I saw the four men's tainted faces as if from a far-off world, listened as their voices drowned in pressing silence. The cold shocked my body so immediately that I couldn't even will my limbs to struggle, to press toward freedom.

A long time seemed to pass as I drifted down. I began to wonder if I might already be dead, because at the center of the brilliant ice shone a white light. It lit up weeds swaying along the floor down below, and hidden among them, a glint of silver that looked like, of all things, armor.

It was a body.

Above me the ice cracked with a deafening sound. Fractures crept through it, splintering it into shards that burst down through the Water like a deluge of jagged rain. Only one of them fell slowly while the others raced back into the depths. The elicrin stone settled softly in my hand, illuminated by the white light and surging with warm energy I could feel in my blood.

I fought toward the surface, at last emerging into the biting air. The Water swirled with waves that gently nudged me toward shore.

✳

The ache in my lungs slowly faded as I sucked in precious breaths. I rolled over and looked at the jagged treasure in my palm. It was a translucent blue-gray, like the color of the sky muffled by wispy clouds and falling snow.

Elwood lay panting in the snow next to me, blood smeared across his face and one eye swelling. He must have tried to save me.

Footfalls approached. I looked up to see Trumble standing over me with his knife, cold eyes fixed on my elicrin stone.

He had been right: I had more to fear from him than the Water. He was determined I would die today, fate be damned.

But no sooner did he pry the stone from my fingers than he discharged a vile curse and dropped it in the snow, the flesh of his palm seared. He glared at me before lurching forward as if to seize me by the hair, but I scrambled away and sprinted dizzily into the cover of the trees.

As I reeled through the mist, I felt a pang of regret at leaving the elicrin stone behind. But I wouldn't let them kill me after I had survived the Water.

My surroundings pulsed in my vision and I felt as if I were learning to use my legs again. Whether the Water had made me more powerful or muddled my senses, I couldn't tell. I only knew that it had changed me.

The kidnappers gave fierce chase, but their ungainly footsteps sounded far behind me. I swerved to avoid trees and sprang through the snow with less noise than a whisper, tearing on until it seemed the kidnappers had lost my trail. As I came upon a clearing, I slowed to a canter, barely even short of breath.

The silver pool waited before me. I had unknowingly circled back to the Water, where Elwood stood alone at the edge. He held the precious object in a fold of his cloak.

From across the clearing, his eyes met mine in awe. Hand trembling slightly, he lifted the stone, offering it to me.

A whooshing sound followed by a swift thud made me lurch back—an arrow striking a nearby tree. The shot had been meant for me and narrowly missed.

Near the tree line, Hagan drew back another arrow. He let the string slip and before I could escape, a piercing pain wracked my side. I collapsed in the snow with a cry.

Fingers trembling, I reached down to feel the shaft of the arrow underneath my ribs. I registered with shock the sight of dark blood on my fingertips and, more absurdly, my unclothed body. But none of that seemed real. Only the sharp, cold, pain sinking through me was real.

The other two emerged from the wood. At the creak of a bowstring, I shut my eyes and waited for death again.

But light pierced the wintry haze as a strange man launched himself in front of Trumble's drawn bow. Before Trumble could react, the man tore the weapon from his hand and, without so much as touching him, sent him reeling across the clearing.

The stranger whipped around. He was tall and broad-shouldered, built like a soldier, with hair blacker than midnight. An emerald elicrin stone hung around his neck, marking him as one of the two remaining elicromancers in Nissera. But his most notable feature was the deep, disfiguring scar that ran diagonally from his right temple, over the bridge of his nose, drawing to a jagged end near his left ear. His eyes locked on mine.

Meanwhile, Hagan stretched for the quiver on his back. He aimed for the scarred man's broad chest, but before he could let fly, a thin branch whipped down from the treetops to wrap around his wrists and neck.

Someone gave a little jerk of laughter. I looked up to see a young woman stride into the clearing and approach Hagan. She yanked one hand upward and the branches suspended Hagan high in the air, straining his arms in opposite directions. His face filled with blood and his screams were wrought with unsettling desperation. I knew that with any more pressure his body would rip apart.

"Tamarice!" the scarred man barked.

The young woman froze and calmly met his eyes. Her hands relaxed, and the branches slid away from Hagan's limbs, dropping him inelegantly on the ground.

When she noticed me lying in a pool of blood, she sprinted gracefully to my side. Her thick brown plait swept across my face as she leaned over me and studied my wound with the forced composure of someone who has seen worse.

"Hold on," she whispered.

A red gem swinging between her ribs lit up and the ground beneath me transformed from packed snow to soft grass. She laid her cloak over my body, careful not to let it touch the arrow, and gripped my hand in hers. Her eyes were soft and gold as nectar, warm with astonishing affection that comforted me even while I writhed in agony.

Gilroy attacked the disfigured man from behind with a

dagger. Tamarice turned to watch the struggle, unruffled. I saw a knife pressed against my male rescuer's throat and for a moment thought he had been overpowered. But an unseen force compelled the dagger and coaxed it from the wielder's hand. I heard the crack of Gilroy's bones as the knife bent back his fingers and tore from his grasp, lodging itself securely in the frozen ground at his feet.

Realizing they were outmatched, my kidnappers slowly rose to their feet, shoulders hunched in surrender.

"Drop your weapons," the powerful man commanded.

Soft thuds broke through the silence as the two who still held weapons obeyed him perfunctorily.

"Leave or die."

With one last awestruck glance at me and then the elicromancers, Hagan and Gilroy trudged toward the spot where the gates had once been, the second cradling his broken fingers. Trumble, seething with anger, spit blood on the miry snow and followed.

Elwood approached the disfigured warrior who had saved my life, taking a knee before him. Cradling my elicrin stone in his cloak, he lifted it toward the elicromancer. "Lord Brack, forgive me," he whispered, head bowed. "I wouldn't have done it if I'd had a choice." He looked at me, writhing in grass blotted with dark blood. "Forgive me."

The elicromancer's expression was cold. I feared what justice he might exact upon my kidnapper. But he used his own cloak to accept the stone, tucking it away in his tunic, then took a small leather pouch from the same pocket and offered it to Elwood.

Mystified, Elwood stood and accepted the mysterious gift.

My eyelids grew heavy and I flickered in and out of consciousness as I met his rueful gaze and watched him depart from the clearing.

The scarred man was a blur as he knelt at my other side.

"I'm going to take out the arrow," he warned me. "So I can heal the wound."

I squeezed my eyes shut and screamed as he ripped the point from my flesh. My consciousness reeled while the light from his green elicrin stone spread over me. He enveloped me with his cloak and lifted me.

Held against his chest, I felt his voice resound. I was unable to make sense of his remark as everything faded away. In fact, I was sure I imagined it.

"That was a clever trick, transforming into a deer. Clever indeed."

TWO

"They thought they could use her." A voice emerged from the profound silence. "As if an elicrin stone simply belongs to anyone who happens upon it. If we hadn't intervened, she would be lying there dead, her power wasted."

I wanted to climb out of the black fog in my mind, but the warmth of sleep held me captive. I recognized the voices, but they sounded distant.

"Yes, they were men without consciences," Brack said. "But the last man was merely desperate."

"Desperate?" the woman called Tamarice demanded. "Is that why you gave him a whole bag of gold aurions? You sympathize too easily."

"His children were nearly starving. He didn't want to take part. If you had heard his thoughts—"

"Whatever he was *thinking*, he still dragged a young woman to her probable death."

"The gift was mine to give." Brack's voice was firm, but gentle.

"The point is that he deserved death and you rewarded him."

"The last generation erected the gates around the Water for a reason: so that only those meant to open them would open them. She was meant to have an elicrin stone, to be here with us now. For all the things they did wrong, the kidnappers delivered her to her destiny."

Tamarice let out a frustrated sigh. "I'll get the old woman so she can tend to her."

"That 'old woman' is an elder of this city, not a servant, and she deserves your respect. . . ." Brack trailed off as the other elicromancer's resolved footsteps faded. He sighed wearily, turning toward me.

"She is clever, Bristal," he whispered, though my eyes were closed and heavy with fatigue. "But I hope you are wise."

After he left, I heard only a hearth fire crackling and mountain wind wailing at shutters.

*

An unforgiving ray of evening sunlight tinted the back of my eyelids red. The soreness of the arrow wound ranged from the tight, itchy flesh to the depths of my belly, forcing me to groan through cracked lips. As I blinked at an unfamiliar room, a face materialized next to my bed, edging closer as though inspecting me. The cloud of fatigue cleared and I took in a little girl's straight orange hair and round eyes of glistening blue.

"Grandmum, she's awake!"

"You made sure of that when you opened the shutters, Deirdrel." The second voice belonged to a tall old woman whose gray hair held hints of faded auburn. She stood up from her seat by the fire and tested my skin for fever with a feather-light hand.

"I was just letting fresh air in," the little girl argued. "It smells like sickness."

"Where am I?" I croaked.

The old woman spoke. "A citadel in the Brazor Mountains called Darmeska. I'm Kimber, an elder of this city, and this is my granddaughter, Deirdrel."

"Drell," the girl corrected.

I had heard of Darmeska before. Patsy had shown me the map on display in the manor study and explained that it was where the descendants of the ancient elicromancers lived.

"Try to eat up while it's hot," Kimber said, placing a bowl of vegetable soup in my hands. The woman and her granddaughter's Northern lilts were strong, much more colorful than my Volarian accent.

I sipped until I realized the breadth of my hunger, then began slurping the steaming broth, which ran down my chin as I swallowed spoonful after spoonful. I tried to sound polite between ravenous helpings. "Do you happen to know where my elicrin stone is?"

"Brack is keeping it for you. He will send for you when the healing spell has completed its work."

Grimacing, I recalled the painful wound and my stark naked body in the snow.

"Do you want to see the best view of Darmeska?" Drell interrupted my thoughts, pointing at the window beside me.

I followed her gaze and my breath caught in wonder. The citadel must have been built into vast cliffs; I saw a dizzying view of the sprawling wilderness in the distance, glistening with ice and snow. The stacked lower levels spread out below us, an entire city staggering down the slope of a mountain.

"Are there galleries full of magical artifacts? That's what people say."

"Yes, we have preserved the culture of our ancestors, even if the magic has thinned in our veins." Kimber closed the shutters, blocking out the chill. Her proud posture exemplified her status as an elder, and yet she was tending to me like a servant. Either the people of this city were very kind, or I was very important.

When I finished the soup, Kimber placed a teacup full of dark-ruby liquid on a saucer at my bedside. "Briarberry tea. It's likely stronger than what you're used to."

It was bitter, much more robust than the peppermint tea we drank in Popplewell, but I detected a tad more sweetness with each sip. When I'd emptied the dregs, Kimber changed the poultice covering my wound. She took pains to ensure I wouldn't see the brown-stained cloth, though I saw it anyhow. I gingerly traced my wound with my fingertips, surprised to find the beginnings of a taut, shiny scar and a stippled bruise rather than a jaggedly stitched wound.

An abrupt knock on the door signaled Tamarice's entry. She looked even younger than I remembered, perhaps only a few years older than me in body, though the legends said she was a century old. Ladylike features—soft cheeks, a round nose, long lashes and lips so full and pink that other women would have pinched and painted theirs for the same effect—clashed with her powerful stance and wild dark braid. Her circular vermilion elicrin stone was set in a gold pendant that hung on a thick chain around her neck.

She strode up to me and examined my wound. "Are you feeling better?"

I lowered my dressing gown. "Much. I can never thank you enough for saving me."

"I would have stopped that arrow if I'd gotten there in time. I'm just happy you're alive." Her eyes snapped to Kimber behind me. "Get her dressed. Brack is ready for her."

"Brack said to send her when she's well. Cheating death is no small matter."

"She looks well enough to me."

After a tense pause, the elder turned her back on the elicromancer and opened a massive wardrobe sitting against the stone wall of the bedchamber. She rifled through a small selection of winter dresses and picked out a dark blue wool dress, a pair of boots and a cloak.

"She can't train in a dress," said Tamarice, who wore a leather tunic, sturdy boots and a fur cloak.

"I doubt she will have any rigorous lessons today. Drell will go down to a clothier to buy her something more suitable."

Drell narrowed her blue eyes at Tamarice. Her thin lips and straight orange hair made for overall peculiar features, but they were somehow pleasant on an otherwise plain face, which she screwed up in a frown. She moseyed out of the room, shoulders prouder than her grandmother's.

Tamarice begrudgingly accepted the clothes from Kimber and helped me get dressed. She finished by tossing the cloak over my shoulders. "Follow me," she said, already on her way into the stone corridor.

"Thank you," I said to Kimber, feeling torn about Tamarice's poor graces. The old woman smiled and nodded, and I hurried out of the room.

My bedchamber overlooked the city below, as well as the foothills and the forests beyond that eventually met civilization. But when I wiped away the condensation clinging to the windows on the opposite side of the corridor, I saw a snowy plateau surrounded by cliffs that jutted higher still than the citadel. Whatever unknown wilderness of mountains and sea lay beyond them was unseen even from the topmost level of Darmeska.

I ignored the pain of my mending wound as Tamarice led me down a drafty stone stairwell, moving slowly for my benefit. "High as we are, the slightest wind can sound like a howling storm," she said. "So don't be frightened thinking the fortress is going to come crashing down."

"Where are the other people?"

"The common folk live down below. Thousands of elicromancers once filled these halls, but now it's just you up here."

"Where do you live?

She removed a heavy latch from the wooden door and a burst of cold air raced around us. We walked through a small passage onto the mountain plateau. "Brack lives in that stone cottage set in the cliff face," she said pointing to a stone hut with smoke pouring from the chimney and warm light from the windows. "And I have a home outside of the citadel, down by the river. Being an elicromancer isn't much to boast of anymore. We don't live in the extravagance many would expect."

My dark hair blinded me as it whipped around in the freezing wind. I tightened the fur around my shoulders, gazing up at the mountains. "It's extravagant to me."

Tamarice led the way over the snowy plateau, which turned to grass beneath her feet. She was lean and powerful-looking, but as I watched her cross through the cutting wind, I realized that the look of power came from within rather than without.

It struck me then: I was like her. I was now one of the three most powerful beings in the realm of Nissera. Soon everyone from Calgoran to Yorth would know my name.

My life in Popplewell suddenly felt as distant as a childhood memory. I wondered if I would ever go back to the manor, if I would have a chance to thank Patsy for her charity. I smiled to myself, thinking of Hazel's reaction to the news that I was an elicromancer. Knowing that in every shadow she would imagine me returning for vengeance was satisfying vengeance enough.

When we reached the hovel, Tamarice opened the door without knocking, casting a gold prism of light on the grass. She allowed me to step inside first. A sitting room with mismatched furniture held untidy stacks of books and loose parchment. In the corner near the fireplace stood an entrance to a winding stairwell, and to the left sat a small kitchen with a simple square table and other crude furnishings.

Remembering Brack's scar, I prepared myself to look on his marred features. But rather than a massive, marked young warrior, there sat a middle-aged man with cropped graying hair and a neat beard. There was no scar—just light eyes of an indeterminate blue-gray. He had a squarish face crossed with the leathery wrinkles that come to the weary too young.

Tamarice brushed past me to warm herself by the fire. Brack stood up from his ratty chair to welcome me.

"Brack . . . sir?" I ventured.

"Bristal, good evening. I'm surprised to see you up and about." The friendly voice was different from the one I had heard before. He set a chair near the hearth and gestured for me to sit. "I'm sorry if my appearance startled you," he said, removing the damp fur from my shoulders and replacing it with a blanket. "I find it makes things easier to be young and strong when I have to fight. Otherwise, I don't mind this." He gestured at himself. "Care for briarberry tea?"

"You change your appearance?" I asked. "Oh, and yes, please."

"It took me more than a hundred years to learn how, and as of yet I've only managed to create two guises."

"One hundred years . . ." I repeated.

"Indeed. You must take pity on the rest of us to whom the power of changing forms doesn't come so naturally." He chuckled at my astonished look. "You're pale. Something to eat?"

"No, but thank you." My mind was far from my full stomach or my injury. "If you don't mind my asking, is this your . . . true self?"

"No. I've haven't appeared as my true self in many years."

I studied him as he hung a tea kettle over the fire. Though older now, he looked sturdy and square, like a retired soldier. The gentleness of his manner agreed with the mercy he showed my kidnappers by sparing their lives. I found it easier to believe he and the man who helped save me yesterday were one and the same.

I looked at Tamarice, now suspicious that her beauty was contrived. "Is that your real . . . ?"

"Yes, it is," she said.

I turned back to Brack. "Why do you appear as either old or scarred? Can't you choose any form you wish?"

"I've found arrogance comes too easily to a young, handsome man. It's not worth the trouble." The kettle screeched. He retrieved it and poured me a cup of briarberry tea, then sat facing me, his eyes bright amid somewhat weatherworn features. "So you have received an elicrin stone."

My heart cantered. "Yes."

He pulled a wrapped object from the pocket of his wool tunic and gave it to me. I unwrapped the cloth and saw the glistening surface of my pale blue gem catching the firelight. Feeling all was right with the world again, I tested its weight in my palm.

"We elicromancers have a purpose," Brack stated carefully. "As gifted beings, we are destined to guide the kingdoms of men to prosperity and peace, to come to their aid when disaster or war threatens."

"Or when Calgoran and Volarre cannot play as friends," Tamarice said. "We like to slap their hands like strict governesses."

"Yes, we aim to prevent proud, powerful men with armies from growing hostile," Brack retorted. He looked at me. "I suppose you're wondering where you come into play."

I nodded.

"There's been magic in your blood since you were born, magic that manifested itself as it chose, outside of your control. Until now." Brack paused, his eyes alight. "The gardener claimed to witness something strange, something you did that only a very powerful being could do."

"I turned into . . . a rabbit?" Watching Brack nod yes to my question felt even more absurd than saying the words aloud. I gasped, finally fitting truths together. "A few days ago, Hagan drank before thatching the roof. He knocked his ladder down but he mumbled something about one of the maids doing it to trap him. I was outside feeding scraps to the dogs, and I tried to hide before he could blame me." I remembered going dizzy, briefly losing my grasp on reality. "But . . . how did you know?"

"Brack is extraordinary, even among elicromancers," Tamarice said. "You and I can manipulate physical matter. He can read and manipulate the mind."

I tensed. Brack's pale eyes shifted from me to Tamarice. "We are all equals. I have promised never to discern your thoughts." He looked back at me. "And I promise the same to you."

I realized I had been holding my breath since Tamarice last spoke, trying to keep my mind from producing thoughts for him to discern. "Um, all right," I muttered. "Thank you."

I didn't know whether I could trust his promise. But when he smiled at my response, the soft wisdom in his eyes made doubt seem unnecessary.

"Though elicromancers have the same broad range of magical abilities," he went on, "each one of us possesses a single gift that is accentuated more than the others. It could be mastery over fire, duplication, prophecy, the ability to turn one's body into impenetrable crystal. . . . There are specialties beyond number. This gift usually manifests itself in some way, often uncontrollably, before the elicromancer claims an elicrin stone."

"Brack is a Sentient," Tamarice said. "I am called a Terrene, because my dominion is over the land and what grows from it. You're a Clandestine."

"Clandestine?"

"Even in the old days the gift was rare and greatly revered," Brack added. "Until now, your talent for disguises has been muddled, unchecked and sporadic. But with an elicrin stone to harness your power, you should be able to assume the form of any human or animal, and even change the appearance of other objects."

A gasp of disbelief escaped my lips. How had so many people drowned in the Water if someone like me could emerge from its depths a hundred times more powerful? I looked at the emerald elicrin stone that hung around Brack's neck. "Who were you before?"

Brack's smiled ruefully. "The arrogant son of a wealthy man. I heard the thoughts of others incessantly, and while I delighted to use it to my advantage, it also plagued me. I knew that if I survived the Water, it would allow me to control my Sentience rather than be at its mercy. In the end, braving the Water also gave me a new sense of responsibility to this world. I no longer saw it as my own for the selfish taking."

I turned to Tamarice, expecting to see her fixing me with the same meaningful look as Brack. But she walked away from the fire to pour herself a cup of tea.

Brack leaned toward me and placed a firm hand on my shoulder. I looked into the depths of his kind eyes, sensing a commission.

"As an elicromancer, you have the responsibility to keep peace between the nations and their people. Your life will no longer be measured by years or the span of mortal lives. Instead, you will mature until you reach the age at which your body ceases to grow, and you will remain that way for a long time."

"A lonely time," Tamarice amended quietly.

"You can choose to be mortal again, giving up your magic along with your responsibility to keep peace in these lands,"

Brack continued. "But if you choose to keep your elicrin stone, you will be challenged, frightened and endangered. You will put yourself aside over and over again, sacrifice the life you want to live for the life you must live. You may even wish you were never brought to the Water. But we promise to prepare you the best we can for whatever comes." His voice grew calm, intent. "I must ask you now: Will you commit to seeking the good of this world?"

At once I knew that this question would weigh on me all my life, no matter my answer. A prick of loss threatened to dampen the exhilaration of the moment. Beginning a new life meant saying a sad farewell to my old one, humble though it was.

More disturbing than that was the memory of the terrifying power hanging in the forest air. What if the unknown path held even greater terrors? It felt too soon to make such a promise.

But a force of pride and purpose rose up from somewhere deep in my chest, a place even deeper than where my heart thundered against my ribs. The elicrin stone in my hand pulsed with light as if to encourage me. It had chosen me. Now I would choose to become worthy.

All I managed at first was an affirmative croak. I swallowed and looked directly into Brack's unfaltering gaze. "Yes, I will."

A quiet moment passed during which I thought of how much power this small room contained. My eyes followed the crimson glow of the fire as it rose and fell like an engulfing tide.

"Then consider this your home." Brack squeezed my shoulder and stood up. "Do you wish to write your guardian? Do you need me to transcribe a letter explaining what's happened?"

"I can write it," I said. "The lord and lady of the manor prefer their servants to be educated."

Brack smiled, hauling a desk with ink and parchment toward me. "Well, that will make your elicromancy training much easier. If you can manage without your elicrin stone for now, I'll have a jeweler make you one of these." He lifted the heavy silver chain and setting that held his jagged emerald stone.

After I reluctantly lay mine back in the cloth he held, he bid us good-night and went out the door.

Dipping the quill in the silky ink, I began my letter to Patsy. After crafting the first sentence, I glanced up at Tamarice. She stood staring blankly into the flames, her red elicrin stone twisting with firelight and her pale fingers tight around her teacup.

"What was your life like before the Water?" I asked her.

The lovely elicromancer smiled, but the humor didn't reach her shining bronze eyes. She took my empty teacup and turned away to pour us each another steaming cupful. "A tale for another time."

✳

With morning sunshine thawing the bitterness in the air, I smiled as I hiked back to Brack's homestead a few days later. The low-lying mists had thinned, revealing silvery peaks jutting into a blue morning sky.

Taking the spiral stairs to the study as Brack had instructed me, I reached a circular room with a lofty ceiling made entirely of glass. Thousands of books lined the shelves, dense and cocooned in dust.

Brack stood amid the clutter, his pendant gleaming white.

Books slunk off the ledges and drifted about, their pages turning as he looked from one to the other, brow furrowed. With a flick of his hand, he sent one to a teetering stack while another soared to a shelf on the second landing.

My stone lay on a square of silk on the desk by the door. The jagged edges had been artfully foiled in silver with thin prongs to hold the stone in place. The pendant was attached to a long, sturdy chain. I brushed it with my fingertips, amazed that so fine a thing belonged to me. It had required years of trust for Patsy to let me wash the fancy dishes trimmed with gold roses.

"It's beautiful."

"I've enchanted it to adapt to your size so that you can wear it with any guise," Brack said, halting the books in the midst of their dance and turning to face me. "Concealing it will be up to you, however. Concealing spells are simple, and you can hide it according to the situation."

I slid it ceremoniously over my head, noticing that the cool metal chain on my nape didn't feel as burdensome as expected. I anticipated a flash of light or a burst of powerful magic to surge out of it, but the elicrin stone just hung lightly against my ribcage. "So, how do I use it?"

"With the language of the ancient elicromancers. Every enchantment and spell corresponds with a phrase in Old Nisseran, which your elicrin stone interprets to an action. What you command, it will make happen. It's as simple as that." He placed his hand atop the wobbly stack of books. I had an ominous feeling that they were for me.

"So I have to learn a language before I can even use it?"

"This isn't a simple fairy charm or a witch's potion."

I nodded, staving off disappointment.

"But since creating disguises is your natural domain, we can jump right into that discipline without words or spells."

"Oh," I perked up, circling my fingers around my elicrin stone.

"Let's start now. Take off your boot, please."

I slid it off and plunked it on the floor.

"Now, close your eyes, breathe in and concentrate on turning it into a slipper. Nothing fancy."

Power swelled up within me like a river during spring rains. I felt my elicrin stone reacting, the magic within it and within me working in tandem. When I opened my eyes I found the boot was still a boot, though made of silk. Next, Brack asked me to turn a teacup into a teapot. I watched it grow, beginning to take on the shape I had envisioned—just before it burst into shards. I covered my head, but the porcelain pieces morphed into silken pink ribbons and fluttered to the floor. I lifted one from the sleeve of my tunic and rubbed it between my thumb and index finger in wonder.

Brack propped his fists on his desk and sighed deeply.

"I'm sorry," I said. "I'll do better next time."

"No, you did very well. Forgive me. My mind is on other matters."

I bit my lip, wondering if it would be audacious of me to ask for more information. Remembering that he had called us equals, I straightened my shoulders and opened my mouth, but he spoke first.

"You haven't happened to visit the library yet, have you?"

"No, my lord."

"You don't need titles among friends, Bristal. I know acting subservient is a difficult habit to break."

I lifted my chin. "Why do you ask?"

"Certain volumes and artifacts have gone missing, ones kept locked up by me and the elders of this city. Far be it for me to judge scholarly pursuits, but it seems someone has taken a rather fastidious interest in the kind of elicromancy we don't ascribe to or permit." He sighed. "I hoped it was simply you, being a curious novice."

I shook my head. "No, I'm afraid it wasn't me." The phrase felt empty without a *my lord* at the end.

"If you . . ." he hesitated. "If Tamarice makes you uncomfortable with her ideas, don't be afraid to tell me so. She's always been fascinated by what some would call *gray areas* of magic. Now that we have you in our midst, her progressive ways put me ill at ease. I don't want you to get overwhelmed."

"I will look out for that," I said. If the three of us were truly equals, I didn't want to promise to report on Tamarice's doings like a spy.

Brack nodded, the shadowy look on his face fading a bit. "Please do." Footsteps clunked up the stairs. "That's Drell here for your next lesson."

"She's going to watch?" I asked, heat rushing to my cheeks. "But I've only just started. . . ."

He strutted toward a cabinet holding an array of weapons. He chose a small sword with an enlarged pommel that was probably meant to keep it from slipping from my hand. "She's going to teach."

I blinked at him. "A child is going to teach me to fight?"

"I started learning when I was three," the high-pitched, heavily-lilted voice said from behind me. Drell waltzed into the room with her fists planted on her hips. "When was the first time *you* held a sword?"

"I never have," I admitted.

"Exactly." She unsheathed the dirk at her waist and struck a pose of readiness.

I laughed, thinking perhaps this was a joke, but Brack held out the lightweight sword for me to take. Drell stalked out of the room, leading the way down the stairs and out the door.

"Will your wound permit rigorous exercise?" Brack asked. "I can tell Drell to take it easy on you."

"Don't bother." I smiled, looking up into his strangely sad eyes as I accepted the weapon. "Thanks to you, there's not even a scar."

THREE

After an hour of winding through staircases and dark, unused passages, my shoulders and back ached from carrying the satchel of Brack's oversized history volumes. I began to fear that I would never find my way to the inhabited areas of the citadel, and worse, that no one would find my corpse for a century.

At last I reached the galleries, where Tamarice waited for me. The vast stone halls could have housed giants. As it was, colorful tapestries and paintings stretched the length of the walls, and endless rows of glass cases held ancient artifacts. The grand entranceway opened to the main courtyard, where a small crowd milled about at the market.

The galleries were empty, however, and my footsteps echoed as I approached Tamarice. She stood before a battle mural so large that its many subjects matched her in size. Her thick brown hair was no longer wild, but in a sleek plait, allowing me a full view of her refined features.

She gestured grandly. "The last battle of the Elicrin War."

I transferred my gaze to the painting, realizing that the vivid reds and greens I had noticed at a glance depicted blood spilled across grassy hills. Bodies littered the lush landscape, so lifelike I wanted to look away. White feral cats and black wolves prowled the battlefield, a macabre dance of ghosts and shadows. Enormous birds with hooked claws and feathers black as pitch circled overhead. A glistening black serpent with four legs and rows upon rows of long, pointed teeth lay lifeless, its dead yellow eyes open, its belly slit from throat to tail. I knew from legends that these were not ordinary animals. They were creatures from Galgeth—the land in the west that only the dead or immortal could reach.

"The Battle of the Lairn Hills," I said, my voice graver than I wished it to sound. I reminded myself that it was distant history, and that these warriors were long dead, their suffering past.

Tamarice eyed the heavy satchel drooping from my shoulder. "What do you know about the Elicrin War?"

"Some elicromancers wanted to use their power to become tyrants over mortals instead of peacekeepers. The good elicromancers challenged them and the conflict culminated in a final battle"—I gestured at the mural—"in which the two leaders killed each other. The good side won." I slid the bag off my shoulder and dropped it heedlessly on the floor, wishing there were somewhere to sit down.

"If only war were as simple as its summation," Tamarice said.

"What do you mean?"

She turned to face me directly, her tawny eyes earnest. "History likes to call one side good and the other evil. But is it bad to want to use your power to bring clean order to the world? To achieve the peace in this land that mortals can't achieve on their own?"

"No, I don't suppose enforcing peace is a bad thing."

"The books you have there, the ones that Brack gave you, will tell you that the revolutionary elicromancers wreaked havoc on Nissera. But it was the traditional ones who began the fighting. They refused to take their natural roles as leaders." She took a deep breath, and the sharp passion in her voice softened. "I'm not saying the revolutionaries were right. I'm not saying they went about things well. I just want you to learn that not everything is as clearly defined as Brack—and those books, written by men like Brack—would like to think. I want you to have an open mind."

"All right," I said. "I've lived a simple life, but I understand that not everything is simple."

Tamarice smiled and pulled a small, clinking bundle from her tunic. She reached inside carefully and her slender fingers emerged holding an elicrin stone by the chain. The metal of the pendant was so tarnished, I couldn't tell whether it was bronze or gold, only that it was old. She lifted it into a shaft of light falling from a high window, examining the colorless, foggy surface of the stone. "Your elicrin stone is the most precious friend you will ever have. It is your lover, your servant, your superior. You are so intertwined with it, in fact, that if you were to die or to give it up, it would lose all but a wisp of its power. And if you lost it, the same would be true of you. You need one another. Which is why this is such a strange phenomenon."

"What is?"

"Most abandoned elicrin stones have only a trace of magic

left, like the one that guards the gates to the Water. That one belonged to Cassian, the leader of the 'good side,' as you called them. It helped him heal any injury within seconds. The last generation of elicromancers put it on the entrance to protect the unworthy. It stops those who are likely to die from ever entering. There is so little power left in renounced stones that royalty have bought them up and wear them like ordinary jewels. But this one . . ." She lifted her other hand and slowly closed it over the pendant.

She let out a cry of pain that made me jump. She pulled her hand back to show me a raw, red burn on her palm. "It burns to the touch. Only elicrin stones with living masters do that."

"So you think there's another elicromancer out there?"

"I don't know."

Soft steps brought us both to attention. I recognized Kimber's long shadow against the light of the courtyard.

"Bristal," she said, approaching us. "Drell said your sword-play lessons have been promising."

I chuckled. "I interpreted her critique quite differently."

"You're just who we needed to see," Tamarice interrupted, holding out the relic. "I'm hoping to determine to whom this once belonged. Isn't there an index of elicrin stones some-where? A record of their descriptions and owners?"

Kimber's eyes widened in alarm. "Where did you find that?"

"Brack took it out of the vault in the library for one of Bristal's lessons." I sensed that Tamarice had found it when rummaging through the vault without permission, but I said nothing. "Do you know whose it was or what it did?"

"This has been dragged through the shadows of black elicromancy," Kimber said in a low voice. "Whatever its original purpose, it's long lost now."

Tamarice raised a shapely brow. Tall as the elder was, the elicromancer stood nearly eye-to-eye with her. She took a step closer. "You know, don't you?"

Kimber's tone was final. "Please put it back where you found it and do not desecrate the memorial halls of our ancestors again."

"You are so committed to revering your dead ancestors, yet you hardly care to treat their living likenesses with any dignity." Tamarice gestured between herself and me. I held my breath.

Kimber maintained a look of cold poise and gave no response. Replacing the pendant in the sack, Tamarice brushed past her. Since I had walked all the way to the galleries for a lesson with Tamarice, I picked up my book bag, bowed my head to Kimber and trailed the elicromancer from the hall.

"She lets that crude little girl do whatever she wills, and I'm not even permitted to archive an historical artifact," Tamarice spat as we left the empty galleries and emerged into the busy marketplace. "I remember when Kimber was a young woman. I should have stepped in before Brack recommended her to the council of elders."

This served as an astonishing reminder of my own agelessness. I stopped short in front of a vegetable vendor's stall. "You knew her when she was young?"

Tamarice had seen a child grow old and gray. How many centuries would pass with so few people for enduring company? Would I have to choose to give up the source of my immortality someday—or would I be too cowardly, clinging to life until I was centuries old?

Raking in breaths, I bent double and nearly lost my breakfast. Tamarice rubbed my back and spoke soothingly. A few people slowed down and stared at us—stared at the elicrin stone around my neck. Already, word that a young kitchen maid from Popplewell had survived the Water to become an elicromancer would be trickling through the realm, gaining momentum as it went.

"It's all right," she said, removing the satchel of books from my shoulder. "I had a moment like this. It's odd, at first, to think of your life in centuries rather than years." She laid a gentle hand on my elbow and steered me forward. "Come."

By the time we reached the open city gates, I had mostly collected myself—just in time to realize the bridge leading away from Darmeska stood over an immense ravine that swallowed the bottom of gray cliffs in shadow far below. We began crossing it, and I focused on taking steady steps even though ten men could have walked abreast.

"You're going to break your back lugging this around," Tamarice said, shifting the weight of my bag.

"I thought I might need materials for our lesson."

"Brack has rather archaic ways of going about things, but my lessons will be different." Though she had noted its heaviness, the satchel appeared light hanging off her arm.

"What do you have in mind?"

She stopped and cocked her head. "Iron must endure fire to be made deadly." She placed her hands on my shoulders. "I trust you not to burn."

She drove me backwards with surprising physical power.

My mind reeled as I took a final step back, and then there was nothing but air beneath my heel.

I thought I knew how it felt to be utterly out of control: to drown, to bleed, to be dragged through the woods at the whim of violent men. But this was true helplessness. Rocks would break my fall and my body.

I screamed until the wind caught underneath me, just barely at first, like a breeze brushing an autumn leaf sideways as it twirls to the ground. The sides of the ravine slid by more and more slowly. Feeling hollow, yet strong, I gorged my lungs on cold air. A current under my arms lifted me, and I used my outstretched limbs to get another, more forceful push upward.

I labored desperately to reach the light above me, and the narrow stripe of gray that was the bridge from which I'd fallen only a second before.

As soon as I drew level with it, I flung myself forward, landing with a smack on the hard stones. My knees and forearms took most of the impact. I groaned and rolled over, relieved to be alive but in fierce pain nonetheless.

Tamarice knelt beside me. Her elicrin stone lit up and a little of the pain faded from my stinging cuts and already tender bruises. She grinned and placed a soft hand on my face. "Barely a second with wings and you looked as if you were born with them. You shifted so gracefully."

"Why did you do that?" I growled.

She helped me up. "Our first lesson: don't dabble in your power like a coward. Test the limits before you learn to fear them. Do you trust yourself more than you did a moment ago?"

Now that I was recovering, I could begrudgingly nod my head.

Tamarice beckoned me forward. I limped after her and we reached the end of the bridge, where a stone staircase wound down a hill into the white-shrouded woods.

"Do you know what *elicrin* means?" she asked, pausing at the top step and turning to face me.

"Peacekeeper?" I guessed.

"It's Old Nisseran for *god on earth*." She faced the woods and waved her hand before her as if wiping frost from a window. A section of icy evergreens burst with fresh green and bright flowers blossomed. The shock of color snaked off into the distance like a pathway, beckoning us forward.

The last trace of my anger faded. Tamarice gestured for me to go down the steps before her and we crossed into the shade of the trees, following the path of fresh growing things in the midst of the winter wood. We reached a flowing stream, where a small boat was nestled by the icy riverbank. She grabbed a handful of briarberries from the thorns before heaving the boat into the water. Stepping in dexterously, she motioned for me to follow.

We floated quickly downstream, paddling along and eating berries until we reached an arcade of trees. It formed a sort of house with flower-speckled leaf canopies that acted as walls. Tamarice stepped out and tugged the boat to shore so I could disembark.

Once on the banks, I parted a section of the tree canopy and entered the house. A curtain of white flowers covered a four-poster bed. Rather than chairs, hammocks of woven leaves hung from the branches high above. The shelter's most ordinary features included a table with wide stumps for chairs, a freestanding kitchen cupboard holding pots and wooden bowls and a filigree mirror.

I caught a glimpse of our faces in the glass. As I had guessed before, we looked nearly the same age. Both of us had dark hair and round features. But next to her I looked less grand, more mortal than elicromancer. Maybe it was an air that came with time and experience—or perhaps it was simply her.

"I see why you chose to live outside the citadel," I said, turning in a full circle.

Tamarice smiled as she set down my satchel and the sack with the colorless elicrin stone. She straightened an impressive stack of books on the table and sank into one of the hammocks.

"Our second lesson: enjoy the unique pleasures your gift permits."

I perched on one of the smooth stumps, delighting in the freedom of leather breeches as opposed to a dress. "Being a Terrene must be magnificent."

Tamarice leaned toward me, emphasizing every other word. "The Clandestine's gift is one of the most coveted and rare forms of elicrin magic. Surely you see how one might do practically anything she chooses with such a talent?"

"I hardly know anything about it yet."

She leaned back. "Once you endure enough of Brack telling you precisely what to do, you will begin to believe your gift has very strict limitations. You will not press boundaries if you are stuck on rudimentary assignments. What did he have you do yesterday?"

"I turned my boots to silk slippers. And I tried to turn a teacup into a teapot."

Tamarice snorted.

"What do you suggest instead? Please don't say jump off an even higher cliff."

Tamarice shook her head, looking past me. "No. It is much easier and yet much more complicated than that."

She got up from her relaxed position and pulled one of the green curtains aside. Darmeska looked imposing in the near distance, the cliffs behind it even more impressive. "Don't think me self-important for saying that under the right circumstances, I could bring those cliffs crumbling down." Her honey brown eyes transferred to my face, and she tapped two fingers on my breastbone. "The heart is even more powerful than elicrin magic. Have you ever been so angry, so torn, that you felt everything and nothing all at once?"

I shook my head. "Only frightened before I touched the Water. And the arrow wound . . . feeling so much life slip out of me was like nothing I've ever known."

She gripped my shoulders, forced me to stand up straight and corrected the slightly off-kilter hang of my pendant so that it touched directly between my ribs. "I want you to close your eyes."

I narrowed them. We may not have been on the edge of a precipice, but I was no fool.

"I will do nothing but speak to you," Tamarice assured me, raising her hand as though pledging fealty. I sighed and obeyed her. "Feel that fear again. Pretend you are once more at the Water."

Even though only days had passed since my kidnapping, I felt I had become someone else entirely. But a thin wind hissed between tightly woven branches, and suddenly I recalled with disturbing detail the rough hands on my nape, the cold that bit at my fingers and toes and sank into my soul. The helplessness paralyzed me like a poison.

It must have shown, because Tamarice said, "Whatever you feel, let it melt to anger. Those common cowards were willing to toss you out like rubbish for nothing but a few gold aurions."

My fists clenched. I thought of Gilroy's disgusting teeth, the evil glint in Hagan's eyes and Trumble's threat to kill me himself if I didn't go into the Water.

My ragged breaths sounded far away. I grew lightheaded, but noticed the tingling in my skin, an itching for something to happen. I could hear my blood rushing like streams of fire in my ears. My mind was loud, deafening and yet somehow tranquil.

"Beautiful," Tamarice whispered. "Beautiful, Bristal."

Without warning, I collapsed against the writing desk, tossing a book spine-up onto the soft grass. Breathing as if I'd just run up and down every staircase in the citadel, I opened my eyes.

Tamarice gripped my elbow and helped me up, grinning in disbelief. She put her hands on my cheeks and exclaimed, "Your face changed dozens of times in the space of a minute! You changed forms so smoothly, took on each disguise so completely. It was a wonder to watch." She laughed in glee and yanked me back outside and toward the citadel.

"We have to tell Brack," she said, releasing me and picking up the pace. "We have to show him! You can get close to anyone, anyone at all—the most important people in Nissera! Why waste time turning boots into slippers? We'll have to teach you court manners, of course, not that I'm an expert in those matters." She walked faster as she talked, until I was jogging to match her long strides.

"Think about it," she continued. "Posing as the right person, you might have the power to give a command to anyone and see it carried out. Of course, we'll have to teach you to materialize, as well. No need to waste time traveling when you have much more important things to do. Together we can reclaim the glory that elicromancers once had."

I sprang forward and caught up to her. She continued to innumerate the possibilities, her golden brown eyes glittering with excitement.

By the time we reached Brack's homestead at the top of the fortress, it was clear to me that I was in poor shape. "Brack," Tamarice said, bursting into the library, causing the older elicromancer to glance up from the documents he scrupulously studied. "Stop frowning over maps and assigning this poor girl hundreds of chapters to read. She should embrace her gift."

Brack's features did not mirror her enthusiasm. In fact, his frown deepened, forging paths of wrinkles across his forehead. "What do you mean?"

"She let go of her reservations." She circled his desk so that they were facing one another. "She changed from woman to man, young to old, beautiful to plain to ugly. She took on the appearances of her kidnappers, you and me, among so many others, all in the span of a moment."

Brack appeared weary as he turned to me. "That's extremely promising, Bristal," he said. "I look forward to seeing for myself what you're capable of. But you've had a long day of lessons, and you ought to rest. Tamarice and I need to have a word."

While he spoke, Tamarice's joy turned to mild surprise before darkening to irritation.

"Yes, of course," I agreed, unable to hide my disappointment. I bowed my head and turned to go, shuffling slowly down the first few steps so that I could catch the beginning of their conversation.

"I'm surprised I have to remind you of the danger of unbridled emotions," Brack said.

"It's unfair of you to bring that up. It was a century ago. I was a child."

"And Bristal is only a child as far as elicromancy is concerned. She has not yet had a chance to develop control, just as you hadn't."

"This is nothing like that."

"It could have been."

As I continued reluctantly down the stairs, their arguing grew indistinguishable.

I bumped into Drell on the bottom step and gave an "*oof.*" Drell shushed me and spoke a phrase of gibberish in an exaggerated whisper.

"What?" I demanded.

"*Seter inoden,*" she repeated, tugging on my pendant. "Old Nisseran. It's a concealing spell. Say it. But grab my hand first."

I did as she asked. My elicrin stone lit up, but nothing seemed to change.

"Don't touch anything," she said in full voice. "And don't let go or they will see and hear me. Come on."

She jerked me up the stairs. I hesitated before we stepped onto the stone landing at the top, but Drell tiptoed into the room, gripping my hand like an iron vice.

Neither Brack nor Tamarice so much as twitched in our direction. Having half-expected the spell not to work, I froze, feeling naked and so very strange. I looked at Drell, whom I could still see, as she pressed herself against the wall and stood completely still. She squeezed my hand reassuringly and I posted up next to her, trying to believe that the flesh I could still feel and see was invisible to other eyes.

"Before the day I found you at the Water, your power had made your life a tragedy." Brack both looked and sounded so tired, so worn.

Tamarice gestured fiercely at him. "And you have grown ever more tragic since I met you. You've taken on burdens you don't need to bear and become a weary old man, worrying about whether generations of kings are getting along. You've exhausted yourself trying to hold back your power, in the name of 'honor.' "

She seemed to suddenly realize her tone had intensified to a yell. She fell silent, smoothing back the fallen hairs that obscured her face, and sighed deeply. Her eyes closed for a long moment. When she opened them, she looked at Brack with deep tenderness.

Rounding the desk that separated them, she knelt before his chair and took his hand in hers. "I'm sorry. I just wish you would stop hiding behind lectures on responsibility and a head of gray hair. Let go, Brack. Allow yourself to simply be. What you can do, who you are, is magnificent and—"

"It's dangerous, Tamarice." He stroked her hand, but then peeled it off of his with a tormented expression. "Desire is dangerous."

Drell and I looked at one another. She pursed her lips and shrugged to show she was as baffled as I.

Tamarice bowed her head, chest heaving. When she looked up, her features were a hard mask.

"I refuse to lie to her. I refuse to pretend that my will can be bent to the needs of selfish humans. You may have been a ruler in your time, but I was treated like a misbehaving dog before I could even speak in my own defense."

Brack stood up to put distance between them, face drawn. "I would never have let that happen if I had been there. You know my heart aches for what you endured—enough not to scold your begrudging attitude every time we go to help those in need, even enough to let you call them 'humans' as though you are something better. But we are responsible for another of our kind now, and I will not stand by while you contaminate her values. Instruct Bristal according to tradition, or do not instruct her at all."

Tamarice had risen to her feet and squared her shoulders. "What if I refuse? What will you do? Challenge me to a fight?"

Brack's defiant expression wavered, fading again to weariness. He said nothing. His silence seemed less a gesture of surrender than a realization that they could argue for days and forever be in discord.

"You would prefer I had nothing to do with her, wouldn't you? Our training days are long over yet you still treat me like a wayward child."

Brack said nothing in reply. Tamarice tore from the room so abruptly that the whoosh of her cloak stirred the hairs around my face.

As I stood frozen, watching Brack sink back into his chair, questions whirled through my mind.

According to him, elicromancers existed to promote peace. I had promised to seek the good of Nissera, and something about that vow felt right and fitting. Brack's humility somehow made him seem worthy of my trust. But he did not seem to live by his statement that we were all equals.

If Tamarice had known great pain in her life, who was I to judge how she felt about mortals? If they had harmed her, what argument did I have against her hatred?

Drell led me downstairs and released my hand at the door. "Repeat the incantation," she said.

"*Seter inoden.*"

"It's a good thing we listened in," she said. "So you could learn."

"Learn what?"

"That Tamarice—"

Drell paused at the sound of a sniffle. I opened the door slowly, finding Tamarice sitting on the doorstep, staring across the plateau at the streaks of orange the sunset painted across the sky.

She turned and glanced from me to Drell with swollen eyes. "I suppose you both heard all that," she muttered, turning away from us again.

Tentatively, I sat on the step next to her. "What happened to you when you were a mortal?"

Tamarice looked back at Drell, who crossed her arms. I realized the elicromancer wasn't going to share any secrets while she was here. Drell realized it too, and shook her head before stalking off across the plateau.

Once Drell had entered the passage that led into the fortress, Tamarice spoke.

"I was born in Volarre, like you. I lived in a poor farming village. The man who fathered me . . . I would have thought tankards of ale grew in our yard, if I hadn't watched him spend every thesar we had on them. He was so violent and stupid that my mother ran away and didn't even bother to take me with her. Those few early years are just a fog of pain and anger in my memory. I had no idea how to manage such strong emotions, and my Terrene gift had a will of its own. I often caused earthquakes or landslides by accident. My village turned on me, which made the disasters worse. One earthquake was fierce enough to claim innocent victims—children."

Tamarice wiped her eyes. "I went to live in the outskirts of the Forest of the West Fringe. I knew I would be happier there, and that people wouldn't have anything to fear from me. But three foolish boys came to hunt down the 'monster' for a thrill. I was only a little girl. They would have killed me if I hadn't used my power to protect myself.

"I had heard of the Water, of how it either killed people or increased their power. I wanted the ability to master my gift rather than let it master me. So I set out to become an elicromancer."

"You went *looking* for the Water?"

"Not all of us are lucky enough to live comfortable lives as kitchen maids," she said. "I went in, received an elicrin stone and then saw Brack waiting on the shore. He brought me back here and made me his protégée."

Eyes dry now, she placed a hand on my wrist and said, "Tomorrow, I will actually teach you something or other about history, all right?"

I offered her a half smile. "All right."

The elicromancer stood, looking imposing once more against the backdrop of a darkening sky. Then she disappeared.

I hiked back across the snowy plateau to the citadel, not

realizing it had grown bitterly cold until I stepped into the shelter of the corridor. From the hallway I could see that my room was warm with firelight, and I walked in to find Drell sitting cross-legged by the hearth, stirring a pot of stew. Kimber sat reading in a chair.

"What did she tell you?" Drell asked skeptically.

"She told me why she chose to go to the Water."

"What did she teach you today?"

"Drell!" Kimber scolded.

"She taught me how to embrace my gift. She didn't do anything wrong."

"Strike flint and tinder just to see a spark and someday you'll start a fire," Drell said.

"What do you know about it? If you want to be an elicromancer, go jump in the Water."

Drell set her chin. Kimber looked at me as if she hoped she'd heard me wrong. Sickening regret immediately rose up in my throat like bile.

"I'm sorry," I blurted, flattening my palm against my forehead. "I'm so sorry. I don't know why I said such a thing."

"I do," Drell said, hopping to her feet and bowing sardonically. "You've already chosen whose student you want to be. See if I offer to help you again, Your All-Powerful-ness." She strutted from the room.

Kimber stood and approached me. I braced myself for her wrath, which I much deserved, but she patted my hair in a motherly way.

"I thought I could learn from both of them," I said.

"You can try, but your very presence has heightened their discord. It seems you may soon have to make up your mind.

But no matter what you choose, remember this: Don't play with darkness. Don't even touch it, because someday soon this world will need you. I can see through your eyes to your heart, and I know you are the type of person—the type of elicromancer—to rise to the occasion."

The elderly woman surprised me by pulling me into an embrace. I laid my head on her shoulder, noticing that she smelled like rose leaves. "I hope I am."

FOUR

Concealing a yawn, I refocused my attentions on the thick volume entitled *The Elicrin War*. The dust tended to make me sneeze, but the words themselves had the power to put me to sleep.

Tamarice and I were back in front of the painting of the Battle of the Lairn Hills for an evening lesson. Since her fight with Brack, she had been a perfectly well-behaved tutor, walking me chronologically through elicromancer history and teaching me phrases in Old Nisseran so that I could begin to perform spells.

Brack had been the only one to address my shapeshifting, and I had learned much within the span of a few weeks. I had succeeded in changing water to briarberry tea and even managed to take on Brack's alternate appearance momentarily, from his scar to his stature.

I was quickly learning that my gift came with limitations. I could not make something out of nothing, nor could I make natural elements out of a manmade thing, like iron ore out of a sword or goatskin out of parchment. A living thing had to remain living and a non-living thing to remain nonliving. Riches were fickle as well. I had tried replicating a copper thesar by plucking a button from my tunic and giving the command, but not even an hour passed before the coin changed back to a button, not an ounce heavier or a tad shinier.

It was best to keep something as similar as possible to its first form. A scrap of cloth would serve better than a leaf if I wanted to make a blanket; though the second might look as much like a blanket as the first, perhaps only the first would keep me warm and dry.

Tamarice snapped her fingers, startling me. "If you can't pay attention during this part, there's no hope for you."

"Sorry," I said, stretching my shoulder and neck, which were sore from lessons in archery, staff combat and swordplay. Drell had forgiven me for my harsh words and was proving to be an apt instructor.

"Don't be sorry, be attentive."

"I'm listening."

Tamarice went back to pacing as she lectured. "Klaine was the leader of the revolutionaries. He was one of the oldest elicromancers, and had earned the respect and awe of many. He believed that solving mortals' problems and cleaning up after them was a waste of elicromancer potential, so he decided to leave Darmeska and establish his own city. He gave his many followers high positions and allowed them to use their powers freely to keep mortals in line.

"Cassian was younger than Klaine, but more powerful, and he had a slightly larger force on his side. At the start of the war, it seemed that both sides had an equal chance of victory. But by the final battle, it became clear to Klaine that Cassian and the peacekeeper elicromancers would prevail. Klaine was desperate. He turned to one of the most condemned acts of magic: a fate-binding spell."

At this point she had my full attention. "A fate-binding spell? What does that do?"

"It's a grueling ritual that ties the life of one person to another so that when one dies, the other dies as well. When Cassian killed Klaine near the end of the Battle of the Lairn Hills, he also killed himself. Think of it as a sort of preemptive revenge."

"What do you mean it was grueling?"

Tamarice stopped pacing and studied the battle mural. "Some spells are not . . . pretty. They can only be performed at great cost."

Someone cleared his throat behind me. I turned around to find Brack with his arms crossed firmly, his graying beard newly trimmed. "I'm sorry to interrupt," he said, looking at me. "But I have some important news."

Tamarice pursed her lips as if pained by his presence, but gestured for him to go ahead. I hadn't seen her and Brack speak once since their argument.

"The queen of Volarre is with child," he said. "The Lorenthi family has had trouble producing an heir, as you know, so this is rather significant. I hope the child will be a girl so that—"

"Volarre can strike up a betrothal between the new princess and one of the princes of Calgoran," I finished. "It would put the two countries on more stable ground."

Through my kingdom politics lessons with Brack I had found out just how much the countries' rulers liked to quarrel and threaten war. The royal family in Calgoran and the royal family in Volarre had long been at odds, using their children as pawns to make statements about who was whose ally.

Brack nodded once, impressed. "Right. I've decided I would like you to attend the name day with me when it occurs, in disguise."

"Truly?" I exclaimed, before checking my childish excitement. An occasion like that would mean feasting, performers and extravagant gifts from royalty. "I never dreamed I'd get to go to the royal city, much less for a prince or princess's name day."

Tamarice shifted uncomfortably in the corner of my eye, but Brack did not seem inclined to extend her an invitation.

"It will be good practice wearing a disguise," he went on. "Not to mention acquainting you with royalty in person, since all of the royal families will be there. I would like to assign you positions of influence in the courts of Calgoran and Volarre in an attempt to strengthen their relations. Your training will continue, of course."

I couldn't hold back a grin. Brack swept his eyes across the mural. "You're learning about the Battle of the Lairn Hills today?"

Tamarice tilted her head. "It is one of the most important events in our history, isn't it? But perhaps you would have liked me to start with something even more basic, since you gave me all of the blandest subjects to teach?"

"Your lesson didn't sound so bland to me," Brack said, unfazed.

I hoped their hostility would dissolve—it was bound to grow tiresome over an endless life span. "Did you know any of the elicromancers who fought in this battle?" I asked Brack by way of intervening.

His voice was softer now as it echoed in the vast gallery. "No. They were of the last generation of elicromancers, and they died shortly before my time. But their stories make me feel connected to them. They remind me of what sacrifice means. Most elicromancers have been wounded by love. After all, we must watch the world change and the people we know pass away, clinging to fading joys or refusing to partake of them at all. Even Cassian and his wife Callista, both immortal, could not flee tragedy. They didn't even try when the battle came. They sacrificed their happiness to fight for the betterment of the world."

"Tamarice said he and Klaine killed each other in battle. Did she die in battle too?"

His expression grew wistful. "No. She was one of the survivors who agreed to give up their elicrin stones and live the rest of their lives as mortals. That way, the existing elicromancers would die off and would no longer present a threat of tyranny to mankind. They could do nothing about the Water and its power to birth new elicromancers, other than try to keep the unworthy from drowning. But the elicromancers chose not to go on living forever, fostering their bloodlines and building their cities. That's why there are just the three of us now."

I had read something to this effect in my history book, but Brack's explanation made surprising loneliness spike through my heart. Darmeska was a hollow husk of lively city, just as we were husks of an entire people.

He sighed. "I'm sure Callista was more than ready to surrender her immortality once Cassian was gone."

I stared at the mural, this time tearing my eyes away from the horrific otherworldly creatures to study the faces of the many warriors. They looked so human, so raw—full of resignation, hope, outrage or despair. I wondered how many sorrows of my own I would have to tell in a few hundred years' time.

Tamarice cleared her throat, snapping us out of the spell.

Voice brisk and overloud, Brack said, "Please, continue with your lesson." With a bow of his head, he retreated the way he had come, firm footsteps echoing into silence.

"Can you believe that?" Tamarice whispered. The irritated edge to her voice had heightened and changed. I now sensed trepidation, perhaps even panic.

"What?"

Without tearing her eerie, wide-eyed gaze from the doorway Brack had passed through, she answered, "You think he couldn't have waited to tell you that news about the name day? He felt he couldn't trust me for even the length of a single lesson."

"I'm sure that's not what—"

"We're running out of time, Bristal." She transferred her intense gaze to me. "I fear I will not be permitted to stay here much longer. We must have one last lesson together, unlike any we've had."

"Um . . ."

"Come." She picked up both our satchels of books and grabbed me by the forearm. I shuffled after her, as unwilling to tear myself from her grasp as to let her drag me into something Brack would disapprove of. But she didn't have far to lead me— merely to the library, whose massive wooden doors stood open right around the corner. Two people of the city sat reading dense volumes in the dusky orange light bearing down from the high windows. Behind them, the grand arcade continued into shadow, lined with shelves upon shelves of thousands of books. I had intended to spend more time here, but my lessons so far rarely permitted free time for exploring.

"Out," she barked at the two mortals, one an old man and the other a young woman. They both scurried away with sore looks, leaving the heavy books where they'd been sitting. Tamarice heaved the doors shut behind them. "We must be quick," she said, taking off toward the farthest end of the room. The light from the lofty windows and torches cast the unlit squares of the library into the darkest shadows, so much that I didn't see the stone statue set against the wall straight ahead until we were upon it. It was of two men, one on the ground and the other standing over him, running his sword through his chest.

"Is that Cassian killing Klaine in battle?" I asked.

"Or Klaine killing Cassian, if that's how you want to look at it. Their fates were bound, remember?"

There was a strange energy to Tamarice's voice and every movement. She knelt down in front of the statue and tried to separate the door of some hidden compartment in its base with her fingertips, only to let out a hair-raising growl. "They closed it up. Stand back and cover your eyes."

I did as she asked, not out of endorsement but out of self-defense. A loud crack sounded and I opened my eyes to find the square base of the statue broken in two. The scene the artist had created slumped down to the floor on one side, making the sprawling villain Klaine now stand on two feet.

She peered down the gaping secret vault and gestured for me to join her. I took a few steps through the debris and crouched down. The vault held sparkling elicrin stones of every color, rich white furs, weapons with glinting jewels and boxes full of nameless other treasures. Tamarice tore out the white furs with little care for how pure and fine they felt and tossed them on the rubble as she kept searching. I picked one up, admiring its beauty until I realized it had a face. It was a pelt, with pearly fangs the size of small knives, glassy silver eyes and an expression of rage that would haunt my dreams that night.

"What is this?" I demanded.

"A korak, one of the feral cats from Galgeth that you saw in the battle mural. This vault is full of spoils from the Elicrin War." Her voice grew strained as she reached for a small box on one of the stone ledges. "The peacekeeper elicromancers weren't much for flaunting victory."

After retrieving the small wooden box, she backed away from the vault, rising to her feet. "I'm going to show you a vision. You must trust me. Nothing will harm you."

I didn't say yes or no. I didn't know what to say. She opened the box and turned it toward me.

It held a heap of dried blue-black leaves with a pungent, unfamiliar scent. I knew plenty of plants and herbs from my walks in the woods as a child; between that and my few weeks of training in herb lore, I was acquainted with a fair number of species. But these were foreign to me.

Tamarice's eyes glinted as she picked out a single leaf and pressed it into my palm. "Place it on your tongue."

I hesitated, casting a glance over my shoulder. "Is this from Galgeth too?"

"It won't hurt you, trust me. We are together in this."

I felt a drip of sweat roll down my neck as I brought the leaf to my lips. Closing my eyes, I placed it on my tongue. The taste, like the smell, was pungent and sweet, but it didn't take long for the fire to set in.

I gripped my skull and collapsed to my knees as the flames licked through my veins. My own screams sounded distant to my ears. My eyes were locked shut, lost in blackness, until the blackness became fog and the fog became a figure.

Its garments were tattered and its skin ashen. As it faced me, I saw the murky whites of its eyes, the tiny black pupils that were no larger than the point of a quill. Its teeth were long, jagged, smeared with what could only be blood, black and foul. A scar the shape of a near-perfect circle, made up of markings I didn't recognize, shone dark on its pale skin. The beginnings of a scream issued from my lips, but I was jerked from the haze.

I lay curled up on the cold floor, coated in sweat, sputtering out damp remains of the leaf that had caused me so much agony. Tamarice rubbed my back, her voice rich with hope as she asked, "Did you see it, too?"

"What was that?"

"Astrikane leaves from Galgeth. They are very dangerous, very poisonous to ordinary humans. Only a supernatural constitution can survive their effects." I coughed again as she helped me stand. "Did you have the same vision I did last time?" she demanded. "Did you see what the world will look like when we elicromancers take our rightful place as leaders?"

"I don't know what I saw. . . ." I trailed off with a shudder. The hopeful arc of her brow dropped. "It was someone, some-*thing* with white eyes and a scar in the shape of a circle on its chest."

Tamarice looked surprised. "The fate-binding spell. The same one that Klaine performed on himself and Cassian leaves that type of mark." She ran her delicate fingers over her mouth as she thought deeply.

"What was that creature?" I managed to ask.

"I don't know. Maybe a blight, an elicromancer who uses dark magic so extensively that it decays them from the inside out. They're in the old legends."

Chills coursed through my body. "Are the visions real?"

"Were, are, will be, could be."

I sighed and closed my eyes, sickened by the lingering taste of the astrikane leaves.

"Bristal," Tamarice said, her urgency returning anew. "Elicromancers like Brack have long condemned certain practices as black elicromancy—dark magic. They don't understand how complex it is, how whole and beautiful a picture elicromancy makes before you segregate its disciplines. Imagine training to have access to it all, Bristal. Training with me."

I breathed in deep. "With only you?"

She placed her hands on my shoulders and looked into my eyes. I had the urge to squirm away. "Yes. You have been given an extraordinary gift that deserves more use than thanklessly mediating kingdom quarrels. I wish you could have seen the glory I saw . . . the shining realm we will build together." She looked past me with a lost, awestruck smile, then drew in a sharp breath. "I have to go now. There's something I must do. After what I've done here, given what else Brack and the elders know of me, I may not be able to return for good. But I will be back for you. In the meantime, I need you to hold onto something for me. None of my possessions are safe."

I nodded, unable to utter any words, much less make a promise. But when she handed me a threadbare book bound in black material with a gold circle embossed on the spine—a circle that I hoped didn't correlate to the mark on the creature's chest—my hands accepted it. I was beyond refusing her demands, even if I couldn't quite wrap my head around what she was asking of me.

She strode off and pushed open the doors, leaving me alone in the library. The dusk had deepened without my noticing, and now the torches supplied the only light in the room. I opened the book and found text in Old Nisseran that I couldn't decipher. But something about it made my pulse thrum in fear and realization. I knew what I had to do.

Hands trembling, I grabbed one of the torches off a metal sconce, flinching at the shadows it cast in the empty room. The vision of the blight haunted my every step as I scurried across the shadowy galleries brimming with cold moonlight to the wing where the elders resided.

I shivered as I waited for Kimber to open her door.

"What is it?" the old woman asked, wrapping a robe tightly around her thin frame. The light of the sconces cast shadows on her wrinkled face. I held up the book so that the symbol showed, and those shadows grew deeper.

"Tamarice." The name was nothing more than a hiss on her tongue, but it was full of knowing accusations.

Grim-faced, Kimber beckoned for the book. I gave it to her and followed her inside. Drell lit a candle. Though she already wore her dressing gown, she stood at the ready with her sheathed dirk in hand.

"I think it has something to do with Cassian and Klaine's

fate-binding spell," I said while Kimber opened the book with the pained determination of someone pouring alcohol on a wound.

The elder shook her head. "Spells can be summarized in a few pages, a chapter at most. Fate-binding is no spell. It's a ritual. A curse. It involves sacrifice. See here: there are many steps, and hundreds of components required to make the elixir. Primarily, ground roots of a fallen tree, ash of a pyre, much blood of a gifted vein."

"Gifted vein?"

Kimber fixed me with a grave stare. "Elicromancer blood."

"A lot of it," Drell added.

The hairs on the back of my neck prickled. I had been alone with Tamarice more times than I cared to recall.

"I've only heard of dark elicromancers using it in the face of eminent death," Kimber said. "As in the case of Klaine and Cassian." She turned over a handful of pages and skimmed them, reading silently. "It appears that completing the ritual involves carving your name and the name of the person you want to bind to yourself in the shape of a ring on your own skin," Kimber said. "And then you drink the elixir, saving the last drop for your enemy. Once the enemy swallows it, the ritual is complete."

"Bristal, have you drunk anything Tamarice gave you lately?" Drell asked.

"Not that I can remember."

"There's a page marked," Kimber said. "It looks like instructions for binding fates of others, without involving yours. You mark one party's name on your skin but leave your own name out. And then you give the last drop of the blood mixture to the other recipient."

"But this is all just theoretical as far as she's concerned, right? She wouldn't drink blood?" My stomach churned at the thought. "Should we tell Brack?"

"She had plenty of chances," Kimber said, only somewhat reassuringly. "Tamarice has always shown a curiosity for shadowy magic. But Brack cannot reason with her. He's been trying to do that for a hundred years. A confrontation between them right now will only escalate." The old woman's blue eyes met mine. "Yet she trusts you."

"It seems that way."

"There's a spell you can perform to follow someone's materialization trail," Kimber went on. "It should be easier for you to materialize this way because you already have a precise destination. We just have to hope she was in enough of a hurry to leave her path traceable."

I had only materialized a few times, but part of my trouble, according to Brack, was that I did not visualize myself at the destination clearly enough. If the destination was decided for me, perhaps I would manage to come out on my feet and ready for whatever I would meet.

"If you appear to be in danger, come right back," Kimber said. "You know how to do that, don't you?"

Mingling fear and urgency made my "yes" sound impatient. Drell handed me her dirk.

"Aphanis halak," Kimber said.

I closed my eyes and braced myself. *"Aphanis halak."*

The spell yanked me violently sideways through biting-cold

air. Dark trees, hills and towns whisked by as if I'd just spun around until I could stand still and watch the world move on its own. I half-landed, one foot on the ground, in what appeared to be a packed tavern, before a nauseating jerk set me off again. When I halted this time, I didn't so much land as tumble into deep snow.

I picked up Drell's dirk, fingers tingling from the cold, as my eyes gradually adjusted. By the time I could see trees in the darkness, I had already sensed the presence of the Water.

I might not have noticed it otherwise. The trees that made up the silver gates did not stand at attention, but instead made an unassuming circle. Someone had opened the gates. The Water appeared so black in the twilight that it barely caught so much as a hint of the moonlight.

That's when her voice rang out, melodic as notes on a lyre. "Please do not swallow this one," she said. "I believe she is gifted. Please give me what I desire."

Following the sound, my eyes found Tamarice crouching at the edge of the Water, stirring it with her fingers. She stood up, her lithe body nothing but a shadow to me even thirty paces away, close enough that I was thankful for the snow that had softened the noise of my fall.

Another figure emerged from the darkness of the trees. Thin branches were wrapped around a woman's arms, tugging her toward the dark surface. She whimpered as they snaked away from her.

Tamarice's hand hooked around the back of her neck, driving her to her knees at the Water's edge. And then, as though deaf to her desperate pleas, Tamarice shoved the woman's head under the surface.

The Water pulled the woman into its depths like a predator gulping down its prey. I scrambled backwards in horror, toppling onto my backside in the snow.

After a taut moment, the elicromancer roared in frustration, kicking a spray of snow in the air.

In a burst of terror I whispered, *"Aphanis."*

I must have pictured Brack's cottage well enough, because I landed on my back on his dining table. I groaned and rolled off, trying to fill my lungs back up with air. Brack rushed in from the den, catching me as I stumbled.

"Tamarice killed someone. I saw her do it. She brought a mortal to the Water."

Brack's pale eyes entertained a full range of emotions. I saw a hundred years' worth of guidance, rebuke, trust broken and rebuilt over and over again. I saw a deep sense of failure strike him like a blow.

"Are you hurt?" he asked.

I shook my head. Brack steered me toward the den, where we sat and caught our breath.

"She gave me a book about a spell," I went on. "I mean, a ritual. It requires the blood of an elicromancer. She must have been testing the woman in the Water."

"Why didn't you come find me?"

"Kimber thought I would be able to reason with her. I didn't know until I arrived that she was already neck-deep in dark magic."

Brack closed his eyes, wounded by each word. "Tamarice obviously thinks that with you on her side she would have enough leverage to overpower me. We are fortunate that she sees promise in you, or you may have been in grave danger."

I shivered, thinking of being alone with her in the deserted, dark library. "How could she do that to an innocent woman when she spoke with such fury about the way my kidnappers treated me?"

"The difference to her is that you are an elicromancer. If she turned out to be wrong about the woman, the tragedy wouldn't move her. She sees mortals as expendable."

"But I was mortal too. It's no different."

"She is beyond reason, Bristal." He stood, his wrinkled face a mask of resolve. "Come with me."

We hurried to the main halls, where all was still and dark. Brack's elicrin stone lit up as enchantments poured fluidly from his lips. We left the galleries and crossed through the marketplace, where the shops were closed and the streets were silent but for the stirring of sleeping animals and Brack's humming chant. The icy wind cut through my clothes as I ran.

When we reached the enormous wooden gates marking the entrance to the city, the gatekeepers were cranking them open to allow someone to pass through. They creaked to a stop against the stone frame, and I saw Tamarice striding toward the bridge where she had pushed me from the ravine, her soft face etched with angular shadows in the light of the blazing torches.

"*Acasar im doen. Halonir tacaral gemisk temorrah,*" Brack said. A shimmering partition began to spread across the open gates. "The other side, Bristal! Say what I say."

I rushed to the opposite end of the gateway and repeated what Brack had said, stumbling over my words. The partition began to seep across the air like honey sliding off a spoon.

"Good, Bristal." Brack's partition crept toward mine.

Through the small gap between them, I saw Tamarice reach the bridge, mere yards away from us.

My voice cracked as I called Brack's name. He looked at Tamarice, and then back at his partition. "Focus," he said.

I glanced up, realizing my enchantment had slowed. I resumed chanting, but Tamarice was now striding across the bridge with purpose in her steps and smoldering heat in her eyes. I couldn't shake the image of her gripping the frightened woman by the neck and shoving her under the surface for the Water to swallow whole.

Our two partitions had nearly melted together when Tamarice shot a delicate hand through the open space. The barriers paused in their paths.

I scrambled back, fearing she would reach for me. But she seized Brack's hand and dropped to her knees in front of the glistening enchantment. Her dark hair fell around her face as she bowed her head and pressed his hand against her cheek, clasping it earnestly.

Brack looked as if he could weep, but he merely took a deep breath and said, "I always seem to understimate the depth of the hole inside you."

Tamarice looked up, her tear-filled eyes shining like flecks of forgotten gold under a clear river current. "No, you misunderstand me. You always have," she said, gripping his hand more fiercely. "From the moment I questioned your teaching, you punished me for thinking I could be *more*."

Her desperate whisper sent shivers down my neck and shoulders.

"How many innocent people have you killed?" Brack asked.

Tamarice swallowed hard. A dark strand of hair clung to

her snow-kissed cheek. "Dozens. I took them to the Water to find more of our kind, until Bristal fulfilled my need for a comrade. Her power is more striking and rare than what I could have hoped for in this day of diluted magic." Her eyes flashed to me, and then back to Brack. "Then I learned about fate binding."

"So you needed elicromancer blood—from a new elicromancer who couldn't fight back." Brack shook his head, as if he wished he could reject the thought and go back to believing Tamarice was no more than misguided and brash. "What do you plan to do with the ritual?"

"Will you forgive me if I tell you? Will you listen to me, for just one moment in a hundred years, listen to me? If you had accepted me," she went on, her voice breaking. "If you had seen reason in my beliefs, I wouldn't have had to harm anyone in my quest. Together, we could have found an easier way to control the kingdoms of men. But you cling to the lie that we were created to serve and not to rule, when you know in your heart it isn't so. Don't blame me for wanting more."

There was that word again: more. Emerging in her smooth voice from her rounded lips, it was all but ambrosial.

Brack wavered, sadness deepening the lines around his mouth. His other hand closed over hers, not in agreement or submission but in protest, as though he were tempted to seize her and pull her close through the enchantments he had just laid to lock her out.

But he dropped her hand and his warm, pain-filled eyes iced over. "You have no home here, and no ally in me."

Tamarice's hand hung in the air, reaching for him. For a

moment she looked utterly forsaken, her rich eyes full of broken hope.

But they narrowed into slits, and her calm feline inflection tightened to a growl. She rose to her feet and squared herself before Brack. "Then you must kill me. Or someday I will have you on your knees. I will bleed the coward out of you and leave you to die in regret."

With a cold whisper, Brack sealed the barrier. The two partitions merged and shot off in opposite directions, trailing light across the walls before disappearing.

I could almost feel the pulse of rage in the air a beat before it manifested. And then Tamarice roared, thrusting her hands away from her body. Every inch of stone not covered by the barrier, from the frame of the city's gates to the bridge beneath her feet, began crumbling. Brack yanked me back by the arm, but there was no need—the barrier held.

As the bridge collapsed beneath her feet, Tamarice summoned a thousand branches reaching out to carry her across the abyss and place her gently on the ground. Then she melted into the darkness of the night.

A moment later, I felt a hand on my shoulder and glanced up to find Kimber, looking haggard yet resolved in the merging of moon and torchlight.

"The fight could have been much worse, right?" I asked, still trembling.

The old woman looked at the empty place that the bridge had occupied. Her wrinkled fingers felt like ice on my neck, even against the chill mountain night.

"The fight hasn't begun."

FIVE

The first day of spring was warm and bright when I materialized to find Volarre's royal city upside down in the distance. I spat out dirt, untangled a twig from my hair and rolled over for a better view. Landing tended to be the most difficult part.

Pontaval sat on a hill and splayed onto the surrounding flatlands. The streets and structures of the city all seemed to rise up toward the palace, which reached its elegant blue turrets into the cloudless sky, each bearing a flag with the silver lily of Volarre. It was the name day of the newborn princess, and even from afar the city felt alive.

Brack materialized next to me in the woods disguised as the scarred man. His pale eyes caught the sunlight as he looked at my dirty, scraped hands. His sense of urgency had spiked like a fever in the month since Tamarice left, and we had tirelessly explored herb lore, spells, languages, weaponry, astrology and current affairs, barely covering the essentials of one subject before moving on to the next. I worked with enthusiasm, hoping to prove to Brack that I would never make the mistakes of my predecessor.

While my Clandestine powers grew more impressive, materializing was not getting any easier. Letting my imperfect landing go without a lecture, Brack started off toward the city. He did not approve of the king of Volarre's recent choice to betroth his new daughter to a prince of Yorth rather than a prince of Calgoran. Volarre was already on good terms with Yorth; its relationship with Calgoran was in need of diplomacy and tact more than ever. Volarre had promised the princess's cousin to Calgoran as a consolation prize, but Brack didn't see this as sufficient progress.

I followed him to the edge of the sparse grouping of trees where I had landed. From here we could see the crowds, no more than splotches of color filling the streets. Banners trailing ribbons and garlands protruded from the parade, making their way toward the palace. A bell tolled the hour.

"So, Daffodil Dimplesworth, then." I sighed, resigned.

The smile lines on Brack's square face didn't get much use, so even the hint of a smirk reminded me of a ray of sunlight nudging dark clouds aside. "One of seven fairies chosen by the queen to give a blessing to the princess."

"Are you sure there's not a more convincing name?"

"I've already spread rumors of Daffodil's magical prowess across the kingdom. You received a royal invitation at your quaint residence in Issabon two weeks ago. I confirmed you would attend."

"The blessing for the princess that you told me to think of . . . Do I have to announce it before the crowd?"

Brack was too restless to give due thought to my anxiety. "Yes, and make sure it isn't beauty or musical talent. Some other silly fool will give those first. Did you form a disguise based on my instructions?"

I changed into a short, plump woman with round red cheeks and curling dark hair pinned in a bun. Fairies were known to be flamboyant on grand occasions, so I wore a blue dress with a purple cape and pink buckled shoes.

Finally attentive, Brack said, "That's your best disguise yet. You're becoming skilled at manifesting clothes."

My cheeks flamed. At first, my guises had been half-imagined at best. But my elicrin stone was learning to anticipate my needs. It was such an extension of my body that I hadn't even noticed my fingers toying with the silver chain.

"Are you ready for your introduction to the world of Nisseran royalty?"

I nodded earnestly. He gave me the gold parchment invitation from which pink confetti sprinkled unceasingly thanks to a simple fairy charm. The curling letters invited Daffodil Dimplesworth to be one of seven fairies handpicked by Queen Lucetta to participate in the name day celebration of her daughter, Princess Rosamund.

"Where will you be?" I asked.

"I'll be in the crowd just outside the palace. King Errod doesn't much like magic, you know. It's a surprise he allowed his wife to invite fairies, but then many kings are fond of tradition. You'll have to show the invitation to a guard to get inside. If you have a blessing in mind, all that's left is to veil your elicrin stone."

I gripped the wintry blue stone and closed my eyes. The

chain loosened and slid from my neck. The round pendant in my hand morphed into a simple wooden fairy wand.

Plodding along with the city crowds would have taken an hour, but those who saw Brack's disfiguring scar and massive shoulders tended to give us a wide berth, and we soon reached the palace entryway. A pink carpet covered the marble steps, and white and purple orchids festooned the extravagant archway.

Brack used his height to drive me toward the guard who kept the spectators behind satin ropes. When I showed him my invitation, he forced the throng to part so I could enter the foyer.

I turned left into the receiving hall and gasped. Tall, broad windows filled the court with sunshine. Layers upon layers of pink, white, gold and sky-blue satin were draped along the walls. On the dais sat two magnificent thrones of marble and gold, cushioned with deep blue velvet. A crib adorned with colorful ribbons stood nearby. I wished Drell were here, so I could see either her jaw drop in awe or her eyes roll in disdain.

The dais, for now, stood empty. However, off to the side of the courtroom waited a line of short, plump, ostentatiously dressed women. Relieved, I took my place behind the sixth fairy. She was even more rosy-cheeked than I and wore a bright yellow dress with plum stockings and a green cape.

"Good day," was her musical greeting.

I matched her sweetness. "Good day to you."

"It was brave of you to fight the crowds. You could have entered through the north foyer, like it says on the invitation. We were served a delightful breakfast. It's a pity you missed it."

Despite her perky demeanor, she seemed genuinely sorry. It must have been a wonderful breakfast indeed. I was briefly annoyed that Brack hadn't told me where to go, until it occurred to me I ought to have read the invitation myself. Brack didn't seem to like giving me instructions when common sense would suffice. The friendly fairy went on to innumerate the delicacies offered—candied nectarines, raspberry pecan custard, pear tarts with fresh cream—while I thought of a blessing to give to the princess.

The trumpeters blasted a triumphant melody, and the court musicians struck up a song. The procession began, starting with the royal family of Yorth, then the royal family of Calgoran. The children carried gifts for Princess Rosamund.

Volarian royalty were known for their golden hair and delicate features, and when they entered at last, they did not disappoint. The queen's twin, the Duchess Lysandra, wore a purple gown with a long train, and her flowing golden curls surrounded a delicate face. She almost seemed too delicate— her ivory skin too pale, her slender form too slender—though signs of fragile health hardly detracted from her beauty. Her husband, the duke, possessed cool eyes and a calm demeanor. Their daughter, Elinor, who was promised to Calgoran in place of her cousin, hid behind her mother's skirts.

The herald waited for them to take their seats on the dais. "Their Majesties, King Errod and Queen Lucetta Lorenthi, presenting for the first time Her Highness, Princess Rosamund."

I resisted the urge to stand on my tiptoes as the Lorenthi trio graced the receiving hall. King Errod was beyond regal: young, muscular and golden-haired. Queen Lucetta looked just like her sister, except that she seemed so happy and healthy that she fairly glowed. When they reached the dais, the king took his queen's hand and they sat on their tremendous thrones.

The princess was bundled in silk and lace that seemed to go on forever, but the nurse who carried her managed it with poise and placed the princess in her crib. The baby cooed as her ceremony began. The other six fairies extracted handkerchiefs and sniffled tears of joy. I wrung mine nervously until it wilted.

We approached the dais to give our blessings. The herald announced Posie Fairfield, who sauntered up the steps, bowed low to the king and queen, and flourished her wand extravagantly.

"I give Her Highness the blessing of grace, that her steps may be light and sure."

A few tufts of a sparkling dust emitted from the tip of her wand and hovered like a cloud over the crib before disappearing. As the court applauded, Posie curtsied and descended.

The second, Alice Odetta, gave beauty. However predictable, this blessing earned many a pleased sigh. Mabel Moorwinkle gave courage, Cassandra Appleberry gave a talent for horseback riding and Angelica Brightcastle gave honesty. Ophelia Hopehaven, my new acquaintance, gave Rosamund the blessing of a generous spirit. I thought it quite nice, though it failed to excite the crowd.

A hush spread as Daffodil Dimplesworth was summoned, no doubt the result of Brack's mysterious rumors. The King and Queen beamed at me as I approached the princess, who studied me with round green eyes as I raised my wand. "I give

Her Highness the blessing of joyfulness, that she may have a cheerful spirit even in adversity and trial."

I waved my wand, wincing inwardly out of fear that the vivid white light of my elicrin stone would burst through and expose my farce. But, like the others, my wand puffed out shimmering dust that settled over the princess.

The time came for the royal attendees to present their gifts. From Yorth, Rosamund received a set of milky pearls. She would wear the pearl diadem on the day she married the prince, who was now only an infant himself. The family also gave her a cape of rich green velvet with gold stitching and a superbly crafted mahogany spinning wheel. Queen Lucetta was fond of the craft and was especially pleased by this gift, as her mother had been a humble spinster.

After the royals from Yorth sat, the princes of Calgoran came forward. The elder prince gave the princess a fine leather saddle embossed with vines. To his own betrothed, Elinor, he presented a dainty glass tiara she would wear on their wedding day.

The younger prince shuffled forward last, bearing a silver box inlaid with purple velvet that held an amethyst tiara for Rosamund. But as he approached the steps, he didn't look at the princess. His wide eyes locked directly on me in what could only be described as utter bewilderment. I froze and glanced surreptitiously down at my clothes, worried my disguise had decided to slough off like snakeskin. I tapped Ophelia's shoulder and asked her if she had an extra kerchief just to see her expression. Her syrupy reaction toward my sentimentality as she handed me one told me that my disguise was still in place. Perhaps the young prince had simply never seen fairies before.

As he sat back down, bursting applause and cheers filled the courtroom. My heart turned over strangely as I thought of how these children were not yet aware of the responsibilities they would inherit and the tumultuous political seas they would navigate. I would watch them come of age, rule and die—and I would remain the same.

The ovation spread to the streets outside, shaking me from my reverie. I belatedly clapped my hands.

But my spine bristled with a shiver. I heard something over the din—a whisper? Shadows fluttered in the corner of my eye, but as I glanced around me, I couldn't seem to chase them down.

Soon the earth began to rumble beneath us. The garden trees spread their branches across the glass windows, their leaves filtering the light until the court was shadowed in green, tarnished with only stray patches of glowing sunlight. The boughs thrashed and writhed as if overcome by a fierce wind.

"Tamarice," I whispered.

At the sound of her name, the simple fairy wand in my hand morphed into my elicrin stone once more. I put on the pendant and slipped it down the neckline of my dress, but no one saw me, short and tucked behind the other fairies. The name had been no more than a quiet intake of breath.

From the front of the courtroom, I looked to the entrance hall and saw a shape coming together out of nothingness, like a figure in a tapestry weaving itself out of vivid threads without fingers to guide the shuttle.

Terror chilled my blood. I felt as though I was once more inching reluctantly toward the Water, toward some strange danger beyond my comprehension.

Tamarice stepped into the grand hall, tranquil as a warm breeze, and the massive doors closed behind her with a thud.

The elicromancer's dark hair hung loose over her shoulder, plunging straight and thick to her waist, nearly indistinguishable from the sheath of rich brown silk that flowed around her bare feet. Her dark red elicrin stone flashed at her white throat. She looked savage somehow, and yet more beautiful than ever, shoulders held proud and bare as she strode like a queen to the dais. I realized that her lovely eyes had once looked haunted, hiding a past of pain and a present of forbidden desires. Now, she was free. And darkness clung to her, threading through her like vines.

Tamarice's golden eyes searched the faces in the audience. Each gaze averted. King Errod opened his mouth as if to set his guards against her, but vacillated and gave no orders. Queen Lucetta froze on the edge of her throne, eyes on Rosamund's crib. At my side, Ophelia Hopehaven swallowed ragged breaths.

"I hope you don't mind my intrusion," Tamarice said, her voice as musical as ever as she approached the dais with much more forthrightness than her words alone demonstrated. She turned to speak to the crowd. "I could not miss the opportunity to see Volarre welcome its next generation of royalty."

As she turned, I noticed a scar spanning the entire breadth of her back—a circular scar, with words upon words carved in so minute a script that I could have scarcely made them out had I been able to study them from inches away. The strokes looked fresh, red cuts barely puckering to white, a cross between stunning embellishment and terrifying mutilation.

"Tamarice," Queen Lucetta recovered gracefully, pasting a

nervous smile on her pale face. "It is an unexpected honor to welcome an elicromancer to our daughter's name day."

Ignoring Lucetta's pleasantries, Tamarice strode up the dais steps to the pedestal where the gifts lay. She stroked the pearls, seized a delicate handful of the velvet robe and ran her fingers along the spinning wheel. She pricked her fingertip on the sharp spindle and flinched, causing the whole court to recoil in response. But she merely chuckled and sucked on the fresh wound, searching the faces of the royal families with amusement.

"I'm here to give the princess my own blessing of sorts," she announced, facing the crowd. "She will have the opportunity to act as a sacrifice, allowing a better world to rise from the wreckage of this one."

Rage taut on his face, King Errod jumped to his feet and growled, "Seize her."

The guards standing along the walls rushed forward, filing around the elicromancer and gripping her arms. The royal children huddled near their parents, who challenged Tamarice's ambiguous threat with defiant expressions. The queen and nurse hurried to stand in front of the princess's crib.

Tamarice shook off the guards like a loose garment. Sinewy tree limbs burst through the windows, wrapping around the guards and yanking them back through the broken glass. Their screams tore through the court, echoing against the haunting thud of their broken bodies hitting the stones of the courtyard. Noises rose from the crowd, but no one dared move as Tamarice walked deliberately toward the princess.

Sweat drenched my palms. Why hadn't Brack arrived? I knew that the fate-binding ritual would play some horrific role in Tamarice's plan, but knowing that wasn't nearly enough to stop her.

"Those of you who wear crowns, who bear titles, who call yourselves kings and queens, lords and ladies, who flaunt your riches as though they are tantamount to power, hear this: Soon there will be no kings and no lords. The fate of all of Volarre's . . . *nobility*"—she said this with a disdainful glance at a cowering minister who had earlier seemed rather pompous—"will be tied to Rosamund. I will kill her when and how I please, and when she dies, Volarre's nobility will perish along with her."

I realized it like a blow to the chest. The words on her back were names. The names of every living noble in Volarre.

Swift as a spider, Tamarice yanked the queen and nurse away from the crib by their hair. The king shouted and lurched forward, but the flowery vines that decorated the dais roped around his hands and feet, anchoring him in place.

Tamarice extracted a glass vial from a fold of her silken gown. She removed the stopper and reached into the princess's crib, tipping the vial so that a single drop of reddish-black liquid slid down the glass, poised to fall between the child's lips—the last drop of the mixture produced for the fate-binding ritual.

I jolted out of my spectator's reverie, realizing Brack would not make it in time to stop her. In the space of a breath, I mounted the dais and thrust Tamarice aside with the sort of strength only desperation can bring about. *"Sokek sinna!"* I shouted, throwing my hands out just as Tamarice snarled an abrasive-sounding curse. A shield of white light burgeoned out from my elicrin stone and deflected her attack.

My former mentor regained her composure. She placed the

stopper back in the vial, the drop still inside, and fastened her eyes on mine. They were lovely and soft as before. But everything within them made my blood run like ice. "The Clandestine. Sweet Bristal of humble Popplewell . . . I hoped you would come."

I heard muttering in the crowd, a question hanging ripe in the air: was the new elicromancer they had heard of powerful enough to keep them safe?

I knew Tamarice's words were meant to make me feel like the novice I was, to blind me with my inexperience like dirt in the eyes. And they succeeded. I wasn't strong enough to stand against her yet. I could emit another shield, but eventually, one of her spells would overpower it. She would reach the princess. The ritual would be complete.

Choking back the fear threatening to keep me motionless, I swept the princess from her crib and leapt from the dais, changing forms in mid-air. Whom I became didn't matter—I hadn't the slightest idea anyway—as long as my legs were fast. As I pushed through the crowd, bystanders dove out of the way, leaving the princess and me vulnerable to Tamarice's curses lashing through the air.

I took on another guise, hoping to confuse the dark elicromancer's eye. Cracks widened along the length of the floor. The princess wailed in my ear, making it difficult for me to concentrate on my next move and impossible to hide. People around me gasped, ducking behind chairs and nearly trampling one another to offer me a wide berth. By fleeing through the room like a mad fool, I was risking their lives. But I didn't know what else to do.

The ground beneath me rumbled and caved. People scattered

to safety, and a few unlucky ones tumbled into the darkness, their shrieks abruptly silenced.

I paused to leap over a widening fissure in my path, landing on my side to shield the princess. With my free arm, I managed to drag us away from the chasm. But before I could find my feet, Tamarice stood over me. The arrogant smile in her eyes had been replaced by pulsing anger that made me want to curl up and disappear.

The princess wiggled and whimpered in my left arm, but the elicromancer didn't look at her. Her eyes clung fast to mine. *"Asas nila."* I shot a spell at her, but she deflected it as if swatting away a gnat. With her bare foot she kicked me soundly on the side of the face, dislocating my jaw and nearly knocking me senseless. The world spun violently and I nearly loosed my grip on the tiny princess. My skull felt like it had burst into a thousand pieces. The tang of blood filled my mouth, and I wondered how someone who had appeared so authentically fond of me could show me such violence.

Tamarice lowered herself to one knee, leaning over me so that strands of her silken hair brushed my face, trailing through my blood. Her lips neared my ear. I cringed and closed my eyes.

"Come with me, Bristal," came the honeyed whisper. "And I will never hurt you again. We will create a bright kingdom of power and light. There will be many elicromancers, as in the old days, and we will rule with love."

She pulled back to look in my eyes, her own warm with affection as they had been when she first found me wounded.

"We will begin a new age together. But first we must dismantle this pathetic order of men, sweep away the chaff of prejudice and fear. We will wipe this realm clear and start anew, sister."

My heart kicked inside my chest with every beat. The calm passion in her voice threatened to melt me like flames melting iron, to shape me into something I would never become on my own.

"We can have everything we desire. We will rule together for countless ages, and I will teach you more than Brack ever could. Come with me."

She stood and held her hand out to me, the hope in her eyes taunting me. In their momentary softness I saw a sister, a friend, a fellow elicromancer damaged by scorn.

But I heard my voice cease to tremble as I croaked, "No."

Tamarice's jaw hardened. Her eyes grew dark like sugar burning in a pan. A second shock rang through my body as she stepped on my right hand, which desperately clutched my pendant. I lurched and cried out in pain as two of my fingers snapped under her weight.

She lifted me by my collar and spoke quietly, her voice full of unbridled hate. "I will *obliterate* Nissera. Every last trace. You will see mountains leveled, kings dethroned, great cities trampled to become the soil on which a new world is built. And I will make dust of you."

Then she dropped me. My head struck the marble as the light of her elicrin stone blinded me once more. I managed to bite through the pain and thrust out a shield just in time, but this attempt emerged much weaker than the last. As I viewed the world through a fog of tears and the dazzling white pool that covered the princess and me, I saw her elicrin stone's light encircle us, folding my feeble shield back on itself like a withering flower. The clash of our brilliant lights shrouded the rest of the court in darkness. My shield contracted, shriveling until it was useless. Tamarice's hand pushed through it, forcing the vial to the princess's lips. . . .

I concentrated on funneling one last gust of energy into my shield, fighting the gut-wrenching pain that ripped through my body. Anger built in my chest like steam in a kettle until I couldn't see anything but blackness. A roar of rage ripped out of me and my elicrin stone lit with a light so bright that I had to close my eyes.

I heard Tamarice shriek. I opened my eyes to see the remaining windows burst. Shards of glass descended like rain, but halfway down they turned to snow and swirled through the court.

The rage in my chest dissipated. I deflated, curling into the pain as the tiny princess whimpered against my shoulder. Amid the snowflakes, I spotted shards of Tamarice's elicrin stone lying on the floor, slowly losing their vibrant hue as they morphed into ice. Soon no trace of their old form was left except for wine-colored veins running like cracks over the clear surfaces of the ice.

Tamarice roared as the shards trembled and flew into her palm. Then she vanished like a wisp of smoke.

The guests stood timidly as sunlight filled the hall once more. My battered head pounding, I turned to look at the princess. Her lips were smeared with red.

The fate-binding ritual was complete.

SIX

Someone extracted the baby from my arms and helped me find my feet. I was dizzy, barely able to see through an unfamiliar veil of blonde hair matted with blood. I bent double and spit a mouthful of blood on the cracked marble.

The doors burst open. People scurried out of the way, making a path by which Brack could reach me.

He cupped my injured hand and laid a cool palm on my jaw. "Are you all right?" he asked, steadying me. I nodded unconvincingly, watching Queen Lucetta collect her daughter in a frenzy of sobs. "I couldn't reach you. Tamarice must have spent weeks since she left laying enchantments around the palace to keep me out."

"Why didn't she keep me out?" My mouth could barely form the question. Brack turned my face to the side and I felt the soft power of a healing spell. He took my hand and repeated it. It would probably take me hundreds of years to perform a spell of that caliber, but he did it easily. Even so, these injuries would need hours if not days to heal completely.

"I expect she didn't know you could destroy her elicrin stone if provoked."

"Neither did I."

"And she wanted a chance to persuade you."

"The princess is cursed," I said hopelessly, Tamarice's whisper echoing in my ears. "I couldn't stop it. Tamarice bound her fate to all the nobles in Volarre. She wants to destroy Nissera."

Brack gripped my shoulders while I swayed. "There may yet be hope for the princess. And there is certainly hope for Nissera."

He turned to King Errod and Queen Lucetta as they approached. "Your Majesties."

"Lord Brack." King Errod's eyes brewed with his famous temper. "You nearly arrived in time to help."

"Is she safe now?" Queen Lucetta asked, burying Rosamund's head in her flowing blonde hair.

"Tamarice will be weak without her elicrin stone," Brack answered. "Since she has turned to darkness however, she will have ways of recuperating her power. I fear that she will journey to Galgeth to access even deadlier magic than what she's already made use of." Brack looked around. "We should gather with the other kings and their ministers to discuss how we can protect the princess from her."

"In what way does it concern them?" King Errod demanded. "It is Volarre's princess and noble countrymen who are at stake."

"All of Nissera is at stake," I said, though the sounds barely resembled words. I bowed my head. "Your Majesty."

"And who are you?" the king asked, but the edge in his voice had softened.

"My name is Bristal, Your Majesty."

"She is one of our kind," Brack added.

"I had heard there was another," the king said, as though we were multiplying roaches. Remembering himself, he added reluctantly, "Thank you for protecting our daughter. We'll summon you when we're ready."

He waved one of the guards over and gave him instructions. Guests filed out of the room as the royal families of Calgoran and Yorth huddled together, still in shock.

Brack and I followed the guard out of the receiving hall through a side door, down a corridor covered in rich blue carpet. We ascended a grand, curving staircase with a marble balustrade and arrived at a room with double oak doors and golden handles. Beyond the doors sat a lavish suite. A balcony overlooked a small courtyard, formal gardens and the hill country beyond.

When the guard closed the doors, Brack's guise changed and he was once more the gray-haired man. I changed into my true form and collapsed into a chair, massaging my jaw with my uninjured hand.

"She plans to destroy Nissera," I said numbly. "And then rebuild and rule it."

Brack was unshaken by this news. Of course, it wasn't news to him.

I couldn't seem to form the words to tell him about her whispered invitation. I couldn't let him know that her summons struck a dissonant chord in my heart, that her words had briefly made me feel like liquid metal burning for a new shape.

But it didn't matter now. I had refused. She was my enemy, and now I was hers.

"You said a moment ago that you fear she will journey to

Galgeth. I thought only immortal creatures could go there. I broke her elicrin stone. How could she make the journey?"

"Performing a curse like the fate-binding ritual leaves a mark and might help her cling to her power. Even the ancient elicrin stone that she found—the one that still burns—is like a severed lizard's tail, useless but still squirming long after its master's death."

"I wish we had known what she was planning. Maybe we could have stopped her."

Brack sat on the edge of the windowsill and crossed his arms. "Regret will do no good. You did your duty. Tamarice kept me from doing mine." There was a swift knock at the door. "Veil yourself as the fairy. We cannot afford to intimidate them further at the moment, and you resemble Tamarice."

I did as he asked so that he could admit a servant with trays of food. After washing the blood from my face and hair, I sat down to eat. Though I felt empty, I found I had no appetite and picked at the roast duck on my plate. Brack drank one sip of tea and set the cup on the saucer with a brisk clank. I wondered if he ever even tasted food and drink or if consuming it was to him just a compulsory chore of being alive, an unwelcome distraction from his thoughts.

When we reached the meeting hall, King Errod, Queen Lucetta and three royal ministers were arranged around a long table in varied poses that betrayed their anxiety.

"Why can't you undo the curse?" Errod demanded.

"I would have to use black elicromancy. That I will never do, not even in the most hopeless of circumstances," replied Brack.

Errod tossed up a hand. "You do nothing but meddle until we need you, and then you are utterly useless."

"The fate-binding ritual means your daughter's life is tied to the lives of your country's nobles," Brack went on. "But it doesn't mean she will perish—not on our watch."

"Why should we trust you? Your kind are—"

"Errod," Queen Lucetta cut in, laying a hand on her husband's arm. "Think of our daughter and our people. Anger will accomplish nothing."

A guard opened the door and plump, kindly-looking King Thaddeus of Yorth entered. He went straightaway to the queen and patted her hand. "I'm so sorry, my dear. I'm certain we can all figure something out."

King Riskan of Calgoran entered with two of his ministers. The king had dark, curly hair and a full black beard. Like Errod, he was muscular and tall, impressive enough to remind me that I wore the guise of an unexceptional fairy. "The betrothal between my son and Elinor must be immediately annulled. I will not be bound by blood to a country that has invited the wrath of an elicromancer."

Brack and Errod both opened their mouths to speak, but it was one of Riskan's own ministers who reacted first. "That would be unwise, Your Majesty. This threat only proves that now is the time for our three kingdoms to stand united."

Brack nodded. "Commander Cyril is right. All of Nissera is in peril. It is a time to honor agreements and make amends."

I should have known the militant bronze-haired man next to King Riskan was a commander rather than a minister. His hooked nose and sharp blue eyes made him more imposing than all three kings combined, in spite of his dusting of freckles.

Riskan flashed an icy look at Brack. "I don't accept counsel from creatures who deal in curses."

"Your father trusted Brack," the commander said, walking around the table. He looked from king to king. "And your grandfathers. Theirs was a time of peace."

"True, Cyril, but at the time, his protégée had not attempted to destroy half a kingdom," said Riskan. "These days, elicromancers are hermits with untimely caprices to meddle in the affairs of men. This concerns no one but Volarre, and my kingdom will have no part in it. Neither will my son."

"You coward," Errod spat through his teeth as Riskan turned his back.

The other king let out a fuming breath and continued down the hall, barking for the guards to gather his family's entourage. Looking thwarted, Cyril lingered for a moment before bowing to the remaining royalty in the room and following his king.

"This is a civil discussion about the fate of a realm," King Thaddeus said to Errod in a fatherly manner. "Let us save our tempers for a time when less is at stake. Have confidence that I will not annul the betrothal between the princess and my dear Nicolas."

Errod nodded. Thaddeus patted his shoulder.

"Let's return to how we will protect Rosamund, in case the curse took full effect," said Brack. "My plan is simple. Black elicromancy may be cunning, but it is also extravagant, and can therefore overlook simplicity. We'll do something Tamarice won't expect: give the princess a new name, a new home and a new guardian. She will live as a peasant in a country village, ignorant of her true identity, until I have dealt with Tamarice." He met my eyes. "And who better to be her guardian than an elicromancer in peasant's clothing?"

"Me?" I asked, voice small.

"Yes," Brack answered.

"That is out of the question," Errod said with a dismissive gesture. "Rosamund will remain in the palace."

"Stone walls and locked doors will not stop Tamarice when she has regained her strength. And your daughter would grow miserable kept under lock and key at all times."

"What about your citadel?" Queen Lucetta asked. "Rosamund and I could live at Darmeska."

Brack cupped his chin in his hand thoughtfully. "I'm afraid that even centuries' worth of strong enchantments around that city can't make it utterly impenetrable, and it's a predictable plan."

"Wherever she goes, I am going," Lucetta said. "She's not even weaned yet. She cannot be without her mother."

"Your face is well known, Your Majesty, and Bristal does not yet have the skill to change it for you. If you truly want your daughter and your kingdom to be safe, you must make this sacrifice. Bristal can pose as the aunt of a child whose parents passed away. She will hire a wet nurse to wean the child early. Meanwhile, I will hunt down Tamarice and destroy her as I should have years ago. I will visit frequently to continue training Bristal and to ensure Rosamund is safe. Let us hope this arrangement will not last long."

I could only listen as my fate was decided. The queen seemed to feel the same sense of powerlessness. I watched the sadness in her eyes deepen as Brack and Errod discussed the details, and it moved me to pity.

"A kind woman once took me in and treated me as her

own," I said to the queen. "I promise I will care for Rosamund just the same."

Queen Lucetta managed a weak smile. "Thank you."

Finally, Brack and the king stood. "Well, it seems everything is in order," Brack said. "I'm sorry it's come to this."

King Errod offered Brack his hand, and they shook. "We are grateful, Lord Brack, Lady Bristal," he said. Hearing a king speak my name, regardless of the circumstances, was bizarre. Even though he moved stiffly, the gratitude in his voice was unmistakable.

I bowed my head. As I turned to follow Brack, the queen placed a hand gently on my arm.

"May I speak with you a moment?"

"Yes, Your Majesty."

The others compliantly left the room. Queen Lucetta waited until the door closed before she turned to me. "I'm sorry that the kings do not give elicromancers the respect they deserve. I know you are not responsible for the actions of your former comrade."

"Thank you."

"I would like to ask one more thing of you, even after all you have done and will do." She looked regal with her delicate face and her long golden hair, but her eyes held the pain and fear of any mother losing her child.

"Anything, Your Majesty."

"Allow me to see your real face."

I nodded and stepped away from her to transform. As myself, she and I were the same height. Lucetta gasped as she took in my appearance.

"You are a lovely young girl. Something about your face

assures me." Her hands felt cold and small as she folded mine inside them. "Thank you for your promise to keep her safe."

※

Evening had come by the time Brack and I returned to the sitting area of our suite. The sky was an exquisite violet, and from the balcony I could clearly make out the thin, glowing sliver of a moon. I dropped my guise and collapsed on a chaise, resting my face in my hands and thinking of the responsibility I had taken on.

For all his composure when speaking with the king and queen, Brack looked beyond exahusted now that we were alone. "The fate-binding elixir requires a large amount of elicromancer blood. She must have used her own, healing herself as she bled out. And then she would have forced someone to carve all those names on her skin." He winced and shook his head, bereft. "How did she stray so far?"

"Did you ever fully trust her?"

He sighed deeply, wearing an indecipherable expression. "I always had hope for her, but no, I never trusted her. Elicromancers are meant to help mortals, not exercise our authority over them unchecked. However, some of our kind have always considered it a desecration to use our magic for the benefit of so-called lesser beings. Over time, power lust can ripen even in the noblest of people. Usually it takes many years. But on the day Tamarice became an elicromancer, the lust already ran deep in her."

Brack paced across the room to the window, pausing with his back to me for a moment before going on.

"When I first met her, I wore no disguise. I didn't want my fellow elicromancer to feel deceived. But then I saw the way she looked at me. I thought it was my appearance that drew her to me, but no: it was my power. She grew to love me, Bristal—desperately. Not as a pupil loves her mentor."

More pieces of the story slid into place. I should have known all along. I had seen traces of envy, respect, resentment. It was clear how these feelings could form hatred, but the deciding ingredient was missing: hurt. "You didn't love her in return."

"I recognized her affection as something to fear. She admired me only because she saw something powerful and wanted to force out its potential. When she confessed her love for me and I couldn't return her affections, she called me a coward for not embracing my desires, be it love, riches or power. That was when I knew her claims were not merely juvenile convictions, but that she was becoming everything I feared she would be—blind to the price of her actions. The golden realm she envisions under elicromancer reign would be nothing but a kingdom of ash and briars."

I looked out the window again. The torches stretched the shadows of the guards as they kept their watch. How was it that a matter of months ago my greatest worry was avoiding a vicious, spoiled girl on a manor in Popplewell? How had my world shifted so much that I was now helping to protect the entire realm from someone I thought I could trust?

I longed to lighten the moment, to hear a word of hope from Brack. "At least we know that with those tempers, the kings will not go down without a fight."

Brack flared his nostrils the way one does when suffocating anger into something a little more productive. "It's their tempers I worry about. Calgoran and Volarre have often disputed, but they have always, at heart, remained allies. Giving

their children to one another openly expresses and perpetu-
ates the alliance. Without the betrothal between Elinor and
Prince Charles, they have no reminder that they are better off
as friends. If rifts form between these nations, how will they
stand against Tamarice and what she brings upon them?"

"Can't you do something about King Riskan? Can you use
your power to compel him to keep the betrothal?"

Brack's solemn gaze met mine. "I will not pretend the
idea hasn't crossed my mind. But the road to treachery begins
with the slightest of compromises. I cannot give myself free
reign over the thoughts of powerful men. I also will not cause
anyone to go mad—rearranging a mind can inflict irreparable
damage. No, I must search for Tamarice, and it will be your
duty to build influence in Calgoran. She may be debilitated for
the moment, but the kingdoms' enmity will make it easier for
her to tear this realm to pieces when she recovers."

"How will I protect the princess and be at court in Calgoran enough to make a difference?"

"I will return often to watch over her while you are gone.
I've been perfecting a third disguise that Tamarice hasn't seen.
You can help me reinforce it if it starts to waver."

He pulled a lumpy square of velvet from the pocket of his
cloak, which hung over a chair. Unfolding it, he revealed the
exquisite amethyst tiara that the younger prince of Calgoran
had given Princess Rosamund. I could now appreciate its every
detail: the way the dainty pattern of the silver mimicked lace,
the tiny diamonds studded along its contours. "It's so beautiful," I said, feeling oddly sad that it didn't belong to me.

"It's extremely fortunate for us that Tamarice did not
recognize its value during the ceremony. The amethyst is an

elicrin stone." Brack held it up in the frail light falling through the window. Purple shapes raced back and forth on the walls. "This belonged to the elicromancer Callista—Cassian's bride. Whoever holds this can see the truth through all barriers: deceitful words, enchantments, even disguises." He gave me a long look. "It is too docile a thing to appeal to Tamarice. She underestimates the power of renounced elicrin stones, and how very lucky we are for that. If she possessed this relic, you might not have a chance of remaining hidden, even with your gift." He covered it back up. "But there's another reason to be wary. It's come to my attention that Prince Anthony held the diadem before he presented it to the princess. Young though he may be, he is still a prince of Calgoran. That means one of the most important figures in the realm knows your true face, as do those in your home village, your kidnappers and of course, Tamarice. Regardless of intentions, any one of these people could put you in danger. You must not reveal yourself, even when you perceive no imminent threat."

I hadn't suspected that when the young prince looked on me in awe, his gaze had locked the door already shut on my freedom.

Brack held out the beautiful artifact. "Take it with you. As long as you and Rosamund are safe, it will be safe." He placed it in my hands and turned away.

"If it's that important, don't you think it belongs in your care?" I asked.

I couldn't see Brack's face in the shadows as he retrieved his cloak and staff. "I believe it's exactly where it belongs."

His voice met my ears strangely. As I cradled the truth-seeing elicrin stone, I thought of how the scarred warrior and the gray-haired man were appearances Brack had scrupulously designed, without a gift like mine to help. I suspected that if I were to look deeply into the shadows on the far side of the room, I would see him in his true form.

I realized I had only thought of him as a sage old man with a heart full of noble convictions. But deeper than that, who was he?

Remembering that he had promised never to read my thoughts, I resisted the urge to search the shadows. I would respect his secrets.

I said goodnight and went to my chamber, hoping to free my mind of the night's events in order to rest.

Tomorrow morning would be the start of months, perhaps even years of wearing disguises, and losing myself in them. But who was I, anyway? I was once a cook's helper with a surprising stroke of magic. I didn't know what could be said of me now.

※

We woke up before dawn and began creating a guise for Rosamund's guardian. I would be her Aunt Amelia, a plain woman with graying blonde hair and a kindly face. My story would be that I had taken in my young niece after her parents' deaths. I would age my guise as the years went by.

Examining my new form, I felt a small part of myself tear asunder and drift away.

After breakfast the day felt fresh somehow, a little less hopeless. My headache had eased and I could now bend my fingers, so I was in decent spirits as Brack and I prepared to leave with Rosamund.

Disguised as a servant, I walked to the queen's private

quarters. The lavishly furnished bedchamber, bedecked in deep blues with accents of gold and silver, was the size of an entire cottage. Double doors opened into a private garden filled with sunshine. A figure lay on the canopied bed, blonde hair spilling over a silk pillowcase.

"Your Majesty?" I asked without venturing farther.

"She has already said farewell to Rosamund," said a languid voice from the garden. My eyes adjusted to the light and found Lucetta's twin sister, Lysandra. In spite of the illness that made her fragile, the duchess's green eyes held a sharp look that spoke of profound inner strength, shining brightly beneath dark, refined brows. "Rosamund is with the wet nurse. She will be ready in a moment."

Lucetta lay on the bed, shoulders shaking with silent sobs. I crossed the room to her and reached out as if to touch her shoulder, but hesitated. Lysandra gave me a soft nod of encouragement and I timidly reached down to grip the queen's delicate hand. Without opening her eyes, she squeezed mine in return. All that I had learned about the boundaries between peasantry and nobility slid away, and my responsibilities as an elicromancer erected themselves more clearly in my mind.

"Keep her safe," Lucetta whispered.

"I will."

The queen released my hand. Lysandra beckoned me to the garden.

We sat outside, surrounded by the mingling scents of spring flowers. Lysandra's daughter, the one who had lost her marriage arrangement after Tamarice's attack, tried to pour me a cup of tea even though she hardly looked old enough to walk. "Let me help you, Elinor," the duchess said, patting the girl's flaxen blonde hair. I watched the woman's hand tremble as she filled my cup. The tea pervaded the air with the scent of sweet cherries.

"Dark times, are they not?" she asked, glancing in my direction as she struggled to set the teapot down and push the cream and sugar toward me.

"I'm afraid so."

"You showed great courage. I am not so selfless. All I want is to protect my family. I've asked my husband to take Elinor to Calgoran when I die. Perhaps the curse cannot touch them there."

She spoke about her death so cavalierly that my teacup paused halfway to my mouth. "That might not be for some time."

"When death slowly draws near, you feel it in your soul. You see shadows everywhere, more every day. I saw them bending over Rosamund's crib last night. They flee with light or sound, but it makes them no less real."

Holding back a shudder, I glanced at Elinor, who was humming to herself and thankfully much too small to understand her mother's words.

A young servant approached, Rosamund hanging in a sling around her chest. The princess awoke and regarded me with a steadfast stare as I took her into my arms.

"Lucetta made this herself." Lysandra gave me a white silk handkerchief embroidered with an *R* in blue thread. "She wants her to have it."

I tucked the handkerchief away in my small knapsack and curtsied. "Farewell, Your Grace."

Lysandra's yellow hair caught waves of sunlight as she

leaned down to kiss her niece goodbye. She then straightened and bowed her head to me.

Once I left the garden to meet Brack, Rosamund began to fuss. I shushed her and hugged her tight against my chest.

"There, now. We'll be all right, Rosie. I'm going to keep you safe."

Part Two

SEVEN

My golden braid whipped against my back as I laced through the colorful streets of Arna. I was late for a meeting, but not so late that I could resist chasing the tantalizing scent of fresh bread to the baker's shop in the square. The baker was fond of blondes, and it wasn't below me to cater to his fancy in the name of a quick breakfast at no charge.

I tore into the warm fig pie and smiled as the coarse lyrics of a tavern song met my ears. I adored Arna, the jewel of Calgoran. The city's complex web of streets led to a grand palace, which sprawled majestically over the Roac River. Endless flat, green country surrounded the city on three sides, while a network of smaller cities and farming towns speckled the rich land southward. I knew Arna like I'd know the face of an old friend.

Passing behind a curtain of clean laundry, I took on my latest courtier guise, all bouncing light brown curls and long legs, one of countless others that had suited my purposes during years of political meddlesomeness. I entered the vast palace courtyard and arrived at the never-ending succession of wide marble stairs leading from the gardens to the entryway. I joined the nobles meandering in the enormous domed receiving hall and passed by a series of majestic marble pillars that looked dense enough to keep the mountain halls of Darmeska standing.

Before entering the music parlor that branched out of the main ballroom, I glanced down at my neckline and made a few adjustments. There was no such thing as too much skin showing when it came to male courtiers—as long as it didn't involve the ankles. That would be in poor taste.

"Lord Yornell," I said over the music of a lute badly played. My voice sounded pouty and childish. "Have you heard that your wife accosted me yesterday in the gardens?"

The sweaty, mustachioed man beckoned me onto his lap while three other courtiers laughed. "I'm sorry, my dear."

"You did explain to her that we've had no . . . relations, didn't you?"

He squeezed me hard around the waist. His voice tended to come out as a soft growl, which many of the women liked. "Of course, my darling Catleen. She is merely envious of your beauty."

I used the excuse of a deep sigh to push out my chest. The man didn't even pretend to have anything better to look at. The unfortunate reality of influencing men, wealthy or poor, smart or dull, was that it often required seduction. I had thought the courtiers of Arna would grow tired of Catleen Boulstridge once they realized I was playing them one after the other, but the reserved nature hiding under my forward pretense made me quite a marvelous tease. Rather than seeing my reputation as a disgrace, the men of Arna had grown fonder of me. Catleen had more power over the male nobles than all the royal ministers combined.

"She knows there's *nothing* to be concerned about." Yornell said this with a theatric eyebrow raise while stroking the curve of my breast with one finger. I had trained myself not to cringe during such moments, but if he pushed any further he would find himself a slimy fish flopping on the tiles.

"You must do something to throw her off the trail." As Catleen, I rarely ceased to sound like a spoiled child attempting to whine her way out of trouble.

Yornell played with one of my light brown curls. "What shall I do?"

"Didn't you refuse to entertain your wife's cousin who is coming for a visit? The Duke of Prude?"

Yornell laughed belittlingly. "The Duke of Prue, you silly girl. He is an arrogant ass who renounced Calgoran because of high taxes, and now is King Errod's lapdog in Volarre." He emphasized the word *lapdog* by squeezing my backside.

"If you make him feel welcome again here in Arna," I said, teasing out his mustache, "your wife will be in better spirits and will no longer be suspicious."

"I would be a laughingstock."

"Perhaps so." I leaned forward to whisper in his ear. "But you will be rewarded handsomely."

Yornell narrowed his eyes repugnantly and took another long look at my neckline. After a moment, he sighed as if annoyed, but his devious smile gave his true feelings away. "Very well. I will show the duke a fine time and try to salvage his reputation. And you," he delivered this with another emphatic smack, "prepare to show *me* a fine time."

I made a very Catleen-esque exit by casting a glance over my shoulder on the way out.

Back in the receiving hall, I crossed behind one of the marble pillars and changed into my anonymous emissary disguise, wishing the feeling of being inappropriately fondled could be scrubbed off like dirt.

The commander of Calgoran's army waited for me on the balcony that functioned as our meeting place. Cyril's bronze hair was silvering prematurely but he had the same muscular, stocky build as when I'd first met him on the princess's name day.

"For someone who can be anywhere at any time, you make quite a habit of being late," he said.

"Rosie is as curious as a cat," I said, straightening my red tunic. "She doesn't let me leave anymore without asking a dozen questions. I suppose I should be thankful she still believes her peasant aunt has any reason to travel for days at a time. I'm fortunate my reputation as a local healer has blossomed."

Cyril handed me a neatly rolled bundle of parchment.

"What's this?"

"His Majesty's plans for increasing border security."

I unrolled the documents with a sigh. "You mean His Majesty's latest attempt to villainize Volarre."

"Precisely."

My eyes grew wide as I studied the documents. "A hundred new guard towers on the border? Imprisonment of any foreign persons deemed suspicious? What is King Riskan thinking? Volarre will not see this as a friendly gesture. Even Yorth will take offense."

"And eventually take up arms." Cyril faced the city, clasping his hands behind his back. Above us, red banners bearing

Calgoran's white crest and red stag fluttered on their posts in a breeze. "Can you clean this up?"

"I can take a diplomatic approach to delivering the news. Let's hope they don't kill the messenger."

The corner of his mouth twitched. "I'd like to see them try." I answered his smile, but it fell quickly when Cyril asked, "Has Brack returned?"

Years had flown by, and yet Brack remained resolved in his search for Tamarice. He rarely left for more than a month at a time, following his instincts or traces of the supernatural, pinpointing places where she might hide and recuperate. I had personally begun to wonder if she had died when I destroyed her elicrin stone, but he grew more and more convinced she had traveled to Galgeth.

This time, I had not seen or heard from Brack in more than three months. A letter from Drell had told me those at Darmeska had seen no trace of him, either.

I pushed it from my mind as well as I could, but Rosie had begun to ask why her Uncle Warrick hadn't visited lately.

"No. No word from him." I rolled up the documents and returned them, staving off my worry. "I could use your advice, Commander. For the past few years I've hoped to gain the Calgoranian princes' friendship and confidence, but I've struggled to find a way to get close to them. Do you know Charles and Anthony Ermetarius well?"

"Well enough to tell you that Charles is as reserved a man you'll ever meet. Anthony is witty and wise, but too restless to stand in one place for more than a minute. I could see why even you might have trouble winning the friendship of the princes."

"I'm afraid I've gotten nowhere close. Having their mother as a friend at court is of nearly no use to me. Queen Dara holds no sway over King Riskan's political decisions. And finding my way into Riskan's confidences is as difficult as I expected."

"Few can tread lightly enough to win his trust."

I massaged my temples. I had accomplished a great deal when it came to preventing disputes that could easily turn into a civil war. Intercepting notes, forging documents, impersonating aristocrats and planting ideas in heads had become elements of my daily life. One of my proudest accomplishments was convincing King Errod to draw up a military treaty that had kept the realm's armed forces at a healthy equilibrium for years.

But there had been no opportunity to plant myself in the life of an influential person. True, Cyril was a powerful man, but the moment he claimed friendship with an elicromancer or publicized his belief that Tamarice planned to destroy Nissera, he would find himself deposed. Riskan didn't like talk of elicromancers.

I hardly saw much of either prince lately. I often glimpsed Charles from a distance, since he made all the customary appearances in court. He possessed the commanding presence and strapping build one would expect of a Calgoranian prince. He stood a few inches taller than the average man, and had clean-cut brown hair and eyes the blue of dark waters. His handsome face offered few expressions besides a habitual look of calm attention but had more than its fair share of admirers.

Anthony I had seen even less. A few years ago, he had requested to live with the soldiers in the barracks. He had grown bored of ceremonial swordplay lessons and wanted to learn real combat skills—in case of real war. King Riskan refused to let him live among common soldiers, but Anthony did as he wished without his father's permission. Everyone behaved as though King Riskan had thought a stay in the barracks was a proper chastisement for his hotheaded and warmongering son and sent him there himself. But it was common knowledge that Anthony chose his own path.

Now Anthony had his own delegation of troops, with a penchant for turning criminals and renegades into respectable soldiers. His mother and father disapproved of his tendency to neglect courtly duties, but he made enough appearances to appease them.

"Anthony has begun to call his small troop the 'Realm Alliance' in hopes that their success will spark some sentiments of unity," Cyril said. "He's convinced that a war with Tamarice is coming. Many find his passionate dialogue on the subject unsettling."

"He sounds wise. But if he's losing favor with his family and the public, it will do me little good to ally myself with him."

Cyril's eyes gleamed with pride. "On the contrary, I've heard talk that he's likely to be instated as commander after me, whenever Charles is king."

"Is that so?" I looked off to the west, where at the far end of the palace grounds sat rows upon rows of military barracks. A shadow of an idea crept into my mind.

I knew a way I could get close to Anthony Ermetarius.

"They're both of marrying age now," Cyril went on. "Riskan will be pressuring Charles to take a wife. The choice he makes could impact the political climate for the better."

"Yes, arrangements for a grand ball are already underway. Every eligible Calgoranian maiden will be invited. If we could just . . ." I trailed off, my mouth falling agape. I turned to Cyril. "Elinor."

"Who?"

"The deceased Duchess Lysandra's daughter. Remember when Brack tried to convince Riskan to make good on the betrothal to no avail? Now that Charles is a man, there may be another way."

"But the duke and his daughter disappeared. No one knows where Elinor is. She's known as the Lost Duchess, and she's been all but forgotten about."

"Lysandra told me her dying wish was for the duke to get Elinor out of Volarre and bring her here to Calgoran."

Cyril cocked an eyebrow. "That's hardly specific."

Leaning on the balustrade, I looked downriver, then at the city and the green land beyond. Calgoran was a vast country. "Even so, there must be way to find her."

But I had other arrangements to make first—arrangements that would put me in a position of greater access to Calgoran's more defiant prince.

When Cyril and I parted ways, I materialized to Volarre, and then Yorth, to deliver the message about border security to King Errod and King Thaddeus. My words as the emissary were tactful enough that I saw only a hint of Errod's thinly veiled temper. Thaddeus's response was more cooperative. "I've been planning to visit both of our friends in the north," he said, concern wrinkling his round, jolly face until it looked like a week-old grape. "It seems a good time to do so, before our relations worsen. Yes, now seems a good time."

It was high noon by the time I materialized to the cottage in Plum Valley and heard the melodic sounds of Rosie's singing drifting through the open kitchen shutters. Our home stood against a green slope, flanked by poplar trees and tucked in a quaint wooded valley in the northwestern corner of Volarre.

Rosie leaned over the windowsill to toss seeds to the garden birds. Her thick strawberry blonde hair nearly trailed through the flower box soil. "Make sure to share," she scolded an over-enthusiastic tawny-tit.

I sighed. When she was a child, I had made a habit of following her through the woods veiled as animals. Once, while in the form of a deer, I made the mistake of absentmindedly nodding my head yes when she asked if I was following her. From then on, she seemed to believe all animals could understand her—and that they were quite solicitous. There was no doubt I would be handing a beautiful yet rather peculiar young woman back to Errod and Lucetta.

Rosie smiled and waved. She wore her fairy gifts like fine jewelry, but her loveliness was something else entirely, something natural. Her sage-green eyes were deep-set, fringed with thick brown lashes and framed by regal brows. Her body was curvaceous yet thin, her face lightly freckled from afternoons in the sun.

Her curious nature led her into conversations with any type of person—a gnarled beggar, a hard-faced blacksmith, a tavern girl, a royal messenger—and this made me anxious, reminding me that I was right to never give her even the slightest hint that she wasn't who I said she was: an orphaned peasant girl. Unfortunately, now that she was older, my persistent warnings to avoid strangers were not well received.

Seeing Rosie grow into a young woman was like watching a flower bloom the same day the seed was planted. According to the lifespan of an elicromancer, I was an adolescent, perhaps even a child. But every few months, I added a few gray hairs to Amelia's head or barely deepened one of her wrinkles. When I needed to be reminded of who I truly was, I would reach into the back of the deep cabinet in my bedroom where behind all of my clothes and hidden by a concealing enchantment, lay the amethyst tiara. When I held it delicately in my fingers and looked in the mirror, it showed me the truth: long dark hair that reached my elbows, pale and youthful skin, a slender frame. My body had ceased to mature and had settled into its permanent state.

Rosie extracted the cumbersome packages from my hands, humming to herself as she organized them on the kitchen shelves. She never doubted my excuses for leaving. Her impressionable nature, which caused me so much concern for her safety, became a blessing every time I had to leave Plum Valley for pressing tasks—or whenever she found me hiding evidence of magic.

"We received a letter from Uncle Warrick," she sang happily.

I froze. "What did it say?"

"He said he was sorry for not having visited in a while. He's been in the Southern Islands. I do hope he has good stories to tell." I could see the hunger in her green eyes, hunger to hear about anywhere besides the quaint town nearest our home.

"Did he say when he's returning?"

Rosie pulled the letter out of her pocket and handed it to me. "He just said soon."

Taming my every gesture so that I didn't seem too eager, I took the letter. "I will be visiting soon, and I look forward to telling you about my adventure and all the things I have learned and discovered," I read. "Please go about your everyday business rather than staying home expecting me. Illness does not take a holiday, and your remedies and healing touch are ever in high demand. Give Rosie my love."

My heart galloped through my chest. I tucked the letter away so that I wouldn't be tempted to stare at the seemingly mundane message.

Brack mentioning things he had "learned and discovered" meant he had gathered information about Tamarice's whereabouts. Since he was able to write—and stressed that I should continue with my diplomatic schemes—it was likely good news.

Continue with my schemes, I would.

The magic books hidden by a concealing enchantment in my wardrobe hadn't seen much light since my lessons with Brack following Rosamund's name day. Feeling like I was stepping back across years, I reverently smoothed the creased, dusty pages of *Travel by Magic* and began to tinker with the details of my boldest plan yet.

My satchel sang a tune of clanking glass vials as I left the apothecary that night. Walking back through the woods to the valley, I stopped to scrape wet bark from a yew tree and didn't notice the cloaked figure on my trail until it was upon me. I gasped and nearly muttered a defense spell before the figure tore off its hood, revealing a long mane of wet orange hair.

"Drell!" I cried, embracing her in disbelief. "You've grown!"

"As mortals do," she said, laughing as she wrapped her thin, strong arms around me. Somehow the familiar proud chin, the thin lips and the wide-set blue eyes—which had made her as coarse-looking of a child as she was coarse-minded—had yielded agreeable looks. She stood small, shorter even than me in my Amelia guise, but I didn't doubt the presence of hidden might on her frame. Though she was a woman now, something girlish endured in her features.

"What are you doing here?" I asked, unable to stop smiling. "I've hardly received any letters from you lately."

Brack had given us permission to write each other in code when we had news to share. But what I had written to Drell over the lonely years hardly qualified as news—until Brack's absence.

"Sorry about that. They're buttering me up to be an elder before my time, which makes for a lot of studying. But when Grandmum and the elders saw your letter about Brack's extended absence, they sent me here to help you."

"Help me? How? I mean, I'm certainly grateful for the company."

"Until Brack returns, you need someone to look after Rosie while you're in the royal cities. I've been thinking." Drell wore her familiar smug smile. "And what I've been thinking is this: you can disguise me as Aunt Amelia while you go about your business. I'll be your relief, and stay here to watch over Rosie. I see that you're cooking up a plan." She pointed at the wet bark in my hands. "Bistort and arrowroot from the apothecary, and fresh yew bark—sounds like you've cracked open a few of the old books recently. Let me watch over things here while you do what you have to do."

I pursed my lips, thinking. My own guises lasted indefinitely, but I wasn't sure how long one might last on her. The elicrin magic in her blood could possibly prolong it, I supposed. And she could make herself scarce when the guise wore off.

"You know I'm skilled with a sword," she said. "A little protection is better than none. What enchantments have you laid?"

I stuffed the yew bark in my sack. "Misdirection, protection from darkness and fortification."

Drell blinked hard at me and massaged her forehead.

"What's wrong?" I asked.

"Misdirection spells are obvious—you can practically bump into them like a pane of glass if you get too close. Brack doesn't believe there's such a thing as being too cautious, but there is. We'll get rid of it."

I shook my head. "You've always known when I needed you. It's why I couldn't take three steps without bumping into you at Darmeska, isn't it?"

Drell laughed. "Grateful now?"

When we reached the slope that overlooked the cottage, we lay flat on our bellies. I whispered the words that would retract the misdirection spell. *Fricara inoden therast iole te herana.* I felt something in the air change and heard a faint wind whistling, and then all was still.

Drell fixed her bright eyes on me. "So what are you cooking up?"

✳

Past midnight I stood outside a tavern on the seediest street of the outskirts of Arna: Halfhand Square, so named for the threat of leaving short a body part you came with. I wore a nondescript disguise—a young man neither short nor tall with brown hair, pale skin, a sinewy frame and a peppering of dark moles.

For the past hour I had watched men laughing, singing, fighting and pawing full-bosomed women. At last I had come across what I believed to be the only sober souls in the whole town: two robust bald men, one with more scars than a whole army could boast. They stood on either side of the entrance to the tavern and extracted anyone who got rowdy enough to cause trouble, unruffled by any attempts to rebuff their jurisdiction.

Drell and I had refreshed my memory with knife, sword, staff and bow, even listened to hours' worth of vulgar dialogue exchanged over countless pints of ale. I had diligently practiced spells and memorized my elaborate story until I nearly believed it myself. I didn't leave for Arna until I had Drell's utter approval on every aspect of my new character.

I strutted forward. "Gentlemen, would you be willing to attack a man for a gold aurion each?"

The one on the right with the scars chuckled. They were symmetrical incisions that had to have been some intentional form of mutilation. "I'd stick my head up a horse's ass for a gold aurion, mate."

"That's hardly necessary." Drawing one of the coins from my pocket, I watched their eyes glint in the lamplight. I considered that the two of them could easily confiscate the coins by force; I was strong, but lean and young, and clearly not as seasoned in combat as they were. A sturdy young man with the accoutrements of a huntsman and a bit of brazen wit would perhaps be a threat to some men, but not these. I was relying on the gold to demonstrate a measure of authority.

The other asked, "What would you have us do?"

"I need you to attack a man, a particular man. Gain the advantage, get a knife at his throat—but don't kill him. No more than some minor cuts and bruises. I'll interrupt, point an arrow at your head. You will release him and walk away rich."

The one with the scars looked back over his shoulder at the tavern, where things seemed to be tame for the moment.

"What man?"

"Does it matter?"

"It matters. There are fires around here you don't piss on, boy."

"Prince Anthony Ermetarius."

The other laughed and ran a hand over his face. "You're joking!"

The scarred one shook his head. "Sorry, mate, but no gold coin can put my head back on after a meeting with the royal executioner."

I drew out three more aurions. "This should be enough to replace even your bollocks if they come to harm. And enough to ensure your silence at the end of this affair?"

I had them now. Both stood mesmerized, mouths agape. It was likely more than a year's wages for each of them. Errod and Lucetta had given me so many gold aurions when I became Rosie's guardian that I was still having trouble getting rid of them.

"Who are you?" asked the other.

"Now, that really doesn't matter," I said. "Half up front and the other half in about a quarter of an hour when it's all well and done—or I'll go find some lucky drunk bastard and pay him one silver."

They waited around the corner from the tavern, where only one lamp flickered. Concealed in the shadows, I consulted my map. Back home, I had pored through *Travel by Magic* to find a basic tracing spell. The one I'd chosen was called a tracker map. It was intended for catching enemies unawares. However, it only responded to good intentions and didn't penetrate even the simplest of protective enchantments; thus, the method had been generally abandoned by elicromancers, according to Drell.

After coating the map with my homemade resin, the final step was to throw it in the fire and say the prince's name aloud. It didn't burn, but a spot of ash indicated Prince Anthony's location.

Now that mark drifted closer and closer to me.

I hoped Anthony wasn't accompanied by a group of his men. Even just one could spoil my plans to waylay him. But this was the second time I had seen this path drawn across my map, and I had spied on him from afar the time before. He had traveled alone, disguised in a frayed cloak, and disappeared into the deserted alley where my cronies were now waiting for him. I looked up to see the hooded figure approaching on a horse and put the tracker map away.

The prince dismounted next to a decrepit structure tucked between two darkened shops. While the prince tied his reins to a crooked post, I watched the two men emerge from the shadows, each gripping a dagger that gleamed menacingly. For being largely built, they moved stealthily. The man without the scars advanced first, gripping Anthony from behind with little effort, forcing his knife at the prince's throat. I leapt forward, ready to play my part. I was surprised by how easily we had succeeded.

But I was mistaken. Anthony pushed his chin down against his attacker's hand and thrust out his right arm in one unexpectedly swift movement, trapping the other man's forearm and turning the knife away from his throat. He twisted the immobilized arm until they were facing one another and the attacker's right shoulder hunched in submission. I hadn't accounted for this turn of events.

The man used his free arm to block the kick Anthony intended for his groin, then grabbed him underneath his raised knee and tossed him flat on his back. The other came forward and together they towered over Anthony, looking more sinister than I could have hoped. The prince rolled to his feet to face them, gripping a knife of his own now.

His cloak had slipped off and I almost gasped aloud. The last time I caught a good look at Anthony, he had been a thin, average-sized youth. The young man I watched now had a sturdy build like his brother. Had I somehow mistaken Charles for him? But I recognized the profile in the flickering light as Anthony's: strong-jawed and as handsome as the elder prince, but with fuller lips, a more expressive face, eyes that held his every emotion at the surface. There was no trace of Charles's removed stoicism.

They had reached the stage in the fight when, if I were in Anthony's place, I would have used my status to make threats, or perhaps pleaded for my life. Yet he merely waited, poised and energetic, knife ready.

I shrugged my bow off my shoulder and inched along the wall. It didn't take the two of them long to overcome Anthony, though it took longer than they had expected. They would both be paying for it later in bruises and cuts. At last, one of the men punched Anthony in the face so hard that even in the dark I saw red spit fly from the prince's mouth. Before Anthony could recuperate, the other man pressed the point of his knife to his heart.

"Let him go," I demanded darkly, the point of my arrow nearly touching his temple. I had stolen upon them, making one swift movement of nocking an arrow and lunging from the shadows.

The attacker gave me a sideways glance. "Let him go," I repeated, voice deep and taut.

I could almost hear his thoughts: *About damned time.* He looked back at Anthony as if he were thinking it over and released him with a sneer.

I looked at the other man. "His knife."

He tossed it to Anthony, who caught it by the hilt. The two thugs strutted back down the alley toward the tavern. The man with the broken nose offered me the most infinitesimal nod as he passed, but the other gave me a look of death through a swelling eye. He would recover; as we agreed, I had hidden the rest of their payment in a crack in the mortar just around the corner.

After they left, I lowered my bow. Anthony caught his breath, eyes fixed on me underneath his sweat-soaked brow. "Thank you," he said, sheathing his knife at his waist. "Thank you for saving me." He ran a hand across his chest and looked down. A dark stain spread across his tunic where the knife had shallowly pierced his flesh.

"Any decent man would have done it."

"Folks in this town are hardly decent." He reached out so we could grasp one another's right forearm, the customary man-to-man greeting in Calgoran. "I owe you my life. Who are you?"

"Tomlin Happer, of Faywick. And you?"

"Anthony," he laughed breathlessly, wiping his bloody left hand on his shirt. "Ermetarius."

"Forgive me, Your Highness. I didn't recognize you." I bowed my head.

"Nothing to forgive. I haven't made a habit of going to court in years. My own mother hardly recognizes me." He collected his cloak and approached his anxious chestnut coarser. His tone was coaxing and gentle as he untied her from the post and stoutly patted her withers. "It's all right, Arsinoe," he said. "Chance was on our side tonight."

Chance indeed.

We walked side-by-side back toward friendlier streets. I glanced behind us at the unmarked building between the shops. He was abandoning his errand.

I repressed my curiosity and turned back to him. I couldn't see the details of his face, but I realized my hired men must have been enormous to tower over Anthony. He was quite tall, even compared to me in my disguise—Tomlin Happer from the poorest village I could think of.

"Faywick is a long way off. What brings you here?"

I couldn't sound too eager to spill my lies. "That's, uh, quite a tale to tell."

"Ale, then." I could hear the grin in his voice. "I think that's a fine way to start repaying you for my life."

"A very fine way," I agreed as we emerged from the darkness and entered a tavern. The crowd here was less rough and sotted, and Anthony earned a few stares for the blood on his face and shirt as we found empty seats in the corner of the den. He didn't seem to notice.

I hadn't perceived the chill outside until we sat near the fire. The ale was good, and the first sip warmed me all the way to my toes. I looked at Anthony, examining him for the first time in the light as he used his sleeve to mop away the blood on his lip before taking a grateful swig.

His face was well defined and handsome. He and Charles looked plenty alike—sturdy yet lean, of a similar imposing height—but Anthony wore his strength differently, carrying himself with a sort of casualness I would have thought uncharacteristic of royalty. He had dark brown hair like the rest of his family, barely long enough to hint at curls, and his skin was slightly sun-browned. His eyes shimmered bright in the firelight, hazel-green rather than blue like his brother's. He barely resembled the boy I remembered. This thought made me wonder how much he himself remembered, if he had committed my face to memory or if he even recalled glimpsing it at all.

"How fortunate for me you decided to journey across the country," he said, clanking his flagon down and resting an arm over the back of his chair.

"Fortunate for us both, actually." I took another deep gulp, my heart racing with the knowledge of what I was about to commit to, of how cleverly I would have to improvise to live out this role as Anthony's confidant. "I have three younger brothers and sisters. My father was a weapons maker. He died three years ago, and we nearly starved."

My words flowed out naturally, convincingly. I found Anthony pleasant, and knew it was due to more than his appearance. He was affable and . . . comfortable here, as if there were no better place he belonged. I could see why he was able to travel alone without trouble—at least, usually. I saw nothing marking him as the son of the king.

"I made and sold a few weapons, but I couldn't afford the materials to make more. I spent all my time hunting for food to keep us alive. But I'm better with blade and staff than bow and snare."

He understood immediately. "So you left to be a soldier and send home your wages."

"Indeed, and here is why I, too, am fortunate in having saved your life tonight: I'm not interested in joining the king's army. Two tedious years of service, chained to the barracks or to the borders—"

"—Play-fighting like that witch Tamarice isn't coming back for us all." I saw something bright in Anthony's eyes as he crossed his arms on the table and leaned closer. I hadn't expected him to be so candid, even after all I knew about him. Calgoranians didn't often speak of the elicromancers, or really any form of magic. "You came to join me, didn't you?"

I leaned in too, lowering my voice. "These are strange times. Not everyone seems to know it, but Nissera could be in great danger from Tamarice, especially with the kingdoms turning their backs on each other. I want to follow someone who's worth my loyalty."

Anthony sat back in his chair. "You know, my father thinks my men and I are agitators. They all think us bored, war-hungry boys who need something to do. But you know better, don't you?"

We grinned at one another in perfect unison. "Yes, I know better."

Anthony raised his flagon. "To the man who saved my neck tonight—to my new brother. Welcome."

We clanked our cups and drank, and the bitter taste of ale was sweet as honeyed mead in the joy of my success. My eyes met with my image mirrored in the window over Anthony's shoulder and saw a genuine smile on my face. It was the smile of a young man with the kind of tough spirit that a difficult life couldn't stomp out, one who thirsted for change. But deeper down, beyond the ruse, it was the smile of a lonely girl at last finding a sense of belonging.

EIGHT

 B y saving Anthony's life, Tomlin of Faywick had earned a place in the small twelfth contingent of Calgoran's army—or as they preferred to be called, the Realm Alliance.

Anthony told me there were but nineteen of them, twenty including me. When he and I made the short journey back to Arna, only two were still awake and sitting next to a dimming fire on the edge of the smallest training field. They looked up as we approached, fingers twitching toward their weapons until they recognized Anthony's face. They wore no uniform and looked to be a few years older than him.

"What poor fellow have you recruited?" said a black-haired young man with a charming smile. "Does he know we're all thought to be mad?"

The big blond man with a beard laughed. "He looks half-mad already. I'm sure we'll get along."

I chuckled in response. Tomlin's face did have a drawn look about it, with dark circles under eyes that looked continuously alert. I had attempted to look unexceptional. With this crowd, it mattered more who I was and what I could do with the weapons weighing down my belt and strapped across my back. We joined them, thankful for the warmth of the fire in the first of the cool autumn air to come.

"Orrin, Weston, I give you Tomlin of Faywick," Anthony said. "If he had found me any later than he did, he'd be tracking my blood on his boots. He was on his way to join the Alliance and found himself battling cutthroats for my honor."

They both reached over to grasp my forearm in greeting. "Well met, mate," said black-haired Orrin. By the name I recognized him as Anthony's cousin, whom I had spotted several times in court. "I told you, Anthony, you should have let me come with you. What sort of idiot goes to Halfhand Square alone, without his sword?"

"Look at how you've made your mother sick with worry," Weston mocked, laughing through a mouthful of pork. Orrin kicked glowing embers at him and Weston brushed them from his shoulder-length hair with a grunt.

"I'm conspicuous enough as it is without a pair of henchmen," Anthony said. "And you know any man carrying a fancy weapon in Halfhand is likely to get his face cracked in. I'd rather go undisturbed."

"Seems to me someone felt obliged to crack your face in either way," said Orrin, reclining again.

Weston offered Anthony and me generous slices of roasted pork. Even though we had already eaten at Halfhand, I put aside everything being a courtier had taught me about manners and ate like a man who had nearly starved a few times in his life. Afterwards, we dragged ourselves up the stone steps of the barracks and I collapsed on an empty straw mattress.

As I drifted off, I felt that there was something right about being here. I missed Rosie, and the old fear crept in as it did every time I left—what if Tamarice came for her? But somehow I fell to sleep without worry, oddly at home among nineteen strange men sleeping with weapons at their bedsides.

✳

Before dawn, I woke up and glanced at the inert forms around me, alarmed and confused. I had slept deeply and dreamt of unsettling whispers and shadows. I looked first at my hands and then ran them through my short hair, recalling last night's events and the reason I was here.

Bow and quiver in hand, I slipped outside. I found a trough next to the well and splashed cool water on my face and bare chest. I planned to squeeze in some target practice before everyone woke up, because even on my best day I was still a mediocre archer. I stretched my arms, getting a better feel for the way this body operated.

My first shot flew weak, barely making the edge of the target. I gritted my teeth. Rescuing Anthony in Halfhand would only gain me so much respect. If I failed at basic combat . . . well, I didn't want to consider how foolish I would look.

Relax. Breathe out.

The next shot struck true, and the one after even closer. The light was getting better. I extracted a fourth arrow from my quiver.

"You must be the new recruit."

I whipped around and found myself facing Cyril in the hint of early light. We had been working in tandem for so many years, sharing information and ideals, that I had to refrain from offering him a familiar smile. I accepted his outstretched arm with the customary greeting. "Tomlin Happer, sir."

"You've aligned yourself with good men, Tomlin. If I had the freedom to do what Anthony does, I would. Well, with discretion," he laughed. "That boy is as reckless as they come. But he's smart." Cyril fixed his blue eyes on mine. "Even if he says he's going straight to Galgeth unarmed and you think him the biggest fool to ever own a sword, follow him anyway."

"Understood, sir."

I had already decided against telling Cyril. Knowing the truth might cause him to treat me differently—to favor me, or to compensate for favoring me with silence or severity. I couldn't risk being noticed. It would be better for my mission if he didn't know.

He studied me briefly, from the hand that clasped my bow to my tense shoulders and peculiar eyes.

"Archery isn't your strongest art, is it?" He drew his sword. It caught the hint of sunlight spreading over the training fields. I sighed discreetly and went to retrieve my weapon from my heap of belongings. At least no one was watching.

I blocked his first strike, then a second and third, but it took great effort. Cyril was applying more speed and force, and I was hardly managing to be a worthy opponent. But strength and rudimentary skill kept me parrying.

It was a cool morning, but sweat ran into my eyes. Cyril took advantage of my distraction and struck the sword from my hands.

A crowd gathered outside of the barrack. The noise of our competition had drawn them out. I felt my face grow hot as I met their eyes. I had fooled myself, thinking I could play this part.

I saw Anthony, Orrin and Weston standing on the steps and felt an odd twisting in my chest of shame and defeat. Then I caught sight of the armory nearby. I wiped the sweat from my face. "Swordplay isn't my strongest either."

Cyril relaxed and nodded his head in the direction of the armory. "By all means."

I jogged inside and soon reemerged with a metal staff. Cyril raised his sword again. It reminded me of healing, the calm that swept over me when I took up a staff. My hands were sure, no longer weak or shaking. Brack had capitalized on my natural talent by emphasizing this art most in my training.

This time, I made the first move.

I swung my staff downwards and Cyril turned his blade to thwart the powerful blow. I blocked and evaded his strikes, answering him with equal force. He put off my over-the-head strikes by dropping to his knees, responded to my low blows by jumping. I spun out of the way of his quick swipes. I earned a cut along my collarbone, and I made Cyril stagger with a jab that met his ribs and a smack against the back of his shoulders. Eventually, every member of the Realm Alliance shuffled out of the barracks in nothing but their breeches to watch. Cyril blocked my staff and pushed me hard with his free hand. I hit the ground and before I could recover, his blade was at my throat.

"Well fought," he said, extending a hand to me. The others hollered, and I sighed in relief. Perhaps I would get by long enough to get close to Anthony.

"Men, welcome Tomlin Happer to your ranks," Cyril

shouted when I stood up. He grinned and clapped me on the back. "Somebody teach this boy to use a sword."

My every muscle felt sore before the first day of training ended. We rotated opponents until I had fought half a dozen of my comrades with sword, knife or staff. I was given leather armor rather than mail because, as Weston explained to me, the Realm Alliance's effectiveness depended on its members being inconspicuous. "Heavy armor protects, but it hinders," he said. "Just don't kill anyone in practice, eh?" He slapped me roughly on the back.

Most of the men were young, as more seasoned men favored joining the traditional army over this barely franchised group of rangers. Some were brawny like Weston and others more lithe, like me, but all were fit and apt fighters. I evened out in the middle rung as far as skill, while others like Weston, Anthony and Orrin clearly had the expertise to take on a seasoned fighter like Cyril and have a chance of coming out the victor.

Nearly half of them were former thieves who had chosen the Alliance over prison and not regretted it. One man, who was short a few teeth but was not otherwise unsightly, told me that stealing three goats from a farmer out in May Acre had been the best decision of his life. "What did I have before?" he said to me when I met him, drinking from a dented flask that he put down only to fight and sometimes not even then. "An empty belly. Now I've got a sword, friends, food and ale."

Come dinnertime, we sat around the fire at the edge of the field once more. My tired body was limp as a wet reed as I relaxed against a log, listening and watching.

"When I first asked for my own troop, my father refused

to issue us supplies," Anthony explained to me. "We were practicing with discarded weapons and hunting for food every night in the woods a few miles out. But when we managed to prove ourselves useful to him by tracking down marauders, he started paying us wages and giving us rations—a good deal less than his other soldiers, mind, but it's better than nothing. And now . . ." He gestured at the chickens roasting over the fire with a smile. "We dine like princes."

I raised my cup. "To the king's provision."

"Here, here." Anthony chuckled and took a drink of his wine before wandering off. Cyril hadn't exaggerated about the prince's restless nature.

Orrin lay his sword belt on the ground and sat next to me. I had been told to "fear the wrath of Splendor," and soon learned that Splendor was the name of Orrin's sword. He was the best swordsman among us, but not the only one to give his weapon a title. Anthony called his own Zeal, while Weston's knife was dubbed nothing other than Lace Cleaver—in honor of the occasions on which he'd grown impatient with clasps and cords while undressing a lover.

I thought of my real weapon, which sat between my ribs concealed by the power of a spell. Shaking off the desire to hold it again, I glanced up at Orrin. Like his cousin Charles, he seemed intense, almost humorless. I remembered him as a foppish child, proud of his status as Calgoranian royalty. He had always been on Charles's heels.

I was curious as to when this shift in his loyalties had occurred. When was it that he decided to abandon luxury in order to follow Anthony?

"Anthony took a beating when he first came to the

barracks," Orrin said, looking at him across the fire. "At first the boys his age hung back, thinking they would get in trouble with the king himself if they roughed him up. They soon learned better. Anthony told Cyril he wanted to be treated like every other fresh soldier—didn't know what he was getting himself into, but he meant it. Weston was the first to oblige him." He laughed, running a hand through his dark curls. "The first time Charles and I saw him bruised and bloodied up from fighting, we swore to him he would come slinking back to the palace soon. But he didn't."

My eyes gravitated toward Anthony as well, who was laughing with Weston while one of the younger boys sprawled on the ground, weary from Weston's strength training—which involved toting lead weights and sacks of grain across the field until you collapsed where you stood. I smiled at the irony that Weston had been Anthony's first enemy in the barracks and was now one of his closest friends.

"He made me feel like a coward, and I didn't like it," Orrin said. "But when someone believes in something that strongly, it catches on. I realized that rather than envy him, it was easier to simply admit I respected him."

I transferred my gaze from Anthony to Orrin. "What makes you all so sure that Tamarice is returning? Her elicrin stone was destroyed." Through all of Brack's doubt, I had clung to the hope that Tamarice would never be able to reclaim her power, even by way of the darkest of dark magic.

"But *she* wasn't," Orrin said. "Anthony was there the day she cursed the Princess of Volarre. He said he heard Tamarice promise to destroy Nissera. A vow like that is not easily set aside, even without the aid of an elicrin stone."

I fixed my gaze back on Anthony. It was hard to picture his young face at the name day, its expression of fear and awe as he looked at me instead of the princess. There had been so much chaos that I hadn't noticed anyone close enough to hear the twisted promise she had whispered for my ears alone. Through the haze of smoke, Anthony met my eyes. I averted them.

"Since the elicromancers have all vanished, no one even speaks of them anymore. But I believe the name day was not the last we'll see of them, for good or ill." Orrin crossed his arms, unintentionally making an exhibition of their well-formed muscles. "During the Elicrin War, the rebellious elicromancers summoned creatures of Galgeth to fight for them. What if Tamarice does the same? They say terrors we couldn't even dream of lie there."

"They do say that," I replied in a thin voice, remembering the image that the astrikane leaves showed me of the dark elicromancer with gray skin and white eyes.

"At least we have two elicromancers on our side. Though it'd be a little more encouraging if they showed their faces."

"Maybe they're working in ways we don't see or expect," I suggested.

"Perhaps so." After a moment, Orrin chuckled. "When we were children, Anthony used to talk about the Clandestine's attempt to save the princess the same way he would talk about the feats of the war heroes of olden days."

Sitting up a little straighter, I chanced another glance at Anthony. So much had overshadowed my efforts to save Rosie and the nobles. Tales had been told of me, to be sure, but all presumptions of victory against Tamarice had been brought into question by Volarre's missing princess. If the Clandestine had defeated Tamarice, I had heard some say, then why is there any need to hide the poor princess? Certain variations of the story even entertained the idea that Rosie's protector at her name day was not *one* person changing forms, but several bravely banding together to save their vulnerable monarch.

And with none of the elicromancers making any appearances of late, it was easy—and comfortable—for many to assume we had simply ceased to try.

So far this had worked in my favor. But upon hearing my title, my gift, mentioned in the same breath as the word "hero," a spark awoke within me.

These men associated my name with hope.

✳

Since Drell remained in Plum Valley with Rosie, I decided to stay for a second week of training. Anthony worked on swordplay with me for two hours each day, and in return requested that I show him my quarterstaff techniques. He both taught and learned patiently, picking up new maneuvers in seconds. He was purposeful with his instruction, often reminding us that we would one day be facing enemies much more sinister than thieves and outlaws.

Two blond brothers named Rook and Maddock, each an excellent tracker and huntsman, began teaching me the skills I *should* have known all along as someone who claimed to hunt every day to keep his family alive. I picked up on their techniques quickly enough to cover my own tracks of untruths before anyone could sense them.

Each day I grew more physically capable. I heard myself laugh more than I ever had, and foul words flowed freely. I didn't remember until after ten days with the Alliance that

I had promised Drell I would materialize home to check on them after a week. Brack would be returning to Plum Valley soon and I would need to speak with him.

I planned to tell to Anthony that I would be journeying home to make sure my family fared well, but I found myself riding out with the Realm Alliance when a mission arose.

King Thaddeus of Yorth had commissioned us to track down a group of men who had mercilessly murdered two Yorthan nobles and ransacked their estates, taking the daughter of one of the nobles captive. They were thought to be heading north to Calgoran. I suspected they weren't the sort of men who would be offered the choice between the Realm Alliance and execution.

When we caught up to the thieves two days later, we moved ahead of them and waited to ambush them in the mountain pass. Four of them we caught on the spot, and I managed to catch a fifth who had escaped. We escorted the outlaws and the freed girl south. The offenders had hidden their spoils so as to be able to flee more easily, and Orrin rode ahead of us to Yorth to inform King Thaddeus of the location at which they could be recovered.

When we stopped for the night, two men were to keep watch over our captives in shifts. Weston and I took our turn first. The rescued girl was tall and thin as a weed, with long blonde hair and delicate features. Before she settled down in the makeshift shelter, which Weston and Anthony had rigged for her out of blankets and branches, with the whole camp separating her from the men who had kidnapped her, she touched my arm so gently I could barely feel it.

"Thank you," she said. "That man you caught today was the one who killed my father."

"I'm sorry," I said bleakly. She reminded me of Rosie so much I had to fight the urge to embrace her. "He will be brought to justice."

"I wish we could offer you better after what you've been through." Anthony gestured at the shelter. "You'll be home soon enough."

"Yes, but it won't be home anymore." She laid a hand on his arm. "Thank you." She slunk away and soon disappeared into her shelter.

Her fragility incited a peculiar sadness in me, not entirely on her account. She was like a flower, lovely yet so easily trampled or destroyed by heat and cold. She needed a savior, and we had come to her aid.

I realized I could never be like her. I could never allow myself to be the one who needed saving, not as an elicromancer.

Weston and I sat in companionable silence for the next two hours, eyes on the six prisoners. "What will happen to them?" I asked him.

"Execution, or life imprisonment. In Calgoran, I know it would be the first. But I'm not sure what King Thaddeus will do."

Weston yawned and got up to relieve himself on a tree. I stared at the toes of my boots. Over the past few days, I had grown as comfortable as a woman could be living among men in a man's body. I preferred to give the men around me as much privacy as I could manage, and sought out my own privacy when I needed it.

Anthony settled down next to me and offered me a full wineskin. "Good work today, Tom. I have another reason to be thankful you're around."

I smiled at him and we fell into silence. He looked at the fire, eyes following the swell of smoke up to the stars.

"Tomorrow will be cold," I said, pointing at the heavens. "According to the Lioness." The constellation shone prominent in the northeast, which I recognized as a sign of a stark weather change.

"Is that true? Can you predict the weather that easily?"

I shrugged. "Wait until tomorrow and decide for yourself."

"We ought to keep this fire going then," he laughed, tossing another log into the flames. "What other mystic arts are you familiar with?"

I bit my lip, wishing I hadn't said anything. "I just read stars. It's simple enough."

Anthony's bright eyes sobered. "My father thinks magic can only be used for mischief and evil. What do you think?"

I took a swallow of wine. My thoughts went back to the snowy clearing, the Water still and dark under my fingers.

"Magic is given to the wise and unwise alike, just like titles and crowns. You could no more say it's only used for evil than you could say every king is corrupt. But I can see why your father thinks that way. He's busy minding his bloodline and borders. Something outside of his control is not only inconvenient but frightening."

Anthony nodded. He looked around at the captives and lowered his voice. "It's not just magic my father fears. He makes a habit of using spies to keep tabs on Volarre and Yorth. It's an abhorrent way to treat his allies. I detest subterfuge. I learned to be wary of it growing up in court, where everyone wears a mask . . . where everyone is manipulating someone."

I couldn't help but crumple a bit beneath his words. I

thought not only of my current elaborate camouflage but of my last sultry performance as Catleen. "Chicanery has noble purposes every now and then. What were you doing sneaking around Halfhand Square the night we met?" I chuckled and looked at him hopefully, but soon wished I could scoop the words back into my mouth as possibilities crossed my mind. What if he had been seeing a woman? It was far from appropriate to ask a prince what he did in secret.

Anthony stoked the fire intently, unperturbed. "I was investigating. A few weeks ago, when I came to counsel with my father, I saw him speaking with a man in minister's robes. Hardly anyone gains his trust without years of working for it, but I didn't recognize him."

"You're not exactly an active member of court," I pointed out.

"That's not all. He seemed . . . common. He brushed past my mother without even bowing his head. His manners are coarse and his hands and face like leather. That's not the type of man to whom my father usually gives the minister's mantle. There was something so unusual about him that I chose to trail him from the palace. He entered that little unmarked building in the alley, so I snuck in and searched the whole place. No one was there. I even checked for false walls and trap doors. The night you saved me, I came to search again while he wasn't there."

He tossed his stoking stick in the fire and brushed the bark off his hands. "I fear he might be up to something more nefarious than what my father asked of him. . . ."

Anthony trailed off, but the silence felt loaded with unspoken words. I could see in his cold stare into the fire that he feared his father might have asked something nefarious of the spy in the first place.

My thoughts were interrupted by the girl emerging from her tent, walking purposefully into a grove of pines. I wondered if she'd ever pissed in the dirt before now, or spent a night under the stars. I wondered if her father had always told her he would keep her safe, as I had always told Rosie, only to fail to keep his promise.

What was I doing, leaving Rosie for weeks at a time? There had been no sign of danger over the years, but I knew that didn't preclude it existing. If danger set upon them, though, Drell could protect her as well as anyone could—anyone except for me.

I took a deep breath. "Anthony, I thought I might visit home to see how my family's faring."

"Of course. Take some provisions and leave as soon as you like. You could wait until after we've gone to Yorth. I'm sure Thaddeus will arrange for an incomparable feast. Yorthan feasts are . . . well, I won't talk of it now, since it will only make us hungry. But you deserve your share of the recognition."

I chuckled. "I'm sure my share won't go to waste."

"Oh, before I forget . . ." He stretched to rummage through his pack, producing a leather pouch. "I sent a courier to Faywick with this, but he wasn't able to find your family." He handed me the pouch. It was heavy with coins. "Take it to them when you go."

I held it incredulously. "I can't—"

"Tom, I owe you my life. And even if I didn't, I would still make you take it."

I closed it in my hand. "Thank you."

In the firelight, his body filled up the space next to me. The strength of his jaw was softened slightly by full lips, and his dark brows and the dimple on his cheek hinted at his usual expressiveness, subdued now by tired contentment. As I studied his profile, his earth-colored eyes caught the light of the golden flames.

I enjoyed his company, and more than that, I was terribly grateful for it. While I was confined to a body not my own, there was a freedom that being a member of the Alliance afforded me. The more valuable I became here, the more that feeling grew.

The next morning, when no one was awake besides the third watch, I set out for home, with the strange sensation that I was leaving home behind.

NINE

*D*rell was nowhere to be seen when I returned, but Rosie was busy spreading bark in the garden in preparation for cold autumn ahead. When she saw me, she brushed the dirt off of her hands and ran down the path to meet me.

"Aunt Amelia!" She threw her arms around my neck. "Did you heal the family?"

"Yes, they're doing much better." I hoped she wouldn't ask for details in case my story failed to align with Drell's.

"That's wonderful!" She clapped her hands and shouldered one of my bags. "I was so worried about them. Where did you get the horse? I thought you took a coach?"

"They gave him to me as payment," I lied. "They lived too deep in the forest for coaches." I would have to pretend I planned to sell the black coarser, as it belonged to the Alliance.

"He's beautiful," she said, patting his neck. "I'll take him to a stall after we get you warm."

"Any goings-on here?"

Rosie pursed her full, pink lips and tossed her long hair. "Not really. My flowers sold well at the market. They've been especially lovely these past few weeks."

Rosie was the most beautiful girl in the surrounding towns, and certainly in a much wider territory than that. I knew her success at the market had little to do with the flowers, but she didn't seem to.

"I brought you a present," I said. "You'll adore it."

I had kept Anthony's gift in my pocket during the journey, the weight of it beating against my thigh as I considered what to do with it. I had traveled through Faywick in the morning, and found myself placing the pouch on the doorstep of a one-room cottage whose windows were covered only with tattered curtains nailed to the walls. Six filthy children slept on one straw palette.

I later discovered that one of the silver aurions had fallen into my pocket, so I decided I would buy a present for Rosie: several yards of rose-colored silk, so dark pink it was nearly red.

When I showed it to her, Rosie gasped and ran the fabric through her fingers. "It's so beautiful!" she exclaimed. "Can we start making a dress tonight?"

"We can start as soon as you like."

We gathered our sewing supplies and Rosie made tea that was, as always, quite weak by my standards. She held the silk against her, describing her designs for the dress. As I nodded along, admiring how well the color suited her, Rosie's face dropped.

"What's the matter?" I asked.

She sank into a chair. "It's just . . . you bought me this, and it's the most beautiful thing I've ever owned, but what occasion will I ever have to wear it?"

I hadn't thought of how the gift would serve as a reminder

that she lived a quiet, dull life in the country. I wanted to tell her she would have a chance to wear it. I wanted to tell her she was the princess and that she was betrothed, that the whole kingdom might see her in that dress one day. But in the same breath, I would have to tell her she was cursed.

"You never know what things come up," I managed.

"Never mind. It doesn't matter, because it's going to be so beautiful." She smiled and went back to planning with muted joy.

After dinner, Rosie walked upstairs with weighted steps. I knew something preoccupied her thoughts, because at night she usually liked to read downstairs by the fire.

I knocked gently on her door. "Come in," she answered. She lay curled up on her side on the bed. The beginnings of the silk dress rested on the chair in the corner of her room.

"Are you all right?"

Rosie sat up and stared at her fingers, twisting a loose thread of her quilt. "Have you ever been in love, Aunt Amelia?"

I cleared my throat, hesitant to answer as I sat beside her. What woman lives to have a head of gray hair and never falls in love? It's not as if Amelia conceivably had more important things to do. Rosie looked at my face, green eyes expectant.

"Well, no, not in the sense of the stories you read." I picked up the book on her nightstand. "There are different kinds of love. If you mean in the sense of admiring someone for his quality, then yes, I suppose."

"I mean the kind in the stories. Romance, marriage, children—didn't you ever want those things?"

I sighed, wishing I could simply tell her my life was too complicated for that. But Amelia's life was as uncomplicated as anyone's could be. A familiar melancholy that I kept at bay threatened to weigh on me again. "Not everyone is built for true love."

"What else are they built for?"

"Duty. Others are built for power, or for selfish gain. Some mean to love and can only manage passion. But you . . ." I wiped a tear from her cheek, "you were built for love of a pure and timeless sort, you beautiful, kind girl."

"But I've no one to give it to."

I wished I could tell her about Yorth, her future home with Prince Nicolas. I wished I could describe the palace at Beyrian, stretching across land that dropped into sand beaches reaching out into the infinite gray-blue sea, the wide arches of its courts open to the balmy ocean air. I wished I could tell her all about the Yorthan people, friendly folk with a fondness for fine cuisine. There, even peasants would pay their last thesars for a cockle in white wine sauce, and richly dressed merchants with dark skin and eyes frequently delivered shipments of fruits and spices from far-off islands. And most importantly, a prince waited to make her his wife.

"You know, Rosie, we don't have to live in Plum Valley forever. Maybe we can move to one of the bigger towns someday."

"I don't want to leave Plum Valley. . . . I just wish there were someone . . ." She looked out the window at the nearly full moon.

"No need to decide now," I said, patting her hand.

She smiled half-heartedly. What would she think of all these lies if she survived?

I kissed her forehead. "Goodnight, Rosie."

"Goodnight, Aunt Amelia."

I extinguished the lamps downstairs and went back up to my bedroom. Locking the door behind me, I shed my Amelia form, something I rarely did here, and dropped onto my bed.

The last image of Anthony resurfaced in my thoughts. I shook my head as if to make it disappear, but it had been lingering there unbidden for days. He was likely still in Yorth, receiving Thaddeus's thanks, drinking the best wine and eating the most excellent seafood the kingdom had to offer. I smiled at the thought of my ruffian friends feasting and collapsing on luxurious beds.

I suddenly felt too restless to sleep. Somehow I wasn't quite at peace without the rumbling breaths of heavy sleepers around me. But the silence allowed me the luxury of thought, and I remembered my idea to track down Elinor and guide her to Charles in hopes that he might choose her for his queen. I began making a tracker map in order to find her.

When I crept downstairs in disguise to start a fire for heating the map resin, I found Drell sitting in the kitchen. "Did your plan work?" she asked through a mouthful of pear.

I couldn't keep the grin off my face. "Better than I could have hoped."

I recounted the tales of the last few weeks and she listened eagerly as I described my new friends and our exploits. She told me her guise had faded a few days before and she had been waiting for my return to reemerge.

"You're becoming quite the strategist. I noticed you're making another tracker map." Her eyes sparkled with curiosity. "What for?"

"To find the Lost Duchess. I'm going to make Elinor the

queen of Calgoran. Charles could usher in a new phase of strong alliances within Nissera. If he marries a well-known royal figure of Volarre, we might no longer be a few missteps away from a war between kingdoms."

Drell looked at me with disbelief. "You better have a good plan."

"If she's half as pretty as her cousin, I won't need one."

"I'm beginning to think beauty a prerequisite of royalty. This Ermetarius, does he fit the mold?" The answer was plain on my face. Drell chuckled, jerking her head toward the stairs. "I hope you haven't been reading the same storybooks that one has." She bit the cork out of a wine jug and filled two wooden chalices. "She's made too much room in her head for them."

"She's a smart girl, just whimsical." I sat down and accepted a chalice. "She's speaking of marriage and children and romance. What am I to say?" I leaned my chin on my hands, delighting in the soreness of my muscles and the itch of healing cuts. I studied my friend's face. "Why haven't you married?"

Drell took a swig and smiled passively. "I haven't found a man who knows his mouth from his ass and a bow from a blade."

"I may know a few."

"Tell me if you need a stand-in at the barracks." She grinned. "But truly, who has time for such things these days? Even you don't, and you'll be young forever."

Such thoughts had been weighing on me for years, but since joining the Alliance they had grown heavier still. I recited the same names every day, the names of those I would have to see grow old and slip from my grasp. *Drell, Rosie, Kimber, Cyril,* I thought as I watched Drell's lightly freckled cheeks turn red from the wine. *Anthony, Weston, Orrin, Rook, Maddock...* The list went on, and as it did, I realized what joining the Alliance meant: I had given myself more people to mourn.

I heard myself ask Drell the question I had wanted to ask since I met her all those years ago. "Have you ever thought of trying to claim an elicrin stone?"

Drell fixed her gaze on me, flecks of light and sadness swimming in the blue of her eyes. "I never wanted to, Bristal. The heart grows old even if the body doesn't."

I realized with a pang that Drell had never envied me. Back at Darmeska, I thought she was so involved in my training because she wished herself an elicromancer. But she had truly been there for me because I needed her help.

Drell squeezed my shoulder. "When war comes, I'll fight with you, bleed for you, die for you if I must. You will survive these days to see better ones, and then you can live the life you want to live." She put a hand on the side of my face, her warm expression filling me with hope. "Let's find Elinor."

Drell and I were leaning over the fire when the door opened and startled us out of our wits. I dropped the pot of resin I had just pulled out of the flames.

"Brack!" I launched myself into his arms.

"Happy to see you, Amelia." He patted my back, emphasizing the fake name in case Rosie heard him enter.

Brack's Uncle Warrick disguise was a blend of everything that made someone forgettable. His features were neither pleasing nor ugly. He was neither short nor tall and carried a little extra weight in his face and belly. Usually, he came bearing an eccentric gift for Rosie from his fabricated travels, but tonight he was empty-handed.

Ushering him onto the sofa next to the hearth, I cast a concealing spell that swathed us like a blanket.

"Did you find her?" Drell asked, taking a seat next to him.

"She's in Galgeth. Not only has she been recovering—she has been gathering servants."

"Servants?" My voice rose an octave.

Drell's expressive face froze. "You mean . . . an army?"

Brack drew in a deep breath. He had never looked peaceful, not for a single moment in the years I'd known him. "That's what I'm afraid of."

The news sank into my belly like a sack of rocks. I realized that I had leaned into the hope that ruining Tamarice's elicrin stone had ruined *her*, made her mortal and powerless. Yes, I had worked to keep the kingdoms united, but that noble cause stood on its own two legs. But Brack had known that Tamarice wouldn't give up. He had sagged under the weight of that knowledge. "How do you know?" I asked quietly.

"A hooded traveler came to a small village in western Calgoran. He lodged at the inn for a night. Before morning, every other guest and the innkeeper had caught . . ." He closed his eyes. "An unsightly disease. Word spread, and I tracked down the creature. It was an elicromancer who had used black magic to the point of ruin."

"A blight," I breathed. "I saw a vision of one when Tamarice made me eat astrikane. So they're not just legends?"

"No. Many of the rebel survivors of the Elicrin War fled to Galgeth to escape punishment. They used magic to try to devise ways to overpower the victors, but the body can only support so many dark rituals before it begins to waste away.

They won't be a threat to the realm if they remain in Galgeth, but it seems Tamarice has stirred up evil at rest there. Just before I killed the blight, I asked it why it had come—and it traced a circle on its chest."

"The shape of the scar from the ritual," I whispered. "So there's no doubt that they serve her."

I noticed fear burning deep in his pale eyes. This did little to comfort me. "I tried to heal those afflicted with the disease, but nothing I did improved it. That is the kind of tenacious darkness that can only come from Galgeth."

"What about Tamarice herself?" I asked. "Has she returned?"

"She's still recovering from losing her power after your attack—no doubt relying on dark rituals to retrieve it. Her spirit is growing more twisted. It's beginning to decay."

"So one day she may be a blight herself, inside and out?" asked Drell, who had gone pale. "Did you see her?"

"Yes. I discovered the hard way that she's laid out traps for Bristal and me—snares to catch us on our materializing paths. When we materialize, we enter an in-between place. There, her spirit can reach out to us."

"But it's not truly her, is it?" I asked.

"Yes and no." Brack closed his eyes. I heard a low grunt in his throat, as though he were suppressing the pressure of tears rising. "It's not physically her, but her spirit state reflects how she has deformed her inmost being with black elicromancy. She has changed in a way that only the strangest, darkest magic can change a creature. That's what I saw. Materialize as seldom as possible."

My hands shook fiercely enough that I had to clamp them together to keep my whole body from doing the same.

"I have to go to Galgeth," Brack said. "It will not be an easy journey, but I must do what I can to stop her. If she's building an army, I need to intervene now."

"I'll go with you."

"That's noble, Bristal, but you are needed here. I only wish I had had more time to train you."

"If we are both fighting Tamarice in Galgeth, Rosie won't need any more protection than Drell can offer. We can take her to Darmeska where Kimber can help watch over her."

"It's much bigger than protecting the princess now. I care for her as much as you do, but more than a thousand Volarian nobles and a princess's life are at stake. You must stay so that you can find a way to merge the armies of Nissera into a unified force. Time passes differently in Galgeth; it moves far more slowly. If you and I were both to go, we might come back to a realm so weak and torn by petty wars that it could offer no resistance."

A few moments of silence passed. I realized I could no longer entertain the belief that the realm was its own worst enemy, or that Tamarice was nothing but a weak mortal because I had broken the source of her power.

"I will try to uncover what is known about Galgeth in the libraries at Darmeska," Brack went on. "It's not an easy thing, traveling through a world that is partly spiritual, even for an elicromancer who has lived for a few hundred years. The more I think about going, the more my heart warns me against the journey." He reached out for both of our hands. "Take care of one another. There are things in the world that evil does not understand and cannot overpower, selfless love being one of them."

I squeezed his hand hard. Not a day would pass that I wouldn't worry about Brack journeying to such a place. When he stood up to leave, I nearly didn't let him go. "When do you think you will return?"

While his eyes told me he didn't know whether he would, he said, "Hopefully within a few months."

"I'll take that as a promise," I said.

He squeezed my hand. "Bristal, you must work ever harder. The word of elicromancers is held in low regard these days, as you know. You will have to be more cunning than ever. Do whatever you think will make Riskan and Errod act like allies again."

He stepped back into the night. "Be careful," he added, drawing up his hood. "We never know what sorts of dark servants do her bidding."

The new tracker map showed me that Elinor lived in May Acre, a town in the farmlands of eastern Calgoran, not far from Arna. I knew that making her queen of Calgoran would do good for the realm, but I hadn't formulated a plan beyond finding her and making sure she attended the ball thrown in Charles's honor. The king hadn't yet set a date, so for the moment I decided to focus on building up Anthony's influence.

Returning to the barracks was a painful decision after Brack's news, but I knew it was the right one. Drell would take care of Rosie. I couldn't lock us both up and hide in safety while the world around me threatened to tear at the seams.

The men welcomed me back warmly, and I had the

opportunity to release some of my tension and worries while wielding a weapon. Afterward, we sat down to an appreciable amount of food and ale. Those who had gone to Yorth recounted the adventure, describing the feast in such detail that my mouth watered even though I had just eaten enough for two men. Anthony was pleased with the journey for different reasons; he felt Thaddeus's commission was a gesture intended to improve Yorth and Calgoran's friendship.

"Statecraft of that sort is respectable in a time like this," he said, his voice muffled as he shaved his face with a knife. "Errod and my father would rather melt their crowns into codpieces than call on each other like that."

He was quite right. The latest theatrics between Calgoran and Volarre were the result of rumored military alliance between King Errod and the king of Perispos, a country with a large army that lay to the east, across the Mizrah Sea. It wasn't true, from what I could gather, but the scandalous rumors had already caused damage, and that damage had placed Thaddeus, peace-lover that he was, in the difficult position of proving he was as much a friend to Calgoran as to Volarre.

Because our mission had been so successful, Thaddeus planned to send his son and Rosie's betrothed, Prince Nicolas, to Calgoran for an extended visit with Charles and Anthony.

As Anthony recounted this news to me, I heard in his voice and saw in his eyes a resilient hope, the same hope that had brought him out to the barracks to sleep on a hard bed and allow other boys to beat and mock him before he was finally accepted: the hope that he was capable of doing something good for Nissera.

Being around him strengthened that hope in me as well. His vision for the Realm Alliance was to recruit soldiers from all three kingdoms and become a unified guard for all of Nissera—one that defended the innocent and helped solve disputes. My vision for it, which had newly developed, was to make it into a full-size force, a united army of Nissera.

While Rook, Maddock and I fletched arrows one day, I wondered how best to persuade Nicolas to contribute some of Yorth's finest warriors to the Alliance. Since Yorth wasn't nearly as troubled as the other kingdoms, I hadn't visited often and hadn't seen Nicolas since he was a boy.

As I was wondering which approach would work best— sweetness and seduction or authoritative advice from someone he trusted—Cyril and Charles approached the barracks. I hurried to finish my last arrow, recognizing an opportunity to learn more about Charles. I thought of Elinor's tracker map, rolled up and tucked away in my wardrobe with that little ashy mark poised over May Acre.

The brothers greeted one another with a grin and a sturdy embrace. Charles grabbed Anthony by the scruff of his neck. "Little brother," he said, his voice a resounding bass. "It's been too long. You've been busy, haven't you? What will you do with yourself when you've vanquished all wrongdoing in the realm? I happen to know of a few court ladies who would like their mischievous husbands spied on."

Having only ever seen Charles stern-faced and removed, I didn't realize this was a joke until Anthony laughed and slapped his brother on the back. "Only if business gets too slow."

Orrin and Charles embraced. The three of them were

quite a sight, standing shoulder-to-shoulder, so similar that if the sun were any more blinding they would be impossible to tell apart.

"You have some new blood," Charles said, noticing me.

Anthony motioned for me to join them. When he introduced me, I bowed my head and accepted the elder prince's extended arm.

"Well met," he said. "Anthony, I'm here because I know you'll refuse to come to court unless I ask you myself."

"Go on."

"Nicolas Veloxen is on his way to Arna, and Father would be pleased if you made a few appearances when he arrives. Thaddeus specifically mentioned hoping Nicolas would have a chance to see your company in action."

Anthony smiled. "I suppose I could parade around the palace a bit for that opportunity."

"Good. Also, Father has set a date for the ball in my honor."

"And so the hunt for a worthy bride begins. When is it?"

"The night of the winter solstice." Charles gave him a long look. "You will be there?"

"In honor of my brother and future queen, yes, I'll come."

Charles looked satisfied. "It's a convenient opportunity for you as well. How often do you have the chance to meet every eligible noblewoman in all of Calgoran?"

"Not often."

"So you will come?"

"I'll come."

Cyril had an announcement, too. For the first time, the king had invited the Realm Alliance to participate in the annual Stag Tournament, a competition for the soldiers in the king's army.

The victor of each event was awarded three year's wages on the spot, but most fought for the honor.

"The king is making the most of your growing renown," Cyril said while Anthony read over the list of events.

"Yes, I suppose he's attempting to coax me into more agreeable pursuits than making ready for a war he believes imaginary. I'll see if my men are interested. It could be a good chance to gain respect for the Alliance and grow our numbers."

Cyril recorded the names of the members who would participate in each event. Our men would compete across the board in archery, sword combat, mounted combat and hand-to-hand combat. I volunteered for staff combat and earned a firm nod of approval from Anthony.

With two weeks to prepare for the tournament, I focused on Elinor and the ball. It would be the perfect opportunity to draw her and Charles together. But that only led my thoughts back to Anthony being in the presence of every eligible beauty in Calgoran, and I fell into bad spirits.

I would go that night, if only to observe Elinor—to determine if she was everything I hoped she would be. More than ever, Nissera needed Charles's original betrothed to sit on Calgoran's throne. The news Brack had brought burned within me, making me eager to set these events in motion.

It was easy to slip away from the barracks without raising questions. Men left on occasion to see their families, to make love to women, to incur or settle debts. I stomped out the fire after everyone went inside, but hesitated when I saw Anthony emerging from the barracks again.

"I couldn't sleep," he said as he approached me. "That spy that I followed was the one who fed my father the rumors about Volarre's alliance with Perispos. He disappeared soon after. I got to thinking: what could be his reasons for inventing and spreading such a rumor? He must have some higher agenda—one that benefits from causing chaos."

The weight of this thought settled like a boulder in my chest. Brack's last warning about Tamarice having servants in Nissera came to mind. "Do you know his name?" I asked feebly, thinking maybe I could track him down.

"I doubt my father even knows his real name. A person like that may use a dozen different aliases. He looked the type to sell his soul to the highest bidder. My concern is: what if the highest bidder isn't a king?"

"You mean Tamarice?"

"Yes. My father won't be convinced that Calgoran is in danger of her. I need the counsel of the elicromancers. But he refused to listen to them and now they're gone. I can't blame them—it's like trying to reason with a raging bull."

His frustration could almost be felt, roiling off of him like heat waves from a fire. I wanted to tell him that I knew how it felt to see hardheadedness loosen all the political ties that I had meticulously laced.

"Sometimes I feel directionless when it comes to the Alliance," he worried aloud. "I don't know how to grow our numbers or get more clout. If Tamarice came tomorrow, we wouldn't even trip her up, much less have any hope of defeating her."

I studied his face, from the gleam of his freshly shaved jaw line to the fine night mist catching in his furrowed dark brows and hair. Elinor would have to wait.

"Come on," I said, tossing on my cloak. "Let's get a drink."

TEN

The morning was cool and bright as I materialized back at the cottage. A light mist cleared in the sunlight and songbirds heralded the morning. The cottage door opened and closed. Rosie followed the path to the river in her yellow cloak, humming as she walked.

All seemed well. I peeked my head inside the open kitchen window, still in Tomlin's form. Drell nearly attacked me with a rolling pin before she recognized the guise she helped me create.

"Is everything all right?" she asked, tying her apron around Amelia's plump middle.

"I'm just checking in."

"Brack said you need to avoid materializing. You shouldn't be coming back to check on us so often."

I shrugged helplessly.

"The news didn't sit well with me, either," she said. "I don't like Brack going to Galgeth alone. Tales of that place and the spirits that lurk there used to scare me out of my wits as a child. And the fact that time moves slower there . . . it's the most unnatural thing."

The thought of the fire-headed girl with

her sweltering ego being frightened of Galgeth was almost more unsettling than anything else I had heard about it.

"I'm just going to watch Rosie for a bit," I said. "It will put me at ease."

Drell nodded. "I'll keep an eye out in case I need to hide."

I changed into a fox and loped after Rosie. Despite the crisp beginning-of-autumn air, the earth was warm with sunlight and still overrun with flowers. Padding through the grass, I followed her as she cut through the woods to the river.

Leaves rustled as I slithered through the undergrowth. Rosie's head snapped up.

"Oh!" She smiled. "You frightened me."

She attempted to beckon me out of hiding, but I was stubborn and she soon gave up. She threw off her cloak and pranced along the slick stepping-stones, singing a song I had taught her. It was written about the lovers Cassian and Callista by a bard who told tales of the Elicrin War. Something about the song made my heart ache so.

Rosie's voice softened. She cocked an ear and looked around. I heard it, too: a rider moving urgently through the wood, a rare sound this deep in the valley.

She grabbed her cloak and scurried back toward home. She never seemed to listen when I warned her against speaking to strangers, but at least had the wisdom not to be caught alone in the woods with one.

I followed at her heels, but we didn't make it far before the rider emerged from the trees on the far side of the river and called out to her. While the good sense that sent her running in the first place should have seen her safely back to the cottage, the curse of curiosity made her stop and turn around. If I, as

Daffodil Dimplesworth, had known what I knew now, I would have gladly given Rosie the gift of disinterest.

The rider turned out to be a young man not long clear of boyhood. He was tall and thin, sitting straight on his golden horse, wearing a green cape fastened by a gold clasp at his collar. His hair was sandy brown, his face so cleanly shaven I guessed he hadn't yet had reason to take a blade to it.

He was clearly well bred. This became even clearer when he opened his mouth. "Forgive me, my lady. I did not intend to startle you."

Rosie bit her lip. She shifted her weight, torn between leaving and lingering, all the while eyes wide and swimming with admiration. She had never seen a gentleman of this sort, only village boys who liked to put insects in her hair when she was a child and who felt unworthy to speak to her ever since she had come of age.

I suspected Rosie was hearing echoes of my warnings to be cautious. She may not have known the reasoning behind them, but the gravity of my admonitions had been unmistakable. She turned to leave.

"Wait! Please!" the young man said, his voice somehow both cordial and desperate. He dismounted and approached the riverbank. "I heard you singing. It was so beautiful—"

"Who are you?" she demanded.

He laughed sheepishly, taking off his hat. "Just a fellow lost in the woods. Who are you?"

"Well, I'm not lost, so I suppose I'm just a girl in the woods."

I shook my head. If I hadn't been paralyzed by worry, I might have snorted.

The young man looked hopeful. Rosie took a step closer. "I could help you find the town," she said. "If you would like."

"You would do me a great service."

Rosie stepped onto the rocks and he hastened to assist her. The water rushed into his boots, but he extended his hand as if he were merely helping her from a coach. She accepted it and leaned her weight on him as she crossed the stones on which she had been dancing carelessly only minutes before.

"I'm journeying north and was supposed to have passed through a town by now," he said, releasing her hand when they were both safely on the other side. "I've never traveled these parts before."

"These woods can be a maze if you don't know them well." Rosie's cheeks flushed. She smiled coyly at her hands.

"How kind of you to help me solve it. Shall we?" He gestured at his horse. Rosie stroked its face and black mane. The young man lifted her up with ease before swinging himself expertly behind her. They reminded me of King Errod and Queen Lucetta, both so lovely and regal, that I almost couldn't bring myself to stop them, despite my trained reflex to shield Rosie from any outsider.

But I remembered Rosie's betrothal to Nicolas Veloxen, which prompted me to take on my Amelia guise and scramble from the bushes. "No, you don't!"

"Aunt Amelia!" Rosie's reaction was no more than a squeal. "I'm just showing this young man to the town."

"Dismount right this moment, young lady. What have I told you about speaking to strangers, much less climbing on the horse of a man you've only just met?"

The young man swung his horse around. "Perhaps I can escort you both home and you can point me toward town."

I crossed my arms for a moment, letting them both sweat,

but finally nodded curtly. Stranger or no, it wasn't like me to let a person wander through the woods without direction.

"What's your name?" I asked as the young man dismounted to help me up behind Rosie, who stiffened indignantly at my presence.

"Forgive me. My name is Bay Sandborn. And you are?"

"Rosie."

"Tomlin," I said. Rosie snapped her head around just as I realized my mistake. I cleared my throat. "Tomlin, you said your name was?"

"Bay Sandborn," Rosie corrected in a tone the townspeople often took with the blacksmith's dull daughter.

It was a long ride back to the cottage with Bay's horse carrying three on its back. The dangerous what-ifs reeled through my mind in the tense silence. What if Rosie were to elope, or worse, return to the royal city with child? The king and queen would never forgive me. And with everything I knew about Tamarice's intentions, there was no way to gauge whether this person could be trusted—even though I felt in my heart that no one in Tamarice's service could look so thoroughly virginal.

Once we reached the cottage, Rosie slid down into Bay's arms, gawking at him as though her deepest fantasy had been brought to life. Feeling like a dreadful person for what I was about to say to her, I went inside to give them a moment of privacy. Drell went to hide in the cellar.

My mood turned sour as I watched the young man walk Rosie to the edge of the garden and give her a chaste, lingering kiss.

When she came in, she pressed the door closed and sighed. She looked as if she might faint of happiness until she noticed me sitting in the kitchen with a dark and troubled expression.

"Rosie, you mustn't see that young man again."

"I don't understand," she said. "Why mustn't I?"

I massaged my forehead. In the long moment that had passed while I waited, I hadn't thought of any good reason to offer her, except the painfully obvious one. "A young man who becomes fond of a young woman so quickly is only after what she should not be offering."

A fierce emotion crossed her face. "What do you know about it?"

"More than you." My voice sounded pitiless to my ears. "I can't explain everything right now, but you'll understand someday."

Rosie shook her head. "No, I'll never understand. I'll never understand why you don't want me to ever fall in love just because you can't imagine what it's like. It may mean nothing to you, but it means everything to me, and this is my one chance."

Again, I longed to tell her the truth. My tone softened. "Rosie, there will be more chances. In fact, your mother and father had someone in mind for you when you were born. The son of a friend back in the town where you used to live—"

"I never knew my mother and father. You are my mother, and you are making me miserable."

The strength of her conviction took me aback. I never expected she would feel this strongly about the young man after only a few minutes, but I hadn't accounted for her capriciousness. She had waited for this too long to take it lightly.

She calmed down, wiping the tears from her eyes. "I know you have a lover."

"Pardon?"

"You leave for weeks at a time, saying you're going to heal sick people. But you returned from healing the family with wind fever saying their house was deep in the woods, when before you said their house was in the mountains—where people actually catch wind fever. You were so involved that you forgot to get your story straight. You've denied ever loving someone but I know you do! Why is it so wrong to simply admit it?"

This conversation had taken a strange, albeit amusing turn.

"Rosie, my dear, sweet girl, I do not have a lover. I have responsibilities. I'm needed elsewhere, and that's the truth."

She looked doubtful, but she allowed me to take her hand. Her eyes averted to the floor. My next words emerged in a voice that didn't sound like Amelia. It sounded like Bristal, leaking through my disguise as I felt I had done so much lately.

"You may think you see one thing in the dark, but in the light it's something entirely different. You're young and in the dark right now, but not for much longer. Please, please trust me and do as I say."

She lifted her eyes. They were the polished green of ripe summer apples, and full of sorrow. But what could I do? Allow her to delve into this love affair with everything I knew and didn't know about her future?

Silence stretched on until she tore her hand from my grasp and ran upstairs.

Drell emerged from the cellar. "That sounded awful."

"I'm sorry to leave you to handle this. Prince Nicolas is coming to Arna, and Anthony plans to ask him to contribute men to the Alliance. I have to get back."

"Your idea, I'm guessing?" My friend smiled wryly. "Don't apologize for doing your duty."

"Thank you, Drell, truly. I'll see you in a few days."

I braced myself to materialize and said the command, expecting to land in a spot of woods near the barracks.

But in the midst of my journey, a fierce pain bolted through my arm and I was wrenched sideways. With a howl, I hit the ground and opened my eyes to find my forearm staked into the dirt by a thorn as thick as a knife. I looked around and saw that I was in a dense, dark wood, tangled up in briars and wearing no guise at all.

A wave of fog flooded over me. The wind picked up, cool and full of whispers. Lightning threaded through the dappled sky. A thin, shadowy shape slid through the trees, but only in the corners of my vision.

I bit my teeth together and got a grip on the base of the thorn to try to pull it out. But I nearly fainted. In my swimming vision I saw blood bubbling up from the wound. I knew an attempt to materialize away without removing the stake would do much more damage than ripping it out, but I couldn't seem to gather the courage to yank it from my flesh.

The shadow scuttled by on my right, and then my left, but I could only see enough to recognize it as human—or at least humanlike.

The figure stopped and stood still at a distance. Her long dark hair fluttered in the wind like a ratty curtain. Her skin was grayish and pale, her muscles sucked against her bones like lean, dark meat. The lovely eyes that had once been the golden russet of autumn leaves were white as milk with tiny black pupils.

I drew in a shaky breath, too panicked to even scream. Tamarice must have learned after Brack materialized out of her trap that she would need to tether me to this waking nightmare. The thorn piercing my arm was meant to keep me from escaping before she could reach me.

She flickered like a candle flame and was suddenly right next to me, leaning over me. Her breath blew hot and damp into my nostrils. When she spoke, many voices echoed in various octaves, reciting a familiar invitation. "Come with me, Bristal, and I will never hurt you again."

Her thin fingers reached out to touch my face. But it was as if she were wading in water, so weighed down that she couldn't quite command her limbs to do as she wished.

"We will create a bright kingdom of power and light. There will be many elicromancers as in the old days, and we will rule with love."

"No," I growled—and ripped the thorn out of my flesh.

Through my screaming, I managed to give the materialization command. I thudded hard on the ground once more.

When I opened my eyes, I lay in a peaceful wood in the sunshine. Since I was neither at the cottage nor the barracks, I figured my journey had been halted halfway through.

Blood surged out of my arm. I knew I needed to get up so that I could tend to my wound and make sure Rosie was okay, but peaceful rest drew me down into its warm clutches.

✳

An unfamiliar voice came out of the darkness. Arms reached for me and I blinked my eyes open, gripped against a solid chest.

"Rosie," I mumbled. "I have to—"

"She's safe," said the voice.

"Brack?"

I received no answer. I knew Brack's voice well, in all its forms, and this wasn't his. This voice was husky and low, with a young, playful lilt. But I had hoped.

Before long, the arms released and steadied me on the doorstep of the Lonely Lord Inn, which I recalled sat in a small town north of Plum Valley. A glimpse at my left forearm showed more blood than the rain could wash away.

"Don't forget a guise," said the voice.

The hand on the small of my back disappeared before I could get a look at its owner.

I half-heartedly mustered a male disguise and entered. I barely registered the gasps that greeted me in the tavern as I made my way to the innkeeper, a fat man leaning on the counter with ale foam in his moustache. "What happened to you?" he grunted.

Covered in blood and sucking in labored breaths, I propped my weight on a chair and muttered, "Thieves."

The man raised a bushy brow. Of course, he wouldn't serve someone with empty pockets. I started to feel lightheaded, and was in no condition to haggle. After sluggishly digging around in my bag, I produced two silver aurions, which probably made him wonder what sort of lousy thieves nearly cut a man to pieces yet fail to lay a finger on his purse. But coin was coin. With a series of suspicious glances, he showed me to a room upstairs and told his daughters to gather supplies to treat my wound.

After they tended to me, I lay on top of the covers, body stiff and sore, bandages soaked taut with dry blood. I stood up to leave with a wince and a groan.

The voice returned: smooth, low and unfamiliar. "Rest awhile."

I spun around to look for my mysterious helper, but the room was empty. After a second's delay, my brain seemed to slam into my skull, the price for so abrupt a movement. The voice had been everywhere and nowhere.

"Brack—or whoever you are—how am I supposed to do my duty if I can't materialize?"

The voice didn't answer. My stomach rumbled loudly, and I scratched at a patch of crusted blood on my face. Perhaps he was gone.

I ate the meat pie the daughters left for me and took a deep swig of water. Never at ease undressing in a man's body, I dropped my guise and started painfully untying my tunic to bathe.

"The traps are laid at random. If she knew your destinations, much worse things would have already happened. But it's still best if we travel by other means as often as possible."

I knew by the speaker's matter-of-fact inflection that he had to be Brack. Perhaps he had managed to adopt another guise in light of the increased need for secrecy. I began retying my tunic. "Can you heal me? I'll be fighting in a very important tournament soon."

"I wish I could heal you. It was unbearable to feel you in pain and be powerless to help."

"What do you mean?" I knotted the laces and turned to face the window, where I had seen a flicker in the corner of my eye. "You did help me."

"Did I?" he asked, as I gasped.

The form that Brack had taken on was not fully corporeal. The indistinct shape of a body was hidden by what seemed to be floating partition, shifting and shimmering, making his appearance about as discernible as a smudge.

"What—?" I began, but then my vision turned inward, and I was led back through the journey of reaching the inn as though reliving it. But this time, I was the one who picked myself up, who materialized at the inn and staggered to the door.

"You weren't there at all?"

"Not in body. I bent your perspective. You were delirious and wouldn't budge."

I shuffled back to grip the table for support, upending the water basin and feeling the scald of hot droplets through my clothes. For the first time, I comprehended how easily he could enter a mind and rewrite its very thoughts. My voice wavered. "Didn't you promise you would never intrude on my thoughts?"

"My mind forges connections to people who are dear to me—it's one aspect of being a Sentient that is still beyond my control. I sensed that you were in trouble, and I acted. I manipulated you and saw through your eyes, but I didn't read your thoughts. I couldn't leave you there, nearly bleeding to death."

I walked forward, studying the blurred outlines of his body. "Your voice sounds different because we're speaking with thought. You must be in your true form right now."

"Yes. My mind isn't vulnerable to disguises, but I can hide from you what I do not wish you to see." Though the young voice held a naturally playful inflection, I recognized Brack's clipped tone attempting to steer that matter to an end. I squinted at the changing wall of air, discerning nothing beyond it.

I sighed. I wished Brack were truly there, wished for his gentle healing spell erasing the evidence of pain and darkness.

"Crushed hawthorn berries speed the healing of wounds caused by dark magic."

"Where are you?" I asked. "Have you left for Galgeth yet?"

"I've been in the libraries at Darmeska, preparing for my journey to Galgeth. I leave tonight."

A low wind moaned at the window. I thought of a dark land full of unimaginable terrors and hoped Brack was strong enough to return from such a place.

"Tamarice asked the same thing of me that she asked at the name day, in the exact same words," I muttered quietly.

"Perhaps her spirit is muddled. When I saw her, in spite of trying to kill me, she was . . . she was confessing that she loved me in the same words as before."

I grimaced, imagining the gruesome mockery of a heart-rending moment.

To my surprise, I was able to reach directly through the blur surrounding Brack and touch the solid form behind it. I found his arm and felt the soft skin of a young man, and under-neath, cords of muscle. I wanted to break through the mystery that swathed him, that always would in so many ways. But feeling his large, warm hand covering mine was enough.

"I have to go," he whispered. "Farewell, dear friend. I'm so grateful for the day the Water washed you ashore."

ELEVEN

"Something troubling you?"

I ran my fingers through my short Tomlin hair, snarling it into curls. Orrin looked up from sharpening Splendor.

"I'm fine," I said.

"You're not fighting like it. I've never seen you hand over three matches in a row. And don't go blaming that wound on your arm. You're not even left-handed."

Wiping the grimy sweat from the back of my neck, I gave up and sat next to him, soothed by the repetitive sounds of metal against stone. My wounded arm was sore but, thankfully, I would still be able to fight in the Stag Tournament. The application of the hawthorn berries mixed with one of my homemade salves allowed the puncture to heal quickly. I had told everyone who asked about it that a man who owed my father a debt had pinned me to a table when I went to collect from him. But in case they got any ideas about justice, I assured them he had eventually paid up during the course of our meeting.

"You're a good fighter, Tom. I've seen you take down men twice your size. You shouldn't worry about the crowds." Orrin's dark blue eyes darted away from his work to focus on me.

Wishing the tournament were the reason for my uneasiness, I propped my staff on my knees and gripped it tightly. Orrin raised his immaculate blade with lethal precision and pointed it at my nose. "Practice will soothe your nerves."

I stood no chance of winning against Orrin, but I could at least forget the burden of my thoughts as we sparred.

After losing to Orrin, I fought Maddock and won, but he bested me in archery immediately afterward. I had never known one could sweat so liberally when the air was cold enough to redden skin, but we were all dripping with it. I took a break to watch Anthony and Weston swordfight, listening to the music of their parrying and grunting. Abandoning my brooding for a time, I sat mesmerized by their violent dance, struggling to drag my eyes away from the bulk of Anthony's arms and shoulders. I focused instead on the footwork, but found my gaze drifting upward again. I had told Rosie that some people were built for mere passion while others, like her, were built for lasting love. I decided I was built for neither, and chose not to contemplate it further.

The dark mood that had followed me from Plum Valley hovered. For the next few days, which were rainy, cold and miserable, I struggled to come up with any shining revelations that would help the realm's cause. Anthony would ask Nicolas to contribute soldiers to the Alliance as we had discussed, and I would contact Elinor—but I knew there was more to be done.

But a distraction came my way late that evening. The members of the Alliance would be attending court to welcome Prince Nicolas. This meant I would have a chance to see if he was worthy of making Rosie forget about the boy she met in the woods and be happy in Yorth. Who wouldn't be happy in Yorth? And if Nicolas were anything like his father, he was a man of good spirits and good manners. In any case, as Queen of Yorth, Rosie would live around kind people and eat well—if we all survived to see her married.

Weston snorted when Cyril brought us our formal livery, but we accepted it and donned the mail and black tunics like dogs putting on boots. While I hoped we wouldn't have to fight in such heavy wear at the tournament, I admired the white crest with its dark silhouette of a stag. Many men had died wearing this symbol; many white crests had been washed with red. I found that I felt proud to bear it across my chest.

We rode to the castle in a pale drizzle. Anthony took the lead as we walked in pairs up the endless marble stairs and took our place in the great hall amid the crowds awaiting the prince of Yorth.

Not long after we settled in at the banquet tables, the herald announced Nicolas's arrival. I agitated my fingers. I hadn't seen Rosie's betrothed since he was a boy.

The tall, thin young man strode into the great hall, wearing a green cape clasped with gold over a tunic bearing the emblem of the gold sea serpent. His light brown hair was the color of Yorth's beaches, his face that of a kind and well-bred gentleman—a face I had seen only days ago in Plum Valley.

My jaw dropped. I then laughed aloud and Maddock and Rook, sitting on either side of me, each gave me a sidelong glance.

Bay Sandborn. What a snarky little name Nicolas had assumed for Rosie, as if he wished to give himself away even while keeping his secret. How in the world had they stumbled across one another? I couldn't have arranged it any better myself—a thought that put me ill at ease.

But Tamarice would have had to know where Rosie lived to send Nicolas there. If she had known, Rosie and Drell and even I would be dead or in her clutches by now.

Perhaps it was truly coincidence, or fate—like the fate that had brought me to the Water. I wanted to trust that fate, to be happy that Rosie was happy. I didn't have space in my heart for any more worries, not with Brack in Galgeth and the mantel of political responsibilities resting on my shoulders. So I chose to trust fate for now—and interrogate Nicolas later.

With at least one small weight lifted, I was able to enjoy the evening of feasting with my friends. Anthony sat at the head table with his family. He and Orrin looked regal in red and black, a far cry from their usual garb of worn brown breeches, dull tunics and leather armor. It was strange to witness Anthony playing this role, to see his father put a hand on his shoulder and smile as though they were not estranged.

I recognized the highborn daughters of my acquaintances in court, daughters who were expected to capture Charles's attention at the ball. But for the first time, I noticed many of them coyly watching Anthony as well.

"I've never seen anyone frown like that while eating braised lamb shank at the king's table," Rook said, breaking through my cloud of thoughts. I tore my eyes away from the royal table and shrugged.

We drank wine from Yorth, a gift from Nicolas. It was heavenly. With every sip my blood warmed and my troubles eased.

That night we returned full, drunk and content to our beds

in the barracks. I looked away as each man noisily stripped off his mail. Anthony stood at the hearth for some time, bare back turned to me. He was the last to collapse on his bunk at the far side of the room.

I wondered if he ever fully rested—if he, like me, could not escape the question of how soon war would come, ending the feasts and the laughter.

*

After he had been amply entertained around the palace, Nicolas visited our barracks with Charles. He remembered the names of every man he had met in Yorth. Weston, who seemed the sort to bear contempt for a privileged boy like Nicolas, greeted him jovially, and they spoke briefly about the quality of the Yorthan wine.

"There's more where that came from, my friend, I assure you," said Nicolas. He turned to me. "And Tomlin, is that right? I heard you captured the murderer. Though you were unable to share in our feasting, accept our gratitude all the same."

"Thank you, Your Highness," I said. Surely it would not be a stretch to convince Nicolas to contribute troops to the Alliance.

Nicolas and Charles spent the day at the barracks and participated in some of our drills. While Nicolas's skills were limited to swordplay, he at least impressed us in that regard. Charles was a formidable fighter, but had been conditioned to direct his rigor and strength into artistry rather than affecting damage. Anthony adapted his technique to match his brother's, holding back on strikes that would have been considered unethical according to the ceremonial style. Charles was slightly stronger than his younger brother, and so the fight, according to these unstated stipulations, went in Charles's favor.

But we understood that Anthony had, on some level, allowed this outcome; the Alliance knew how he fought because we had faced him ourselves and had the bruises to prove it.

But Anthony seemed to think it important that the fight remain stately and dignified, and that Charles emerge the victor. I secretly wondered if Anthony had forfeited other things in life, being second born. I realized that he had given up everything to protect Calgoran; if only Riskan and Charles could see what he saw.

"Three years' wages for a win," I heard Rook say to Weston as everyone settled down and started talking about the Stag Tournament again. "Of course, it wouldn't be saying much for us—you would need three years' worth of Realm Alliance wages just to afford a night in a whore's bed."

The idea struck me so suddenly I had to catch myself before slapping Rook on the back with appreciation. Anthony sat in the grass, wiping sweat out of his eyes with his sleeve when I approached him.

"Is your father fond of wagers?"

He looked up at me through his eyelashes. "Aren't all boring, wealthy men?"

"What if you made a wager with him over the tournament? If three of our men fail to place, you will take your rightful position back at court and stop embarrassing him."

Judging from his expression, one might have thought I suggested he start wearing women's underclothes on his head.

"If three of our men *do* place, he raises the wages for members of the Realm Alliance, and allows you to openly recruit members from the other two countries in addition to Nicolas sparing a few of his best men as a gesture of goodwill."

Anthony narrowed his eyes in thought. "It's risky, but I like it. There might be many other men who would join us if we received the same wages as the other soldiers, men who can't afford to because they have families." He looked up at me again. More and more lately I had felt the urge to look away when his steady eyes fixed on mine. "You have your head on right, Tomlin."

"I knew you would like the idea."

"My father will demand five men instead of three. I'm counting on you to place in staff combat."

I smiled. "I'll do my best, captain."

✱

The day of the tournament was unusually warm for autumn. We stared into the sun as we made our way to the arena. My mouth went dry when I saw the colorful, enthusiastic crowds.

Anthony noted my unease. "You're better than any of those lugs, Tom."

I tried to relax my shoulders. There would be hours of eliminations to narrow the competition from hundreds to dozens, and then a break for the noonday meal. After that, six finalists for each event would compete.

I won all of my preliminaries, advancing to the next round. Though weaker than many of my opponents, I had learned my skills from Brack over our secret training sessions in Plum Valley, and this, I found, compensated for any shortage of brute strength.

Before the second round, I took a walk to see how my friends were faring. The Alliance boasted plenty of successes so far. Rook and Maddock had advanced in archery, while Anthony, Orrin, Weston and several others had advanced in their various events.

I winced while watching Weston trounce four opponents in knife combat. From what I understood, grave injuries were rare during the Stag Tournament thanks to good arbitration, but a few of Weston's opponents would be wise to stop at the healer's tent.

In the final round of eliminations, my luck turned. A blow to the ribs forced me to withdraw from one of my matches. That luck ended entirely when I misread a strike during the following match. I ducked rather than dodged and my opponent's staff met the side of my face with a crack. When I came to, three images of Orrin's face swirled in my vision.

I staggered to my feet with his help, cursing.

"Well done! You finished seventh."

"But I had to make sixth to go to the next round."

"Don't worry," Orrin said. "We'll be all right. Seven of ours are fighting in the final rounds. And no matter what happens, we've earned respect for the Alliance today."

This did little to comfort me. Failure was failure. Anthony had depended on me.

On my way to watch the other events, I passed a man by the healer's tent with both eyes swollen shut. I recognized him as the first man who defeated me, one of the six finalists in staff combat. He staggered along as if blind.

"He looks awful," I said to Weston as he approached.

"Anthony just thrashed him in hand combat. He's withdrawing from his other events, which means . . ." He poked me in the chest. "You're advancing."

Seconds later, one of the arbiters told me the news: I was now one of the six finalists. The pressing urge to contribute to our victory thrummed in my chest.

Weston took to the field first. He won his first match, and

then fought another winner while the one with highest score waited to fight the winner out of those two. Weston survived this rapid elimination and won the whole event easily, and the crowds cheered wildly as an arbiter declared him the victor. There was one.

My event came next. My head felt like it might split in two and I strongly suspected that one of my ribs was broken, but I knew every man in the finals had garnered injuries. As I took to the trampled field, I stole a glance at Anthony. He watched me with rapt attention. I reminded myself that there was a chance, however small, that someday he might know who Tomlin really was.

A grin crossed my lips. The pain in my ribs and my face morphed into the inspiration I needed to earn my spot on the platform.

This fire of determination lasted long enough for me to defeat my first two opponents, but the last was too strong, too quick. I came in second, which would at least get me to the platform. That made two placements from the Alliance so far.

The roar of the crowd sounded like an army marching to war. My friends hollered and celebrated. Weston made lewd gestures about my masculinity. I cracked a smile and took my place among my friends, who cheered and threw their sweaty, hairy arms around my shoulders.

Rook placed third in archery. Maddock finished fourth, which didn't count. That made three of us.

Orrin and Anthony took the field next for the swordplay finals, facing one another. They fought hard, holding nothing back, their swords cutting through the air and thwarting one another's strikes. One would advance, the other would drive him back and all the while their faces held barely suppressed smiles. They read one another too well. They even seemed to be chatting when they managed to stand shoulder-to-shoulder, Zeal and Splendor entangled, before Orrin sent Anthony staggering. Orrin bested Anthony, just as I predicted. He helped Anthony up and clamped a hand around the back of his neck, saying something in his cousin's ear. Anthony nodded and left the field to answering cheers.

Orrin earned the highest score and was able to sit out while the other two victors determined who would face him. His first challenger was fierce, but my comrade could take him. As the fight began, Orrin was energetic, indomitable. Yet as the end neared and his final opponent weakened little by little, Orrin started backing off. It was nearly imperceptible; we who had seen him fight one man after another for hours in a day knew that when his movements became slow and labored, he was choosing to lose. I glanced at Weston to see if he had caught on, but he didn't seem surprised. After a fight that wasn't near lengthy enough considering each combatant's skill, the opponent held a sword at Orrin's throat.

I grew even more frustrated watching Anthony in hand-to-hand combat. Bulkier men wailed on him, but he wore them out and attacked once they tired. He took blows that made me cringe and elicited gasps from the crowd. He waited until the perfect moment to strike—to crack a head on his knee, to bury his fist in a set of ribs, to throw his elbow to a nose—and then, with just a few more hits, he would win.

"Smart man," Weston said proudly. "I taught him how to take a hit, but that strategy is all his own."

But as Anthony faced the last opponent, he suddenly seemed unable to recover from the blows in time to make his riposte.

"Why are they throwing their matches?" I demanded of Weston. "They do know what's resting on these fights, don't they?"

Weston uncrossed his beefy arms to dab away a drop of blood leaking from his nose. "Sure, mate. But they're royalty. What use have they for three years' wages? They'll still place."

Frowning, I watched Anthony take second rather than first place. That made five men from the Alliance, but even so: winning would have meant gaining more respect from Calgoran's people and from his father.

Weston eyed me sidelong. "He's not trying to be their champion, Tom. He wants Charles to be that."

As much as I squirmed watching Orrin and Anthony lose, I saw the sense in their motives; they were able to show their excellence without superiority, to flaunt the Alliance's talent without inspiring fear. While Anthony had no trouble undermining his father, he didn't hunger to overshadow his brother, the future king.

We received medals on the victors' platform. A roar of cheers burst out when Anthony strutted forward to accept his, smiling even though one of his eyes was swelling with violet-black bruises and his cheekbones and lips were streaked with cuts. His eyes flickered to the box where his family sat. His father bowed his head, an indication that he would honor their wager.

Anthony looked satisfied as he shook with the third and first place winners of his event. The cheers intensified.

He was generally labeled reckless, and that was true in some ways. His current battered smirk said as much. But what those outside of the Realm Alliance didn't know when they called him hotheaded and war-bent was that, when it came to his country, he was the most careful and discreet diplomat there ever was.

TWELVE

One month remained before the ball. The sense of anticipation throughout Arna became more palpable each passing day.

I grew impatient to find Elinor, but it took two weeks for the visible bruises from the Stag Tournament to heal. Scars and bruises remained even when I changed forms, which had never been a problem until I joined the Alliance. Thus I was tied to the barracks and Tomlin. Anthony's wounds took even longer, passing through a greenish phase and settling at yellow for days. I would always cherish the memory of the tournament day, after the feasting and the prying off women that clung to us as we made our exit to the barracks. Exhausted, aching and bloody, we basked in the victory and in the priceless pride on our leader's swollen face. Whether it could be blamed on my high spirits or the soft firelight in the cool night, I had deemed Anthony more handsome in that moment than ever before.

"The Realm Alliance was well-spoken for today, men," he had said. "I'm honored to call every one of you a member of this fine contingent, and more importantly, a friend. I believe we'll see the fruits of this effort soon enough."

I had been proud that night too: of my bruised ribs and busted face, of the medal swinging at my chest, of my role among these men. Drunk on victory, I was at last able to admit that my swelling pride was grounded not only in our successes, but in Anthony; and though he was no more mine than the faces I borrowed or the titles I donned, I was ready to admit that I wished him to be.

As much as I tried to let wisdom suffocate the admiration I felt, the thrill of that moment unhinged my grip on those struggling emotions. Every time our eyes met, I became overwhelmed with what I wished to see in his glance, what I caught myself vainly seeking even though I knew I wouldn't find it: a sign that I had his attention. My instincts drove me to search for this within our every interaction, and I had to remind myself not to look. I waited impatiently for my face to return to normal so that I could wear other guises and bury myself in my new task.

My ears perked up one night when Cyril and Nicolas visited the Alliance training grounds. Rook, Maddock and I were mending arrows when Anthony and our two guests joined us and spoke freely of their own predictions concerning Charles's future wife.

"If there's anything he's learned from our mother, it's that wisdom suits a queen well," said Anthony. "Charles is too careful to choose based solely on beauty or birth."

Weston tossed two dead doves on a stump, plucked away a few feathers and slit their undersides. "My coin's on Lord Goodenouthe's youngest daughter. There's a worthy lass." He wiggled his blond brows and demonstrated the size of her breasts. Even though my current form held nothing of interest there, I instinctively glanced down at my chest, convinced Weston exaggerated. Surely the girl would have met her end falling down a staircase by now. "In the end, he can only pick one, leaving you with your choice of beauties."

Everyone but me chuckled, including Anthony. I scowled at my arrow. We all left the barracks privately from time to time for various reasons, some to see lovers. Few of us had wives. I had even pretended to go see a girl once myself when I had let my eyes ponder too frequently over Anthony. Anthony left least often of us all, and when he did I found I was rather tense until he returned. It wasn't my place to mind his business, but I was grateful that neither he nor the other men said anything to confirm my fears—fears I had no business having.

"No, this is his time," Anthony said. "I have more important matters to attend to than choosing a wife."

"That's what I said at your age, and now I'm nearly forty," Cyril said. "We don't know when the war will come, or what it will do to the kingdoms. Some would advise you to be happy while you can."

"Nonsense. I'm perfectly happy."

Cyril smiled. "That's what I thought you'd say."

Somewhat assuaged, I forced my tension to morph into concentration and loosed my fierce grip on an arrow shaft.

"What of you, Nicolas?" Anthony asked. "And your betrothal to the cursed princess?"

Nicolas's bright brown eyes turned dark and his jaw tensed. He looked a little older now, closer to Anthony's age, with the boyish joy stolen from his face. "No word in over fifteen years. As a child, I didn't understand her curse or why they had to hide her. I thought that any day she would visit with her family and we would become friends." Nicolas sighed heavily. "But we're both of marrying age now and no one mentions her."

"Isn't that the idea?" I chimed in. "Keeping her hidden?"

"I suppose. I hoped to find her on my own a few weeks ago, so I asked a fairy to create a charm that would lead me to her. She told me that if the princess were protected by elicromancer enchantments it wouldn't likely work, but I asked her to make one for me anyway. Since everyone believes the princess is hiding in Darmeska, I decided to start by journeying north. But on the way, I met a peasant girl in a village in the woods, and . . ." He shook his head in disbelief. "I fell in love. She is the most beautiful girl I've ever seen."

That explained his detour through western Volarre on his way to Arna, and of course his happening upon Rosie the way he did. But I was not comforted by the reality that a fairy charm had overpowered my enchantments. I had spent all this time protecting us from dark, deep magic, but not from the simple, sparkly, trivial magic one could purchase like a new pair of shoes. I would have to place all manner of low-level enchantments upon the cottage when I returned.

"If things were better in Nissera, I would ask my father to annul the betrothal, but . . ." Nicolas shrugged. It was clear from his resigned expression that he had already thought this through.

We all silently finished his thought. *But it wouldn't be wise.* Anthony wasn't the only prince making sacrifices in these times.

I recognized pity on Anthony's face. I couldn't imagine any circumstance in which he could be forced to take a woman of his father's choosing, except the one: if it kept the scales balanced, helped protect Calgoran and the rest of Nissera.

I thought of Rosie weeping and shrinking away from my touch. What if she only had a short time to be happy, to live her life, before dying at Tamarice's hand?

I couldn't give Rosie her parents. I couldn't give her all the possessions or luxuries to which she was entitled by her birth. I couldn't give her back the previous years of her life, or the promise of years to come. But I could give her this—tell Nicolas the truth and send him back to her.

I would do it on one condition.

When Nicolas said his farewells and began making his way back to the palace, I excused myself and jogged after him in the dark. I took on the form of a young woman, one I had never used in Calgoran, and changed my garments to flowing robes.

"Bay Sandborn," I called out as the Veloxen prince walked alone across the courtyard.

Nicolas jolted out of his thoughts to whip around and stared at me. "Pardon?"

"Does your love have hair of spun gold and rose petal lips? Eyes greener than a spring morning?"

"How do you know?" he drew closer, squinting in the dark. "Who are you?"

"A messenger, sent by the Clandestine."

"The Clandestine? Everyone says she has disappeared, that perhaps she even joined Tamarice."

"I can assure you, she is at work—protecting the realm *from* Tamarice. And protecting a cursed princess in hiding."

Nicolas stood with his mouth slightly agape, puzzling

together my implication. "The girl in Plum Valley . . . she couldn't be my betrothed, could she?"

"She is. The Clandestine has an agenda that goes beyond protecting Rosamund. She has adopted many names and faces to try to keep Nissera intact. But you must not doubt that Rosamund is extremely dear to her. She will not take kindly to you being frivolous with this information." I had been circling him, and now let my voice grow dark and my eyes bore into his. I feared the boy would take my words too lightly. "You must not breathe a word of the truth, not even to Rosie herself."

"I am permitted to see her then?"

"Yes, but you must do something for the Clandestine."

"Anything." It was clear by the earnestness in his voice that he meant it.

"Anthony plans to request that you convince your father to assign soldiers to the Realm Alliance as a gesture of unity and support, to grow our numbers and give us more credibility. But you must persuade him to send some of his *finest* and most intelligent warriors and officers. Men of such caliber that he would personally trust to protect his own life."

"I will do what I can, with pleasure. These men of the Alliance are honorable and willing to fight for the good of the realm. My father has seen that. And I shall do everything in my power to protect Rosamund. I will give my life to keep her safe from Tamarice if I must."

I stepped forward and placed one hand on Nicolas's shoulder, savoring the taste of truths on my tongue, even if they were only half-truths.

"Farewell, Nicolas. Please be wise and careful."

Nicolas kissed my hand. "Thank you. Tell the Clandestine I am grateful."

He took off with feverish haste toward the stables, unwilling to wait until morning to set off toward Rosie again.

As I walked back to the barracks, I wondered how it would feel to tell Anthony the truth. If I were a stranger, the lies I had told might be of little consequence to these men. But I was a trusted friend, a brother. I couldn't help fearing I would be viewed as an infiltrator.

No, I couldn't entertain the thought of spilling my secrets to Anthony. But with Nicolas taken care of, I could turn my attentions to Elinor and on the ball that had the whole kingdom talking.

I wanted them to be talking of her when the night came to a close.

✳

Elinor's hometown of May Acre sat in the midst of miles of pure farmland. It was flat and sunny, small yet affluent. One could reach it from Arna by way of a leisurely two-hour journey on country roads, but that was of little consequence to me as I materialized to Youngblood Manor. I'd delicately asked the townspeople about the duke and learned he had taken on the name Youngblood before establishing himself here, then married a woman named Nellica Placett. He had since passed away and left Elinor and his new family a dwindling fortune.

The estate was a typical country manor house, not vast but not small by any means. Endless fields, an apple orchard and a garden filled with autumn fruits surrounded it. Ivy climbed the walls and flowerboxes, and light blue shutters framed the windows.

Shortly after I arrived, a servant emerged from the house to clean the stables, her face covered with a dusty rag to block out the stale must of the hay and manure, but there was no sign of Elinor.

I had just transformed into a bird and perched on a windowsill when I saw a young woman emerge from the house. Though it was almost noon, she wore a nightgown. Her frizzy brown hair was woven in an erratic braid and her face was plain as a glass of tea, no prettier than it was ugly, scrunched in exasperation. My heart dropped. If she were Elinor . . . well, even my meddling wouldn't likely make her queen.

"Ella!" the young woman called out, traipsing toward the stables.

The servant I had seen earlier emerged, loosening the cloth to reveal flaxen hair and a delicate face. Not even the plain clothes and dirty apron she wore could hide who she was. Though she had been a young child when last I saw her, I knew without question that she was Elinor.

Her hair was the fairest shade of blonde. Though dainty, her body had been shaped by hard work, her pale skin kissed by sunlight. Like Rosie, she resembled both Lysandra and Lucetta. But while Rosie had inherited her father's fire and the spark in his green eyes, Elinor seemed to have inherited the duke's solemn poise. Her gray-blue eyes were cool and smart, her chin held high with ingrained dignity.

"Ella, you could at least help me see to my mother just this once," the other girl said. "She can hardly sit up."

Elinor wiped the sweat from her forehead, leaving a smudge of dirt its place. "Just this once?" she repeated with an incredulous laugh. "Do you even know how she takes her tea to calm her spells?"

"All I know is that I've been tending to her for hours—and that if I don't make it to town for my dress fitting today, I won't be properly attired for the most important social event of the decade."

"You're free to go, Bianca," Elinor said, pushing past the other girl to go inside.

I flew impulsively to one of the open windows and found a gray-headed woman lying in bed, massaging her head. Even her reclining posture was stately, and her features suggested a frosty demeanor. But when Elinor entered the room and knelt at her bedside, the older woman patted her hand tenderly and smiled. "I raised her dress allowance just to get some peace," she said with a low chuckle. "Yours is there in the drawer. I'm afraid we don't have much to spare, but you never know whom you'll meet on such occasions. He could make every thesar worth it."

Elinor slid open the drawer of a nearby vanity and pulled out a velvet pouch of coins, weighing it in hand. "Mother! I couldn't possibly—"

"There won't be another night like this in your time, my girl. And you've taken such good care of us since your father died." The woman, who I guessed to be Nellica, leaned toward Elinor, but sank back down with a moan. "Oh, the whole world is churning."

Elinor stood gracefully. "I'll make tea."

"Please do, dear. With—"

"Ginger and mint," Elinor finished. On her way out, she gently placed the pouch of coins on the vanity. Then she changed her mind, clutching it against her apron. "Thank you."

Elinor left her stepmother's room. I materialized to Arna, barely even noticing when two chatty women saw me appear in the street and fell silent. Elinor's situation weighed heavily on my mind. I suspected she didn't know who she was or where she came from any more than Rosie did. If Elinor had known, surely she would have had the sense to go to Volarre when her father died.

Determination burned through me. I would make certain this ball was the most spectacular night of Elinor's life. Lysandra's daughter would sit on the throne of Calgoran.

✳

I returned to the barracks more absorbed with dress, slipper and hair details than a lady's maid. With the weather getting colder and the whole kingdom anticipating the selection of its future queen, the Alliance didn't have much to do besides "drink and piss," as Anthony put it. The king had honored the wager by raising our earnings, and would allow us to go on a recruiting journey in the spring. Under his banners and with his blessing, we would request that the other countries send soldiers to the Realm Alliance, as well as invite unenlisted commoners to join. But for now, our missions were sparse, which made Anthony restless. He looked hopeful any time a messenger came our way and disappointed any time the message turned out to be trivial. While the others were content this slow time of year to visit nearby family or seek the warmth of taverns and pleasure houses, I obliged Anthony's restlessness by plunging into the forest with him to hunt.

The wood smelled of coming snow. We sat by a fallen tree in the velvety black of a night lit with cold moonlight, hearing no sound besides my breathing and his. I knew when he spotted something, because he would silence even that, hand creeping toward his quiver.

The doe lifted her head, frozen in fear, before leaping off into the shadows.

Anthony sighed, filling the air with the fog of his breath. Even the hunt couldn't keep him from his worries. "Why haven't we seen the Clandestine yet?" he asked. "Why hasn't Brack been seen since my father was fool enough to ignore his counsel? I can feel darkness closing in, but no one else seems to feel it. And sometimes I fear the good elicromancers have abandoned us."

His earnest eyes met mine in the vague light. I saw a stroke of vulnerability in them I had never seen before. He yearned to hear the truth as I yearned to tell it, and in that moment, when we were so close in the dark that the fog pouring out of our mouths combined and disappeared as one, I nearly did.

But I had to see Elinor crowned, and I feared that any revelation of my identity could upset those chances. And there was a deeper fear, much less significant in the scope of the realm's events: that when I told him the truth, I would have to own every one of those painful desires rising in me like fire in a closed furnace. I might even have to lose him.

As long as I was Tomlin, everything could stay as it was. I could be near him in the lonesome forest that smelled of snow not yet fallen. As long as I was Tomlin, I didn't have to think about how love and grief were inevitably and perpetually intertwined.

With everything as it was, I couldn't have him the way I wanted him. But I wouldn't have to lose him either.

"The elicromancers have sworn to keep peace," I said. "To fight with every last breath to protect mortals in this realm. Yes, Tamarice will come full force. But you won't be alone when she does."

Anthony nodded, still staring off into the shadows, not

seeming to notice that my words of reassurance contained a direct promise. "It feels like we are."

I rested my arm on my bow and closed my eyes. "I believe the Clandestine is working—probably has been all these years. She will reveal herself in time."

We started the trek back to the barracks in silence. Finally, Anthony spoke.

"Tell me, Tom, what do the stars say tonight?"

I looked up at the lights that sparkled like jewels, like slivers of ice in the Water. "Snow."

And snow it did.

✳

On the eve of the ball, I arrived at May Acre just before sunset. Lamps were lit throughout the manor house, and by their light I saw Bianca's figure rushing frantically past the windows. I heard indistinguishable yelling, a crash and weeping. I waited, certain this didn't bode well for Elinor.

I touched my pendant. I could feel my stone's energy pulsing through my blood, and the magic in my blood flowing back through it, a never-ending loop of power. Tonight would be magnificent.

As the sun set, a coach arrived and Bianca paraded down the snowy path. She climbed inside a carriage with two giggling girls, a difficult feat in such a large gown and a fox fur-lined cloak that must have cost a handful of silver aurions. One of the girls wore deep purple and blue, as if to proliferate an air of royalty, while the other looked decisively patriotic in ruby red with touches of brocaded gold at the collar and sleeves. Bianca wore lavender with a central panel of midnight blue, an unexpectedly nice pairing, though her hair couldn't manage to look appropriately tame for the occasion.

I waited, but Elinor didn't come. The young women shut the door of the coach and departed, leaving Youngblood Manor silent.

My feet crunched over the snow as I walked through the garden. I dressed as a regular old fairy—something like Daffodil Dimplesworth—though I decided to forego the pink buckled shoes this time. I disguised my pendant as a white wooden wand with a foggy blue jewel on the handle, but it surged with power in my hand.

I was debating whether I should knock or make a more mystical entrance when Elinor burst out the door in a flurry of sobs, barely clothed, and dropped onto her knees in the snow.

She didn't cry for long, pressing on her eyes until all the tears were gone, sniffling and snotting on the back of her hand. Her blonde hair tumbled freely about her bare shoulders, damp with fresh snowflakes. She curled her knees to her chest and dropped her head to them, and would have remained thus for some time if she hadn't heard a voice and glanced up, startled.

"What's become of your plans to go to the royal city?"

She wiped away a straggling tear and looked around, wondering where I'd come from. "My dress is ruined." Fingering the pale pink fabric, she half-laughed as though it was silly, but the effort ended as a sniffle. "Who are you?"

"Who am I not?" I offered her my hand. She accepted it and stood up. "Tonight I am your clothier, your cobbler, your coachman and, most importantly, your friend. I also happen to be a fairy."

Her eyes widened with anticipation. "A fairy?" she asked in amazement. It was likely she had never met one—at least not since she was old enough to remember. "And you're going to help me go to Arna? Why?"

"Like I said, my dear, I'm your friend. Now, you can't go like this." She shivered in the cold. The pink bodice was partly laced over ivory petticoats, slipping off of her nearly bare chest, and the skirts looked as though they had been severed carelessly with a knife. "What happened?"

She cast her eyes down. "My sister spent too much on her gown. I had to use my dress allowance to buy our mother her tonic. My mother told me to borrow one of my sister's old gowns, which I knew would cause trouble, but I hoped that just this once . . . I'll admit I like to test her temper from time to time, but tonight was different. Now I've missed the coach." She sighed. "I don't even know why I wished to go so badly. Everyone would know I don't belong."

My stone pulsed under my touch. "We had better hurry."

"How . . . ?" she began, crossing her shivering arms and gesturing meekly at the empty place where the coach had stood only moments ago.

I stalked through frosted plants and found two snow-capped wagon wheels leaning against the stables. I rolled them toward a garden bench and set them on either side, muttering nonsense words that sounded like fairy spells. Sparkling dust poured out of my wand, and in spite of its disguise my elicrin stone still did its work; the bench and wheels turned into an all-white covered coach with blue curtains and silver filigree foliage. It wouldn't last long—the objects were too large and their changes too detailed—but it would do for the evening.

Elinor's mouth dropped. I certainly wasn't taking pains to hide my magic, but a lonesome country girl who had never even encountered a real fairy probably wouldn't know the difference between elicrin magic and the ordinary kind.

"Do you have any horses?" I asked.

Elinor looked toward the stables. "Just one."

"What about dogs?"

She trudged through the snow to the stables and returned leading a white horse, three hounds at her heels. I whistled at the dogs and they nearly bowled me over.

Elinor winced as I raised my wand again. "This won't hurt them a bit," I assured her.

It took longer than the coach transformation, but the dogs' features changed and grew until four white horses stood at our disposal rather than just the one.

"My goodness!" Elinor gasped, rushing forward to pet one on the muzzle. "Fairy magic is more powerful than I dreamed."

"You must not stay too long lest the larger items begin returning to their original forms."

She nodded eagerly, and then looked down at her torn dress. "Must I go in this?" she asked, a little humiliated.

"Of course not," I said with a knowing smile. I had visited every clothier in Arna, studying the most intricate gowns on display. For Elinor's, I had settled on a glimmering blue silk, the color of Volarre's crest and of my stone. Elinor would attend the ball covered in a secret tribute to her homeland— and my own signature of pride in my work.

I concentrated hard to transform the tattered pink garment. The result robbed me of my breath. The color manifested just as I imagined. The material had an almost glass-like quality, silky and full of movement as it nimbly followed the arcs and bows of her lithe body. The silver-white embroidery across the breast held such fine detail that it looked as though someone had slaved over it for hours. The false sleeves were crafted of the same silver-white of the silk stitching, but covered only her shoulders and then split away, falling delicately at her sides like relaxed wings.

I told the speechless Elinor to plait her hair and bring me jewelry and a cloak of any sort. She ran inside and did as I asked, gathering one of her stepmother's necklaces and a circlet of Bianca's, and emerged with her long pale tresses fixed complexly. I turned the cloak into white wool, lined on the interior with sapphire satin. The necklace I turned into silver and glass, and to Elinor's shoes I did the same: silver satin with clear embellishments. The last touch was the best feature: I transformed Bianca's gold circlet into a tiara of silver and glass identical to the one Charles had given Elinor on Rosamund's name day in honor of their betrothal.

"It's so beautiful," Elinor whispered, her shapely lips dark pink from the winter air. She bowed her head and allowed me to place it in her fair hair.

At first sight she had seemed as beautiful as Lucetta and Lysandra. Now I wondered if she might be more beautiful. She could have worn the rags in which I found her and Charles would have inevitably thought her lovely—but now she looked undeniably majestic.

Elinor grasped my hands. "How can I possibly thank you for tonight? I don't even know why you've done this for me."

I patted her hand. "That's not important. All that matters is you reaching the palace in time."

I opened the coach door for her. She embraced me and kissed my cheek. "You are the loveliest person I've ever met."

"Only because you haven't yet looked in a mirror tonight, love."

After Elinor climbed inside, I harnessed the horses to the coach and took the coachman's seat, tightening my cape around me as fresh snow began to fall.

THIRTEEN

My heart raced as we entered through the gates and sped down the endless tree-lined drive leading to the palace courtyard. Lights lined the road, twinkled in the gardens and edged the marble stairs to the palace, a thousand distant moons against the clear black night.

From afar, I watched the silhouettes of a few lingerers entering the great foyer, but most of the guests had arrived some time ago. Ours was the only coach traversing the courtyards at this hour. I pulled to a stop and left the coach in the care of an attendant. I then took the form of a palace attendant myself, hurrying ahead of Elinor so that I could observe her entrance like a director sitting back to watch her theatrical piece unfold.

I had attended court in Arna on many occasions but had never seen the great hall bedecked so illustriously. Under thousands of sparkling lamps, garlands wound with silver and gold ribbons draped from the walls. White banners had been erected for the occasion in place of the usual red, and crisp white linens covered banquet tables dressed with gold and silver place settings.

King Riskan and Queen Dara sat on their thrones while Charles stood at the foot of the dais to greet guests in a receiving line. He looked resplendent in a white doublet worn under a gold jerkin with a deep red sash across his chest. Calgoranian tradition stipulated that on grand occasions the heir don a sash of red, while the king's other children don a sash of white. I glanced at the royal party, noticing that Nicolas had returned for the occasion and kept company with Cyril, Orrin, the royal ministers and Anthony.

Anthony. My heart overturned at the sight of him. He wore a dark red doublet ornamented with gold, the traditional white sash crossing his chest. Zeal was sheathed in black and gold at his hip. I found myself astounded by how suited he looked to the occasion, by how much he resembled Charles. He seemed radiant, imposing and out of reach—like a different man entirely from the one who had confided his doubts to me in the dark of a winter night.

I dragged my eyes back to Charles, commanding myself to focus. By now most of the guests had made it through the line and were partaking of the wine and food. As soon as Charles welcomed the last guest, the musicians would play and he would choose a woman with whom to dance.

Behind me, an attendant took Elinor's cloak as she reached the top of the stairs. I heard the herald ask her name. His booming voice filled the hall. "Lady Elinor Youngblood of May Acre."

Earlier, when hordes of people had arrived all at once, this announcement would not have turned every head in the hall. But it did now. I could tell Elinor wished to shrink away from the stares, but some innate dignity led her forward with her chin held high.

Drifting to the flanks of the room, I watched with smug satisfaction as Charles became enraptured with her.

I decided to disguise myself as Catleen so that I could gossip about this new arrival without raising suspicions. Disappearing behind the wall décor, I took on the appearance of the sultry courtier. As I assimilated into the whispering crowd, I accepted a glass of wine and wove through the maze of skirts to get a better view.

Elinor turned out to be the final guest in the receiving line. She curtsied to Charles as if she had been doing this all her life.

"Your face is familiar, Lady Elinor," Charles said, "though I do not remember having met you." His eyes found the glass tiara and he furrowed his brow as if trying to decide where he had seen it before, but he couldn't look away from her face for long. A slight hush settled over the hall.

"I don't see how, Your Highness," she replied coolly. "I've never been to Arna."

The sudden flux of intrigued whispers around me made it impossible to catch the short remainder of their dialogue. But soon Charles offered her his sturdy hand, and the musicians took the cue. An insuppressible grin slid across my face.

Elinor smoothly transformed her fearful hesitation into a curtsy and accepted his hand. I exhaled with relief when she knew the first steps of the *laureat*, a dance with somewhat complicated steps. Even though the duke had never told her the truth of her origin, at least he taught her something useful.

I wove back through the multitudes of people. A few of the women who had come tonight expecting or hoping that Charles would give them this sort of attention stuck out like weeds, wearing scowls, while less disillusioned women looked wistful at worst.

Relaxing my shoulders, I looked down at my gown to make sure it manifested properly. It was light green with yellow-gold teardrop patterns and false sleeves—pretty, but not conspicuous like Elinor's. I pulled a strand of hair in front of my eyes and saw Catleen's light brown curls.

I easily located Bianca in the crowd. She made a fierce sound through gritted teeth. "How did she get here? In *that*?"

"You should inform the prince," said one of her friends. "If he knew she spent her days covered in dirt and cinders and working like a serv—"

"And have him think me a snitch?" Bianca snapped. Anger burned in her eyes, but something else too: fear. Did she know Elinor's true identity and hope it would never be revealed? Or was her envy so powerful that she didn't have to know of her sister's origins in order to resent her potential?

Forcing a path between Bianca and her friends, I allowed a servant to replenish my wine.

"Pardon," I said with a sour smile. "Are you speaking of the Lady Elinor? I quite agree she's not what she seems to be."

Bianca's smile resembled a snarl. "See? She's fooled no one."

"Right you are!" I exclaimed, squeezing back between them. "She is clearly the Lost Duchess of Volarre."

A chorus of gasps followed. Bianca dropped her wine glass. I glided away, trusting the news would spread.

But my moment of triumph was cut short by the realization that it had been a mistake to attend the ball as Catleen. As I roamed the edges of the dance floor, someone firmly grabbed my buttocks and spoke in a low voice that wasn't quite low enough. "Decided to grace us with your presence again, I see. Were you banned from court for being too"—he squeezed again—"devious?"

Resisting the urge to send whomever it was crashing onto a table, I turned to find the Duke of Joliff, one of my previous conquests. He was too wet with wine to realize he had caught the attention of Prince Nicolas and a minister who conversed nearby. Oblivious, he stumbled off, leaving me to acknowledge their attention by curtsying.

I located a lush settee against the wall, from where I could watch the dances. I had never seen Anthony dance before, but it didn't surprise me that he did so skillfully, considering his princely upbringing. Seeing a dark-haired beauty in his arms made my stomach sink. With every sip of wine, my eyes drifted more liberally toward his face, appreciating the indented lines around his smile. I longed for his familiar gaze to find me among all these people, even though I wouldn't see the recognition or admiration I wished for.

I sighed and left the receiving hall, making my way past the guards and down the stairs. Leaning against the balustrade of one of the open archways in the foyer, I closed my eyes and breathed in the snowy air, shutting out the sounds of the muted celebration that followed me. I wished I were somewhere far away, like in the heights of Darmeska, where I couldn't see those eyes or that smile.

"I don't much enjoy a *racade*, either." Anthony's voice cut short my musings. I emitted a grunt of surprise. "Forgive me," he said, laughing a little, "I didn't mean to startle you. I just need the fresh air."

I smiled at him, but it was a friendly, crooked Tomlin smile, and I didn't know how to greet him as anyone else. I finally managed, "Such occasions overwhelm me," and added nearly too late, "Your Highness."

"You're not alone in that," he said. I had trouble believing that thanks to his flushed cheeks. "What's your name? I don't remember Charles greeting you, but I do remember that you were the only woman in court fairly beaming when he chose his first partner."

Naturally, Anthony was vigilant enough to notice me grinning like a madwoman at the forefront of a sea of awestruck faces. I should have expected that. I gestured overenthusiastically toward the top of the stairs. "The . . . uh . . . the Lady Elinor is a dear friend of mine from childhood. I'm Catleen Boulstridge."

"Pleasure to meet you, Lady Catleen." He bowed his head. Out of habit I started to reach my hand out for a man-to-man greeting, but it found my skirts instead and I managed a half-hearted curtsy. "What can you tell me about this mysterious lady of whom my brother's enamored? I've never seen him look so captivated. By anything, really. He tends to be a rather somber individual."

"She's courageous and kind as she is beautiful. In dark times like these, that's all anyone could hope for in a queen."

"In dark times like these?" Anthony repeated.

I hadn't meant to say anything that would pique his interest, but I relished the gleam in his eyes. I covered my tracks. "Calgoran and Volarre are hardly friends, Your Highness."

His shoulders dropped slightly. "True. And you recommend this Lady Elinor? My brother holds my opinion toward his choice of bride in some esteem, though it appears he has already—"

"Anthony," Orrin interrupted, jogging down the steps. He looked comely in dark blue with touches of gold. Upon noticing me, he shot me the ghost of a disapproving expression that proved he, unlike Anthony, knew something or other about Catleen's reputation. "That woman, Lady Elinor—I just heard she's the daughter of Lysandra and Aidric. She was once betrothed to Charles."

A shocked smile broke out on Anthony's face. "The Lost Duchess? What will the king say?"

"He and the queen have already claimed to be charmed by her. I don't believe they've heard she's Volarian royalty."

"Oh dear," I muttered, for Elinor suddenly fled down the steps, passing us without a second glance before making her way through the entrance hall.

"Pardon me," I muttered, scrambling off after her.

As I ran, I nearly tripped over one of her shoes that slipped off on the way. The guards standing at the crest of the marble steps outside flinched when I passed, but didn't pursue me. I caught up to her just as she stumbled on the last stair.

"It's all right, Elinor," I said, steadying her. "I wear a guise, but I am the one who brought you here. Come, let's get you home and I'll explain."

She leaned back to look at me, blinking away warm tears that forged glistening paths down her cheeks. Awe, confusion and clarity passed through her blue eyes before she finally said, "You're an elicromancer."

Charles shouted from the top of the palace steps. I feared

he would give the command for the guards to chase us down. "Let's go," I said, urging her toward the coach.

We had nearly made it back to May Acre when the coach started shrinking. By the time we could see the manor, the three counterfeit horses changed back to hounds. I gave poor Elinor my cloak, and she rode the horse home while I made a fire and waited for her in the sitting room.

When she arrived, she immediately marched up to her stepmother's room. I crept up behind her and stood in the shadows outside the door.

"You knew who I was," Elinor whispered to her stepmother.

Nellica's eyes flickered open. She groaned deeply. "Knew what, Ella, dear?"

With startling vigor, Elinor swept a bottle from the vanity. Tonic and shards of glass splashed across the room. "You both knew that I was a duchess from Volarre."

Nellica's bleary eyes widened. She forced herself to sit up, but soon turned pale and closed her eyes. "Your father didn't want you to know. I was honoring his wishes." She opened her eyes. "And I didn't want you to leave. How did you find out?"

Elinor's chest heaved, something between a sob and a cry of anger caught in her throat. "I saw it in Bianca's eyes. She denied the rumor so fiercely that it could only be true. You told her but not me?"

"It was an accident," her stepmother said. "A tonic loosened my tongue. I thought she would tell you, that she would try to exploit your relationship for wealth and fame. But jealousy is a powerful thing." As she looked up at Elinor, I couldn't tell if her gray eyes held regret or resolve. "As is love."

"Love?" Elinor demanded.

"Yes. My love for you and yours for me, which led you to care for me when the daughter of my own blood wouldn't." The older woman's voice grew thin with desperation. "Who would I have if you left me? I would waste away. The manor would fall to ruin. You are the only good thing here, the only light in the dark. I loved you more than my own daughter." Tears spilled down Nellica's parchment-like cheek, and she dropped her head to her bosom.

Elinor's scowl softened. She slowly knelt beside the bed, taking her stepmother's hand. "I would have always cared for you. If I had known, we could have had wealth to keep up the manor, to pay for your treatments. . . ."

"You wouldn't have stayed," Nellica said, pressing on her temples with a grimace. She lay back down, unable to keep herself aright any longer. "You won't stay now. . . ."

Elinor shushed her, combing back her gray hair. "Of course I will. I will never leave you." The girl stood up, wiping tears from her eyes. "I'll make tea."

Down in the kitchens, I sat Elinor down while I made the tea myself. She held her cup with trembling hands. Much of her fair hair had fallen free of the plaiting and clung to her face and neck. I sat on a stool across from her.

Her blue eyes held mine steadily. "You knew who I was, didn't you?"

"Yes."

"Bianca once told me the tale of the duke who disappeared with his daughter after his wife died. What do you know of Lysandra? My mother?"

I recalled my meeting with the duchess in the queen's garden long ago. "I only spoke with her once. Some thought her frail, but she was strong. Truthfully, she was the loveliest woman I ever saw. Until tonight."

Elinor's eyes filled with tears. One slipped out and she wiped it away.

"You were once betrothed to Charles, Elinor," I said.

A laugh burst out from her, harsh and robust for someone so exquisite. "To think . . ." But then she sobered and looked into my eyes. "You planned for all of that to happen tonight."

"I did."

"Why? Why did you go to the trouble?"

"There were many reasons for my actions, Elinor, not the least of them being that I feel you deserve happiness."

"But that's not all, is it?"

I shook my head.

She sat back in the chair. "You are very powerful."

"Yes."

"How did I ever gain such a friend?" she asked. "And what could I ever do to repay you?"

"Only this: if Charles comes for you, don't refuse him. Let him make you his queen."

Elinor laughed wistfully, blowing a stray strand of hair from her cheek. "Royal heirs don't marry rough palms and empty pockets."

She leaned forward and grasped my hand, and I felt the calluses she spoke of. Yes, by blood she was a duchess, but she had lived as a commoner. Had I been so exempt from the confines of peasantry since becoming an elicromancer that I had overlooked an insurmountable obstacle to Elinor reaching the throne—and therefore to Calgoran and Volarre holding fast to their friendship?

"I know who you are," Elinor said. "I've heard your name, but I will not speak it if that's your wish. Thank you. For the most remarkable night of my life." She untangled the glass tiara from her hair and removed the necklace and remaining slipper. "We ought to change these back."

I did as she asked with the necklace and circlet, but left the shoe as it was. "Keep it as long as it lasts, to remember tonight."

She smiled sadly and held it to her chest.

"Go to Volarre, Elinor. I'm certain Queen Lucetta would give anything to have her family back."

Elinor shook her head. "And my father's estate would fall to ruin, and my mother would probably die. And as much as I dislike Bianca, I don't wish poverty upon her. They're my family."

"Much bigger things are at stake than your father's estate. Do you realize what this could mean for the relationship between Volarre and Calgoran?"

I felt no better than the men who had argued over her marriage years ago.

"I didn't think of that." She licked her lips and stared at the floor. After a moment, she raised her eyes again, resolute. "As long as he will provide for my family, I will marry him if he happens to inquire. Or command."

I stuffed down my guilt and gestured at my body. "For now, this is the form I will take. I go by Catleen Boulstridge. I claimed tonight to be your dear friend, which I hope you will consider me to be."

The low rumble of someone approaching drew our gazes to the window even though the shutters were closed and braced against the winter cold. Elinor met my gaze as we rose to our feet. "It's only Bianca and her friends returning from the ball."

We rushed to the door regardless. Elinor opened a wooden slat to peek outside. She sucked in a breath and slammed the slat closed.

"What?" I demanded.

"I think . . . I think it's him."

I peeked outside for myself. Sure enough, five men approached the manor on horseback—something only people with sure intentions and no time to waste would do on a winter night like this.

"I'm not ready," Elinor squeaked, combing back her ratty hair. "Can you help me? Wait . . . no . . ." She marched to the kitchen, where she seized her apron and a sooty cloth and tied them around her waist and hair. After sliding her feet into too-big leather boots, she finished up by smudging dirt from the apron on her face. "If he still wants me as his bride after seeing me like this, I will marry him as you asked."

A swift knock resounded at the door. Elinor approached it, chin held high, and swung it open. A windblown royal attendant stood before us. Charles waited on horseback in the small courtyard, flanked by Anthony and two other attendants. Elinor and I both curtsied, though hers was more extravagant and, in this context, rather facetious. She didn't believe he would still want her.

"Is the Lady Elinor present?" the attendant asked.

Charles dismounted, looking slightly timid for all of his princely height and broad shoulders. No trace of disdain surfaced in his blue eyes at recognizing Elinor in such condition.

"Elinor," he said softly as he approached. "My father told me that with one glance I would know my queen. And I did. It wasn't only your beauty, though you mustn't doubt I find you terribly beautiful. It was knowing at once that you were royalty, whether or not the blood ran in your veins."

He drew close and gently tore away the cloth that covered her head, releasing her soot-streaked blonde hair. She looked up at him in wonder.

"We were betrothed once. The troubles of our kingdoms divided us, but I find I don't mind that they did, because now I am able to choose you freely." Reaching inside his cloak, he withdrew the glass slipper that had slipped off on the palace steps. He knelt down and unlaced her oversized shoe. She clung to his shoulder for support as he slid the slipper onto her dainty foot and took her hand. "Will you be my queen?"

Elinor stood speechless, unable to wipe the look of surprise from her face before finally spitting out a "yes" that emerged with too much enthusiasm to be wholly influenced by her promise to me.

Beaming, Charles stood up and leaned down to kiss her. "Oh, but," she interrupted, "my mother must come live at the palace and receive treatment for her illness."

"Of course."

"And the manor will need to be kept up in my absence, and a small sum must be allotted to my sister for personal expenses."

"Anything you ask, consider it done."

Elinor laughed in disbelief. Charles smiled, admiration erasing all the placidity of his demeanor, and leaned down to kiss her soot-covered mouth.

My eyes strayed to Anthony, sitting tall on Arsinoe and smiling to himself. The gold accessories of his decorative attire gleamed underneath his winter cape.

I held in a sigh and returned my gaze to the future king and queen of Calgoran. I would allow no room for pain in my heart on such a night.

✳

Nicolas and Rosie had already discussed marriage. He had returned to Yorth, but Rosie still talked of nothing but their wedding in the highest of spirits.

My spirits, on the other hand, sank lower each time I left the Alliance. I cherished my talks with Orrin during sleepless nights, Weston's gruff banter and cheeriness, Rook and Maddock's vast knowledge of the wilderness, Anthony's passionate yet easygoing nature. These men were my brothers the way Rosie, in a way, was like a younger sister. But trouble stood around the bend like a dark wave mounting, and I couldn't bear the thought of losing anyone—in Galgeth or Nissera.

Without much to do in the winter, only Anthony and Orrin's insistence on staying sharp kept us from growing fat on food and ale, and it paid off one frigid, dark day. We went in pursuit of a pack of wild animals that were prowling through towns out west, attacking folks in their sleep, leaving only blood as a trace.

Reasoning that the thunder of horses would spook our query, we traveled on foot. The going was slow. The unremitting snow covered the beasts' tracks, immediately vexing Rook and Maddock. I had never seen the brothers so thwarted. After a long day of traipsing through harsh weather with no trail to follow, we at last made camp a little distance from the town where the most recent attack had taken place and hunted for fresh meat to use as bait.

Rook and Maddock were quick to make themselves useful by constructing a trap featuring the bloody deer carcasses Anthony and I had hauled back to camp. During the night, an outer circle of men remained awake while an inner group was permitted to rest in safety. Fearing a fire might keep the beasts at bay, we wrapped ourselves in thick furs and did without. With only half a moon and no firelight, we waited in utter silence.

Sword drawn, I stayed alert as part of the outer circle for four long, hushed hours, knowing that we might not be equipped to defeat whatever we would face. After that, I dragged myself to the inner circle and slept close to Weston's large, snoring shadow.

In the morning, we woke and found the bait undisturbed. The watch reported they had heard and seen nothing. We kept moving, hauling the deer carcasses along in case the beasts might still catch the scent.

An eerie feeling haunted me as we continued to traverse the empty white wilderness. I constantly reached up to touch my pendant even though the concealing spell made it feel and look as though nothing was there. There was an eccentricity to these attacks that the villagers had described, and it had given me pause when we set up the trap. I didn't want to lure in strange creatures that feasted on human flesh in the night and left no marks besides the blood spilled. In one case, a woman had been attacked and dragged from her bed, while her husband slept beside her. Most could only guess it was the work of a pack of wolves mad with starvation. But to me, the cunningness and soundlessness suggested something else entirely. I thought of the battle murals at Darmeska that I hadn't even dared look at in the dark. For the first time, I wished the Alliance would give up and go home where we would be safe.

We crossed a frozen creek and came upon a meadow. The woods stood at a distance on either side. The hair along my nape prickled. I stopped and glanced around at the trees, expecting to see dark forms lurking, but I spotted nothing.

"What is it, Tom?" Orrin whispered, lips tinged blue. We would need to stop and build a fire soon.

I shook my head and forced my feet to trudge onward, but glanced involuntarily back toward the woods.

Then I saw movement amid the white trees, so subtle it might have been a clump of snow drifting from the boughs. I spotted another movement, and another: white shifting at the edge of the forest. I found a pair of eyes fixed on me and realized what sort of creatures these were. I had seen them in the battle mural at Darmeska, had held their fearsome pelts in my hands. An unuttered scream rose in my throat.

The attacks made sense now as I watched the ghost cats from Galegth creep steadily closer, the same shade as the snow. We were no longer the hunters.

"Koraks!" I yelled, drawing my sword. The few who knew what that meant—knew where these had come from—scanned the woods in alarm.

They stole sinuously closer, their silver eyes shrewd and hungry. What I first believed to be three or four turned out to be eight, nine, ten, each seeming to materialize out of the snow. Their black lips curled back to reveal gleaming fangs.

The nearest cat lunged for Weston and tackled the big man to the ground, clawing at his face and chest.

The Alliance came to life. Weston buried a knife in the animal's fur, but it merely retreated with a shudder and lunged at Maddock, who was poised and ready to shoot an arrow into its skull. The arrow pierced the animal's chest. Maddock dropped his bow and drew his sword just in time to block the set of teeth that nearly closed around his neck. I didn't see what happened after that; someone shoved me and I whipped around to find Anthony fending off a korak that had pounced at me. No longer stunned, I lurched forward to help Orrin, who was blocking a korak's teeth with only his arm while his sword lay out of reach. I stabbed the creature through the side of its head, and it slumped over. Orrin scrambled to pick up his sword.

I looked around. Some men had already received wounds and I saw a great deal of blood in the snow. I hoped little of it was ours, but it was difficult to tell.

A fresh surge of koraks emerged from the trees, their tensed muscles as frightful as their calculating, hungry eyes. Something about their configuration, about the sheer number of them, made this attack seem anything but random.

That's when it struck me: it wasn't random. The Alliance was the only force openly preparing for war with Tamarice. She wanted to silence us. So she had set a trap. The sporadic attacks had been a trick to draw us out, to make us think *we* were the hunters—to isolate us in the middle of the wilderness.

Arrows whizzed across the meadow, hitting two of the approaching cats between the eyes while the others sidestepped easily. I traced the arrows to Rook and noticed that he couldn't shoot swiftly enough to handle the new onset alone.

"Rook!" I cried. His eyes darted to mine while his hands moved mechanically. "I'm going to lead them away."

Rook nodded and adjusted his aim to cover me. Abandoning the scuffle, I staggered forward. It was almost laughable to hope I could outrun them, but I had to try. I sprinted through the snow between two koraks. Each lunged at me, but Rook sent an arrow through one of their throats and I buried my sword in the other's head. I left my weapon lodged in its skull and ran on desperately. I heard a cry behind me—a human cry, guttural—but I couldn't turn around. I had to lead them away.

I ran harder, occasionally hearing the whoosh of an arrow as it struck down the creatures at my heels. My battle strategy wasn't quite on par with one of Anthony's, but it was working. When I reached the cover of the wood, I whipped around to find eight or nine koraks strewn bloody across the meadow behind me. Three had survived to face me now.

I unveiled my elicrin stone. The glow made the cats shrink back, but their retreat didn't last long. They circled me, leaving faintly bloody tracks in the snow. One of their muzzles was striped with red—*which man's blood?* I asked myself in revulsion.

"*Matara liss.*" The nearest cat burst into flames, shrieking and dancing as it met its end. Sheer force of will kept the bile from rising in my throat. I had never performed that spell on a living creature, and my own power to kill frightened me. The other two snarled, baring their pointed, gleaming fangs that I could too easily imagine ripping through my flesh. I waited for the attack, but they exchanged throaty growls and tore off through the woods, their sinewy legs carrying them west— toward Galgeth.

I couldn't let Tamarice find out I was helping the Alliance. She would target them with even less mercy. I took off in pursuit.

But before I could take three strides after them, I heard a yell and whipped around. The sight that met my eyes terrified me more than anything I had encountered in my life: more than the Water, more than the koraks or even Tamarice herself. I would go to Galgeth and back happily if it meant I didn't have to see what I was seeing now.

Anthony lay heaped on the ground at the tree line, unmoving.

FOURTEEN

I stumbled forward and crashed to my knees beside him. There was so much blood. My hands were soon covered in it as they peeled back his tunic, trembling. I pressed my ear to the slippery, torn skin of his chest and found the faintest of heartbeats.

Choking back sobs, I examined an enormous bite on the left side of his chest, a messy one. The korak had sunk in its teeth and dragged him. The bite mark extended over his shoulder and ended near his collarbone, too near his neck for my comfort. I tore off my cloak and pressed it to the wound. Nearby, Weston grasped the fur of the animal's severed head. It seemed he had dragged the animal off of Anthony. He dropped it and raced to help me, lifting Anthony while I wrapped the cloak around him with shaking hands. I whispered a novice healing spell I knew would hardly help.

I felt Weston go still as he watched the light spread out from my pendant. Though unconscious from blood loss, Anthony moaned when we lifted him and laid him across Weston's cloak. I swallowed back more tears, willing

Anthony to live with silent, panicked pleas. *I love you*, I thought to him. *You can't die. I refuse to let you die.*

Whatever Weston wanted to say, assuming he was not too overwhelmed to speak at all, he held back. Getting Anthony warm took precedence, so he hurried off to gather wood for a fire while I tucked away my elicrin stone. The remaining koraks were dead and our men regrouped in the clearing around a motionless form, a friend whose life had been taken.

When the fire was warm and glowing, I melted snow and mixed it with wine to wash Anthony's wounds, whimpering faintly when I saw a flash of bone. I had silk thread and a needle in my pouch of herbs and set to work stitching the deep gashes, covering them in dry comfrey leaves. His skin felt cold and clammy, so we swaddled him in our cloaks and kept him close to the fire. With Weston watching over him, I allowed myself to leave Anthony's side and venture toward the desolate clearing, fearing what I would find.

Maddock sobbed silently over Rook's lifeless body, his face buried in his younger brother's chest and his blond hair stained dark with blood. Shoulders shaking, he pressed Rook's eyes closed.

Another sob caught in my throat. I almost collapsed to my knees, but other wounds needed swift attention.

They brought Rook to the fire and covered him with his cloak. "Bear our friend home to rest," Orrin said to the others. "Tell the king about the attack. Weston, Tomlin and I will stay with Anthony until he's able to make the journey." I saw in his eyes the same fearful thought in mine: *If he is able.*

We watched the group travel slowly out of sight as the western sky dimmed. Orrin and I skinned the deer carcasses and made a makeshift tent of skins and cloaks while Weston roasted the meat and watched over Anthony. When we were finished, I touched Anthony's forehead lightly, grimacing at the heat of his skin and the rapidity with which the blood had soaked through the leaves. I would need to change them soon.

When I went to gather firewood, I found myself on a hill facing west. Rage burned through me, searing and violent. I shook with it, my sweaty, ice-cold palm clutching my elicrin stone.

The words that had haunted me for years resonated inside me—her words, now mine.

"I will obliterate you," I growled into the night. "Every last trace. I will make dust of you."

※

When I returned, Orrin, Weston and I sat in silence. I opened the flap of the tent often to look in on Anthony and eventually crawled inside to change his leaves. Weston studied me through fresh eyes, but I cared little that he knew who I was. All that mattered was keeping Anthony alive.

He wrenched awake while I peeled off the bloody leaves. Hating his suffering, I soothed him until his eyes fluttered closed again. He woke once more when I lifted his shoulder to wrap it, and he was able to take a few sips of water from my pouch. After that, I left him to sleep.

"His fever is raging," I said as I reemerged. "But the bleeding's slowed. We have to find warmth and shelter soon."

Orrin ran a hand through his dark curls and over his bloodstained face, then went to gather more wood. Weston stoked the fire. I had been staring at the blood under my fingernails as I warmed my hands, but my eyes met his cautiously.

"What did I see earlier?"

Timidly, I crossed my arms beneath my cloak. "You saw an elicrin stone."

"You're the Clandestine," Weston breathed.

I studied Weston's massive form across the fire. My voice cracked when I finally muttered, "Yes."

"Anthony, he—this would change everything. Who else knows?"

"Elinor, Charles's betrothed. Cyril might have an idea. Nicolas knows I'm involved, but he doesn't know how."

Weston nodded, still mystified. "I'll always think of you as Tom," he said. But the encouraging look in his eyes couldn't quite reach through the fear and weariness.

We fell into silence. I knew I didn't have to ask Weston not to reveal my secret.

The next morning I noticed that the leaves Anthony wore overnight were not nearly as bloody as those he wore for an hour yesterday. I felt it when I touched his skin and his eyes flickered open briefly: he would survive.

Though he didn't see me in his delirium, I smiled at him, but my smile grew weak. Whenever he woke up, he would have to learn that Rook was dead. We would return to a broken brotherhood.

By afternoon Orrin suggested we move on. We crafted a litter out of branches and a cloak and shouldered Anthony's weight, walking carefully to prevent jarring him. It took us until nightfall just to reach the nearby town. For the first time, we used Anthony's princehood to make demands, and the first house we happened upon became our shelter for the night.

The owners put Weston and Orrin up in a barn loft while Anthony slept in a bedchamber with a hearth. I lay on a pallet on the floor to minister to him. Our hosts brought me stew, bread and fresh cloth, then left us in silence.

After cleansing his wound and applying a poultice, I sat before the fire, wearied beyond measure. Anthony groaned in his sleep. I did not envy him the pain he felt, but I would gladly have felt it in his place.

The fear of losing him was still fresh and raw. I had gone from aching for his attentions to silently begging him to stay alive, and it suddenly made me feel small and fragile. Losing him would have broken me.

I dropped my guise and raked my fingers through my silken strands of hair, touched the folds of the tunic that now hung loose on my slender body. Appearing in my true form near enough for Anthony to see was like unwrapping a grave wound and expecting the worst—only to find it wholly healed.

Walking to the far side of the bed, I knelt beside Anthony, touching the hardening bandage that staunched the blood on his chest and shoulder. My hand moved of its own accord softly over his neck and face. His eyelashes fluttered, but I didn't retreat. Instead, my fingers traveled over his feverish forehead and brushed back his brown hair. My own dark hair surrounded him as I leaned down and brought my lips against his.

I would have been satisfied with the kiss I gave him, but before I drew away I felt a light touch on my hair and felt his mouth open against mine. He may have been delirious, but when his lips parted and moved with my lips, I couldn't resist his answering kiss. The fire had burned itself down somewhat, leaving us in darkness, emboldening me. I laid my hand against the side of his face and kissed him more deeply, while his good hand traveled down from my hair to the small of my back and pressed me closer with surprising strength for the state he was in. He drew back, straining to see my face in the dark, but I closed the distance more surely, though still gently for fear I would hurt him. He propped his weight on his elbow, leaning further into our kiss and briefly making everything else in the world disappear but my desire for him. But this caused a groan of pain to emerge from his lips while they were still pressed against mine. I helped him ease back down.

"Sleep," I whispered.

I waited until his breaths were even and steady again before I went back to the fire, heart thundering long after he faded out of consciousness.

✳

The next morning I woke to the sound of low voices and found Anthony sitting up in bed, sipping broth. Weston sat in the chair beside him.

I blinked hard and stood up. "You look . . . well," I said.

Weston grinned. "Doesn't he? I was just telling him he'd be dead if not for you, Tom." His eyes caught mine in such a way as to make the name feel ironic.

"And this isn't the first time that's been true," Anthony laughed weakly. "That fever did strange things to me. My dreams felt so real. . . ." He shook his head. My heart lurched. "Are you the only ones here?"

"Orrin," I said, walking around the bed to examine his wounds. When I unwrapped the bandages, Anthony glanced down to appraise the damage.

"Lovely." He grimaced.

"It'll heal fine, as long as it's kept clean. You may lose a little sensation, but it won't be grave."

Anthony looked from Weston to me, the question he dreaded asking in his eyes. His voice was quiet. "And the others?"

Weston and I shared a glance. He cleared his throat and spoke first. "Rook is dead. The others are on their way back to Arna."

Anthony stared into some unknown distance. After a moment, I applied a new poultice and covered it with bandages. I knew it hurt him, but he was too distressed to wince as I tightened the wrappings.

He closed his eyes and muttered, "May light surround you. May goodness follow you wherever you go."

The Calgoranian blessing over the dead brought tears to my eyes. I swallowed hard. When I finished, Weston and I left him to rest.

Over the next few days, Anthony grew stronger and we began our journey to Arna. The others had surely reached the city by now to tell the king what had happened to his son—and that koraks from Galgeth were in his lands. How could he ignore that Calgoran and the other kingdoms faced trouble from the west?

Anthony was impatient to return, and I knew similar thoughts weighed on his mind. He wanted to buy a horse, but his face turned deathly pale after just a few jarring paces atop the saddle. We had to walk on.

I realized that if something could distract Tamarice and her servants, something that seemed like more of a threat to their plans than a growing band of ambitious soldiers, she might let the Realm Alliance be for now. Perhaps my friends could continue on their path unscathed, at least until they grew stronger.

As we journeyed on, my plan took shape. To protect Anthony and the others, I would leave and begin my own campaign against Tamarice for the first time. I would disassociate with the Realm Alliance. I would fight back so that she would have to focus on me, Bristal.

Tom would have to disappear.

*

When we reached the barracks, Anthony embraced Maddock fiercely with his good arm and spoke into his ear. Maddock nodded to whatever he said, eyes watering. My heart ached thinking of the times that Rook, Maddock and I had wandered off into the woods to hunt and discuss plants and remedies, or sat in one another's company fletching arrows. I forced down tears once more and turned away.

Rook's body had been cleaned, dressed and burned on a pyre, his ashes scattered in the wind. But we still lit a torch and gathered around as Anthony spoke eloquent words over our dead comrade.

"He remains our brother, even in death," he said. "And we know he lives on, where we can't follow him now. But we'll see him again in the land of light." Anthony closed his eyes and repeated the blessing over the dead. I felt a shiver travel down my spine, thinking of how the same words might have been said over him.

We drifted away from the heat, but Maddock stayed. I listened as he sang a sad and beautiful song of mourning. The wind carried his smooth voice over the crackling of the flames.

*

"We were so worried."

Queen Dara clung to Anthony, pressing her face into his neck, finding reprieve, as I had, from the anguishing possibility of losing him. She laid her hand on his cheek, her dark eyes straying to the sling across his shoulder and chest.

King Riskan entered and rushed to his youngest son. He gripped the back of Anthony's neck and touched their foreheads together. "My boy," he said, shaking. "My dear boy."

Anthony put his free arm on his father's shoulder. "Father, gather your ministers."

"You ought to rest. Whatever the matter is, it can wait until your condition has improved."

Anthony set his jaw. "While the kingdom's condition worsens? While monsters from Galgeth roam Calgoran and the elicromancer who sent them plans to take Nissera for her own?"

I knew Anthony's disposition well, but I had never seen this sort of fire in his eyes. Whatever passion he held for the truth before was now multiplied tenfold, heightened by grief over our lost friend and by the reality of our encounter with the koraks. Our enemies in the west could no longer be ignored.

Queen Dara's face paled. I knew this wasn't the first time she had seen tensions mounting between her husband and her youngest son.

King Riskan's features stiffened until he looked like a stone effigy. "Calgoran has greater concerns than a pack of wild animals. You dealt with the disturbance admirably, now let me deal with the real threat to Calgoran. My intelligence tells me that Volarre has initiated trade negotiations with Persipos to obtain their iron ore from across the Mizrah Sea. If Volarre no longer needs our iron, it no longer has any reason to give us wheat and grain."

Looking truly astounded, Anthony demanded, "Perispos and Volarre? Truly? You must realize you are a victim of false information. It makes no sense to trade iron ore across a sea when you have an ally next door with as many mines as it has mountains."

"What would you know?" He drew eye-to-eye with Anthony. Both men were so tall and so proud. "I honored our wager because it served my own purposes—I raised your men's earnings and will allow you to recruit from the other kingdoms with my blessing because the Realm Alliance is successful at policing my lands. Not for any other reason. I will continue to let you do as you please with your brigands. But don't think for one second I would trust you to make decisions for this kingdom, brash and insolent as you are."

Calmly, Anthony said, "You think you are above all counsel, whether it's that of the elicromancers or your own son, who would give his life for you. You're a fool, old man."

The air seemed leaden with his last words as he turned and walked away.

"You will not speak to your father that way, boy!" the king roared to Anthony's back.

Anthony carried his fury all the way to the barracks, but the commotion had so wearied him that by the time we arrived his features had contorted in a grimace. He poured brandy down his throat as I tightened his sling, gritting his teeth in pain. I longed to comfort him, but my hands went obediently about their task.

When I finished, I looked around at our grieving, discouraged men, chest tight with repressed tears. Maddock stared emptily into the distance, Rook's bow in hand. We had thought ourselves invincible, chasing adventure, valuing camaraderie and contest and ale. We had seen combat many times, but we hadn't yet seen battle—and our first taste was bitter. And if the tides didn't turn soon, the Alliance would be facing a war with Tamarice and her army alone.

Sleep finally saved me from my thoughts, only inasmuch as they did not invade my dreams.

The night's rest seemed to restore Anthony's health, and though the wound remained an unpleasant sight, he emerged from the barracks convalescent, bare-chested with Zeal in hand. It was warm enough in the east that the snows of the weeks before melted for a time, but the chill of winter still hung in the air. Anthony looked daft compared to the rest of us wearing wool like sensible people. He didn't wear a bandage even though the hastily stitched gashes across his chest and shoulder had barely begun to heal.

We were eating cold meat and bread for breakfast and sitting in relative quiet when he walked down the steps of the barracks to the center of the lawn.

"Orrin." He held Zeal out with his healthy arm.

"You must be mad." Orrin looked up from his reading. "You can't fight like that."

Anthony waited. Orrin sighed and laid his book down, reluctantly taking up Splendor. He ventured a few cautious strikes, but Anthony answered with speed and ferocity.

"Take it easy, Anthony," Weston cautioned when the din of clanking metal lulled momentarily. "Tom doesn't want to sew you up again."

Anthony parried even faster, holding his left arm across his middle to keep it out of the way.

Thundering hooves announced Charles's approach. Orrin and Anthony ceased sparring and waited for him to arrive.

The older prince dismounted and embraced his brother carefully. "I was so relieved to hear you returned alive and well." He examined Anthony's wound with a grimace. "At least, relatively well. You shouldn't be fighting in this condition, but I'm not surprised."

Anthony laughed wryly, pointing his sword at the weapon sheathed at Charles's side. "Cross blades with me, brother."

Charles made no move to accept Anthony's challenge. "We must speak of your conduct."

"Then speak." Anthony turned his back on him and splashed water on his face at the trough, ready to spar with Orrin once more.

Frustrated, Charles shrugged off his cloak and drew his sword, stepping in front of Orrin so that he and Anthony faced one another. "Your words with Father were unacceptable."

Anthony advanced first and they parried swiftly. I, of all people, knew he shouldn't have been exerting himself this way for another few weeks. But his face filled with color and his every strike proved stronger than the last.

"I only spoke the truth," he said.

They stood shoulder to shoulder, blades tangled, each grunting in their struggle to force the other to retreat. Charles said through gritted teeth, "I hope you plan to make amends for your words to the king. A son of Calgoran cannot act like this." He pushed hard and Anthony staggered back. "Your defiance has made you strong, but it has made you forget whose blood runs in your veins. You wear your authority with embarrassing flippancy—"

"Flippancy?" Anthony repeated, anger now evident in his tone. "What have these past few years of my life seemed to you? Do you think me a child looking for trouble?"

"I think you an ungrateful son of a good man." Charles's hard tone matched Anthony's. "Your heroism has salvaged your reputation, but if you speak that way to our father how can I trust you will respect me when I'm king? I cannot have a commander who stands against me."

Anthony drove Charles back, unleashing everything. He shoved his knee into Charles's stomach, then pounded the fist that gripped the hilt of the sword into the crook of his neck and shoulder. He disarmed Charles within seconds.

Anthony drew so close to his brother that their faces were nearly touching. Though his bare chest heaved, his voice retained its calm.

"Do you know why I disarmed you, Charles? You're stronger and quicker than I am. You always have been. You should have won."

Charles glared at Anthony, breathless.

"It's not real to you," Anthony went on. "War, destruction, the death of your brothers, the point of a sword. I won because I am afraid. Open your eyes."

Anthony turned his back on Charles, who left without retrieving his sword.

✳

Rosie's embrace eased my troubles like salve on a wound. She launched obligingly into a description of every moment spent with "Bay Sandborn." I listened, grateful not to focus on the worries plaguing me.

"He sent word he'll be journeying back this way again soon," she said with a glowing smile. Of course, Nicolas would be returning to Calgoran for Elinor and Charles's wedding. "Can you believe the news about the Lost Duchess?" she went on. "I've never heard of anything more romantic! If only the cursed princess came back and married Nicolas of Yorth, everything would be perfect."

Knowing this was far from true, I forced a smile. But it was encouraging that Calgoran and Volarre would tentatively put aside their prejudices for the occasion—an occasion that would mark my last day as Tom.

As I told Drell about our encounter with the koraks, she clamped her hand over her mouth and pulled me into a fierce embrace. I didn't try to hide how much Anthony nearly dying affected me. I was worn from hiding it.

I rested, too tired to even dream my haunting dreams. A glumness had engulfed me and I could tell Rosie thought I was acting strange.

Meanwhile, I worried about her too. Though she wasn't a timid girl, she had never faced darkness, and darkness was well on its way.

"Rosie, what are you afraid of?" I asked that evening.

She looked at me sideways. "I'm . . . I'm afraid of losing the people I love. I'm afraid of darkness in the woods, though I'm not sure why. I've never seen anything to fear. I'm afraid of my dreams. Sometimes when I wake, I can't breathe." She stared at the fire, the golden flames dancing in her round green eyes. "But I don't know what it is that frightens me. It's all just shadows and mist."

Leaning forward, I folded her delicate fingers in mine. "You've lived a very calm life. I don't think I've taught you about the world the way I should have. I always wanted to protect you from it. But it is full of peril. Can you promise me you'll be courageous if you have to be?"

Rosie furrowed her brow. She looked from the fire to me, her eyes retaining the light. "Yes, I promise."

Those three words were all I required. She may have been

curious, naïve, little more than a girl. But those flames in her eyes, they belonged to her father. And the willfulness in her voice belonged to me. As much as I had always tried to whole-heartedly assume the role of simple Amelia, I possessed intrinsic qualities that no guise could cover. In Rosie now I could see myself holding my elicrin stone by the firelight in Brack's den years ago:

Will you, in this moment, blindly commit to seeking the good of the world?

Yes, I will.

<hr />

With six servants assigned to Elinor's toilette on her wedding day, my assistance was hardly necessary. I sat on a silk cushion and ate cakes while she bathed in scented water and allowed lady's maids to tie her up in corsets and drape her in satin. They drew her hair back and adorned it with diamonds. Her flowing gown of silver and white made her as elegant and whimsical as a snowflake. When she looked in the mirror, her blue eyes caught mine.

"Catleen, what do you think?"

I joined her at the glass, staring back at my disguise. How long had it been since I had seen my own face? "I think the prince would have been a fool not to choose you."

During the warm and tearful reunion of Lucetta and her long-lost niece, I approached Errod. Aside from the gray hairs woven into his golden hair and beard, he had not aged much in the years since I had met him.

"King Riskan is convinced you've formed a trade agreement with Perispos and are planning to shut him out," I said in a low voice.

He looked down at me, his niece's friend of lower nobility, and raised his brows. "What do you know of this?"

It only took the sight of Rosamund's handkerchief with the embroidered *R* to turn him pallid. He reached out and took the silk from my hand, rubbing it softly between his fingers.

"Lady Bristal," he gasped, emotion welling in his stormy eyes. "How is she?"

"She's safe and happy. She knows nothing."

Errod smiled faintly and bittersweetly, but quickly hardened his brow. "Why would I pay to have iron ore shipped across the sea? I would only close trade with Calgoran if our alliance were broken." He shook his head. "Trust me, I'm no friend to Riskan. Part of me thinks he may be somewhat mad. Which is why I'm not going to provoke him, not when there's already so much at stake." He looked down at the handkerchief again, buried grief surfacing on his features. Come to think of it, he did look older.

"I counsel you to speak with Riskan," I said. "Dispel the rumor. Reaffirm your loyalty to the trade agreement and contribute respectable soldiers to the Realm Alliance. Unless Brack succeeds on his current mission, we will be facing war with Tamarice and the army she's forming in Galgeth. We need a unified force, and the Realm Alliance is where it starts."

Errod sighed and ran a hand over his blond beard. "And perhaps where it ends. I had hoped you'd defeated her for good."

"On the contrary, I've discovered lately that I . . . I may have forced her to become stronger."

Errod's face cleared as he returned the handkerchief without hesitance, closing away the tender part of himself. "I'll speak with Riskan before the wedding."

I bowed my head. "Thank you, Your Majesty."

Satisfied, I returned to Elinor's rooms smiling as though I had merely been kind enough to stand aside for her and her aunt's emotional reunion.

As Elinor and I waited to enter the receiving hall, I looked down at my gown. The vivid red material held a metallic sheen that made it appear gold in the light. I wondered if I would ever have a chance to sport anything so extravagant and lovely in my own form.

My heart raced when the doors opened. The last time I had taken part in a royal ceremony, I had left with broken bones, a child to care for and the echo of a threat I had never forgotten.

But the wedding was flawless. When he saw Elinor, Charles's deep blue eyes lit like the sun rising over the Mizrah. Garlands of white delphinium hung overhead, shielded from the winter snows in the palace greenhouses. Silver and glass ornaments glistened in the light of golden sconces.

Elinor had been willing to overlook the scandal of Lady Catleen's reputation in order to make me her witness. The brothers' last confrontation no doubt had left its mark, but it comforted me to see Anthony as Charles's witness. Every guest of note was present, as if there were no tensions within Nissera. Royalty of Calgoran, Volarre and Yorth feasted at the same table. Come spring, dozens of Yorth's highly trained warriors would be joining the Realm Alliance, and that was just the start. Errod would humble himself to speak to Riskan, and then begin contributing to the Realm Alliance as well. By summer, it could very well be a unified force at the command of one of the wisest leaders the realm had to offer: Anthony.

It struck me then that my plans had come to fruition.

But would it be enough?

I quickly learned the answer. The porcelain veneer of the blissful occasion began to crack ever so slightly as I overheard officials discussing a spreading disease in small west coast villages. I immediately thought of the blight that Brack had killed, of the people he couldn't save even with his powerful healing spell. Others spoke of unusual storms from the west ravaging coastal towns, of dark clouds clinging to the western horizon.

That Tamarice could rain such havoc from afar made panic return afresh. How much worse would it be when she set foot in Nissera again?

But I couldn't afford to dwell on how things would be, or what the mounting signs of trouble from Galgeth meant about the success of Brack's mission or, more importantly, his survival. I could only plan for now, and use the blights as an opportunity to step out on my own and lead Tamarice's attention away from the Alliance.

The semblance of a plan and my grim determination to carry it out helped suffocate the dread in my belly. But it wouldn't make leaving any easier.

Though Anthony's eyes caught mine once, for the remainder of the evening I vowed not to look at him. It was much easier to empty and refill my wine glass than to think about how leaving the Realm Alliance would mean leaving a home I had only just found.

As I migrated back to my seat with a third glass of wine, a hand caught mine gently. A voice spoke close to my ear. "Will you dance with me?"

Turning my head, I found Anthony and struggled not to gasp. My "yes" emerged as little more than a murmur. With my blood warming my face and neck, I allowed him to lead me past the long banquet tables while I stared at our clasped hands in disbelief. I admired the roughness of his palm and fingers, and how suitably they encompassed my slight hand. I followed him through the swelling crowd, realizing I had come to think of that hand and every other piece of him as though it belonged to me.

When we reached an open space on the floor, he faced me, wrapping his left arm around my waist and drawing so near that he had to tilt his chin down to look at me. I tried to compose myself as our gazes met and lingered.

"This is quite an occasion: my brother marrying a duchess of Volarre, the woman you were happy to see made queen above yourself. You have a rare stroke of selflessness, my lady."

He truly didn't know anything about Lady Catleen's reputation. "What of you?" I asked, recovering my wits, even though his closeness reminded me of the kiss he didn't know we had shared. "You risk your life to keep Nissera safe."

Anthony's face went dark as he thought of our lost brother. "And the lives of others."

With barely any use of his injured arm yet, Anthony lifted me with only one when the next steps required it, drawing me closer than was customary in order to accomplish this. As he lowered me, I slid against him before we took our proper stance once more. Many familiar courtiers flashed me envious or conspiratorial looks, puzzling over how I had graduated from court tease to Prince Anthony's confidante. A young woman whose husband I had once seduced for my own purposes bumped into me before offering a sardonic apology and a bow.

"I heard you were injured by koraks," I went on, ignoring her.

"That's one story," Anthony said. "The other is that they were wolves. The cold and exhaustion had us out of our wits. That's the rumor."

"That's outrageous," I said through gritted teeth before I checked myself. "You would know the difference."

Anthony tightened his gentle grasp on my fingers, grateful I wasn't one of the many who doubted him. "You spoke of 'dark times like these' when we first met. Did you truly mean the threat of a war between kingdoms? You hesitated before you answered."

He had been listening to me that closely? "No, Your Highness—"

"Anthony," he corrected.

"I spoke of war with Tamarice."

His smile was rueful. "You could become quite unpopular, saying such things. Take it from me. Sometimes I fear I am a fool as people say."

"Of course you aren't. Why would you say that?"

"I always believed when things got bad, the elicromancers would return. I watched one of my men die fighting koraks from Galgeth. Where were they then?"

His forthrightness took me off guard. I had never seen Anthony's faith shaken, and I didn't like it—especially as he seemed to be losing faith in me.

"Many say Brack journeyed to Galgeth to try to forestall the war," I offered.

"Then what of the Clandestine? Don't you wonder where she is? Why she will not help us? I've spent years believing she would show herself and prepare Nissera for war. A few hundred men is an improvement, but how many do we need? Five thousand? Ten thousand?"

I wished I were more deft at concealing the hurt in my voice. "Circumstances are often more complicated than they seem, Your Highness. No doubt she's working in the way she deems best."

"I see no evidence of her concern."

Angry tears pricked unwelcome behind my eyes. I stiffened in his grasp.

"I've offended you," he said softly, clearly surprised by the strength of my response. "Forgive me. Can we keep dancing? We'll talk of less significant matters. The snow is lovely, isn't it?" He glanced at the windows that stretched from floor to ceiling and eased me back against him. "I love snow."

"So do I," I said after a moment, melting in his grasp. "There's nothing like the sight of snow in the mountains."

"Have you been to the mountains?" he asked.

"Only for a short time, but I dream of them every day."

Anthony laughed. "See, we sound like any other pair of courtiers now."

"Then I may as well mention that Lord Goodenouthe looks like a gourd in his green and yellow jerkin."

He laughed again. " 'Lord Gourd-enouthe' does hold a certain charm."

I had to cover my mouth to stifle a loud laugh. Anthony twirled me with his right arm, his left pressed safely against his chest. Afterwards, our hands met, palms flat, and we drifted away from one another, circled around and returned. Before I realized what he was doing, Anthony gently turned my arm to study the jagged puncture scar on my forearm, which was exposed just beneath the edge of my sleeve.

"My lady," he said, concerned. Then his brow furrowed in recollection.

The wine had reached my head. I hadn't noticed my sleeve ruching up as we danced or the scar from Tamarice's trap shining in the light of the high chandeliers—the only mark on my body that could give me away.

Anthony had already recognized it, even if he didn't know where from or what it might mean yet.

I extricated myself and forced my way through the crowd, hiding behind one of the marble columns. I had been safe as long as he thought he was dancing with Catleen. But he had seen a part of me that didn't change with my guise.

I wiped away the fast-flooding tears. "Farewell, Anthony," I whispered.

Before I could change my appearance, Weston rounded the pillar and seized my arm. "Are you her?"

I nodded.

"You love him," he said wonderingly. The expression on my face was all the affirmation he required. He drew me close and pinned me against his hard chest. I accepted his embrace, wrapping my arms around his solid torso. "You ought to tell him you're the Clandestine."

I pulled back, distancing myself from his request. "I can't. It will undo all I have done for the Alliance and for the realm. Goodbye, Weston."

I turned to leave.

I would have no chance to say goodbye to my friends. They wouldn't know that the long looks and wounded smiles I had given them lately were my farewells—not until they discovered I was gone.

FIFTEEN

The child's hand slid from my grasp, dropping lifelessly onto the mattress. Her mother wailed with grief, a sound that tore my heart and echoed in the depths of my being. The rage within me made my breaths uneven as I closed the child's eyes and dabbed the black blood from a sore on her face. "May light surround you. . . ."

✳

"They can only get so clean, Aunt Amelia."

I jumped, nearly upending a vase of flowers as I emerged from my recent memories. Rosie's green eyes were fixed on me. With raw fingers, I swept back stray gray hairs and wrung out the ragged cloth I was using to scour pots. I tried to smile at her through the darkness on my face, but pretenses were harder lately. "That sounds lovely, dearest," I said, remembering that she had been talking about her plans for a modest wedding.

Responding to the attacks in the west the past few weeks had been a gruesome ordeal. I could kill the blight elicromancers without a shred of mercy, but the ravaging sickness they left behind was incorrigible.

I felt as though I had aged a hundred years in a matter of days. I had grown accustomed to the smell of death, to killing and destroying while wearing my true form as a challenge to Tamarice. I hoped she knew I was fighting back. I hoped my conquests had distracted her from the Alliance.

In moments of weakness, I looked at the tracker map I had used to find Anthony at Halfhand Square, brushing the mark that rested in Arna. After a few weeks, I had chosen not to look at it anymore. He would be safer now. No one would know that the Realm Alliance's recent steps forward had been facilitated by an elicromancer, and the contingent would continue growing.

In between handling the outbreaks and the arrival of more blights in the west, I channeled all of my energy into mindless tasks. I waited to see when Brack would return.

Every day, I resisted the urge to return to Arna, to tell Anthony I had been on and at his side all along. But my feelings conflicted so fiercely with my mission that a knot of agony began to build in my chest. Brack had always been clear about the cost I would pay to be an elicromancer. I knew wishing Anthony would love me in return could only end in sorrow. The price of my immortality pricked me like a needle every hour. When all was said and done, I might find myself in a familiar world with only unfamiliar people.

"Aunt Amelia," Rosie tapped me on the shoulder rather aggressively. Clearly she had been trying to get my attention. "I'm going into town. Is there anything you need me to buy?"

"No, thank you, dear," I said absentmindedly.

Rosie shook her head in curiosity at my mood as she clasped her cloak.

A few minutes after she left, a horse whinnied outside. I glanced out the windows to see chestnut hindquarters, but I couldn't see any farther. Perhaps it was the courier—but he had already come by this fortnight. A knock sounded at the door. I flung down the wet rag, as if I could be done with my thoughts along with the dishes, and answered the door.

As it creaked open, I gasped and reeled back. It took me a few long seconds of absorbing his every feature—the familiar scabbard with the familiar sword situated at his waist, the determined set of his brow over handsome features—to understand that it was truly he. The indecipherable expression in his eyes was the sole unfamiliar sight.

"Anthony," I breathed, too startled to pretend to be Amelia even though I still wore her skin and spoke in her voice.

"It is you, then." His green-hazel eyes locked on mine, unwavering. He took a step closer. "Part of me knew all along that you were more than you claimed to be."

I had forgotten how much I longed to trace my fingers along the strong line of his jaw, to press my lips against his charming smile.

He didn't smile now. His face remained unreadable. But being near him again was like breathing fresh air for the first time in a month, and the familiar wave of desire swept over me again.

"But I didn't know what that meant," he went on, taking another step. "I didn't know what it would mean to me. You see, that day that changed me forever—the day Tamarice cursed Rosamund—I held a gift for the princess: an amethyst elicrin stone that showed the truth. While every other guest watched a common fairy give a seventh blessing to the princess of Volarre, I saw something else, something that has stayed with me since. I saw a powerful, beautiful and courageous young woman, not near old enough to be laden with such responsibility. When she was hurt, I came close enough to hear the threats made against her, against all of Nissera." He had drawn close now, his gaze unfaltering. There was nowhere I could go to escape it. "This young woman became my hero. Then she lied her way into my confidences, became one of my dearest friends, saved my life and left me."

My heart wrenched. "I didn't want to lie, or leave. I was just doing what I had to. Will you forgive me, Anthony?"

Strange, how tall he seemed, and I so small. He drew near and lowered his voice to a whisper.

"Only if you tell me I wasn't dreaming when I felt that kiss."

I found it suddenly quite difficult to breathe. "What kiss?"

It was a pathetic attempt at deceit, and he cut me off straightaway. "After all your experience with pretense, I would think you a better liar than that."

I braced myself against his condemnation. "You don't understand. . . ."

"I understand perfectly. You've been at my side all this time. I was convinced you'd failed me, after I'd hoped to see you act all these years—after I'd grown to love the idea of you. But now I know you were my true friend even if you weren't in your true form. I wish more than anything to see that girl I saw years ago, but if you don't want to show her to me, I don't care. I've always somehow known I would love you if ever I had the chance, and I want the chance now."

With no words at my disposal, I shook my head again.

"Anthony, I can't let myself . . . If I do, I'll lose you. Age will take you from me, and—"

"Yes, I will die as all men do. And you will find it in your heart to love another."

"As if it's that simple?"

"It is that simple. You love me already." His eyes were intent on mine. "Show me who you are."

"No," I croaked. Each word tore away a piece of the armor that protected me from him.

He leaned down and pressed his lips against mine, so warm and passionate that I staggered back. For all that I had dreamed of this moment, I answered the movement of his lips half-heartedly, still hiding behind the guise in which I had grown so comfortable. He paused long before I wanted him to, pulling away to study the wrinkled face covering the one he wished to see. Closing his eyes, he laid his forehead against mine.

"Bristal. Show me."

My name emerged huskily, full of longing. I surrendered and let my guise fall like sand washing away in a tide. He looked at my eyes, my hair, my nose, my lips, each my very own, and released a fierce breath just before closing every bit of distance between us. The kiss swept through me and I clung to him, wrapping my arms around his neck, wishing I could pull him any closer.

"I've waited for you for so long," he whispered into my ear. "Why didn't you tell me who you were?"

"I was afraid you'd be angry with me, and I didn't want to lose you—any of you. And there were things I had to accomplish—"

"Charles and Elinor. Soldiers from Yorth and Volarre join-ing the Realm Alliance."

"How did you know about Elinor and Charles?" I asked, already missing the feel of his mouth against mine.

"Really, Lady Catleen? Did you think I was blind?" He interlocked our fingers and lifted my arm, brushing his other thumb over my jagged scar. The light touch of his fingers on the tender skin made a shiver run through me. "The scar, Tomlin's disappearances, you taking offense to my talk of how the Clandestine had abandoned us . . . When I pieced it together, it was as if I held the truth-revealing stone again. I was shaking up and down because I finally saw the truth. But then you were gone."

"I thought it easiest not to say goodbye."

"Not for me. I waited for you to come back. Weston seemed sure you'd return. When weeks passed and you still hadn't, he told me that Elinor and Nicolas knew too. Nicolas knew where Rosamund was and that you were watching over her. He resisted for a long while, but I can be persistent. You know that."

"Yes."

"You've protected the cursed princess, crowned the Lost Duchess and fought for the Alliance. Is there any identity you haven't assumed?"

"I've hardly assumed my own."

He smiled just before our lips met again. "That should be amended."

The voice in my head warning me to resist was utterly silenced. I found my hands moving from his strong shoulders and the curve of his neck to his face and into his hair. His breaths brushed fervently across my lips and filled my mouth.

The door creaked open. Changing back into Amelia, I

shoved Anthony away from me in time to see Rosie's mouth drop open and her green eyes grow round. "Aunt Amelia?"

Scrambling for words, I gestured at Anthony, but only managed to stammer. Rosie's gaze shot from him to me. Her struggle to comprehend the circumstance seemed almost painful as her eyes locked on Anthony and studied every inch of him. No doubt until this moment she believed Nicolas the only handsome man in the world, as she had never seen anyone like him before, but was gradually realizing her mistake.

She looked back at me, bewildered. And then she ran.

"Rosie!" I started after her.

Anthony caught my hand. "Shouldn't you tell her the truth?"

Watching her dash through the garden to the woods, I sighed. "I suppose it's time for that."

I dropped my guise. Anthony wore a tight-lipped smile, obviously trying not to laugh.

"You find this amusing?" I asked, driving my knuckles into his good shoulder.

"Oh, Tom, there you are," he said. "Honestly, the truth will likely be easier for her to swallow than the idea of her aunt being some kind of trollop." He tried but was unable to contain a grin.

"All right," I said, feeling as though I should regret the incident, but finding I was unable to. The lies had grown tiresome anyway. "I'll go talk to her."

"I'll be waiting."

I found Rosie sitting in the grass, elbows resting on her knees. When I circled around and stood in front of her, she gasped. She didn't know my face.

"It's me," I said. "I have a story to tell you."

"What?" Rosie's tearful eyes appraised me. "I don't understand. Who . . . what are you?"

"On the day you were born, the whole kingdom rejoiced. Thousands gathered to celebrate your name day. Your mother and father couldn't have been happier."

Rosie clamped a hand over her mouth as I went on. "You were given gifts from royalty and blessings from fairies, and you were betrothed to Nicolas of Yorth. And when an evil elicromancer came to curse you, someone stood in her way. She has watched over you ever since."

"You're Bristal," Rosie gasped. "You're an elicromancer. And I'm the princess." I nodded. She smiled, but horror soon overtook the eager joy on her face. "I'm cursed."

I opened my mouth to say something, anything that would encourage her. I had so much to explain—that her parents were still alive, that she was betrothed to Nicolas—but the darkness of her last utterance hung in the air. Before I could gather the right words, she stood up, eyes full of tears, and tore off into the woods. I decided to let her be.

As I hiked back to the cottage, the sight of Anthony sitting on the slope behind it tightened the knot of anticipation in my chest. He stood up as I hiked nearer. It felt strange to be in love with that wide-eyed little boy, the one who had seen me in my true form so many years ago. Though when I looked at him now—standing more than a head taller than me, broad shoulders marred by korak's teeth, possessing the kind of courage I couldn't muster even if I lived a hundred years—it didn't seem strange at all.

"How is she?" he asked.

"She just needs time. This isn't the way I always planned to explain everything, but I couldn't leave her to wonder what was happening just then. . . ." I allowed myself to laugh a little now, realizing how odd the kiss must have looked through her eyes.

He grinned at me. "You didn't really save me from cutthroats at Halfhand Square, did you?"

"No. I paid them to rough you up so I could rescue you and gain your trust."

Anthony laughed. "You're even craftier than I thought."

"Do you disapprove?"

"Quite the contrary."

We stood in silence for a moment as he studied my face. I broke our gaze and looked down.

"It's time to stop hiding, Bristal. My men—our men—need hope. Nissera needs someone to put faith in. I'm not enough."

Impulsively, I reached up to touch the jagged scar on his sternum and pulled the collar of his shirt aside to follow it across his chest and shoulder. The sunlight poured through his hazel eyes as he looked down at me and drew in a deep breath. I reached the end of the tender skin and pulled my hand away. "If I came back with you, Tamarice would have more of a reason to target you. And the realm would discredit the Alliance because no one trusts elicromancers."

"Tamarice is coming either way, Bristal. We're not afraid."

"But I'm afraid for you. I almost lost you. Do you know what that felt like?" I crossed my arms and looked away from him, staring into the sun. "I can't bear to lose any of you."

"The Alliance needs hope. Give people a chance to put faith in you."

I closed my eyes, wishing I didn't feel the ache of loss in my chest even though he was here with me now. Even if Brack hadn't strongly warned me against putting desires before duty, I knew better than to think Anthony and I could live happily together. Whether I lost him to war, a more appropriate suitor or old age, I would lose him all the same.

"No one has faith in elicromancers anymore," I said, somewhat coldly. It was so much more difficult to look him in the eye when I had nothing to hide behind. "I'm sorry, Anthony. Secretive work is what I do. If I reveal myself as your ally now, suspicions about me manipulating every king and lord would run rampant throughout the kingdom at the moment when my interference is most crucial—"

"Do you not understand how frightened people are? Since you left, more than a hundred civilians have joined the Alliance of their own volition. They need to hope that victory is possible—whether it's over disease or curses or battle itself." He stepped forward, cupping my face gently with his callused palm. "And I need to know you for who you really are."

I gently pushed his arm away. "You know I struggle to resist you. Please go. I'll return to fight alongside you when the time is right."

Anthony stared at me a moment longer with an opaque expression. "This is what you want? To put the mask back on?"

"What I want is unimportant."

"Or perhaps just not important enough." His dark brows knit a straight line, emphasizing the disillusionment in his eyes. Regret already sank heavy in my gut. But I had clung to my role for too long to let Anthony be the reason I stepped forward before it was necessary.

He stiffly bowed his head in acknowledgement of my decision. Heart aching, I watched him descend the hill, mount Arsinoe and ride out of sight.

I slumped into the grass and wrapped my arms around my knees, gazing at the sinking sun as it spilled across the summits of the distant hills. I wandered back down to the cottage, feeling about as full of life as a dry winter leaf.

When I walked in, I found Drell and Rosie sitting at the table in the kitchen.

"Truth always finds a way out, doesn't it?" Drell said. "Even if a Clandestine is involved."

I sank into a chair across from them. Drell and I wearing our true forms in front of Rosie felt bizarre, but it added to the feeling that the fragments of my life were suddenly reconciling into one whole. "Anthony all but begged me to come back to the Alliance with him."

"How could—I mean, why would you turn him down?" Rosie asked, her face reddening.

I glanced up at Rosie, surprised by her calm demeanor.

"Drell and I talked about . . . about how my situation isn't hopeless," she said. "I know I'll see my parents again, and that I'll get to marry Nicolas. And I know why you were never able to tell me who I was." A small smile lit her lightly freckled face. "I think you deserve all the happiness in the world for being so selfless all these years. Why won't you go with Anthony?"

I dropped my face into my hands and groaned. "For plenty of reasons, none of which satisfied him."

"Or you, for that matter," Drell said. I lifted my head to look at her. "I understand you're afraid. You want to protect these men from Tamarice. But you can't protect Nissera's sole united force from the danger it's uniting against. They need you on their side, not competing with them for her attentions."

She reached out for my hand. Reluctantly, I let her have it, knowing her wisdom would be hard to hear but would be wisdom all the same. "And I know that being yourself with Anthony will be frightening. But in guarding your secrets and refusing to come forward, are you doing what's right or what's simple?"

"I think I'm doing what terrifies me the least."

Drell smiled crookedly. "Hardly a code to live by."

I nodded, leaning back in my chair with a renewed sense of dignity. "You're right, as usual." I smiled. "Will you two get along without me?"

"We have been," said Rosie. "I'm not afraid. You're going to kill Tamarice and I'm going home. There's no other way it can be."

With a wan smile, I tugged on a strand of her thick hair. "No other way at all," I lied.

SIXTEEN

I paced nervously around Cyril's office at the barracks, nearly tipping over the same weapon stand for the third time. I raked my fingers nervously through my long, dark hair. *My* hair. Not Amelia's or Tomlin's or the court siren Catleen's.

Cyril was not surprised that Tomlin and I were one and the same. It had taken him a few weeks to figure out, but his biggest cue was that Tom appeared around the time that I stopped showing up to meet the commander, just after I had asked for advice on approximating the prince.

"Will they be angry?" I asked.

"Surely not," Cyril answered. "They're reasonable men."

I heard footsteps and a knock. Cyril went to open the door while I sucked in a deep breath.

Orrin, Weston and Maddock waited on the other side. Each looked me up and down, eyes clinging to the wintry blue elicrin stone between my breasts before landing on my face.

Orrin and Maddock bowed at the waist, their expressions full of wonder.

Weston, however, took a purposeful step forward and pulled me into a fierce embrace. "I knew you'd come back."

"You're the Clandestine," Orrin said, before snapping his cool, deep blue eyes to Weston in befuddlement. "Did you say 'come back'?"

"Orrin," I began as Weston released me and stood at my side. "Maddock. I asked Cyril to summon you because you are my dearest friends, and I've long owed you a truth I couldn't share."

"Dearest friends?" Orrin repeated skeptically.

"Tomlin is not the man I led you to believe he was. In fact, Tomlin is no man. I am he. I contrived the disguise to join the Alliance while continuing my secretive work."

Orrin's expression of surprise frosted over. Maddock's face clouded with confusion from his furrowed blond brows to his slackened jaw. "You're Tom?" he asked, his voice an octave higher than usual. "Tom is the Clandestine?"

I looked at Orrin, whose reaction hadn't changed.

"I know I misled you. But my friendship with each of you was true to the core. I would have revealed myself sooner, but I was orchestrating sensitive matters. I selfishly feared losing your trust and friendship."

None of them said anything or broke their formation. I continued nervously.

"If you feel manipulated, perhaps you are right. I manipulated you. But I also care deeply for each of you and would die for any one of you if it came to it—"

Maddock caused me to break off by striding forward and placing his hands on my shoulders. "I can only speak for myself, but I require no explanation," he said. "I only wish Rook were here to see this."

"As do I."

All of us turned back to Orrin.

"Does Anthony know?" he asked, his voice betraying no emotion.

"Yes. He came to find me days ago. He should be returning sometime today."

"He's waited for you a long time, you know."

I nodded.

Silence stretched on as Orrin gave me an unreadable look I had come to recognize as an Ermetarius signature in tense moments.

"Just . . . remind him you're the powerful one," he said eventually, a modest smile warming his austere expression. "Don't let him try to be the hero. We all know that's you."

I smiled and extended my arm for him to grasp. Orrin stepped forward and accepted the gesture.

"Let's go spread the word, shall we?" he asked. "The hidden elicromancer hides no more."

* * *

"Oh, Bristal you are so lovely," Elinor said as she entered my chamber at the palace. "Green truly suits you."

I glanced into the ornate mirror, surprised to see my own grayish eyes regarding me with a solemn stare and my dark hair plaited back, revealing every feature of the face I hadn't seen in so long.

"If only enduring a tight bodice were all it took to survive this evening," I said grimly.

"The king is a harsh man, but a good one. He's been in better spirits since mending ties with Volarre. I'm sure you have nothing to worry about."

Elinor poured us tea. One of the maidservants twitched as though uneasy about allowing the future queen to pour her own refreshment, but Elinor didn't appear to notice.

I accepted my cup with thanks and sipped lightly, finding it soothed me a little. "Riskan isn't likely to take my words to heart, since I am an elicromancer and a woman."

"You and I, we appear delicate." Elinor smiled. "But we're not, are we?" She stared at her hands. Her calluses had faded by now. "I miss hard work. Charles won't allow me to lift a finger, but he'll learn soon. Last week I went to Halfhand Square on my own merely to prove to him that I don't need an escort to go only as far as the market. He seems determined to think me fragile."

"Well, that's something I've never had to endure," I laughed. "It doesn't sound all bad though."

"Oh, it's not, please believe me," she said. "I love him so dearly. He's terribly good to me, and he'll learn to understand me in time. Maybe once I birth a few sons he won't treat me like a glass figurine." Elinor eyed me sidelong. "I saw you and Anthony at the wedding." At my nonplussed reaction, she chuckled. "His fondness for Lady Catleen was a shock to everyone."

"She is quite the scandal."

She laughed. "Not just that. He's sociable enough with women—he's polite, at least, and looks at them the way any man would—but Queen Dara feared it would be years before he returned to court and considered taking a wife. Seeing him with Catleen gave her hope, even if she disapproved."

"I doubt he'll ever return to court, regardless," I said, though perhaps I only hoped that. His taking a wife had long been a sore subject in my thoughts.

Elinor sipped her tea. "I should like it if we were sisters."

"We will have to call ourselves sisters regardless. Neither Anthony or I are the marrying sort."

"What sort are you?" Elinor asked.

"The sort that fulfills their duties no matter what the cost, and tries to spare themselves the pain of loss in the process."

Elinor's face fell slightly. She traced the pattern of gold thread on her blue skirts.

"Still, the way he kissed me . . ." I said without thinking.

Elinor looked up. "He kissed you, and then he said he wasn't the marrying sort?"

"Well, no," I admitted. "Then he asked me to come back to the Alliance with him."

She laughed like pealing bells, but changed the subject. "Why does King Riskan distrust all elicromancers? It seems to me you and Brack have only ever done good for Nissera."

"He thinks elicromancers create as much trouble as we solve, which is true." And either of us was powerful enough to crush him with a thumb should we desire, a quality few kings would be fond of.

Someone knocked and one of the servants answered. Orrin stood in corridor, waiting to escort us to the dining hall.

"Good evening, my ladies," he said. "Elinor, may I have a word with Bristal?"

"Of course." Elinor grabbed up her skirts and departed in the direction of the dining hall.

Orrin shut the door. "You shouldn't expose everything you know to Riskan," he said, blue eyes intent. "Don't say anything an intelligent woman with an interest in politics wouldn't know."

"But if I try to discuss war without revealing what I know, he'll think me ill-informed."

"Better ill-informed than conniving. You think he'll trust this renewed peace with Volarre if he knows it was encouraged by an elicromancer who changes forms and has posed as his emissary? Who was an acquaintance of his wife, a friend of his commander and influenced not only his allies, but his own sons?"

I sighed in frustration. "You're right, as usual. I cannot betray my position if I have any hope of having influence at all, although that prospect is looking bleak."

Orrin gave me a doubtful smile. "You, on the other hand, are looking beautiful. Much lovelier than Tom would look in that gown, I daresay."

"I arrive and suddenly you're so disapproving of Tom. I'm tempted to think you never liked him to begin with."

"On the contrary, I miss him, strange as that may sound. I'm merely skeptical of his feminine graces. Which means you played your part well, doesn't it?"

"You'll notice I don't have many to speak of either after spending months with you lot." I gripped his shoulder. "I'm still your friend. You know that, don't you, Orrin? On more occasions than you might think, I wasn't pretending."

"Yes, of course I know. It'll just take some time for us to

grasp the thought of losing one friend and gaining another." He patted my hand. "At least if you're going to seem vapid, you may as well look beautiful."

I snorted. "And thus I'm reintroduced into courtly life at Arna."

Orrin laughed and offered me his arm.

Elinor and Charles waited in the dining hall. Recalling the charm with which I carried myself as a courtier, I curtsied to each of them and waited for them to take their places again before I sat. When the doors opened, I forced a serene expression as I stood and curtsied to the king and queen.

"And here I was under the impression my son and nephew only kept company with ruffians," King Riskan said in his robust voice, looking me up and down from beneath rigid dark brows. "You're no ruffian, are you?"

"You might be surprised, Your Majesty." I said this in earnest, but the king and queen interpreted this as a clever joke. I must have looked as genteel as Orrin and Elinor claimed, if my comment could pass for one.

When Anthony entered and his gaze landed on me, he smiled—at first appreciatively, and then crookedly. Perhaps it was an ill-timed thought of me snoring across the barracks, or of curses flowing unchecked from my mouth as we rode side by side on a particularly cold and rainy day of travel. "Good evening, Lady Bristal," he said.

"Good evening, Your Highness." I said, almost facetiously, and we both smiled. Riskan, Dara and Charles gave us curious looks.

We sat down to dine on poached salmon, and with a few sips of wine my nerves eased. Anthony's hazel eyes glanced my way often, and not at all discreetly. I grew gradually more at ease under his admiring gaze.

"My son has made it clear he intends to marry you," Riskan said to me, his voice expressionless as ever. I felt my cheeks and neck grow hot as I turned to Anthony, heart pounding.

Anthony nearly choked on his salmon. "Father . . ." he began, but Riskan waved his hand to silence him.

"While I admit I would never voluntarily accept an elicromancer into my family, my youngest son has proven himself as hardheaded as I am, and I have always promised my boys they would wed women of their choosing. I thought it may prevent them from acting like the kings of old days, spreading their seed and fathering royal bastards from here to Perispos."

Greatly taken aback by this turn in the conversation, I worked to recover my wits while Anthony reined in a laugh. "That's quite wise, Your Majesty," I managed quickly enough. "Such recreation makes for messy bloodlines and even messier wars."

"Clever young woman," Riskan said as he took a sip of wine. "Ought I to be wary of this one, nephew, as I am of the old man?"

Orrin winked at me. "Not at all, Uncle. I can say with certainty that she has Anthony's best interests at heart."

"Ah, so you are interested in tarnishing the Ermetarius name with your talk of make-believe war? That is Anthony's chief interest."

"Father . . ." Charles began.

"What of your father and mother, Lady Bristal?" the queen asked, attempting to lead us down a smoother path. "Could they perhaps travel to Arna for a visit?"

"I'm an orphan, Your Majesty," I explained. "I didn't even know the common tongue when a village woman in Popplewell found me wandering alone as a child."

"I'm sorry to hear that," Queen Dara said softly.

I looked in King Riskan's eyes and saw what I expected: not only was I an elicromancer, but an elicromancer from Volarre, and a bastard at that—not at all the woman he would have chosen for his son. But I wasn't here to win them over for my own benefit.

"Don't be, Your Majesty," I said, glancing from Riskan to Dara. "Both my childhood guardian and Brack took care of me and taught me well. I was loved and never ill-treated."

"Perhaps they can come to the wedding?" Dara asked.

Anthony and I met one another's eyes. "Actually, Mother, Bristal hasn't agreed to marry me—in fact, I haven't asked her yet—so you can imagine how this conversation puts her ill at ease."

The queen looked horrified. "How dreadful of us!"

"It's all right, Your Majesty," I amended. "There are more pressing matters at hand."

"With you elicromancers, there are always pressing matters," Riskan said. "If Brack had found himself a wife to share his lonely mountain, perhaps he would not have meddled so inappropriately in the affairs of kings. Although I have not seen him in years." Riskan chuckled. "Perhaps the other elicromancers have done away with one other, leaving only you."

"He's in Galgeth," I said coldly.

"Galgeth?" Riskan raised his brows in mockery and turned to Anthony. "The source of this war I've so often been warned of lately?"

"Must we do this, my love?" Dara asked. "Bristal, what of you? What is your duty as an elicromancer?"

I could feel Orrin giving me a long look. "I've been protecting Princess Rosamund of Volarre, Your Majesty."

Queen Dara smiled, happy to have recovered the conversation. "Hers was such a tragic story. I'm happy to know she has been well looked after."

I fixed Riskan's gaze. "Your Majesty, I know you find it difficult to believe in the danger of something you cannot see. But Tamarice swore to me that she would destroy Nissera. I have killed many of her servants in the past months—soulless former elicromancers from Galgeth who are spreading sickness in the west. Your son and nephew were nearly murdered by koraks, and I imagine much worse awaits us still. Focusing on the Realm Alliance, giving us more resources, more credit, more soldiers, would—"

"Enough!" Riskan's tone was severe. "You're no different from Brack, and your counsel is as unwelcome as his. You are clearly lovely, sharp and suitably defiant for my son's taste. If he wishes to marry you, that is his business. But the politics of kingdoms are best left to kings. I will hear no more."

"Don't speak to her like that," Anthony growled. "She's knowledgeable in Nissera's affairs and has only ever served the realm." He looked at me, inviting me to expound on his claim.

But all I said, in a somber, quiet voice, was, "Please, King Riskan. Don't shut your eyes, or you will find yourself rudely awakened from your stupor."

I took the liberty of excusing myself after that, leaving a heavy silence in my wake. Anthony's fierce footsteps cut through the quiet as he pursued me.

"Whatever happened to that Catleen girl?" I heard Riskan ask as I disappeared down the corridor.

"Why didn't you tell him everything you've done for Nissera?" Anthony demanded when he caught up to me.

"He wouldn't have seen it as a service. Your father would think himself a pawn in Brack's game if he knew everything I've done. It's much better that he think me insolent and foolish than deceptive. At least then he can stew over my warning rather than denounce it without qualm."

"I just thought—"

"That the two of us together could make him see reason? That at my command he would march his army west to wait for war?" I squeezed Anthony's arm. "There was never any hope that I could influence Riskan, which is why I sought you out instead. I hoped you wouldn't have the stiff neck of your father." Anthony stared intently at the ground, but I tilted his chin until he met my eyes. "You do have his stiff neck, but thankfully it's turned in the right direction."

The hard look in his eyes softened. He took my hand from underneath his chin and held it to his chest. We stood like that for a time until he said, "Let's walk in the gardens."

When we reached the cool night air, he seemed to relax. "I'm sorry about how my father treated you," he said as he ducked under a weeping willow whose branches crossed the garden path. "And I'm sorry you had to discover my intentions that way. I wasn't going to ask you right away. I just always imagined my life with you, ever since I saw you save the princess that day."

"You have?"

"The image of you stayed etched in my mind, a creature

of myth come to life. I admired you for your heroism, but it wasn't until my governess told me that elicromancers don't age that I realized there was hope for me. . . ." He chuckled. "Of course, it still seemed foolish to hope you would return my affections." His smile faded and he stopped to face me as we crossed the bridge over the river. "I know my proposal seems untimely, but please consider it. You're afraid to lose me, but if we're not together, we will have lost one another all the same. If you want to keep yourself hidden from the world—if that's the problem—you can be Lady Catleen, or Tom around our friends for all I mind. Well, perhaps not Tom. But whenever we're alone, I just want you." He searched my eyes. "We'll do everything we can to stop Tamarice together. Please say yes."

"Anthony, I—I want to more than anything." His answering smile was so joyful I nearly forgot my next words. Holding fast to the balustrade, I could only hope he wouldn't kiss me again, or I would forget myself entirely. "But I can't."

His voice was no more than a rough whisper as he stepped closer to me. "Why not?" He tried to read the reason in my eyes and misjudged. "Is it . . . is it because of Brack? Do you love him?"

"Not in the way you mean."

"Then what is it?"

A yes to his request built up inside me, full of joy and abandon. He had given me company when I was lonely, accepted me when I felt that the real me didn't truly belong anywhere. The Alliance was more my home than anywhere had ever been.

We were so much the same, Anthony and I. We were both just kindling for the flames of our convictions. But we each possessed a spark of selfishness. Otherwise we wouldn't speak of love and marriage in days of approaching war. Just as I had rushed to him when he was hurt, forgetting the koraks that escaped with my secret, I would forget everything else and fold into him for as long as he lived. It was precisely the reason Brack had never permitted himself to love.

If I allowed myself to put everything else aside and love Anthony freely, nothing could ever make me leave his side. That was the most frightening possibility of all.

I closed my eyes, retreating deep into my memories. "Well, it is because of Brack, actually. He warned me, Anthony. He warned me that I would make sacrifices, just as he has. He told me that I would be lonely, that I would often wish I were never brought to the Water. He's in *Galgeth*, and here I am speaking of marrying you." I swallowed hard and opened my eyes, my chest hollow with regret. "I made a commitment to the good of this world at any cost. How can I make a commitment to you when I've already promised all of myself?"

His calm gaze burned me up for a long moment. "I understand," he said eventually. Brushing back my hair, he tried and failed to give me an encouraging smile. My heart fluttered traitorously. "If I must treat you differently, please don't be angry with me. It's the only way I can bear it."

He kissed my hand and walked away. But before he reached the end of the bridge, he turned back and said, "Thank you for having the courage to return with me."

When he was gone, I let out the sob I had been choking back, thinking I might have preferred Galgeth to this.

<hr/>

The next afternoon brought with it an unfortunate turn of events. One of Riskan's spies had returned from the east to tell him that Perispos was readying a fleet of war galleys to cross the Mizrah Sea and attack Calgoran.

Anthony, Weston, Orrin and I were gathered in Cyril's office, leaning over his desk to study the spy's rude sketches of the fleet poised off the coast of Perispos.

"My father is being misled," Anthony said. "I would bet a thousand aurions it's the same informant who convinced him Volarre planned to shut off trade with us. Why would he believe him again?"

Cyril's face was drawn as he studied the sketch. "Let's hope it *is* false information. With this many ships, the first wave would number a couple thousand men strong."

Weston leaned over the sketch. "I know these shores. My father was a sea merchant and when he was short of hands I'd go with him on voyages to Perispos." He brushed a spot on the map. "There shouldn't be any ships here. There are miles of sea stacks off this side of the bay, and depending on the conditions they can be unnavigable even for smaller boats." His tapped the desk furiously. "There is no way these ships could be positioned as they're shown here. Maybe we can use that to persuade the king that his intelligence is false."

"Cyril, do you know anything about the man my father hired?" Anthony asked. "We need everything in our arsenal to convince him he's a fraud."

Cyril scratched his bronze beard. "He is stealthy and goes by an alias, but I did some digging. Trumble is his name. I didn't find out much else."

I gasped.

"What is it?" Anthony asked.

"Trumble," I repeated. "Is he from Popplewell?"

"His accent is Volarian, but beyond that I know nothing," Cyril said. "You know him?"

"He kidnapped me when I was a mortal. He forced me into the Water at knifepoint."

"Then we have an even better case against him," Cyril said. "But the king is no more likely to trust an elicromancer than he is a traitor."

"Riskan doesn't trust me," I agreed. "But there are other kings who do."

"Will it divide Nissera again, if Volarre and Yorth come to our aid instead of Riskan's?" Weston asked. "Errod and Riskan have barely begun playing nice."

"Better Nissera be divided than focus all of its attentions in the east," said Anthony.

"We should go to the king now," Weston said. "Expose Trumble as a traitor to the crown."

"I'm to attend a war council with the king and his ministers tomorrow to determine our next action," Cyril went on. "We must bring Trumble before him to confess. King Riskan speaks of imaginary wars; he'll find himself in the midst of one soon enough. Boys, what say you hunt him down? Bristal, I think you should make for Pontaval and Beyrian in the morning. News of the Clandestine's reappearance is already spreading. Let's see if the other kings of Nissera trust you enough to hold their ground if Riskan attempts to pull their armies east to his defense."

I nodded. My eyes shot to Anthony of their own volition, but he didn't meet my gaze.

As the four of us left Cyril's office, a voice prodded my thoughts.

I'm on my way back.

I took in a deep breath and froze while the others walked on.

Brack. He was still alive.

Meet me at the base of Mount Forlath on the western shore. Come now.

✳

The freezing wind thrashed over the cliffs and raged through my hair. I had to bow my head and surge forward to get near enough to the edge to see the shoreline down below.

My vision stretched to the far reaches of the western sea, where the water was bleak and still.

I sat on the rocks and wrapped my cloak around my shoulders as I waited. This same sea in a matter of days might carry vile creatures I feared to imagine. The sea would bear to us our destruction, the end of everything—unless Brack had succeeded.

"You turned out a pretty one, didn't you?"

The chilling voice came from behind me. I turned, not knowing whose face I would see.

Gray hair and deepened lines on his hard face didn't make him any less recognizable. I would remember his calculating, cold blue eyes for all the long years I had left to live.

"Trumble," I gasped. "How did you . . . ?"

Realization dawned. Somehow, I had been lured here. Brack wasn't coming.

He wore a knowing smile. "You look little more than a girl. How many years have you now? Time is kind to you." He took a step closer, and I curled my fingers around my elicrin stone. "Not to us," he went on. "We die a little every day, doesn't matter who. Kings, peasants, princes of Calgoran. We all end up food for worms. But not you."

"You've been feeding Riskan lies. You serve Tamarice."

Trumble spit. "I serve myself, as she serves herself. We don't shun the shedding of blood in the scramble for victory. Which is why I'm to visit a few of your friends when I've finished my business here."

Rage imbued my body, but I kept my voice calm. "I won't let you touch them."

Trumble crossed his arms, making his muscles swell like full wineskins. "I'm carrying a bit of borrowed power. Did you know about that enchantment? It takes only a few drops of elicromancer blood as sacrifice."

"I find it unlikely that Tamarice lent you a portion of her power."

"Then there must be someone else at her disposal, some other elicromancer who wandered right into Galgeth, someone whose gift could allow one to manipulate the mind of a stubborn king. . . ."

"*Nagak,*" I growled, thrusting his large body back on the rocks in a sudden charge of light. I knelt over him, seizing the collar of his shirt. "You spoke in my thoughts, didn't you? Where's Brack?"

There was another flash of light, but this time I was the one reeling through the air. I landed hard, my shoulders and head hanging off the cliff. The world spun as I sat up and saw Trumble pacing slowly forward, Brack's elicrin stone swinging on its chain around his finger. I scrambled to my feet.

"You made locating the princess rather difficult," he said.

"But alas, she must have found out the truth of her origins—she went to Pontaval to take her place as royalty."

Guilt and horror churned in my chest. How could I have been so stupid? "What did you do to her?"

"I let her reunite with her mother and father. I allowed her to wear her new finery and explore her home. And then I performed a death curse on her with my borrowed power. Tamarice wanted to take from you as you took from her."

The sound that rent from my throat revealed my transition from human to animal. Without knowing what sort of beast I became, I pinned Trumble down with my claws, hungering to tear out his throat. But without warning, the chain of my pendant snapped violently from my neck. My elicrin stone struck the rocks and scraped across the ground toward the cliff, moving on its own.

"Best run and get it," he said coolly.

Barely able to breathe through my rage, I dropped my guise and scrambled for my stone. He took the opportunity to grab a fistful of my hair and crash my head against the rocks. Vision bleary and head pounding, I crawled on my hands and knees. He landed a brutal kick to my side and I collapsed.

"I'd prefer to do this the straightforward way," he said. "No magic."

He lifted me by the neck with one arm. My head spun and I saw three pairs of steel blue eyes rather than one.

"Aye, we'll do this the simple way. I'm going to drop your elicrin stone in the sea, and then I'm going to leave you here bleeding while I kill everyone you know. The princess is as good as dead, but there's still the Lost Duchess, your friends in the Realm Alliance—"

I jammed my fingers into his mouth, choking him and forcing him to drop me. I yanked his head down as I went so that I could strike his face full-force with my knee. As he stumbled, I dove for my stone and grabbed it up. He recovered and charged toward me, but my next spell left him sprawled near the edge of the cliff. The gray water churned below us as I approached him.

"You said 'as good as dead,' " I growled. "Is Rosamund still alive? Tell me."

Trumble said nothing. I dropped my knee on his chest. "Let me put it the way you did once," I whispered with relish. "You have a better chance of living by falling into that water than by disobeying me."

He extended his hand so that Brack's elicrin stone hung over the sea. "Kill me," he spat. "And lose the source of Brack's power that you hope to restore to him when he returns . . . if he returns."

"Give it to me, or I'll slit your throat."

Trumble laughed humorlessly. "Somehow I doubt that. But go on. Just remember I'm the one who had the courage to throw you in. I'm the one who made you what you are. I smelled fear on you that day, and I smell it now. Let me up," he said. "Or I'll drop it."

I held his eyes for a few long seconds before releasing him and backing up a step.

"Poor choice, as Brack is dying outside the gates of Galgeth as we speak. He won't be needing that."

A roar left my lips and I reeled back the hand that held my stone, landing a merciless blow to his face. His nose cracked and he slumped backwards. I reached for Brack's pendant just before Trumble released it and slid off the edge of the cliff, his body striking the rocks before slinking, lifeless, into the tumultuous waves.

Still pulsing with rage, I barely noticed the wounds beginning to throb all over my body or Brack's stone singeing my fingers. For as long as it burned me, there was still life in him. I tore off the broken silver that had left a raw stripe on my nape and slipped my pendant next to Brack's on his chain. I didn't know whether Trumble's last words were a trap or some kind of message. But I *would* put Brack's elicrin stone back in his hands.

✦

I materialized to Pontaval. From the woods just outside the hilly royal city, briars rose up around the palace like a dense forest, casting ragged shadows over the empty streets. The tangles of thorns looked as impenetrable as a wall, the thorns themselves as sharp as spindles on a spinning wheel.

"*Umrac korat,*" I hissed. My spell cut away at the frontage of briars, opening up a narrow passage for me. But as I passed through, repeating the spell as I went, the thorns began to grow back even thicker—faster than I could perform the spell. They tore mercilessly into my flesh, forcing me back outside the bulwark. I tried materializing into the palace, but slammed into a protective barrier and fell flat on my back. I scoured the perimeter and found not a single vulnerability.

The princess is as good as dead.

I clung to these words, twisted them into something like a promise until hope throbbed within me. It was possible, in spite of Trumble's death curse, that Rosie and the nobles were still alive. Perhaps my shield from years ago had protected

Rosie in some way. Perhaps my beginner's defense, the one Tamarice bent but did not break to reach Rosie, had been enough to mute the effects of dark curses, to keep her alive somehow. . . .

I couldn't save both Brack and Rosie on my own. I needed Drell and Kimber. I needed the Realm Alliance.

I materialized and hit the ground at Plum Valley at a run. If Rosie had run off long enough ago to make her reappearance at Pontaval, Drell had probably gone after her and attempted to send me word. Clearly none of the news of the princess returning or her curse had reached Arna yet. And what I had been doing? Admiring Anthony, considering marriage like an ignorant fool.

In the afternoon sunlight I noticed that bushes at the far edge of our property had been trampled. I ran to investigate and found dark stains in the grass. Cursing through a sudden wellspring of tears, I followed the trail, stomach churning as the smears grew thicker rather than thinner the closer I got to our door. My mind and heart seemed suddenly submerged beneath the surface of a black wave as I opened the door, knowing I could never be prepared for what I would find.

But it was Kimber I found sitting in the kitchen.

She stood up from the table. "Bristal," she said, her voice much meeker than I remembered. Her long gray hair had thinned and whitened. She looked so frail.

"What happened?"

The old woman strode forward and wrapped her arms around me. "Drell was attacked. She's alive and resting in your room."

"Koraks?"

She shook her head. "Wolves. One of her spies found her wounded and sent word. Let me tend to your wounds while I explain. We need you at your best."

Ushering me into a chair, she reached for healing supplies that lay at the other end of the table.

"I'm sorry, did you say one of her spies?" I asked as she began massaging salve into the cuts on my face and the burn on my hand.

"You think Tamarice has eyes everywhere? Drell has more. From Beyrian to Darmeska, Mizrah to Marav."

"How bad is she wounded?"

Kimber's expression was so dispirited I could hardly bare it. She pressed her lips together until they turned whitish. "She will survive, but she has a life of pain in store for her. She may not be able to walk for months."

"Is anyone I love safe?" I whispered. "Brack may be dying at the gates of Galgeth, thanks to Tamarice. I can't just leave him there. And Rosie . . . I don't know whether she's dead or alive or in pain—"

"Bristal."

"I should have been here, not Drell. I could have caught Rosie before she went back. I would have been the one to get attacked, not Drell."

"My dear, listen," Kimber insisted. "Protecting Rosamund Lorenthi was honorable, but not your only task. Even all of the nobles in Volarre do not weigh up against an entire realm in peril."

"But how do I save them, Kimber?"

Her pale blue eyes fastened onto mine. The resolve in them

failed to steady my heart. "You may not be able to. But you still have to win this war."

I shook my head. "That's not the answer. No, you're supposed to tell me how to reach the gates of Galgeth and tell me it's possible to save them both and—"

"You can't retrieve Brack. If we lose you, we'll have nothing." Kimber finished with the salve and laid her hand over my wrist. "He forbade me to tell you how to reach the gates. Besides, this could be a trap. Tamarice is trying to lure you there. As for Rosie, I suppose we will know her fate by the state of the country's nobles. If they are alive, then she must be."

I clenched my hands into fists. "But what if it's not a trap? I just let him die there? What if I could give him back his elicrin stone, and he could heal himself and help us? You know I'm not strong enough to lead Nissera against Tamarice on my own. Tell me how to reach the gates of Galgeth."

Kimber took a deep breath and closed her eyes. I waited, heart thudding in the silence.

"It's not a long journey, as Brack led you to believe—he didn't want you to come after him. You must simply submerge yourself in the Marav Sea. The gates will appear before you. Any immortal with death on their hands can enter the gates."

"Thank you." I pushed back my chair and clasped her hand. "I *will* return. I'm not like Brack—I'm not afraid to make promises."

Kimber's shoulders dropped. Her pale eyes seem to stare through mine rather than into them. "All right. But you must know something first. Your power will mute as you approach

Galgeth. Your elicrin stone will be useless, and time will slow. Days or months could pass here in the time to takes to retrieve him."

In my haste to rescue Brack, I had shoved this information from my mind as though it were of little consequence. But it sank in now, adding to the pressure of tears on my chest to which I would later surrender.

"At least war will not come from Galgeth without me knowing," I said quietly.

Kimber stood up and filled a sack with food, water and a salve. "Here. Leave this on the shore. Just in case. Enter at the base of Mount Forlath so we know where to watch for you."

I nodded, enlivened by the idea that Kimber believed our return possible. "Tell Drell I'm—"

"Tell her yourself when you return."

She embraced me. I cringed as I rested my chin on her frail shoulder, wondering how long from now that might be.

There was no time to say goodbye to Anthony, and I couldn't bear the thought.

Shouldering the pack Kimber gave me, I took a deep breath and materialized to the shore.

Part Three

SEVENTEEN

*B*efore me lay the empty Marav Sea. There was little strange about it now, though I knew the gates lay ahead, unseen. Except for the Brazor Mountains at my back, it could have just as easily been the Mizrah Sea, with Perispos waiting on the other side.

My limbs shook as I dropped the pack on the rocks, past where the tide might reach it. As the sea spray misted across my face, I closed my eyes and thought of Brack's farewell, deciphering the fear in his eyes. Was his faith shaken, his faith that the forces of good were stronger than the ruinous darkness of the world?

I lowered myself onto a smooth, wet rock and slid my booted feet into the chilling sea. I knew that every second I hesitated could mean a bit of Brack's life slipping away. After all that he had done, I could not afford to falter now.

Silence cocooned me as I sank down into the cold waves. But within seconds, the still waters began churning around me as if subject to a mighty storm. The fragments of sunlight ebbed away, leaving absolute darkness. I struggled toward the surface, fighting the thrashing waters. Just as the fierce aching in my lungs grew unbearable, the waves heaved me onto something solid.

My palms met a shore of rough pebbles. I crawled on my hands and knees and choked out briny saltwater, greedily gulping air in exchange.

I lifted my head, pulse beating a deafening rhythm in my neck as I took in the sight before me. A wall of jagged black rocks rose up from the flat island where I'd banked. The sky held two moons: a red and a gold, each emitting wan light. Stars scintillated through a mask of clouds in this strange, untimely twilight, making patterns I had never seen before. As when I'd first encountered the Water, I sensed a power so ancient and unruly that I felt inconsequential in its presence. But where the Water seemed fearsome for its power alone, here I could sense a rattling darkness—even outside the gates—that chilled me to the marrow.

A vigorous wave crashed against my back, flattening me on the pebbled shore before breaking on the rocks. Fingers trembling, I touched the pendants at my sternum to make sure they hadn't washed away. But when I held out my stone to better see the treacherous mass before me, its light was faint and flickering.

As my eyes adjusted to the pallid atmosphere, I made out a lump of a shadow sprawled on the shore against a low outcrop. My heart seemed to both leap in my throat and drop to the depths of the sea as I dashed across the soft, sinking surface. "Brack," I cried out, but when I threw myself to my knees at his side, my hope fled as quickly as the receding waves. It was a young man with blond hair and blue eyes that flickered open at the sound of my voice.

Before I could make sense of this, a wave smashed over us, throwing me off balance. I reached for the rock face in an attempt to stay upright, but my hand sank through and I fell forward again onto my chest.

A great roar thundered from afar, the sound of many voices, and the earth beneath me gave a rumble that rattled my skull. But the sight ahead was even more terrifying than the savage sounds.

As I slowly found my feet, I saw a vast, arid valley stretching before me. The rock had been the gate to Galgeth. An army of creatures covered the land, with numbers strong enough to storm from Nissera to the other side of the world. There were lines of wasting, dark elicromancers like the ones I had killed in Nissera. There were koraks, wolves and all manner of other strange creatures to which the battle depictions had done little justice. On a jutting overhang on the far side of the massive swarm stood a figure in red robes, dark hair whipping in a warm wind.

I scrambled back. Though Tamarice was little more than a small streak of color to my eye, I cowered in the shade of some black astrikane trees that towered overhead.

Something in me died then: hope. Strapped to a pyre, scorched until it was less than dust. How vain were my attempts to unite the realm, when either way this force would trample us like crumpled leaves for the wind to carry away? Why had Tamarice felt threatened by me? There had never been any real hope of my saving the realm.

I felt the urge to weep there in the shadows, but something lurched my wrist and yanked me back through to the other side. The wind left my lungs as I toppled onto the rocky sand.

"Bristal." The young man crouched over me. His shadowed face was ashen, his voice barely more than a broken whisper and full of relief. It sounded faintly familiar. I had heard it in my mind once, and briefly when I'd held the Callista's truth-seeing diadem after the name day.

"Brack?" I asked softly as I propped myself up.

He collected me in his arms, answering my question with a fierce embrace.

"You're alive," I whispered against his shoulder.

Brack's breaths were labored as he helped me to my feet. Though I couldn't make out his features in the orange-tinged darkness, I felt rawness on his wrists and heard him hiss in pain. He had been too weak to return on his own. Clinging to one another, we approached the violent sea and submerged ourselves without hesitation.

The battering waves overcame us, but this time, I wasn't afraid. The thought of bringing him home rallied my strength, and that charred little hope inside me still burned like scattered embers. I held fast to Brack and welcomed the emptiness of the endless depths of water over what I had just witnessed. When the water stilled, I fought for us both to reach the surface.

All was still when we emerged and caught our breath. A pure, white moon hung small in the distance, and the paltry light of an ordinary dawn touched the far corner of the horizon.

After we heaved ourselves onto some rocks, I blinked away the sting of salt and realized that the sea had spat me out in the exact place I'd entered. The pack sat safely out of reach of the tide, so I hiked up the rocks to scoop it up. But the bread was hard and stale. How much time had passed during my absence? Did Anthony know why I'd left? Had the Realm Alliance grown or dwindled?

Brack took desperate gulps of the water and tore into the bread. When I tried to rub the salve on his cuts and scrapes, he shook his head and lay back to rest on the smooth surface of the rock. As glimmering dawn smeared the sky, I was able to better make out his true form.

His blond hair swept across his wet brow, spattered with blood and mud. He was long of leg and broad of chest, with robust shoulders and youthful features that made him appear no older than me. He wore a wry, crooked smile as he watched me study his face—a smile that made my heart pulse in my throat.

He chuckled. "Not what you expected?"

The voice emerged husky and deep. The eyes gleamed a livelier shade of blue than the ones I knew. I searched desperately for a shadow of the Brack that I knew so well. There was something painfully glorious about him, like blinding sun glinting off smooth, pure metal. I couldn't see my Brack in him anywhere.

Understanding my silence, he sighed and pulled himself to a sitting position. "Here, drink the rest," he said, offering me the pouch. "How long have I been gone?"

The cool water helped me find my voice. "Three months, when I left Nissera. Now I don't know."

"It was only hours to me," he said. "When I heard your voice, I . . ." He smiled faintly, trailing off as his eyelids fluttered closed over his captivating eyes. I let him rest for a time while I openly studied his features, still trying to make my eyes understand what my mind knew: he was Brack.

I felt as if I had lost him, and yet here he was, with all his secrets. I realized he hadn't been born with unfathomable wisdom and humility, but had once been a youth, full of fears and dreams. He didn't always have such burdens to bear.

"What happened to you there?" I asked, because of all the questions flitting in my mind, it was the first one I could grasp.

His eyelids fluttered, as if he were falling asleep, but he dragged them open and answered. "There is darkness in the deeper places of Galgeth that even Tamarice wouldn't dare stir. I journeyed in and awoke an ancient serpent. It went on a rampage and destroyed a large portion of her army."

I shuddered at the realization that the force I glimpsed was only what remained. "Then what happened?"

"Tamarice organized her troops and had them attack the creature while she hunted me down. But she wasn't alone. Klaine is leading the army alongside her. The elicrin stone she found in the vault was his. She has restored it along with her own."

"Klaine? The rebel elicromancer who killed Cassian in the war?"

"Yes. He was a strong leader, Bristal, and ruthless. Now that she's found an ally in him, you have much more to fear."

"But didn't Cassian kill him?" I asked, almost begging, as if logic could will this reality away. "And if his elicrin stone was here, how did he make it to Galgeth without it?"

"It doesn't make sense—it's dark elicromancy beyond what I can conceive."

When he said the word dark, I remembered my hands and why I had been able to pass through the gates. Brack hadn't asked me whom I had killed.

"What did they do to you?" I asked, examining the raw stripes on his wrist that could only have been inflicted by iron bonds. Tamarice must have been sure Brack would die. Why else would she send word of where he was?

Brack didn't answer me. His eyes lost focus for a moment. The thought of him suffering at her doing filled me with unspeakable rage, the kind that had made me kill Trumble without a second thought.

He swallowed hard and returned to what he considered the more pressing issue, as he always did. "Her army of blights doesn't have the power they did when they were elicromancers, but their numbers are strong." He let out a shuddering breath, and even in his shining youth looked undeniably weary. "We don't have much time."

I tightened my grip on his hand. His skin was burning. "Just rest."

"I know I seem a stranger to you now," he said, ignoring my request. With labored breaths, he propped himself up on his elbows. "It's just as strange for me. There's a reason I never take my true form if I can help it."

"What do you mean?"

"When I was young, I had wealth, women, anything else a man could want. I couldn't be outwitted or outfought. My father took great pride in my skills as a warrior and encouraged me to overtake the lands and riches of lesser families so that ours would grow in power. I was Brack Lyon, Lord of Branwhaite. I thought if only I could control my power of hearing thoughts, it would no longer torment me. I could have everything I desired, and the quiet in my mind I had always longed for."

He swept the wheat-colored hair from his brow, and my eyes followed each movement. "My desires changed, as you well know. But there is still a part of me that thirsts for those things: power, extravagance, glory. When I take my true form, I have the tendency to grow overzealous and arrogant. It reminds me of my old ways. It's too tempting to forget the value of patience and sacrifice, to storm through life heedless of things more important than my own longings. I could have had anything I wanted, but when I was reborn an elicromancer I received a mission and made small sacrifices to ensure I'd carry it out. Otherwise I might have turned out—"

"Like her," I finished. "But even more dangerous."

Brack leaned back and half-closed his eyes.

"I'm sorry," I muttered. "I'm sorry she turned on you . . . that she thought you weak."

He laughed lightly. "I am weak. I knew you would be different. There's goodness in you I wish I'd had as a mortal." His blue eyes flickered open and met mine. He looked so handsome, so youthful and powerful even when weary. "There were moments that I grew tired of being your wise old teacher. If I hadn't had to prepare you so quickly for days of war, I believe I could have loved you very deeply. Not in the way a mentor loves his pupil." He laughed again, a gravelly, charming sound, and my breath caught in my throat. "If I had allowed myself to love you, I would have given everything to protect you. It was better to give you to protect Nissera, even when it hurt me to do so."

"Brack," I whispered, searching the eyes I had never seen before. I found something familiar there, something I had always known: he was a man who would give anything to keep evil, whether in the world or in himself, from prevailing.

"I can see you now," I said, leaning over to brush the hair from his perspiring forehead. "I feel I know you even better than before."

He smiled and sighed deeply, holding my hand against his chest. "I know you're eager to get back, but let's rest here a little longer."

Shadows shrouded the cliffs above us. The way would be treacherous until the sun rose, and he was too weak to materialize. So I shoved away all thoughts of war and death and lay my head on his shoulder, letting the peace of sleep eclipse everything else.

✴

An hour or so later, I blinked my eyes against the risen sun. Warm, wet blood colored my palm. I looked down where my arm had rested across Brack's middle and found a dark stain spreading over his gray tunic.

"No," I said, jolting upright. He was still breathing, but weakly. I tore away his tunic, gasping when I saw the wound carved out of the hard muscle. The waves must have washed away the blood outside the gates.

I looked around helplessly before attempting to tear a shred of his cloak for a tourniquet. He moaned, his eyes blinking open briefly. I remembered his elicrin stone at my neck. He hadn't asked for it back. Now I knew why.

"Brack," I said, trying to shake him to full consciousness. "I have your elicrin stone. You can heal yourself!" I took off the chain and pressed his pendant into his palm.

He looked at me dazedly. "It was used for black elicro-mancy. I can't use it now."

"Yes, you can!" I sobbed. "You have to! Why didn't you tell me?"

Brack's hand lay limp as I tried to force him to accept his stone. His fingers didn't even attempt to close over it.

I sprang to my feet. Darmeska wasn't far. I could material-ize—at least to the point where enchantments protected the city, and run the rest of the way. I could get healing supplies. I could ask for others to follow me with a litter to bring him home.

First I needed to get him away from the tides and sharp rocks. Wiping away the tears that clouded my vision, I scrutinized the steep hills and cliffs above and saw an unexpected sight off to the south: red tents bearing the crest of Calgoran. My heart tried to lift at the sight, but it felt anchored in my belly.

Using all of my strength, I helped Brack slide off the rock and caught him as he swayed. "We don't have far to go," I said. "I see a path that will lead us up."

He stumbled along next to me as I negotiated us over the rocks. We made it high enough that I could wave his blood-ied tunic in an attempt to catch the attention of the camp sentries. I soon saw horses departing from the camp and, a moment, later, men clambering down the steep and rocky hill toward us.

My chest tightened as I recognized the closest one: Anthony.

"Help him!" I cried out as he hurried down. He took on most of Brack's weight and soon Weston arrived at my side to support the rest.

When we reached their camp, Drell saw us and limped off

to the nearest tent, holding the flap open so that they could bring Brack inside. Anthony and Weston laid him on a straw mattress with furs covering his legs, leaving his torso bare so I could tend to his wounds. Drell and Maddock crouched beside me, digging through pouches of plants while I performed the healing spell I knew wouldn't work. When it failed, I growled and cast my stone aside. Thin ropes of severed flesh hung around the wound. It was deep, too deep for a mere herb-soaked tourniquet, but I had to do something.

"Bristal, stop," Brack breathed, catching my fingers as they pressed a cloth to his skin. His grip was firm. I realized the tent flap had closed and Maddock no longer crouched beside me.

I heard Drell gasp from where she sat on the floor. "It's you, isn't it, Brack?" she asked him, taking his hand.

"Drell," Brack said, reaching out for her as she moved to his other side. "You're wounded."

"Don't worry over me. Nothing will stop me from fighting."

"I'm so proud of you. And I have a feeling you'll give me many more reasons to be proud in the days ahead."

Drell fought a sob as she nodded her head. "I swear to you, I will. Goodbye, my friend." She kissed his hand and stood up, touching my head and weeping as she limped out of the tent, leaving us alone.

Brack focused his eyes on mine. "My control is weakening," he said. "I can no longer keep my promise not to look into your mind."

"It's all right," I said, closing my eyes. I welcomed his searching, allowing him to see every part of me: my fears, my regrets, my passions, my admiration of his true form. Breaking the connection, he released me and brushed my cheek with his thumb.

"You love Anthony," he said. "He was a child when last I saw him, but he's a fine man now, deserving of your love if anyone is."

"But—"

"I told you life would be lonely and difficult. I never said you shouldn't love."

"But you said it's selfish to put our desires first, that it could only lead to evil and grief. . . ."

"For me. Not for you." He sputtered and closed his eyes, but the slow rise and fall of his broad chest comforted me. "For many years I regretted sparing her life, knowing that things might come to this."

"No." I buried my face in his shoulder. I pretended not to see the growing scarlet stain on the cloth. "It's not your fault."

"I've learned over the years to never regret showing mercy." He gripped my shoulder. "What has happened is done, but because of you, no dark future is set in stone."

My fingers clenched his protectively. Tamarice and Klaine had tortured him, fatally wounded him, left him outside the gates to die. It wasn't a trap, or an oversight—it was a message. A message that they were in control, that they could crush everything to oblivion, that there was nothing I could do.

Brack may have never overcome his pity for Tamarice in order to destroy her, but I would do it. And I would relish it.

I was tempted to make this vow to him, but when I lifted my head and looked into the strange blue eyes, I knew I could not let my last words to him be a promise of revenge.

"Now it is I who know you better than before," he said. "My weaknesses are not yours. You have the purity of heart to claim your desires without yielding to darkness."

"Your heart is the purest I know," I said, embracing him

once more with a choked sob. Though weakening by the second, he smiled and stroked my hair. My voice trembled. "Thank you for what you did for Nissera."

He released me, shaking, and relaxed against the pallet with a sigh. "You would have done the same if I'd asked it of you. Now, don't be discouraged. I'll see you again. My faith and love go with you."

I gripped his hand as if that would stop him from passing out of my reach. He was so beautiful it wracked my heart. "And my love and gratitude with you."

It wasn't long before the light in his brilliant eyes dulled, the lids fluttered closed and his labored breaths ceased.

✳

The Alliance brought Brack back to Darmeska, where the elders dressed him in a fine tunic and sang an Old Nisseran song over him.

> *Ord elenis portil waena fir sironoell.*
> Light of dawn, lift his soul to the heavens.
> *Halonir gemri li tacaral li iknor li fare temorrah.*
> Where neither cold nor dark nor death can touch him.

With Kimber's gentle hand at my back and Drell crying silently next to me, I watched as Brack was laid atop a pyre in the cliffs and engulfed by flames. I watched as my hope truly did burn to ashes.

✳

"To Brack!" shouted Anthony.

"To Brack!" The answering shout filled the great hall of Darmeska as we raised our cups and drank briarberry wine.

I sat down to the solemn feast feeling numb, my eyes cried out of tears. I hadn't yet shared the news from Galgeth. I cringed at the thought of snatching away whatever hope remained in the face of grievous destruction.

"Did you hear about Rosamund?" Anthony asked as sank into the seat next to me.

"Kimber told me. The Volarian nobles are breathing but don't stir." That meant Rosie was alive and in the same condition. Trumble's death curse hadn't worked—not the way they had planned.

"I've been wondering about the name day," Anthony said. "When Tamarice cursed her and you blocked it with your shield. Perhaps it became a part of Rosie the same way the curse did, protecting her from dark magic and whatever Trumble might have tried afterward to harm her."

"Then why won't they stir?"

"Perhaps her death curse and your shield are warring within her, suspending her between life and death." He leaned in close, his eyes flickering gold in the light of the torches. "I know you feel powerless right now. But that alone should be a reminder that you're far from it."

"It won't be enough." I resisted the urge to drop my face in my hands. "Tamarice isn't alone, Anthony. *Klaine* is still alive, if that's what you want to call it. He's been living in Galgeth as a blight."

His expression dimmed. "Klaine, from the Elicrin wars? How is that even possible? Cassian killed him."

"Not just that. Tamarice restored both her elicrin stone and his. I saw their army myself and it numbers thousands upon thousands. . . ."

I trailed off, closing my eyes until enough moments had passed for his stunned silence to morph into resolve. But when I looked at him again, all I saw in his usually passionate eyes was emptiness. "We'll spread the word soon," he said flatly, setting his jaw. "But let them feast first. It could be the last time."

I fell silent, looking around at the friends and strangers picking at the funereal feast. There were hundreds more members of the Realm Alliance than before.

"How long was I gone?" I asked.

"Nearly a month. My father has fallen ill and Charles is acting as king, though relying on my father's guidance still."

Riskan seemed healthy last I spoke with him—but Trumble had used Brack's borrowed power to manipulate his mind. Brack had once told me this could do damage beyond repair. I winced and swallowed back this explanation that wouldn't help matters. Riskan may have been a rock in my shoe these past years, but I didn't wish illness upon him.

"Charles is marching Calgoran's army east to face Perispos as we speak," Anthony went on, not registering my reaction. "Cyril left a few days ago to make a last attempt to convince him to turn around and come to our aid, so we have yet to see what he decides. But Yorth's army is camping nearby, fully at our disposal, and many of Errod's soldiers have joined us of their own accord since the king and his ministers are under Tamarice's spell like Rosie. Nicolas and a few hundred men are hacking at the briars in Pontaval, trying to reach her. I couldn't convince him to join us."

"Maybe I can," I said softly.

Anthony nodded. I felt his fingers weave loosely through mine, as if he feared to cling to them too tightly.

After the feast, I materialized to Pontaval to find Nicolas. I passed several of his men hacking at the briars to no avail. Each slash caused them to grow back thicker. I found the Yorthan prince scratched and bloodied, face taut with the kind of resolve that's more dangerous than helpful.

"We need every last warrior, Nicolas," I said, stepping in front of him. "Please, move your men west."

Nicolas paused to wipe blood and sweat from his brow. Such grim determination looked unsuited to someone so young. "Are you the Clandestine?"

"Yes, which means I care for Rosie just as much as you do. But I know that this will help nothing."

"I cannot abandon her."

He turned back to continue his fruitless struggle, but I stayed his arm with a spell and forced him to face me. "If every last man does not fight, Rosie may well be alone in a ravaged world when she escapes, if she ever does," I said. "And Tamarice will do as she likes with her."

Nicolas said nothing, but I watched understanding settle. After a few beats, he sighed, defeated. "All right. We will come."

I glanced up at the palace, feeling the urge to have another go at the briars with my own two hands, tear them apart as though they embodied Tamarice herself.

But with one last fleeting look at Rosie's besieged home, I materialized back to Darmeska, where men sharpened their weapons and readied their armor. Except for the clanking of metal, a heavy silence settled over the city.

Drell's wound was deep and still on the mend. As soon as she had been able, she and her spies had met up with the

Realm Alliance. Maddock had been using his medicinal knowledge to continue her treatment. Knowing there wasn't much time before the battle, she practiced walking without the help of a crutch and the pained grimace she tried to hide told me it wasn't going well. The wolf had torn right through her thigh muscle. As we lay on our mattresses on the stone floor that night, I grasped her hand while Maddock stretched out her leg and kneaded the muscles. Her fingernails sank into my skin and she bit the collar of her shirt to muffle a moan.

"I should have been there at the cottage," I said quietly.

"Nonsense. You were right where you belonged. Just as I will be when Tamarice comes."

"Drell, you can't—"

"Don't argue," she snapped. "I wasn't just listening to myself talk when I promised I'd go to battle with you. It was the last thing I said to Brack." She turned to Maddock. "What do you think? Do you think I can fight?"

"I thought you were going to die when I met you a month ago," Maddock said, his eyes gliding across her face and then back to her leg. "But you didn't want to die, and here you are. You shouldn't fight, but my guess is you'll do as you wish no matter what I say."

Drell offered Maddock a wan smile, but he didn't meet her eyes, and I wondered at the hard look on his face.

"Don't take away my chance to die with honor," she said when he was gone, her round eyes earnest. "I'll be at your side, and I'll hear no more of it."

I nodded, crushed by her implication that we were all likely to die. I looked around and found Anthony staring emptily into the depths of the fire in the great hearth. As clever a tactician as he was, he knew that no plan he could conjure would help our poor chances of victory.

I saw Drell lift herself off her pallet in the great hall and limp into the galleries. I got up to join her. She didn't make it far before she had to sit and knead her injured leg, color receding from her face. When she noticed me, she hid her pain and glanced up at the mural depicting the Battle of the Lairn Hills.

The blood did not make me cringe. The beasts did not make me want to turn away. This was our future, painted across the wall.

"If I had known," I said, "I would have been too frightened to continue with training. I would have gone back to Popplewell and pretended such evil didn't exist, like everyone else in Nissera."

Drell sighed. "No, you wouldn't have."

I pulled Brack's elicrin stone from my pocket. It no longer burned me, since it no longer belonged to him.

"You should give it to Anthony," Drell said. "Brack always said to never underestimate the power of renounced elicrin stones."

I searched its glimmering emerald depths. "What power do you think it will offer now?"

She hoisted herself up and limped to my side. "Probably visions or thought discernment of some sort. But I'd like to think selflessness," she whispered. "Rare and utter selflessness."

EIGHTEEN

A few days composed of hopeless hours passed. Every time I met someone's eyes, I saw the same thing: fear masked by resolve. But then I started to see something at work in Anthony. He stared at the battle mural, fingers crossed under his chin. I was shifting my stone, making the sunlight dance in its silver-blue depths, when he stood up. "Come with me."

I grabbed my cloak and followed him as he wandered the hall and found Orrin. Anthony pulled his cousin aside and laid a hand on both our shoulders. "Orrin, lead the Realm Alliance to the Lairn Hills. If we stay here, they will besiege us."

"I know."

I realized that when he said "Alliance" he was no longer referring to thirty men, or even fifty. He was referring to thousands. The Realm Alliance was now a full army.

"Bristal and I will join you there soon," Anthony said, "If I don't come back, you two must lead us into battle."

"If you don't come back?" Orrin and I echoed.

"If I don't, lead them. But I will."

"Anthony, are you mad?" Orrin demanded. "Where are you going at this hour?"

Anthony set his jaw. "Trust me."

Orrin inhaled through his nostrils, but nodded. Bewildered, I let Anthony guide me outside and into the city streets toward the stables. "What are you doing?" I asked him as he tacked up Arsinoe. She whinnied restlessly, sensing the tension at Darmeska.

Anthony didn't answer me. I stayed his arm, fear raw in my voice. "Anthony, where are we going?"

Without an answer, he leaned down and crushed his lips against mine. His arms encircled my waist as the warmth from his urgent kiss raced through me. He grasped my hair and traced the slope of my neck with his fingertips, and then his lips retreated and found where his fingers had touched. He sighed warmly into my hair and pulled me against him, and for a brief, disarming moment I wondered if he meant to lead me somewhere we could be fully alone. But he grudgingly stopped himself.

"Damn this war," he sighed against my lips. "I could do this for the rest of my life. But we have to go."

I could have grown roots and let the fury of Galgeth crash over us where we stood. But he brushed back my hair and withdrew his arms from around me, so I followed him outside, my curiosity growing.

When the guards opened the gates for us, we mounted Arsinoe and Anthony pushed us south through the woods. We left the mountains and entered the shadows of the Forest of the West Fringe. It wasn't until we plunged blindly into its depths that I realized what Anthony planned to do.

"You're mad!"

Anthony turned his head "There are thousands of blights on their way from Galgeth, and there is only one of you."

"No. I won't lead you there."

"I'll find it on my own. You can materialize back to Darmeska."

"Why are you doing this?" I asked desperately.

"Cassian appeared before me in a dream. He told me to go to the Water."

"What does a dream of a dead man have to do with anything?"

"His fate was tied to Klaine's. And you saw Klaine with your own eyes, still clinging to life. Maybe Cassian isn't dead after all."

"Klaine isn't alive, not really. He's a blight."

"What if neither Cassian nor Klaine truly died that day, like Rosie and the Volarian nobles? What if he still exists somehow, trapped between life and death? Wouldn't that explain why Klaine is immortal without his elicrin stone, why he could reach Galgeth?"

I didn't know how to answer such a wild theory.

"Cassian told me that I need to go to the Water to save Nissera," Anthony said.

"But it was only a dream. You don't know it will work."

"I feel certain Brack's elicrin stone brought on the vision. You gave it to me for a purpose, didn't you? You knew it would have power."

"But I didn't know what kind or how much. Your dream may be just a dream. You can't follow it to your death."

"What choice do I have? You can come with me or turn back, but you will not stop me."

I opened my mouth to protest, but Anthony spurred Arsinoe on. As we pressed forward, the woods around us grew dense and eerie. Magic sat thick on the air and trembled through the earth beneath. I could feel us nearing the Water and silently begged the gates to stay hidden, as they had for so many who had gone heedlessly searching for them.

But the Water did as it willed and appeared wherever it desired, just as it had on that grueling winter day many years ago. Within minutes, the silver trees loomed before us. I clutched my pendant, wondering if I ought to stop Anthony with force. It felt wrong to lose faith in him now, when he had never given me any reason to doubt him. But the Water lurked threateningly on the other side. I couldn't let it take him from me, even if we had but one day remaining together before we would be destroyed.

The sapphire stone waited in the gates. Anthony dismounted and approached it with sure steps. He didn't so much as glance my way before pressing his hand against it.

The silence grew denser as we waited. Nothing happened.

"Anthony . . ." I said with pity, feeling surprising disappointment of my own.

He didn't move, so I dismounted and went to his side.

"It's all right," he said. His eyes were such a peaceful color, like a bedding of autumn moss in the woods, but the determination within them frightened me. "You can still open it."

"It didn't work, Anthony. If you were meant to have an elicrin stone, the gates would have opened."

"I'll press my luck." He took my hand in his. I snatched it away, taking a few steps back. "Please, Bristal. Whether or not you trust me now, we may both die tomorrow."

This dismal thought had shrouded my mind since the moment Brack had slipped from my grasp. For as long as no one said the words, it didn't feel certain. But the truth struck me hard now.

If Anthony became an elicromancer, that alone could turn the tides of war. He gripped my shoulders. "Bristal, trust me. I won't die in the Water."

I looked at him long and hard, and finally nodded. He gently urged me forward, sliding his hand over the back of mine as he pressed my fingers against the elicrin stone. The heat rushed through my blood and the silver trees untangled.

I followed Anthony into the clearing, where the Water waited, glassy black and still. When we reached the edge, he faced me.

"I'm afraid," I choked out.

"I'm only one man. Even if I die, it was worth the risk."

"Not to me," I whispered.

Anthony wrapped his arms around my shoulders and buried his face in my neck. "Just promise me that if we survive this war, you'll be my wife."

"I promise."

He released me, smiling subversively. "That was easy. Now I know if I ever want a yes from you, I need only make you fear for my life." He removed his sword belt and placed Zeal in my hands. He then cast off his cloak and shirt, approaching the Water's Edge. "No use tiptoeing in, is there?"

"Anthony."

He turned back. The fear in my eyes wiped the smirk from his face. "All right, if you want to treat this like a farewell . . ."

He returned and touched his lips to mine gently, mere

brushes, and I closed my eyes and let the bliss overtake me, imagining a life after this moment that would never come to be: to thousands upon thousands more words exchanged by the warmth of a fire or in the dark of a wood in autumn, to nights spent in his bed and in his arms, to our dark-haired Ermetarius sons and daughters who would never exist to see the pain and joy that the world had to offer. My arms clung to his neck when I feared he would draw back, but rather than withdrawing, his lips parted mine and filled me with even deeper longing. I was weightless, and he was the only solid thing left in the world.

"*Efrenil*," he whispered, breathing it across my lips.

I had read the Old Nisseran phrase, but hearing it made it feel even more familiar, like a forgotten lullaby. "*Var efrenil*," I answered. *And I love you.*

He pulled away. The cold air took the place of his warmth. I opened my eyes just in time to see the person I held most dearly in the world plunge deep into the Water.

The wind blew. The ice spread. I waited. A long minute passed. With each second, my hope dwindled to despair. My hands shook as I drew out my elicrin stone and dropped Zeal on the grass.

It had been too long now. Anthony wasn't coming back on his own.

I ran and slid to a stop at the center of the ice and tore my pendant off its chain. Light beamed out from it as I drove it into the hard surface and heard the crack of the ice breaking.

Only, it wasn't the ice that broke. My elicrin stone was dust in my hands.

NINETEEN

*H*ours passed. Winds howled from the west.
I didn't shudder or weep. I lay still as bleached
bones and prayed I would die. I wished we
could all simply die, and give Tamarice no enemies to crush when she came to our lands, no
triumph—just mountain crags and forests and
green hills with no blood to wash them red.

Without Anthony, without Brack and without my elicrin stone, I was nothing. I was not
the Clandestine. I was nameless and empty.

The hurt was so deep, and had hit so true,
that I no longer even felt it. But breaths still
filled my body and my heart still beat in my
ears as I lay against the earth. I wished it would
all simply stop.

Arsinoe nudged me with her muzzle until
I stirred unwillingly from my stupor. She
whickered as if inquiring after her master. I sat
up and covered my face with my hands, blinking back burning tears as I rose shakily to my
feet.

Death could have me. And it would.
Tomorrow, I promised myself. *Tomorrow, Tamarice can destroy what's left of you.*

I looked back at the ice that still sealed off

the Water. Fate wouldn't afford me even the chance to bear Anthony's body back to Calgoran for a proper burial. He had been so sure he could tilt the odds in our favor.

But he died in vain.

Feebly, I situated Zeal at my waist, where it hung loose and heavy on my small frame until I made a new hole in his belt with trembling fingers. I mounted Arsinoe and took up the reins. She stamped her hoof, reluctant to leave, but I firmly urged her on without looking back at the traitorous Water. I heard the metallic sound of the gates erecting once more. "May light surround you," I whispered, closing my eyes to trap the tears before they fell. "May goodness follow you wherever you go."

Directionless, I rode through the forest in a daze of despair, no longer intimidated by its strange energy. I didn't make it far before I was intercepted by a figure cloaked in gray on horseback. I reacted little. Indeed, I yearned to see some gray-skinned blight or the glint of a poised dagger.

Arsinoe swerved to a halt as the rider cut across my path. "Bristal," Maddock said, throwing off his hood. "Drell had me track you here with a message." His outstretched hand froze halfway to thrusting the letter in my direction. "What happened?"

When I tried to speak, no words emerged. My chest felt like it was caving in. The realization in Maddock's eyes, the utter despair, seemed to make it real.

I slid limply off of Arsinoe. Maddock dismounted and caught me up in a ferocious embrace. My knees buckled and we sank to the ground together. "No," he repeated over and over while I sobbed into his shoulder.

After we had wept together for ages, he held me by the arms and looked into my face.

"We'll come up with a strategy," he said. "We'll do our best defending Nissera and we will die honorably. Tomorrow, you will see him again. But today, you have to stand and prepare to fight. You have to head south."

"South?" My voice was no more than a croak. "The Lairn Hills are North."

"Drell's message will explain." Maddock stood up and handed me the letter. "You should go quickly. There's a dark cloud covering the western horizon. I'll take Arsinoe back so you are free to materialize."

A fresh tidal wave of despair washed over me. "I can't materialize. My elicrin stone broke on the ice that closed over the Water, and without it I have no control over my power." I shook my head, bereft. "I don't know why I thought I could use an elicrin stone to break the source of its own power."

Maddock's look of shock quickly turned grim. "We still have time. Drell seemed to think this an important errand." He mounted with a sense of purpose. With a last nod of encouragement, he turned and rode northward.

I broke the seal, willing this letter not to bear bad news—as if any misfortune could touch me now. I unfolded the parchment and read Drell's slanted script.

Bristal,

There were things Brack never told you. One of them was his theory regarding your origin. He never knew for certain, and that's why he never spoke of it. He didn't wish to mislead you. I don't wish to mislead you either, which is why you must meet with the one person who was there the day you were brought to Popplewell. Forgive me for being cryptic, and forgive Brack for withholding this from you. Find the man named Elwood in Popplewell. He's the one who can help you find out where you came from. Hurry back.

Drell.

I stared at the letter with my head bowed and realized my hands trembled fiercely.

I supposed there was no better time than hours before the end to find out where I began.

※

When I reached Popplewell, weary beyond measure, the whispers weren't lost on me. The people could feel the storm coming. I could see it in the way they walked with their heads bent and hurried through the streets, lifting their gazes as I passed.

I had changed so much since calling this town my home, it struck me as odd that Popplewell had not changed at all. The same cottages speckled the rich hillsides, and the same quaint shops and booths stood in the town square. As I approached Elwood's farm, seeing endless rows of crops, I wondered what circumstances his family had lived in before I was kidnapped and Brack gave him the gift of gold coins. Perhaps they had been huddling in a shack, children and animals gathered next to the warmth of a pitiful fire. That certainly wasn't the way of it any longer.

A servant escorted me to a library, where I forced myself to eat the food laid out for me. My eyes brushed over the book titles until I saw *The Ermetarius Royal Family History* and clamped a hand over my mouth. Everything in me ached. I could not stop thinking of the way Anthony had kissed me, with all the love built up inside of him that would never be spent.

You can die tomorrow, I promised myself. *But today, you have to live.*

"My lady," Elwood said as he entered the library. His hair was white, his square jaw a little less square and his shoulders bent, but it was undoubtedly my kindest kidnapper. He offered me a chance to rest before we spoke, but I brushed off his courtesies.

"I've been told you're the only man who knows something of my origin." I could barely see him through my swollen, tired eyes.

He studied my face. "I know only what I saw, my lady, something I've tried to understand for many years. Something I believe Brack struggled to understand once he read my thoughts." Elwood's pale eyes fixed mine. "What I saw—or rather whom—was what led me to believe you were unlikely to die in the Water that day. Not that it excuses what I did to you. That's something I've deeply regretted all these years."

"I don't blame you, Elwood," I said. "What did you see when I first arrived in Popplewell?"

"You and a man appeared out of thin air, both bloodied and grim, as if you'd just come from a battle."

"So whoever brought me here was an elicromancer." My heart beat a quick cadence. What if I hadn't been abandoned? What if I'd been saved? "Can you tell me what the man looked like?"

"Couldn't forget if I tried, my lady. He was tall, dark-haired, covered in sweat and gore. He wore mail and a torn tunic—not quite the dazzling silver-clad warrior the battle illustrations make him out to be, but this somehow seemed more fitting."

"Battle illustrations?" I stared at him in disbelief, my heart pounding as I thought of Anthony's dream.

"I believe it was Cassian. The leader of the good elicromancers during the Elicrin War. I knew him from the paintings and books."

"Cassian? But he died hundreds of years ago. Klaine killed him in the last battle."

"I only know what I saw, Lady Bristal. I brought you to the cook and told her to leave me out of it—I didn't want to have to explain what I'd seen to anyone else. But not long ago, Brack came to ask me about the memory he had seen in my mind at our first encounter, the day you became an elicromancer. I couldn't tell him anything beyond what I just told you."

I belatedly accepted his offer to sit down. My heartbeat sang in my ears, full of hope and loss. "Did he think that . . . Cassian was my father?"

"And that Callista was your mother."

I stared at him. "Callista and Cassian both died hundreds of years ago. It's impossible."

"Brack seemed to think it was possible." With an enigmatic look, he walked to a set of double doors with thick curtains that stifled the intruding daylight. He placed a hand on the knob. "The gift that Brack graciously gave me all those years ago—do you remember?"

"A pouch of gold aurions."

Elwood shook his head. "A pouch of seeds."

"Seeds? What kind of seeds?"

Elwood unlocked the curtained doors and pushed them open, filling the library with sunlight. I stood and shielded my eyes. When they adjusted, I heaved a disbelieving breath. The doorway opened to an interior courtyard thick with trees that held striking white leaves.

"White astrikane," I breathed, stepping nearer to the beautiful garden. "I learned they were extinct in Nissera."

"Almost," Elwood said, gesturing for me to go ahead of him. "Of the twelve Brack gave me, I sold only two. That alone was enough to purchase land and livestock and build this house. Unlike its Galgethian counterpart, white astrikane can show visions to mortals without killing them. I sold to the highest bidder."

"I can't believe it," I whispered, passing under one of the sunlit white canopies.

"Brack thought white astrikane was a dangerous tool for elicromancers, especially for you. He worried that what you would see might disrupt your mission and send you on a new path. Without knowing your past for certain, he had no idea what knowledge it would bring you." Elwood joined me as I stroked the white trunk of the tree. I tore my gaze away to look at him. "But I've heard that Nissera will soon fall, my lady. Seems there's no harm in it now."

Elwood bowed his head and retreated into the library, shutting the doors behind him. My fingers trembled as I reached up to pluck just one of the thousands of glowing leaves.

I didn't expect the acrid taste of Galgethian astrikane, or the sensation of swallowing poison. But I certainly didn't expect the white astrikane leaf to taste like the sunlight that glowed down upon it. I felt warm and light as well, like clean laundry drying outside on a summer day. The crippling pain in my chest uncoiled and departed.

The manor house was gone. A clear river ran alongside me, winding away toward distant mountains. The blades of grass felt like strands of silk under my feet.

I recognized the face that greeted me, though I couldn't recall a time or place I had seen it. But the name didn't escape me. When I saw the chestnut hair and eyes the color of a calm sea, I knew two things: that she was Callista, and that she was my mother. "Is this just a vision?" I asked because she was so real—much more real than the blight had felt—that I no longer knew.

"A vision and a memory," said the voice I hadn't realized I had been waiting my whole life to hear. "The astrikane is drawing out your hidden memories of me."

Callista reached out a hand to me, and I grasped it firmly, finding it felt no less real than the hands that had cupped my face that morning.

She was small and thin and strong, with round lips and eyes that only vaguely resembled mine. I wondered if I looked more like my father, if the painters and sculptors had embellished too much, if they had brushed out the nuances from his features that I would recognize in my own.

Callista wrapped her arms around me, pressing my face into her sweet-smelling chestnut locks, a scent not unfamiliar to me. I felt tears well in my eyes and slip into her hair.

"How can you be my mother? You died so long ago."

Callista stood back and lay a hand on my face. "Just before the last attack, the one that became the Battle of the Lairn

Hills, we hid the elderly and children in the barrows under the hills and sealed the passage. We left you there so you would be safe." She dropped her hands and closed her eyes as if mustering the courage to speak the memory out loud. "But our enemies sent koraks to ambush the barrows. By the time we arrived, it was too late."

I saw images as she spoke, vague memories shifting in my mind before locking into place. The dark, dank passages, the scratching and shoving at the stone doors, old women and children huddling in fear around me. And then I heard screaming. I saw blood. I covered my head and urged myself to be smaller, to be invisible.

"You were the only one who survived," Callista said. "You transformed into a fox and escaped through another passageway. But the koraks chased you down and attacked you. You were badly wounded and the battle was pushing back toward us. I saw you from afar and opened a portal for your father to take you through. That was my gift: I could open passages to other places and other times. Meddling in the past or future comes with more costs than gains, so I spent most of my life trying *not* to use my gift. But Cassian needed somewhere safe to heal you, and for once I acted without thinking."

In my memories, the air tore like a piece of fabric, exposing a shimmering light. A dark-haired man covered in blood sprang forward, picked me up and dove toward the portal while enemies closed in around us.

The chaos gave way to silence. My father gripped my hand, his gray eyes watching mine. Light flowed out from his elicrin stone, robbing the pain from my body until it was gone.

We stood on one of Popplewell's rich hillsides, behind the

manor house to be exact, and there was Elwood threshing wheat. He looked on in disbelief as Cassian knelt down and took my hands in his.

"You'll be safer here, Bristal." Cassian looked up at Elwood. "You—find someone to take care of her."

Elwood stared. I could see how witnessing this moment had made him certain I would survive the Water.

Cassian placed a thumb on my forehead and muttered a spell, then kissed where his thumb had touched. He drew his sword and returned through the portal, the rent pieces of air meshing together behind him.

I blinked away the memory and looked back at Callista.

"He wiped your memory so that you could escape the pain and terror of that day and live a new life." Callista brushed my forehead the way Cassian had done, tucking a strand of hair behind my ear. "I didn't expect either of us to survive the battle. But when I *did* survive, I regretted until my last day that I had no idea where or when my gift had sent you. I looked for you every day, but eventually learned to accept that you were meant to be where you were."

I felt the urge to weep and laugh all at once. I always assumed fate had chosen me to be an elicromancer, that my parents had abandoned me and I would never know why. But I was the daughter of elicromancers, the pair whose love had inspired legends.

Long-smoldering grief began to burn the fragile edges of newfound joy. Finding my family after they were already gone was like sewing up a wound from a poisoned arrow. The pain had lessened, but my fate was already sealed.

Yet something Anthony had said prodded and perturbed my sorrow.

"Did the fate-binding ritual cause my father to die when he killed Klaine?" I asked.

"Their fates were bound, but neither of them died. Cassian was too strong. His strength kept them both half alive. I thought he was gone. I thought he was gone until I passed on and didn't find him. . . ."

Callista's image began to fade. I knew astrikane visions didn't last long, but I was far from prepared for this one to end.

"Where is he now?" I demanded, desperate for answers as I felt the lightness and warmth leaving my limbs.

Her last word sounded distant, imbued with regret. *"Efrenil."*

When I opened my eyes, I lay on the grass. The distant mountains and the river had faded, and the ivy-clad walls of Elwood's house had risen around me once more.

Stretching my muscles languidly, I felt the soreness and fatigue creep back into my body. The pain of my wounds from fighting with Trumble and journeying to Galgeth returned, but the hard knot of grief in my chest had lessened, if only a little.

I opened the door to the library and closed it behind me, regretting that I had to leave the ethereal garden behind. "Thank you, Elwood," I said, grasping the old man's hand.

"It hardly makes amends for what I did, but I'm glad to have helped," he replied. "I've seen you cheat death a time or two, my lady. Perhaps you'll manage to do so again."

I lacked the heart to tell him I hoped I wouldn't.

But even as the lightness in my body and soul bled out by

the second, I remembered something vital. Cassian's sapphire stone sat mounted in the gates around the Water.

I had learned that any stone with a living master would burn my flesh if I touched it, and that renounced elicrin stones, or those with dead masters, held mere traces of their former power. Yet neither seemed to be true of Cassian's stone. It didn't burn me, and I had felt its power for myself, its responsiveness to my touch. I thought its role was simply to guard the gates, but perhaps there was more in store for it.

It was no ordinary elicrin stone, after all. It had belonged to my father, the most powerful elicromancer of his time.

✳

I tried not to look at the still, treacherous Water beyond the gates as I dismounted, tried to bury the question of how Anthony could have been so right about Cassian's survival yet wrong about his own.

I focused instead on the object in the gate. Without an ounce of hesitation, I set to prying it loose with a knife. But it took no coercing. The metal encasing its edges folded away and my father's pendant fell into my palm.

The sensation of immense power moving through me nearly knocked me over. Light swelled within the stone. The power both strengthened me and made me feel as though it could split my chest open. I clenched my fists, yoking myself with magic, holding it in and trying to swallow it with my body like a gulp of strong liquor. At last, the power dispersed, spreading throughout my whole being, tingling in my fingertips and toes.

I slipped my new elicrin stone onto the empty silver chain around my collar. I garbed myself like the elicromancer warriors from the battle murals, in a black tunic and mail so light and closely woven that it resembled silver silk. I felt rested, as though I had slept dreamlessly for hours.

I strode back to Arsinoe, stroking her coarse muzzle, fighting back the hot wave of tears as I stripped off her gear. *"Lofthar neranin."* The spell would lead her to a safe place, at least. I pressed my face against her neck. "Goodbye."

When I materialized at the Lairn Hills, the dark cloud of which Maddock had spoken hung low in the west.

My grief returned anew as I wondered if I would have to explain Anthony's fate. I watched him enter the Water over and over in my mind and hoped Maddock had already told Orrin and the others. I couldn't bear to.

From the crest of the hill where I landed, I spotted red, blue and green tents in the distance. Cyril and Orrin had chosen the spot for its high ground facing flat land stretching off to the west—an advantage, but not one that would turn the tides in our favor.

Eyes met mine as I entered the camp. I watched the sorrow and fear welled deep within them lessen, turn into something else—not hope but a question, a reminder of the possibility of victory.

When I reached the center of the tents, Drell was waiting for me. Orrin, Maddock, Cyril and Nicolas emerged behind her.

The expressions of relief on their faces were, for a moment, unadulterated by grief or weariness. I approached them in silence. At a closer glance, the slight movement of a muscle in Drell's neck betrayed the effort it took to hide her pain when nothing else would have given it away. Cyril's jaw was set, which told me the news I already knew: Charles had refused to defy his father's orders and was still at the eastern shore. Orrin's shoulders sagged slightly, as if bearing a weight, though to unfamiliar eyes they would only look proud.

"Bristal," Drell said. Her eyes strayed to the object at my chest. "Is that . . . ?"

"Cassian's elicrin stone. Mine shattered when . . ." I trailed off, swallowing hard as I strove to suppress the grief that tore at my heart. Speaking of it felt like grinding salt in a fresh wound, and I couldn't go on.

"He made you bring him to the Water," Orrin said. At the speechless, pained look I gave him, he took me in his arms. With my ear against his chest, I heard a shuddering, silent sob and realized it was my own.

"I should have stopped him," I whispered.

"No one can stop Anthony once he's made up his mind." I heard a catch in Orrin's voice. Exhaling, I closed my eyes and allowed him to comfort me for only a moment longer as the memories I had been warding off overcame me: Anthony congratulating us after the Stag Tournament, bruised and triumphant; how regal he looked at the ball with the white sash across his chest; the realization that he was going to live after the korak attack; the way my heart and body seemed to catch fire when he kissed me, a feeling more powerful than any elicrin magic.

When I opened my eyes, I looked over Orrin's shoulder and noticed the tendrils of gray clouds sprawling across the sky.

We retreated to a tent, arranging ourselves around a table holding maps and wooden pieces that Cyril had carefully positioned to demonstrate his strategy.

"We'll place spearmen three units deep at the base of the hill to rout the initial onslaught," he said, the calm of a born leader in his tone. "And we'll situate archers and swordsmen behind them, as well as a line of archers on the flanking hills. Once they've broken through, the main cavalry will charge. We'll position light cavalry on the wings as well, to loop and attack the tail of the onslaught."

Orrin leaned his fists on the table. His eyes searched the map of the hills where Cyril's wooden pieces were poised in formation. "We should attack."

"We can't afford to act offensively with so few men," Cyril said. "Right now the lay of the land is our only advantage. We have to kill as many of them as come our way, absorb the damage so that Nissera has a chance."

"No, Orrin is right," I said. "Even if we destroy the entire force, Nissera will still fall to Tamarice and Klaine, especially if our strongest leaders die in its defense. And the lay of the land will do us little good. Tamarice can manipulate the hills and the battlefield the way we can manipulate the pieces on this map." I picked one up and tossed it back on the table.

But an idea came to me, bright and swift, and I had to catch it before it fluttered away. It relied on the memories that Cassian had erased but that the white astrikane had drawn shakily back to my consciousness.

I splayed my palms on the table and looked into Cyril's eyes. "She won't target an advantage she knows nothing of. The barrows where the old kings are buried lay close by. There are two ways out of them: the main entrance and a secret exit that ends in a rock escarpment west of here." I led them outside and pointed at the gray rocks in the distance that broke up the green hills. I remembered emerging from the darkness and scuttling over the rocks into a battle even fiercer than the korak ambush that had driven me deeper into the tunnels. "The loyal elicromancers used them as a hideout for the young and elderly during the last Battle of the Lairn Hills. Let them think our only aim is resistance. Let them miscalculate our numbers. We can assault them from behind. It's far enough away from the battlefield that Tamarice will think nothing of it."

Orrin smiled weakly. "You know who you sound like, don't you?"

I closed my eyes. Orrin gripped my shoulder.

After a moment, Cyril crossed his arms and studied the escarpment. "Will you lead the covert attack, Bristal?"

"No, the overt one. I want to ride out."

My request was met with silence.

"You ought to ride with the cavalry after our spearmen have routed the first assault," Cyril finally replied. "You'll have a better chance of surviving to face Tamarice."

"Tamarice and I will face each other no matter what. Might as well not tarry."

"What about Klaine?" Drell asked.

"I don't know. I have no idea how strong he is. He's half alive, but he was very powerful to begin with."

"Your power has grown," Drell said. "I can see it. Maybe you are strong enough to defeat them both."

"Stronger, yes. Strong enough, I don't know."

A black shadow engulfed the tent. We dashed outside and looked up to find a black bird sweeping over our camp. No sooner had we spotted it than it gave a chilling cry and froze in the air. For a moment it was suspended, wings motionless, before it plummeted to the earth, forcing five or six men to scamper out of the way. It landed with a windy thud, its massive wings sprawled.

"A scout," Maddock declared as he retrieved his arrow from the bird's eye. "They're getting closer."

We looked across the hills and found that the blackness brushed the horizon now. A hot wind stirred and seemed to carry with it the stench of death. Fear curled in my heart and weakened my bones.

Startled by the blast of a horn, I continued to search the west before I realized the noise hadn't come from the far-off enemy host, but from the east. We turned to find a great swarm of human warriors bearing red and white banners, sweeping toward us over the waves of green.

TWENTY

Charles Ermetarius spurred his white horse across the hills, as welcome a sight as any I had ever seen. Thousands rode in his wake. His silver breastplate held the image of a rearing stag and a cloak the color of wine thrashed behind him.

"Lady Bristal," he said when he reached the camp and halted before us. His features looked painfully familiar. But his eyes, which were the velvet blue of dusk, assured me that I wasn't straying into a dream of Anthony.

"Your Highness," I said. "You came."

Charles dismounted and approached me. "I was blinded by allegiance to my father. He is a good man, but relentless. Thankfully, my brother is equally so." His eyes found Zeal at my waist and quickly read the misery on my face. "Where is my brother?"

"I'm afraid . . ." I faltered. I had not yet been forced to explain his fate. "He drowned," I managed, "in the Water."

I lowered my head so I wouldn't have to watch this news register on Charles's handsome face. I heard the clank of armor as he paced away, stopped and paced back. His mournful whisper of the blessing over the dead picked up and carried through the ranks of his men. I pressed my eyes closed.

"We will all drown within the day," he said at last. "I'm here to make reparation for my lack of faith, and I will ride at your side in my brother's stead." Charles laid a hand on Orrin's shoulder. "I'm sorry I shut my eyes."

"We're glad you're here," said Orrin, echoing my silent sentiments.

I grew restive as our last hours waned and men prepared their weapons and horses. Before Cyril left to lead his men to the escarpment for the covert attack, he found me where I sat clenching Zeal on my knees, watching clouds obscure the western sky.

"When Anthony first asked me to train him as a soldier, I sensed nothing but trouble," he said. I wiped a tear away as he sat next to me. "A defiant boy is enough of a problem when his father is a millwright, much more if he's the king of Calgoran."

"But you let him."

Cyril nodded. "I let him. And for my sake as well as his, I hoped he would prove himself. I knew that if those boys were going to respect him, I had to stay out of the way. But I kept an eye on him." His chest shook with a throaty laugh. "One day I saw him sitting alone, rubbing poison climbers over his arms and neck and face. When I asked him what he was doing, he said Weston had promised him a beating. I thought, 'This boy is either a coward or the bravest one of the lot, if he's about to poison himself to escape a beating.' But he didn't tell anyone—no, he let Weston beat on him all he wanted. Then I saw what he was after. He didn't care if he had a body rash and a dozen broken bones. He would bear it all happily if it meant gaining the fear of his enemy."

We laughed together even though everything in me hurt unbearably.

"And he did. They were both miserable with sores for a week. But to him the gain seemed greater than the cost, and perhaps it was."

He turned to me and waited until I met his eyes. "Bristal, your display of courage years ago helped show him who he ought to be. But he had a unique kind of courage that was all his own. No one else might have thought the gain was greater than the cost of going into the Water. But to him, it was."

I took a deep breath and stared at my small fingers as they curled around the hilt of Anthony's sword.

"We still don't know what the day may bring." Cyril stood up and offered me his forearm. I got to my feet and grasped it. With his other arm he embraced me and patted my back firmly, the way he would a son. "Good luck to you, my friend."

"And to you."

I watched him walk away and lead his troops toward the barrows.

When I returned to camp, I ate and drank grudgingly, feeling as though I would lose it all anyway, and sat with a shield strapped to my arm. The leather dampened with sweat in my palm, but I couldn't seem to release it. A spear lay at my side, and every once in a while my fingers twitched toward it, but mostly they clung to Cassian's elicrin stone. While grasping it, I could refuse to let the panic within me rise.

Drell sat next to me, wincing in pain.

"Drell, you can hardly take three steps. Please—"

"Nissera is my home," she interrupted. "I'm riding out."

I bit my lip, realizing it was selfish to try to scold her into sitting out of the battle. If we were all to die, each should be free to choose how.

Only Nicolas, who had never faced battle of any kind, looked as fragile as I felt. Most of my friends in the Alliance, on the other hand, baffled me with their natural sense of calm. Maddock sat across the fire in his leather armor, sifting through the healing herbs in his satchel with steady fingers, his eyes often straying toward Drell, whose face was drawn in pain.

When Weston heaved himself onto a log beside me, I was thankful for his great, solid form. He offered me a wineskin full of brandy, and I didn't refuse.

"I wanted to die," I confided after the liquid burned its way down my throat. "Now I'm afraid."

"Even when you have nothing to lose, there's always something that makes you fear death, whether it's only the wind on your face or the scald of a good draught. Everything suddenly seems precious."

"It's the strange calm that's weakened me."

"That won't last much longer."

We sat in brittle silence until the sentries' horns resounded. The enemy host had been spotted in the distance. I leaped to my feet, frantic, and seized my spear. Weston laid a hand on my arm and looked into my eyes. "Bristal, take a moment. Breathe." He tightened his grip. "Fear must not have the final say in what becomes of you."

I breathed. Suddenly I was the only thing at rest in a swarm of men with steel in their hands and steel in their eyes. Everything seemed to move too slowly and yet too fast. By the time I blinked, my riders sat astride their horses, waiting for me to pilot them into battle.

The spearmen and swordsmen flooded to the base of the hill, and the archers on the summits took their stance. The cavalries of Nissera covered the fields and hills to the east like a vast shadow.

Charles and Orrin fixed their gazes on me. Their dark hair flitted in the wind, and their blue eyes showed a soul-deep determination. Nicolas, who had pulled his face into a mask of resolve, gave me a resolute nod. Drell looked ablaze, her orange hair whisking around her pale face in the warm wind like tongues of fire.

Only one face was missing, but the longing and sadness caused by his death now churned into fury against the evil in the west.

When I mounted, I gripped my spear and let the power of my renewed magic purge the fear from my body and heart. I faced my vanguard.

"Warriors of Nissera! We will be rocks against the crashing waves, with little hope of stopping the surge, but standing firm all the same. Our blood may pour out, but it will mingle with the foul blood we spill. Let it be known that on this day, we rose to meet the black tides of Galgeth!"

A savage cry ripped through the air in answer. I turned to the west, from where a stifling wind raped the green of Calgoran's crests and valleys. Indistinguishable hordes of creatures spilled before us. Shrieks and roars rent the air in a chilling cacophony against the thundering rhythm of their approach. My horse reared his head, and the white light of Cassian's elicrin stone swelled.

The army crested a summit in the distance. I could make out the forms of white koraks and wolves, of birds circling overhead, of gray-skinned elicromancers riding reptilian mounts with countless rows of teeth.

And at the helm, a figure in a candescent white cloak rode waves of churning earth. A mountain rose up beneath her, so that when the riders of Nissera at last dug in our heels and pushed through the path between the ranks of swordsmen and spearmen, we were laboring upward to meet her.

In spite of our many disadvantages, the bright light of my stone blinded the creatures of Galgeth. After charging through the aisle of glinting metal to meet the beasts that waited to rip through our flesh, I saw Tamarice barely squint her eyes— one the familiar molten gold color, the other white as bone. I took this chance to move my shield aside and look at her squarely, and what she saw in my face brought a gleam of fear to her eyes just as my point sunk into the flesh of her arm. On either side of me, my friends collided with claws, teeth, flails and spiked cudgels. The roar of chaos rose around me as I yanked the spear from Tamarice's flesh, causing blood to squirt from the wound. Shock swept across her face and there was a brief, heady moment during which I realized that Tamarice could bleed—and could therefore be destroyed.

But this small triumph ran its course. Before I could take another breath, something solid struck my face, throwing me off my horse. I saw red and felt the sticky warmth of blood rush into my mouth from my broken nose. I rolled over to find Tamarice, the red stone pulsing blindingly at her throat, where a patch of skin had begun to decay. With the arm I had wounded, she lifted me by the neck, drawing me so close to her face that I could feel her breath.

"I am not fond of destroying beautiful, powerful things.

Brack forced my hand." Her soft voice rose an octave as she attempted not to betray emotion. "I beg you not to force my hand, Bristal."

The intersecting hope and sadness in her eyes were so profound that I wished I did not have to be her enemy. But I remembered growling a promise into the night after Anthony was wounded by the korak. I remembered Brack's eyes fluttering closed as the scarlet stain spread across his shirt.

Of all the spells I could have cast and the forms I could have taken on, I mustered all of my hatred and spat a mouthful of blood in her face.

Fury flit across her expression, but she merely sneered, tossed me back to the earth and disappeared. Lost in a tide of black shapes and roars and screams, I staggered to my feet only to be leveled once more by a white blur that sank its claws into my shoulders. The elicrin mail kept them from ripping through my flesh and muscle down to the bone. I turned into a lion and dug my teeth into the korak's throat, tasting blood as the life left its silver eyes. On my left I saw Weston thrust a knife through the roof of a wolf's mouth as it stretched its jaws to snap around his head. I heard a cry and whipped around in time to tear a korak off of Nicolas.

I searched and found Tamarice atop a summit in the distance, facing east, her arms raised. Her expression appeared peaceful, but I turned to see the hills for myself and stared in horror at the destruction she was causing. The earth fell beneath our cavalry, an abyss that spread and swallowed the oncoming ranks of our riders.

I took on my human form in order to materialize, but a cold hand with sallow gray skin closed over my wrist. I looked up and found myself staring into Klaine's white eyes. He towered over me, hot breath snaking through his decrepit teeth, pointed gaze boring into me. The wind whipped back his black cloak, revealing emaciated gray limbs under the tatters of centuries-old Elicrin armor. The tarnished, colorless elicrin stone sat against his concave sternum.

While Klaine trapped my right hand in his grasp, I used my left to unsheathe Zeal and thrust it into his gaunt torso. But he ripped out the sword and tossed it aside, exposing nothing but a hollow hole in his chest. He was stronger than the other blights I had faced. Stronger because it was Cassian's strength, not his own, that had kept him alive.

I felt the tremors of earth crumbling in the distance, and knew I couldn't take time to fight Klaine. I materialized, colliding with Tamarice so violently that we both hit the ground and rolled.

She rose to her feet again. *"Matara liss!"* I shouted. The spell should have caused her to burst into flames, but she cast a firm shield. I tried another, but the shield impeded it as well.

"Why won't you fight me?"

"Stop provoking me, Bristal. You know you cannot win."

"You think that will stop me?"

I hated that my voice shook, that it betrayed more grief than rage when my very soul burned with hatred.

"I gave you a chance to prevent the ones you love from coming to harm, but you were too blind to take it. However, I'm feeling merciful. Take a real taste of war. Watch your friends die for nothing. Come back and tell me if that's what you still desire—or if you would prefer to join me as a ruler of a revived world."

"Such peace cannot be accomplished like this, Tamarice. Love cannot be blood-bought."

Her eyes turned to slits. She swiped her hand through the air and the hill suddenly sloped underneath me. I rolled down, striking ground every few seconds but mostly falling, landing on my stomach in the midst of the battle. I barely had enough time to spit out a mixture of mud and blood before I had to stagger to my feet and prevent the attack of a descending giant bird. I performed a spell that made it catch flame as though its black wings were drenched in tar. It screeched and crashed into a pack of koraks devouring a dead horse and a Calgoranian rider. I looked away quickly and stared eastward.

By now our spearmen had been routed and the cavalry scattered. The landscape had greatly morphed and no longer favored our armies.

I spotted Charles nearby, soaked with sweat and gore as he hacked off the heads of the blights that came at him in droves. I materialized in their midst and started carving through their rotted flesh with spell after spell.

Some distance to my right, I caught sight of Drell's orange mane and watched as a blight raised a spiked cudgel to strike her. I tensed to intervene, but Maddock intercepted the blow with his shield, managing to earn nothing but a superficial gash on his brow that spilled blood over his right eye and lips.

"I know what you're doing!" I heard Drell yell above the din as she slit the throat of another blight and stabbed it in the head for good measure. "I can fight! Don't kill yourself to protect me!"

Without reply, Maddock swung his sword and split the

head of another so forcefully that its blood showered over his blond hair and leather armor.

I saw two koraks bounding toward Orrin, whom I had only just noticed nearby. His sword was lodged in the chest of a monstrous dead wolf, and he struggled to pull it out in time to defend himself. I shifted into a bear and engaged the cats in a clash of claws and a racket of roars and yelps, half of them my own. I didn't notice until after I had killed the koraks that my back leg was gushing blood. I changed back and destroyed another dozen blights. The battle seemed to go on like this for a long time, as I performed spell after spell and those around me slaughtered dark elicromancer after korak after wolf until I wondered if it would ever stop.

At last, we reached a lull in the fighting. Cyril's horn blasted, and soon after he and his men charged from the barrows. Our covert attack was launched. When the enemy flocked to the onslaught, I looked back up at the high, flat summit where Tamarice stood unchallenged. I prepared to materialize and engage her before she could shift the landscape again, or do much worse.

Before I could move, I saw her head suddenly reel back as if she had been struck in the jaw. For a moment her svelte form lay flattened on the earth, but she leaped up again and struck the air with whips of thorns.

They wrapped around something solid, not air—though to my eye it was only a faint glimmer, like of a mirror or glass. Something was fighting her. When it caught the light just right, I saw that its edges took the shape of a man. An elicromancer.

"We saw him up close," Drell said, limping up next to me. "As much of him as there is to see."

"Cassian," I whispered, a new wave of adrenaline coursing through my exhausted body.

Klaine crested the hill to join Tamarice in battling the new arrival. Even if it was Cassian, and his body was somehow invulnerable to destruction, I couldn't leave him to take them both down alone. I materialized to the hilltop again and strode toward Tamarice. "You promised to make dust of me."

The words came out as a roar. Lights flooded from our chests at the same moment. Our spells pushed against one another, their brightness intensifying so much that it stung my eyes. Tamarice thrust her hands out, sending a shock of power through our converging waves that made my ears ring. Both spells dissolved, but she was quicker to the next attack.

She clapped her hands together and two enormous slabs of rock sped toward me. I transformed into a deer, leaping out of the way in time for the rocks to barely clip me when they would have crushed me. But I had exhausted my powers too much to hold a guise. I landed in my own body in the midst of the battle between Klaine and the transparent elicromancer.

Klaine had just struck down the iridescent warrior, forcing me to roll out of the way to keep my ally from crushing me. I studied the newcomer as well as I could in spite of the light that flowed through him. It was as if he truly were made of crystal, pure as glass. I saw no skin, no blood, no bones, no distinguishable feature other than his shape, which was angular but unmistakably human.

I tore my eyes away to look up at Klaine. There were puncture holes in his gray skin where light pierced through, but those didn't kill him the way they would a human. He turned his quill-point eyes on me and reached a long, gaunt arm toward me. Pain throbbed deep in my bones, as though every one of them might splinter into a thousand pieces. Never before had I known such suffering. I hadn't even known that elicromancers could possess gifts whose sole purpose was to cause suffering. There was no room in my body for anything but the excruciating pain, no point at all in trying to move or breathe or go on living.

I watched my ally hoist himself over me on his hands and knees. I closed my eyes.

The pain stopped, and it occurred to me that this mysterious elicromancer was using himself as a shield. I opened my eyes again and saw the world refracted through his translucent form.

Seemingly unable to bear the silence, he let loose a very human cry, one that denoted physical misery as intense as what I had just endured. Though there seemed to be nothing to him but an unbreakable, lucent husk—pure invulnerability—Klaine managed to twist and torture him regardless.

But before I could help him, whips of thorns seized me once more and dragged me out from under his protection. Now exposed, I had no time to react as Tamarice's elegant fingers reached out and broke the chain at my neck, tossing Cassian's elicrin stone aside.

The thorns tightened around my wrist and neck, forcing a cry from my lips. I struggled against them, but they only bit deeper.

Tamarice knelt on my chest and wiped the blood from my face with her white cloak in an oddly maternal gesture. "Goodbye, Bristal," she whispered.

The beautiful woman's skin began to change. Scales

popped out of her flesh before turning black and metallic. She shuddered, and an extra row of sharp teeth emerged from her gums. A shriek of pain tore out of her as her body morphed, but the change continued to rage through her.

My confusion turned to terror as I realized what creature she was becoming. As if this battle didn't hold enough horrors, she gradually, painfully took the form of a giant legged serpent. Whatever dark magic it had taken to accomplish such a feat I knew had cost too much.

She reared her head, exposing rows upon rows of teeth the size of daggers. Her hot breath gusted over me like a violent storm.

I lay there, blinking, unable to breathe. Her scales may as well have been iron for how vulnerable they appeared. My elicrin stone lay out of reach.

One of us had to die today, and I knew now that it was me.

But a newcomer, a soldier, leaped in front of me as Tamarice lunged, clashing a sword against her teeth. With his other hand, the man tossed me my pendant.

I caught it and closed my eyes, letting my magic go unbridled as I had once before, when I had burst Tamarice's elicrin stone. But this time, I was more powerful. This time, her weapon remained intact; it was her body itself that I changed.

I used my mind to reach inside her, to morph and bend every part of her to my will the way I had so many times given new forms to objects. I concentrated on her heart, her lungs, her ribs, distorting them until they would no longer fulfill their tasks of keeping her alive.

Tamarice screamed and shed the forced guise. It fluttered away from her, crumpled and clear. She clutched at her chest, scratching across her skin. Panic lit her eyes, both of which were now white with black pricks for pupils. She collapsed on the ground like a used rag.

The thorns slid from my wrists. I stood shakily and approached my enemy.

Gasping for breath, Tamarice still managed to grit her teeth, fear and anger battling for control of her expression. She reached out a feeble hand to try to regain control but barely managed to cause the earth to tremble beneath me.

A lost, glassy look slowly slid over the horror in her eyes. Tamarice heaved a last shuddering breath before going still.

To my right, the warrior who had thrown me my elicrin stone sparred with Klaine, running him through over and over with a sword until he was more holes than flesh. The man's hair was dark, his features strong, and he wore the same grimy battle gear he had been wearing when he brought me to Popplewell to rescue me from the last battle of the Elicrin War.

"Cassian?" I whispered. I glanced from him to the translucent elicromancer recovering from Klaine's attack, the one I had thought might be my father. But here my father stood, true to my last memories of him.

It took three more thrusts of Cassian's sword for Klaine's grimacing head, with its murky white eyes, to part from his shoulders. It teetered on the edge of the slope and dropped off, landing in the midst of the battle carrying on below. The Galgethian ranks, which had been thicker than tar when last I looked, had thinned out.

Staggering a little, I looked down at my wounds. My leg and wrists bled copiously. My vision started to blacken at the edges.

Suddenly, the translucent elicromancer stood up and hurtled into the warped, shallow valley, where the sunlight was spreading over countless bodies strewn across the grass. I noticed Charles's white horse standing without a rider. Beside it, the future king of Calgoran slumped to his knees, but the elicromancer caught him before he hit the earth. I watched the elicromancer drop to the ground with Charles Ermetarius in his arms.

"Anthony," I breathed as my vision blurred and my knees gave way. Just as Charles Ermetarius released his last breath in his brother's grasp, I collapsed against my father, the man who had abandoned me to save my life.

TWENTY-ONE

When I opened my eyes again, my head pounded vengefully. I knew we had suffered great losses, but the thrill of victory resounded within me.

My hand trembled as it touched Cassian's bearded face. The gentle smile he wore was like a string of dulcet tones fluttering through my memories, pulling together into a familiar refrain. His gray eyes swam with tears.

I pressed his elicrin stone into his palm, but he closed my fingers back over it and helped me stagger to my feet. When he spoke, I recognized the deep timbre of his voice. "It's yours now, Bristal."

He spoke in Old Nisseran. Before the astrikane, I wouldn't have understood. But the release of my memories had brought the ancient language to my tongue. "You don't need it?" I asked, still holding it out.

He hung it back around my neck, drawing me against his shoulder and cradling my head beneath his bearded chin. He whispered my name. I clung to him.

When he drew back, he clasped my hand in his. Light began at my fingertips and surged upward, a faint glow beneath my skin. And as it did, my wounds disappeared one by one until my skin was pure and smooth as marble.

"I need to help the healers," Cassian said.

"Yes," I agreed breathlessly, marveling at his work.

My father kissed my forehead and made his way down into the valley, healing as he went.

In the distance, amid the startling aftermath, I saw Anthony. Waves of elation and pounding grief paralyzed me as I watched. The invulnerable armor had faded, and he looked himself again. One of Charles's men had given him a cloak to cover his unclothed body. He crouched next to his brother, sobbing silently and holding Charles's head in his hands. After a moment, he stood back and allowed Calgoranian soldiers to carry the body to a healer's tent.

I ran to Anthony and pulled him close through a veil of tears. His arms hooked around me.

After a moment, I pulled back and placed my palm against his rough cheek. "How did you . . . ?"

"Bristal," he whispered, eyes sweeping over me. "Are you hurt?"

"No," I said, still awed by the absence of pain. "Anthony, I'm so sorry."

"Charles came," he said. His voice broke. "I didn't expect him to come."

"If not for him, we would have fallen long before you arrived."

He swallowed back tears and looked closer at my blood-stained clothes and skin. "There's so much blood."

"Cassian healed me. But I don't know how you're alive."

"Cassian was at the bottom of the Water. He awoke and saved me. When he pulled me out, this lay in my hand." He held out an amber elicrin stone, round and smooth like a setting sun. "As soon as we reached the fight, my . . . my body just became its own armor. I was invincible. I felt like my skin was made of diamonds or iron or some unbreakable element." He studied his own hands in wonder, still struggling to believe it. "The vision Brack's elicrin stone gave me steered me true. I suppose I was meant to have one after all, and I think this shield is my gift."

I remembered seeing what I had thought was a dead body in the Water just before I had become an elicromancer. Tucking away my questions for later, I went with Anthony to the healer's tent, where one of the old women gave him clothes. He slid the boots from a dead Calgoranian's feet so he could help comb the battlefield for survivors.

Seeing Drell limping about brought me immeasurable relief, as did the sight of Maddock crouching over a cot, stitching a man's wound with steady hands. But as I looked around, I noticed the familiar horrors of the disease the blights carried. My relief washed away. The smell of decaying flesh and leaking sores invaded my nostrils, and I remembered the faces of the diseased victims I had tried to save and couldn't.

"We have to get the diseased away from the others," one of the healers said to Maddock, motioning for him to grab one edge of a cot.

Cassian strode into the tent. He didn't cover his mouth and nose as the rest of us had instinctively done. "No need to move them," he said to the healer in Old Nisseran. She didn't understand, but she did budge out of the way as he fearlessly gripped the sore-ridden forearm of a diseased man. The sores healed up as quickly as my wounds had. Even Brack had not been able to overcome this disease with his healing spell, and yet Cassian was powerful enough to heal without an elicrin stone.

The healers carried in a new patient, reminding me that the other survivors needed help.

The next hour was gruesome and heart wrenching. I found myself crouched and retching on the ground due to the stench and the sights, but I recovered and held a man's hand as he breathed his last breath. I used a spell to drag a wolf from a man who survived underneath it and helped him back to the healer's tent. Outside of it I saw Orrin and Nicolas. Drell and Maddock rested nearby. It was when I realized who was missing that my heart dropped.

"Weston?" I asked, voice thin.

Nicolas looked up at me, and then down at his hands. My heart sank. "We were fighting together. He took a hit for me."

"Cyril," Anthony said as he approached. "He's dead."

Tears welled in my eyes as we bowed our heads. I couldn't imagine a world without either of them; without Weston's high spirits and coarse manner, without Cyril's imperturbable wisdom. I stared at the toes of my boots. *May light surround you, friends. May goodness follow you. . . .*

Anthony pulled me close to him as we watched Cassian hunker down next to Drell. He clasped her leg and the ever-present grimace of pain cleared from her face.

We piled and burned the enemy casualties, but handled our own ceremoniously. There were too many bodies to give every man the honor he deserved, but the healers wiped the blood from Charles's face and polished his armor, and Anthony placed his brother's sword in his hands. Cyril and Weston were laid nearby, and the healers did the same for them.

As Anthony crouched beside them and looked out from his brother, friend and commander to the countless rows of bodies that lay in the grass, I realized he intended to honor them all with this act of service he had done for the three. As the fallen warriors were doused in pitch and the blazes of a hundred torches spread, Anthony's deep voice resonated shakily in the silence:

> *The enemy's fields are razed*
> *No longer will he flourish*
> *Gray ashes from our wrathful blaze*
> *White blooms they now will nourish*
> *When glory earns us songs of praise*
> *Let it be known we brazen few*
> *Followed our king to the end of his days*
> *Till light and shadow parted our ways*
> *As only death can do*

As the company packed up and prepared to journey our separate ways—those of us from Calgoran, back to Darmeska to recover—I found Nicolas standing with his arms crossed as if bracing against a cold wind. I placed a hand on his shoulder.

"I never expected anyone to have to die in order for me to live," he said. "I owe Weston everything, but there's no way for me to repay him."

"There is. Be a good and kind king. Surround yourself with

friends like him." I squeezed his shoulder. "Not that they're easy to find."

Nicolas nodded and stared straight ahead. He opened his mouth to speak, but I already knew what he was going to say.

"I'll go now," I said. "I'll return as soon as I can."

Hope spilled into his brown eyes. "With good news, I pray." He leaned in to kiss me lingeringly on the cheek.

Understanding this as a message I was meant to relay, I nodded and braced myself to materialize to Pontaval.

Seconds later, the palace stood before me. Briars still covered the entire city and crawled up the walls of the palace. But this time, when I hacked at them with spells, they broke and withered away.

When I reached the palace, I found its halls silent. Light from the smoldering sunset stretched in stripes across the gleaming floors. The bodies sprawled every which way appeared dead at first glance, but the color in their faces and the breath in their chests said otherwise. King Errod and Queen Lucetta were eerie sights, sleeping propped up in their thrones with their crowns on their heads.

Two maids giggled in the opposite corner of the receiving hall. They hadn't heard me come in, and they continued arranging a sleeping fat man in various poses and eating fancy food from silver platters without realizing they had company.

"Hirafeth." My softly spoken word stirred something unseen. It was clear that the effects of Tamarice's curse on Rosie and Volarre's nobles had not been completely undone by the elicromancer's death, but my restoration enchantment overpowered it easily. Everyone in the courtroom began to stir.

The maids squeaked and scurried out of the room before they could be chastised for their new hobby.

I searched through the palace, waking up any cursed nobles I crossed. At last, I found Rosie in a room at the top of one of the palace's towers. My heart leapt into my throat when I saw her lying motionless on a bed, her long strawberry curls splayed like silk across the pillow. At least a few of the maids weren't useless.

I collapsed to my knees beside her, noting the rise and fall of her chest before I let myself feel confident that she was alive. I kissed her lightly on the cheek and whispered, *"Hirafeth."*

Rosie's green eyes blinked open.

✳

After meeting with King Errod and Queen Lucetta, I rejoined the victors and brought Nicolas the good news. I searched for Anthony and found him readying his saddlebags to travel to Darmeska. Watching him stole my breath; after I had thought him dead, here he was, in all his beauty and strength. But I noticed darkness in his features that I couldn't read. He moved as if physically burdened and met eyes with no one.

I left him alone to process his grief, an unnamed fear growing in my heart.

As we traveled, the fear took shape. Anthony would be king now, a fate he had never expected or prepared for. And when he had asked me to be his wife, he hadn't been choosing Calgoran's queen. Perhaps he feared that two elicromancers ruling a kingdom would let power go to their hearts, as other elicromancers in lesser positions of power had before. Perhaps he had only loved me because it gave him something to put faith in.

Whatever the reason, my heart felt tight and cold now.

We reached Darmeska in the late black hours. The elder residents and children, who had been ready to tend our wounds when we approached, were astounded to find every last one of us whole and able-bodied. This evidence of Cassian's power could be seen, though Cassian himself was not to be found.

I watched Maddock pull Drell close to him after they dropped onto heaps of straw and blankets in the great hall. I collapsed wearily nearby. Anthony was nowhere in sight.

In the deep of the night I woke suddenly, despite having been so tired I'd barely remembered finding a place to lie down. I crept over the sleeping forms and traipsed up endless stairwells toward my old room. As I followed the familiar path, I conjured all four images I had of Brack now, but found that strangely, the one that lingered most was not the one I had seen for years, but for hours. His wheat-blond hair and immaculate blue eyes were now woven among my other memories as if they had been there all along.

When I reached the topmost corridor, I noticed a flickering campfire light on the plateau and a figure beside it. I went to don a dusty cloak from my old wardrobe and found Callista's diadem sitting on my bedside table. Kimber must have retrieved it from the cottage.

I slipped it in a deep pocket and went outside, bracing myself against the mountain air. As I drew toward the light, I recognized the figure as Cassian.

"Are you hungry?" he asked as I approached.

"Terribly," I admitted.

He gestured for me to sit and I eased to the ground, crossing my arms for warmth. He snatched a seared fish from the flames and lopped it on the stones next to me. I disposed of the succulent meat with almost vicious haste, tossing the bones into the fire and licking the juice from my fingers.

As the wind swept Cassian's dark hair back from his face, I found a bit of myself in every feature.

"Leaving you where you couldn't be found was the hardest thing I've ever had to do," he said quietly. "And as a leader, one must do many difficult things—as you've learned by now."

"What happened to you?" I asked.

"When I killed Klaine, the fate-binding curse left me barely alive, with only a shred of my former power. I felt myself slipping toward death, but I somehow knew I was still needed, that I wasn't meant to die yet. I used the last of my strength to reach the Water, hoping it would restore my life and power— and it did, a thousand times over. Though it took longer than I ever could have imagined."

"Anthony knew you were alive, and I didn't believe him. Even Callista thought you had died."

Cassian closed his eyes, the shadows cast by the fire deepening on his face. "I could feel how much time had passed when I finally awoke to find Anthony in the Water. I prepared myself to find out that she was gone." He looked at me, his expression a dynamic landscape of emotion. "But I didn't expect to find you."

He reached out for my hand, and I laid it in his rough palm. The stories and pictures had painted him as fearless, fierce, stoic. But I sensed tenderness and peace within him, a quiet power with no impulse to prove itself unless provoked.

"You've done immense good for Nissera, Bristal." His words washed over me like a cool salve, calming the burn of my spirit's wounds, carrying a curative power that even his healing hands didn't possess. "I always felt you would."

I balled up the feeling I had right then inside of me like a relic that I could keep for all time.

"Will you return to Arna with us for the celebration?" I asked. "We would not have claimed victory without you, and I can't bear to think of parting ways."

"I wouldn't dare miss it."

"I have something for you." I slipped the diadem from my pocket and held it out to him.

His gray eyes filled with tears as he looked from it to me. "Callista's elicrin stone."

"Yes."

He got up and knelt in front me, taking it from my hands. "My daughter. Nothing would make me happier than for you to guard and cherish and wear it with pride for your long years."

He slid it gently into my hair. Normally I might have felt childish, wearing an emblem of royalty. But for once, I didn't question whether such a fine thing was where it belonged.

❋

As the Realm Alliance approached Arna, a cool wind carried in the scent of a spring storm. Anthony and I strode into the receiving hall at the head of our company, sapphire and amber elicrin stones swinging at our necks. I carried Tamarice's white cloak and Anthony, her fiery pendant.

Riskan's face so filled my chest with a cluster of strong emotions that I was tempted to look away. Sickness had warped him strangely; his face was sallow and his stance weak.

But when he looked at Anthony, something very much like pride shone in his eyes. It made him look healthy and vicarious again for just a moment. Dara's trembling hand covered her mouth when she saw her only living son. Elinor sat with her back straight and gaze steady, but her face was wet with tears that she didn't bother to wipe away.

✳

I kept Elinor company during the seven days of mourning, during which I didn't see Anthony at all. We lingered about her chambers in black gowns and watched the spring storms rage outside.

Cassian and I walked through the gardens when I wasn't with Elinor, sometimes smiling over our memories, sometimes not speaking at all. Having my father at my side, sharing his wisdom, filled a hole in my soul that I had never acknowledged. But I could still feel a distance, a wall he had built up after a few hundred years of missing out on his life. This was not his home.

When the mourning period passed, it was time for the ceremony honoring Anthony as Riskan's heir. Clothiers delivered a trunk to Elinor and me with gown choices for the occasion, but since neither of us cared whatsoever, they happily chose the garments themselves. They put Elinor in pale yellow, as if a cheerful dress might make her skin look less pale or her drawn look of grief less pitiable. For me they chose violet, perhaps to make me look vibrant and feminine despite my grim face.

After they left, Elinor sat back down like a wilted flower. "Is it terrible that I feel relieved not to be queen? I could have done it, I think, but there are many better suited." She smiled weakly, meaning me.

Restlessness took hold of me. I changed out of my dress and freed my hair from the cloth ties that would make it curl in long ringlets. I wandered through the gardens in the late morning sunlight, looking longingly at the barracks across the damp green field.

As I wove through the weeping willows and vibrant flowers, I noticed Maddock and Drell standing side by side on the same bridge where Anthony and I had stood just a few short months ago. I watched them numbly for a moment before continuing on.

Finding myself on a wooded hilltop overlooking Arna, I sat and rested my chin on my knees. The sun shone pleasantly on my shoulders as I watched a great crowd fill the streets. Visitors from all over the realm had come to the city to celebrate our victory and the naming of the future king. Lucetta, Errod and Rosamund had been reunited and were staying at the palace, and Nicolas's family was in Arna as well. I even heard that a prince and princess from Perispos had crossed the Mizrah to Calgoran after hearing tidings of the war.

I let the wind rake through my hair until the perfect curls were loose waves brushing against my face. I sighed as I watched a great concourse of people gather at the palace, knowing I should go back soon.

"What's all this commotion about?"

I recognized Anthony's voice and looked over my shoulder at him. "I hear they're planning to crown some impetuous warmonger as king," I replied, rising to my feet.

"I can't imagine that will go well for them."

"You might be surprised."

Anthony laughed and joined me on the edge of the overlook.

He hadn't donned his ceremony attire yet. Bits of grass clung to his clothes and hair. He looked just like he always did, except for the amber elicrin stone hanging on a chain around his neck.

"You certainly make materializing look easy," he said. "When Drell told me the spell, she failed to mention I'd be eating dirt for breakfast."

"You have yet to taste rocks or poison climbers."

"I'll probably just limit myself to riding Arsinoe. Did you know she found her way home?"

"Yes, I was pleased to hear."

Anthony took a deep breath and looked at his hands. "Bristal." When he said my name, his eyes met mine steadily, unmercifully. He stood so close that I could see the thin webs of gold intersecting the earthy colors in his eyes. "I know that when I asked you to marry me before, neither of us knew I would be king someday."

I looked away, fixing my gaze on the city instead. I had cried so often in my sleep over the past week—over Brack and Weston and Cyril and Charles and every person who had given his life—that no tears came now. I knew for certain I would have to live with Anthony's refusal. As consolation, I thought of the cold and solitude of Darmeska. The mountains would be my escape. Brack's little cottage would be my home.

"I know this isn't what either of us had in mind," he went on. "We're both accustomed to a certain kind of freedom, and being the ruler of Calgoran comes with the administrative duties I was always happy to let Charles handle." He heaved a sigh. "I know when you said yes to me, neither of us was thinking of all this."

I let out a sharp breath and turned to him. "I should

understand. I'm a Volarian commoner, after all, aren't I? And a bastard? Or maybe it's that you fear I might become power-thirsty."

Anthony looked stunned that I would be so angry, as if I were meant to simply accept that I was no longer a suitable choice. I had spoken insolently to the king, undermined authority with deception. I could indeed begin to understand why I would be of better use as a lone elicromancer than ruler of Calgoran, but I was too hurt to stop.

"I am Cassian and Callista's daughter," I went on. "But if my parentage still makes me unworthy, then by all means, marry Lord Goodenouthe's daughter and let her bear you strong sons. Try to learn elicromancy on your own and see how you feel in fifty years when everyone you love—"

"Bristal, stop, stop." Anthony gripped my shoulders, staring at me as if he didn't understand a word. "You think I no longer wish to marry you? You rode to battle against Galgeth. You have Nissera's best interests at heart. You're a hero. And you're one of my dearest friends. What woman could be more equipped to rule a kingdom with me than you? And you're beautiful, as if the rest isn't enough to make me lose sleep. It's a matter of whether or not you want to."

"Whether I want to?" I repeated. "You haven't changed your mind?"

"Of course not. I love you. I've spent the last seven days pondering how unprepared I am to be king. I believe I may have mustered the confidence to do this, but I don't know yet if you're willing to endure all the nonsense and rules and traditions that come with being a queen and living at court."

"Anthony," I breathed, taking his face in my hands. The

warmth in his eyes would have taken me hundreds of years to forget. "I would never refuse you."

He grabbed my hand and pulled me in, tilting my face to his. "So will you marry me? Even if it means you have to be queen?"

"Why don't you threaten to throw yourself off this cliff and see if you earn a yes like you did last time?"

He grinned and leaned down to kiss me, but pulled back and cocked his head. "Cassian is your father?"

"Things happened while you were dead. I have much to explain."

"There will be time for that. And for other things." He closed the distance with a grin.

✳

In the receiving hall, I stood to the right of the dais with my father, Elinor, Rosie, Errod and Lucetta. Rosie took Elinor's hand. She reached for mine next, beaming at me in admiration. I squeezed her small fingers protectively in mine. She hadn't spoken to me since I'd marched in with a bloody cloak in my hands and an army at my back.

After parading through the city, Anthony dismounted at the doors of the receiving hall. He wore white, gold and gray, with the red sash across his chest. The amber elicrin stone hung regally around his neck and petals from the parade clung to his dark hair.

When he reached the dais, he knelt before his father. The king's head minister took the cup of water from the Roac River and poured it over Anthony's head, saying, "I wash you in the water of your kingdom. Calgoran's wounds will be your wounds, its victories your victories, its peace your peace.

Likewise, your kingdom will mourn when you mourn and rejoice in your triumph. You will prosper as a king and man if you do these things: provide for the hungry and the weary and the bereaved. You may stand." Anthony stood. "I present to you Anthony Ermetarius, successor to Riskan and Charles, the heir to the throne of Calgoran, your future king."

※

I let a slew of the finest clothiers, cooks, cobblers and gardeners oversee wedding details in which I took insufficient interest. Rosie was as eager as I had ever seen her, but for once she had more demands for me than questions; she called upon me to feel fabrics, taste wines and food and judge flower arrangements. Drell proved invaluable to me, if for nothing other than her ability to keep Rosie in check without dousing her fire.

Elinor was adamant about helping despite my protests, insisting it kept her mind from grief. She seemed in better spirits as she worked to lace up the green and white bodice of my wedding gown and placed the amethyst diadem in my hair.

The wedding took place in the gardens. All the royalty I could name attended, as well as the elders of Darmeska and even royalty from Perispos, and of course, my father—which I still struggled to believe. After the ceremony, we feasted on springtime delicacies and danced in the light of a thousand glowing lanterns. Anthony no longer had to compensate for his wounded arm, but held me close and tight all the same.

The moon emerged, silver and vibrant, and in the soft light I noticed Cassian standing in an arcade of white flowers.

I managed to escape the crowd and approach him. We fell into step together as we entered the arcade.

"You have seen much in a short time as an elicromancer," he said.

"It's strange, now, not having to prepare for dark times ahead. It's all I know: the meddling, the waiting, the danger. And if Anthony and I are as alike as I think we are, he finds it strange too, and will go looking for trouble."

Cassian laughed. "We are not meant to sit idly atop our accomplishments, but to accomplish new things, and you're in a position to do just that. Your sights have been on Nissera all this time, like a watchmen looking over the streets of her city."

"I don't know what comes next."

He stopped and turned to me, taking my hands. "Become mortal. Live and die as humans do. Immortals don't have a place in this world right now."

"But I . . ." I shook my head, trying to comprehend the idea that my tasks as an elicromancer had been fulfilled. I looked at my gleaming new elicrin stone as I had never looked at one before: a thing that could be tossed away and forgotten. "I no longer know who I am without elicromancy."

"Finding out will be a new adventure." He glanced toward the end of the passage. I noticed that the other end of the arcade didn't open into the night as it should have, but into the soft light of day.

"You're leaving," I whispered.

He offered me a bittersweet smile, cupping my cheek in his hand. "This is not my home."

"I understand, but I thought you would stay for a time."

"In a few hundred years, you will understand better. My body may be young, but my soul is tired."

"I do understand," I said, reluctantly allowing him to pull

me close, burying my face in his shoulder. When we released one another, we looked to the end of the arcade. Stars twinkled even against the pastel blue of daylight. A forest path wound away to some unreachable, distant land.

"She's opened a way for me," Cassian said. He turned back to me. "We'll be waiting for you, daughter."

I smiled through my tears. Cassian wiped them away with his thumb just like he had wiped my memories years ago.

He kissed my head softly, a tear meandering down his cheek. *"Efrenil."*

After he left the arcade, the portal closed behind him. But a familiar honey-sweet scent lingered in the air the way it had lingered in my mother's chestnut tresses.

"Var efrenil," I whispered after them.

The cool saltwater waves lapped against our knees as we stood on a cove off the eastern coast. The sun warmed our backs through a thin veil of clouds, and the sounds of the sea met my ears like music. I held my elicrin stone, gazing over the endless Mizrah before looking up at Anthony. "You should do it first."

He looked at the amber gem in his hands, then hurled it far enough that it was no longer visible when it hit the gray waves in the distance.

Fighting the tide, I walked forward until the water reached my waist. I closed my eyes and pitched my elicrin stone as hard as I could, following its arc until it was swallowed by the sea.

I feared I would feel weak without the power of magic charging through me. But I only felt lighter, as if I could float away on the wind. I didn't mind the sensation. I turned around and laughed with disbelief.

"How does it feel?" Anthony asked as I neared the shore again. "You're mortal now."

Without answer, I threw my arms around him, nearly dragging us both into the water. Anthony regained his balance and cupped my face, kissing me slowly and deeply, his lips tasting of saltwater. My hands slid along his wet shoulders, and his traveled over the clinging linen of my dress.

He cleared his throat. "Now that we're not expecting a war, we're going to have to find something to do with our time. I might have a suggestion."

"Oh, do you?"

"But let's not forget our responsibilities," he said as I twined my fingers in his wet, dark hair. "Now that we're mortals, we're going to need an heir."

"Oh, that's right," I smiled. "Our list of royal obligations is getting out of hand."

Anthony laughed and kissed me again. The waves crashed against us as he swept me up out of the tide and carried me back to shore.

*

I awoke that night, my hand shaped as though there were something in its grasp, recalling a dream of holding my elicrin stone. I sat up in bed, realizing that the feeling of magic surging through me was not merely a part of the dream. There had been power in me before I ever touched the Water.

I got up and ran as a fox through the cold winter woods, feeling the snow settle in my fur, knowing magic would always run in the heat of my blood.

Acknowledgments

No words can do the people in my corner justice.

I have the feeling that anyone who approaches an artistic dream alone ends up a Gollum-like husk of a human. Thank you to everyone who got behind this book; because of you, I still refer to myself in the first person.

Warmest of thanks to Sally Morgridge, whose vision for this work has sharpened it immensely, and the rest of the Holiday House team, who have been all shades of wonderful since I had the privilege of joining.

Deepest of thanks to my agents Sarah Burnes and Logan Garrison, without whose hard work and belief this story might have stayed a big ole pile of words.

I want to thank my gifted critique partner and long-distance soul-friend, Sarah Goodman—our ceaseless text stream has been a constant companion in this process (yay, introverts!).

I also want to thank my soon-to-be husband Vince, who came into my life before this story's fate was certain but has never second-guessed its happy ending.

I owe a huge debt of gratitude to my family, whose encouragement I spent a lifetime taking for granted until I realized: not everyone gets a family like mine.

Kali Katzmann, your enthusiasm means more than you could possibly know. Same to Brooke Buchanan, Lindi VanSlyke and Hannah Crawford—nothing helped me believe in the magic like knowing you saw it too.

Thank you immensely, Julie Scheina, for bringing our villain to the foreground.

I'd also like to thank Ashley Gordon, Caleb Bollenbacher,

Ryan Kirk and Nate Wade for their input, as well as Mary DeMuth and the Rockwall Christian Writers Group.

And last but never least, Dr. Wink—*La joie venait toujours après la peine.*